Accosted by
the Forces of the Dark

The enemy ship was larger than *Wind Dragon* by perhaps thirty feet. Her vanes and stabilizers appeared to be no larger, but the ship itself was much wider and deeper in construction, most likely a small freighter rather than a schooner like their own. If it came to a running battle, *Wind Dragon* did have the advantage of speed and maneuverability. But the other ship also had a couple dozen archers clearly visible on her deck.

"What ship?" Mira called.

"*Blood Hawk*, out of Alashera," the sorcerer at her helm shouted back. "What ship?"

"*Wind Dragon*, out of Bennasport."

"Stand to and prepare to be boarded, woman!"

Lady Mira looked rather indignant. "Stand to and prepare to get your ass whipped, bastard!"

D0050275

THORARINN GUNNARSSON

HUMAN, BEWARE!

ACE BOOKS, NEW YORK

• Prologue •

The Blue-Haired Child

THE RIFT EXPLODED open, the burning edges of space itself peeling back as the Way Between the Worlds expanded wide in the pre-dawn sky. The golden-scaled form of a faerie dragon, illuminated in that yellow glow, shot through the opening pathway between the two universes even as it continued to draw back, and a second followed a moment later. They circled back sharply, spying out the broken, barren landscape in a quick reconnaissance, their keen eyes peering into the midnight shadows among the boulders and ledges of the steep walls of the vast ravine where they had emerged. The morning sun was only just beginning to lighten the eastern sky, but day itself was well over half an hour away. They hoped to be gone from this world by then.

The Way Between the Worlds continued to peel back until it formed a wide oval over a hundred feet across. A vast form emerged from the void: the long, slender shape of an airship's wooden hull. The bright colors of the canvas stabilizers in her bowsprit and the ribbed fins behind each of her four wide induction vanes were as black as the surrounding night in this dim light. She ran silent as a bird of prey, with only the whistle of the cold wind in her rigging, showing no lights.

The smaller of the two dragons dropped back to pace the helm deck of the airship, coming up as close behind the stern as she dared. "All set?"

Princess Merridyn of Elura looked up from the helm, where she had been watching the young sorceress Kerie Wold fly the swift airship. She was a tall, graceful woman, not much older than the young girl who stood at the ship's wheels. She stepped away from the helm to stand at the rail. "All set, Lady Dalvenjah. We seem to have taken no damage coming through into this world. Were we seen?"

"No, I think not," Dalvenjah answered. She was gliding alongside the airship, matching speed with her lift magic effortlessly. A fine blue magical mist trailed her form. "We are perhaps two minutes short of the main entrance, but we must remain in the canyon until the last moment. Allan and I will lead you in."

"Lady Tenika is standing watch in the bow," Merridyn called after the dragon as she moved ahead.

The dark shape of a mountain rose before them, although only the keen eyes of the faerie dragons could see it in the dense night of this world. It was a massive block of solid, dark stone, at one time perhaps the molten core of a vast volcano, riddled with round tunnels and passages. Most of the lower passages were closed in by walls of massive stone blocks or gates of heavy iron, turning the hivelike interior of the mountain into a fortress. The faerie dragons knew the way; they had been through here before, several times in the past week, spying out their path.

They knew of the immense oval passage that opened two-thirds of the way up the towering front face of the mountain fortress. A tunnel opening that had never been secured because of its great height up the featureless, almost vertical face of that portion of the mountain, but large enough that the airship could be landed there. Dalvenjah Foxfire did not know who had built this fortress, a dead race on a dead world. A world that had been dead, dry and barren for untold thousands of years. But she did know who held it now.

After a minute or so the two dragons shot out of the deep ravine and began to ascend swiftly toward the fortress, towering vast and dark barely a mile ahead. The airship followed, coming around slowly at first but accelerating swiftly as it entered open air. They might be seen any moment now and the alarm would be up, but they could at least get in before the confusion created by their sudden attack settled. With luck they could get what they came for before any defense could be organized against them, but there was little hope of that. They had no idea of even where to begin looking, and were dependent upon the considerable magic the two dragons possessed to guide them. Getting back out again would surely be a battle, but there was at least one point in their favor. The defenders were few and widely scattered throughout the wandering tunnels.

The airship rose quickly in the dark sky. Kerie Wold brought the ship expertly through the opening the dragons indicated and settled it gently on the stone landing just inside, although the twin masts barely cleared the ceiling even when it was resting on its four skids. The faerie dragons were already standing guard to either side of her bowsprit with their long-bladed swords drawn, alert for guards, while the others lowered the boarding ramp. But there had been no one within the chamber, only a pair of dim lamps for the guards who might pass here on their rounds.

"Are we discovered?" Princess Merridyn asked as she hurried to join them. She was a trained and highly skilled sorceress and Veridan Warrior, like all the rest. But no mortal could match the talents of the faerie dragons.

"No, I think not," Dalvenjah answered absently. Her sharp ears were perked, although she employed other senses to scan the massive fortress. "I feel no changes in the sleepy calm that pervades this place. With any luck, we might not be discovered for some time. Marie and Lady Tenika will stay to guard the ship."

"I've got my shotgun!" Marie Breivik declared indignantly, then hesitated when the dragon turned to glare at her. "And we will both be very pleased to stay here and guard the ship."

The ease with which she surrendered to the dragon's will demonstrated just how much this business had affected her. Her brother Allan and Rex Barker, her husband-to-be, were both undecided whether to be amused or to feel sorry for her. Then again, she was also on Dalvenjah's turf now.

"We must move quickly," Dalvenjah continued. "Allan, do you sense Jenny's presence anywhere within this place?"

"Yes, very far below," the larger, slightly darker-scaled dragon responded. "*He* is here as well. And his master, the Emperor Myrkan. He does not yet know that we are here, but he may soon."

"Yes, and I must go to him," Dalvenjah said softly, more to herself than the others. She turned to her mate. "You must find

Jenny. You must lead the others to her, and get her out of this place. I must go to him.''

"Dalvenjah, you cannot," Allan insisted, watching her with deep concern. "There is no point in doing so. Nothing can bring him back."

"No, nothing can bring him back now," Dalvenjah agreed sadly. "But I must do this, and you know why. The High Priest has stolen countless bodies in the past, but he cannot be allowed to keep the form and the powers of a faerie dragon. I can defeat him, but it must be now.''

Allan nodded slowly. "I wish that I could fight this battle at your side, more than any other. But Jenny is our reason for being here.''

Merridyn laid a hand gently on the female dragon's long, supple neck. "Do what you must, my friend. We will await you.''

"That you will not!" Dalvenjah ordered sharply. "Find Jenny and get her away from this place and out of this world as quickly as you can. I will follow in my own good time . . . if I am not here before you. Enough time is wasted already. Hurry! And may fortune be with you.''

Allan and Merridyn both considered wishing her well in return, but thought better of it. Dalvenjah turned and hurried away, moving swiftly on all fours with her long sword in its sheath on her harness. Allan sat back on his haunches, his emerald eyes shining as he watched her disappear into the shadows which flooded the passages. The others remained silent, knowing what this meant to her. Dalvenjah's brother Karidaejan waited somewhere within this place. And yet Karidaejan had in truth been dead these last two years; only his golden-scaled body lived on, stolen by a being immensely old . . . and immensely evil.

"Come. We have little time," Allan said as he slipped his own sword into its sheath. "And stay behind me, since I may use my flame.''

The Emperor Aressande Myrkan deftly smoothed the folds of his billowing black robes, checking to see that his face was well hidden within the shadows of the oversized hood. He would allow no one to look upon his true face and form. This was the price of his contrived immortality, that the features of any body he wore soon adapted themselves to reflect his inner nature, consumed as he was with hatred, greed and the destructive touch of raw Dark

Magic. Few knew for certain the secret he kept hidden within the folds of his robes.

The only one in all existence he trusted to any great extent— dared to trust—stood before him now, in the reception room of his private chamber. The High Priest Haldephren was no less evil than his master, but his powers were less and so he always contrived to conceal his own evil within a form of deceptive grace and beauty. Now, for the first time in his own considerable existence, the High Priest did not wear a human form, as he had once himself been human, but the sleek body of a Mindijarah, a faerie dragon. He was grace and power in soft scales of burnished gold and a long, stiff crest of sapphire blue. There was a sharp, cunning look to his jewel-green eyes, half-hidden in the shadows of his forward-facing horns, a predatory look which could not have been more alien to the rightful inhabitant of this body.

Haldephren waited patiently as his master seated himself in a massive chair which stood before the back wall. Heavy hangings and carpets of dark colors covered the cold, naked stone from which the chamber had been carved, and two round glowstones gave off a pale, timid light. This place did not lend itself to the High Priest's jaded tastes; he looked upon it as a form of exile. But the Emperor felt peaceful and protected here, an impenetrable fortress in a world without enemies. But not absolutely secure, it would seem.

"They have come to rescue the child, my lord," the High Priest reported simply. The Mindijaran were tiny by draconic standards. And yet, standing on his hind legs with his head thrust forward on its long, slender neck, he remained an imposing sight.

"Yes, so they have," the Emperor remarked, seemingly unconcerned. His voice was a velvety baritone, smooth and disarming. "Guards have already been dispatched to intercept them. Do not allow that matter to concern you. You must attend to a problem of your own, for she has come as well. Dalvenjah Foxfire is here, and she is determined to deprive you of that which you have stolen."

The High Priest hesitated only a moment. If his first thought had been that he was no match for the faerie sorceress, he would have been correct. But his own conceit could never accept that. He deemed that he possessed too many advantages, especially his belief that she could never strike him. That he, the usurper, commanded the love that she had for the one whose form he now wore. He dipped his head in acknowledgement.

"It must be a fight to the death," the Emperor added almost as a question, as if he doubted such dedication from his chief servant. "Dalvenjah is at this time our greatest threat. She is organizing enemies against us from throughout the many worlds. The Prophecy is a matter for the future, many years yet to come. Dalvenjah Foxfire must die, now."

"So be it," Haldephren agreed in a soft, cold voice. "So be it. Even if it costs me the body I now wear, it will be worth the price to destroy her. I will always return, while she cannot."

"Then hurry, my old friend," Emperor Myrkan encouraged him. "Go to meet her, but in a place of your choosing. For I foresee that you must seize every possible advantage if you hope to defeat her. Keep your pride and hatred under control, for now you must be calm, cold and ruthless."

"That is a lesson which I have learned well through the ages," The High Priest said as he dropped to all fours and turned to stalk away.

The Emperor smiled to himself, a cold, cruel smile of self-satisfaction. He had his doubts that Haldephren could defeat Dalvenjah Foxfire, but that hardly mattered. He had allowed the High Priest to assume the form of a faerie dragon as an experiment, and they had learned much from it. But now was the time to end the experiment, before Haldephren began to think that he could use his growing powers to defeat his old master and become Emperor himself. The High Priest would be returned to a mortal form, and the ancient balance of power that had existed between them would be restored. Ideally, the Emperor preferred that their battle should end in their mutual destruction, and the very real problem that Dalvenjah represented would be solved as well. But however matters turned out, he stood only to gain.

He could never accept that Haldephren truly did not want to be Emperor, that he was satisfied with his own position as second. From there, the High Priest enjoyed all the privileges and rewards, indulging his decadent whims and immense vanities, and all the more so for the lack of the added responsibilities of rule.

The Emperor judged others by himself, and he could not imagine a life in which the gaining and keeping of power was not all-exclusive. But power was only the first of the High Priest's many lusts.

* * *

Dalvenjah Foxfire waged a hopeless battle with her own errant memories. She slipped through the darkened corridors of the ancient structure with all the cunning and caution she could muster, but her thoughts continually strayed, wandering down brighter paths of their own. The memories of her past were infinitely preferable to this horrible present.

Her mind drifted upon the winds of time, returning to events of a distant past. She remembered herself as she had been then, young and insecure, and her earliest memories of her older half-brother. He had been tall and proud, surely the most majestic of all Mindijaran, wise and fearless. By his example, the overly small and very timid dragon that she had been had learned to be clever and brave.

And then, suddenly, he was gone.

Karidaejan had taken his secrets with him, leaving Dalvenjah a mystery that she might never solve. Why had Karidaejan gone into that same mortal world where she had been exiled, ten years before her own brief visit? Why had he set into motion the events that had initiated the Prophecy of the Faerie Dragons, the circumstances which had led to this very incident? She thought that she might never know, and yet she feared that the answer to that question was vitally important to her ability to know how to read the Prophecy and use it to her own advantage.

There was a new light in the corridor ahead, a warm, red glow, while most of the tunnels had been dark even to a dragon's keen eyes. It was the heart of the mountain, the core of the ancient volcano, a round passage two hundred feet across. She paused just inside the entrance of the passage for a discreet look about. The fiery interior was still alive; the bottom of the shaft was lost in a fierce glare several hundred feet below, and acid wisps of grey smoke rose through the shaft to the dark sky far above. A catwalk circled the shaft, opening onto several other tunnels on this level, although this main passage was spanned by a broad metal bridge.

Haldephren stood on his hind legs at the far end of the bridge, sword in hand as he watched her calmly and closely. Dalvenjah was not to be hurried. She rose to her own hind legs and stepped out slowly onto the bridge to meet him. The bridge was a good eight feet wide and made of long metal plates that felt warm even beneath her tough feet. The plates were hinged at the ends and held rigid by solid steel shafts, one to either side. Another set of shafts provided siderails, supporting the lower shafts by connecting rods. She carefully noted every detail, wondering why he had selected this place for their battleground. Perhaps he was still thinking in human terms. But she was a dragon, with no reason to fear the heights.

Haldephren stopped a short distance away and watched her with that same intent, almost hungry stare. But her heart was satisfied that this was not her brother Karidaejan, that she could indeed fight him. That cold, cruel look of pure hate, that lust for violence was so alien to the one she had known and loved that he looked to her now be another person altogether, a face that she had never seen. She no longer doubted that she could fight him, even strike him. But still it would be terribly painful.

"So, you have come," he said in a deep, rough voice that also was not Karidaejan's. "I had thought that not even you would dare to come here."

"Did you leave me any choice?" Dalvenjah asked in return. "I think that you underestimate me even yet. I have fought worse enemies than you, and won. I will not hesitate to fight you."

"I think that you underestimate me," he countered. "I am older than you. I am old even by the standards of your own immortal folk, while you are yet just a child. I have been a sorcerer of the Dark for over three thousand years. Jenny is mine, I tell you."

"No, that is a lie," she hissed coldly. "Say what you like, I know better. You are not her father."

"That is not quite what I meant, and I will not argue the point with you," Haldephren said. "But Jenny is the key to the Prophecy, and the Prophecy can cut either way depending upon which side of the debate she takes. And the fact remains that she is in our possession now."

"I have come to take her back," Dalvenjah answered simply as she lifted her sword. "Nor will I allow you to keep that which you have stolen. You have held that body only four short years. Have you learned its ways well enough to defeat me?"

"We shall see!" Haldephren declared in a voice sharp with hate as he lunged to the attack.

Dalvenjah caught his blade with her own and turned his attack, throwing him back. The two combatants paused a long moment as they prepared themselves for honest battle, calling upon magic to enhance their own strength, speed and agility. Dalvenjah's one disadvantage was in her size; at two hundred and fifty pounds she was small and slight of build for a faerie dragon. Haldephren was much larger of body but not so long of limb for his size, so that he had little more than an extra inch of reach. He certainly did not have her speed or precision, at least not naturally. It remained to be seen which of them was the better when their abilities were magically enhanced.

Dalvenjah waited, letting him press the attack. Haldephren responded by driving at her relentlessly, striking blow after blow like lightning while his blade burned with the misty fire of raw magic. Obviously he thought that he could beat her in either speed or endurance. Dalvenjah did not feel threatened but she preferred to deal cautiously. Her chance would come if she waited and, as long as she did not waste her powers as he did, she could afford to wait. But she held her ground subtly, refusing to allow him to force her to retreat from the bridge.

Allan stopped short as he came to the turn in the passage, sensing several mortals in the tunnel just ahead. He peered cautiously around the corner but saw no one, for the passage turned again only a few hundred feet farther on. So far they had avoided any direct confrontation in this maze of tunnels by simply cutting around any presence he sensed. But they were coming into the inhabited regions, and they were due to have a fight on their hands any moment now.

"They're coming up behind us," Kerie Wold warned nervously. She was the youngest of the group.

"I know it," the dragon said softly. "Fortunately, we are almost there."

He led the way around the corner, proceeding cautiously along the passage beyond. Things were getting tight; he could sense enemies closing in on them both before and behind. Suddenly they heard heavy boots marching along the corridor behind them, echoing loudly in the stone passage. They paused long enough for one quick look back before they turned and ran, hoping to avoid detection one more time before they were forced to fight. Allan rounded the next turn as fast as he could and found himself nose to nose with another party of guards, nearly a score. It was fair to say that both groups were very surprised, the guards most of all, and both did their best to execute a hasty retreat. The soldiers of the Dark had heavy boots, and they reversed course fairly quickly.

Allan was not so lucky. His feet slipped out from beneath him and he fell backwards on his tail. The three mortals, still fleeing the group behind, nearly fell on top of him as they came around the turn in the dim light. The dragon leaped up again in the next instant, scattering all three of them as they did their best to ready their weapons and stand prepared to fight.

''Stay behind me and watch my back!'' Allan ordered sharply.

Already the guards ahead were regrouping, drawing their swords and ready either to stand their ground or attack. Some had bows— Allan's greatest worry. He took a deep breath and sent a fireball straight down the middle of the passage, scattering frantic guards until it detonated near the middle of their group. The explosion rocked the very stone of the mountain itself and sent guards flying, but as the echoes faded away most of their number lay either dead or stunned and definitely singed. Allan had given it all he had, and he looked startled and just a little self-satisfied. He had only been a dragon for a few weeks, and was still getting used to things.

''Look out!'' Rex warned sharply. ''Behind you! Point that fire of yours in the opposite direction!''

Allan stuck his head around the corner and let loose two of his second-best fireballs, catching a glance of perhaps a dozen more guards. The three sorceresses had already advanced to meet the handful of survivors from the first group. Their skills enhanced by magic, the Veridan Warriors made quick work of what remained of the soldiers. Rex and the dragon waited until they were done and hurried them on their way, knowing that the reverberating blasts of his fireballs would bring trouble from all corners of the fortress.

They went some distance without being challenged, but Allan stopped again soon and stood for a long moment casting about for their goal. They were getting very close now, but that made it only that much harder to be exact. He found a wandering ramp leading down. There were no actual levels to the fortress, the passages twisting and rising at random but with chambers and side passages cut at various places.

It was in this passage that they met another small group of soldiers, this time only five. Allan did his best to stop but once again his feet slipped on the cold, polished stone. Instinctively protecting his folded wings, he slid on his belly down a rather steep length of the ramp, scattering the guards as they stood. Princess Merridyn swore a rather dire oath under her breath and led the others to the attack, taking advantage of the momentary confusion. She cut her way through the shaken defense of the tumbled guards and hurried on to join the dragon, who was just picking himself up. Then they both ducked their heads as Rex let loose with three rapid blasts of his shotgun.

"Are you alright?" Merridyn asked.

"Oh yes, I am fine," Allan answered impatiently as he brushed the dust from his belly. He turned his head to glare. "I really wish that he would not do that in these tunnels."

Rex was just standing there, staring at his gun in disbelief.

"Merciful heavens, I've never shot anyone before," he muttered, and sighed heavily. "Awesome."

Allan glanced around, then hurried back up the steps and confiscated the boots from one of the fallen guards. The fit was not good, for dragons had feet which were long but very narrow, and the boots flopped and threatened to fall off. He looked up to see that Rex and Merridyn were watching him appraisingly, while little Kerie was trying hard not to laugh.

He pushed past them and led the way on down the stairs, the thumps of his loose boots echoing through the length of the tunnel. The ramp ended presently, opening into a larger passage.

He paused at the entrance and peered warily around the corner. His ears twitched nervously. "Guards. I was afraid of that. There are at least two dozen guards waiting in the hall outside her door."

"Any recommendations?" Merridyn asked softly, privately surprised that the soldiers had not heard them coming.

Allan sat back on his tail for a long moment, deep in thought, his ears laid back. "I will cut around them from the other side, so that we may catch them between us. But stay in this passage until I call, for I would not have you caught in my own attack."

Before Merridyn had a chance to ask him what he had in mind, the dragon abruptly disappeared. He simply faded to invisibility where he stood, boots and all, and was gone. A moment later the guards shouted in surprise and drew their weapons as they pressed eagerly to the attack. Princess Merridyn was about to hazard a quick glance when the hall was suddenly rocked by a series of tremendous explosions, so fierce that they cracked the walls and ceiling of the passage and raised quite a cloud of grey dust. Allan called out both aloud and telepathically, and Merridyn sprang out of the passage with her companions close behind.

Half of the guards were down already, but the rest were staggering to some attention and seemed ready to renew their attack now that the dragon's fireballs were momentarily exhausted. These were not simple guards but warriors in plate, mail and leather, which had helped them to survive that fiery barrage. The women were themselves only lightly armored, wearing padded leather with vests of mail. But both the main weapon and defense of Veridan Warriors lay in the remarkable speed, strength and endurance granted to them by their magic.

Rex, however, had the advantage of technology. In the swords and armor set, a pump-action shotgun made him something to consider. By the time he had run out of shells, he had also run out of targets. He had also made a startling amount of noise.

"The doctor is in, and the operation was a success," Rex remarked as he began slipping new shells into the gun.

"If you are quite finished, you might come with me," Allan remarked drily. "You and I will collect Jenny. She knows us."

"And so what makes you think that she will recognize that fox's face of yours?" Rex asked.

He disappeared with the dragon inside the chamber for well over a minute while the others watched the corridor outside. Allan returned at last, with Rex following close behind guiding before him a small human girl of about nine years. Her vast eyes were dark, but her scruffy mop of hair, once brown, was now a blue so deep that it seemed almost black in the dim light. She looked up at the two mortal sorceresses rather fearfully, although she was reassured by the dragon's presence.

"Jenny, these are my friends. They are going to help us get out of here," Allan told the girl soothingly. Then he lowered himself completely to the floor. "Can you climb up on my back and hold on tight?"

"I think so," Jenny answered uncertainly as she walked around the dragon's long body, guided by Merridyn. She moved stiffly, almost trancelike as if just awakened from a deep sleep. But she was clearly doing her best to hurry. The Princess lifted her up onto the dragon's back and showed her where to take hold of the straps of Allan's harness.

"All aboard, kitten?" Allan asked.

"Ready!" Jenny agreed with stoic determination. She was becoming more her old self with each passing moment.

"You just be ready to jump off if we have to fight," Allan warned as he rose carefully to stand on all fours. He bent his head around to look at Merridyn. "Now we return to the ship as quickly as we can. You must lead, and let the others go behind me. They have been playing with us so far, thinking that they are in control, and we have surprised them. But if they know that we have Jenny, they will do all they can to stop us. They must prevent her escape at any cost."

Rex stared at him intently, understanding what he was implying. "Surely she is of too much value to them."

The dragon closed his eyes and shook his head firmly. "We must have Jenny if the Prophecy is to work in our favor. But they win two ways. The Dark is nearly as strong as long as they can stop her from serving us—any way they can contrive it. But they will have to deal with me to get at her. I am not greatly concerned. Hurry, now."

Dalvenjah Foxfire held her enemy to the center of the bridge, returning blow for blow with swords that shimmered with misty flames of raw magic. Haldephren no longer pressed his attack with the fury of his initial offensive but he continued to drive at her mercilessly, never allowing her—or himself—even a moment's rest. He did not yet realize that she was easily his match in skill, although she was yet to prove how her magic stood against him. But her sword might have been moving with a will of its own. While her mind was enthralled in the absolute concentration of battle, her thoughts wandered dangerously along paths of their own.

It hurt her to have to see Karidaejan—or at least Karidaejan's form—again, and it hurt her more to sense the evil thing that now dwelled inside him. Her inner senses were infinitely accurate, and she trusted what she sensed in this matter. Her eyes saw Karidaejan, but it was a different Karidaejan than she had ever known. Her heart knew beyond any doubt that it was not him. All the same, this was all that was left to her of the one who had been her brother. She found it hard enough to fight him. She dreaded the thought that she should have to strike him, even kill him.

Haldephren broke off the attack without warning, drawing back a step. "So, Dalvenjah Foxfire, do you tire?"

Dalvenjah did not have to feign surprise, for she could not imagine why he had said that. At least it roused her from her own thoughts. "I tire of this pointless swordplay, I do confess. The time comes to make an end to it."

"My very thought," the High Priest agreed as he renewed his attack. "Flee, Dalvenjah Foxfire, while you yet have the chance. You know that you cannot strike me."

"I do not doubt that I can, or I would not be here," she returned.

How long had she been at this? Were the others already on their way out? The time had indeed come to be done with this game. Their blades locked and she allowed him to press her slowly back, as if she was folding beneath his strength. Then she drew back suddenly. A faerie dragon's weight was delicately balanced on either side of his hips between body and neck and tail. Even four years in that form had not taught Haldephren enough about being a dragon to avoid that simple trick.

He was thrust forward by his own weight, nose first toward the ground, although he caught himself before he fell completely over. But it threw him off his guard, leaving him vulnerable for a desperate moment. Dalvenjah's sword bit deep into the shoulder of his left wing, slicing through muscle and tendon at the same time that her magic ripped through his body like lightning. Then, in the same swift movement, she brought her blade over the top of his long neck to strike his right shoulder as well.

Haldephren stumbled back with a sharp cry and stood gasping with pain, staring at her in fear and disbelief. Clearly he had not thought that she really would find the courage to strike him. His wounds were not great; he would fly again in a matter of weeks, with the proper care. But now he was betting his life that she could not finish what she had started. There was no escape for him unless she allowed it.

"No, you cannot!" he insisted, panting heavily, dazed with pain and the shock of her magic. "You must not. Dalvenjah, if you destroy me, I will be gone forever."

"I have no such hope," she answered coldly. "All I can hope to do now is to deprive you of what you have stolen."

"No, Dalvenjah," he said, softening and gentling his voice in a crude counterfeit of Karidaejan. "Think of all that we have been through, and the good things that we have known. Remember the love that we had. If you destroy me, there will be nothing left but your memories. Why do you even want to destroy me, my sister?"

"No," Dalvenjah insisted desperately as tears came to her eyes. But she was not lured by his words. Haldephren had never known the real Karidaejan. He had no access to Karidaejan's memories, and nothing that had been Karidaejan's but his form was a part of him. And so his imitation was far from perfect.

"You must not do this to me," he continued, pleading.

"No!" she shouted.

Dalvenjah lifted her sword, and the blade burned with magic. Haldephren drew back fearfully, but she did not strike him. Instead she swung the blade fiercely in an arc that shattered the metal rod of the siderail to her right in a shower of sparks, and in the next instant cut the left rail as well. The bridge swayed and dipped dangerously, but it did not fall yet.

"No! You must not!" the High Priest declared. Too late he guessed her thoughts. She had damaged his wings so that he could not fly and the shock of her magic had stunned his own powers, leaving him unable even to levitate. Now she would cut the bridge from under him to plunge him into the fires below, sparing herself the necessity of destroying him by her own hand.

"Lye assanda min, Karidaejan," she said softly as she wept.

She brought her sword down once again in a double arc of flame, cutting the two remaining siderails that supported the floor of the bridge itself. The bridge broke immediately below her, parting in two even halves that fell away. Her broad wings snapped out as she began a slow ascending spiral about the perimeter of the core, but Haldephren fell helpless into the depths. He cried out only once as the bridge parted, a cry of rage and frustration rather than fear. He knew that he did not go to his own death, just the end of the body he now wore. Then he fell silently for what seemed a very long time, while Dalvenjah circled slowly and watched, before he disappeared at last in a sudden flash of flame.

Dalvenjah wept in silence as she began the long, spiralling climb up the core of the ancient volcano.

Allan pulled himself to an abrupt halt, this time without falling, while the three sorceresses stood defensively behind him. They had just come around another sharp turn and now stood at the entrance of one of the largest natural chambers they had yet seen within the mountain, a roughly oval room several hundred feet long which had opened along a wide fissure. A wide stone bridge spanned the fissure, and the bridge was guarded.

But it was no mortal guard that stood facing them on the center of the bridge. It was roughly human in form but broad and short-legged, its armored body like some immense crab standing man-like, with long plated arms ending in powerful pincers and a tiny head with glowing eyes peering at them from atop wide shoulders. Its entire form glowed with a pale, sickly light, as if it was some misty phantom. All the same, it looked very real and solid. It was much larger even than Allan, standing nearly ten feet tall and perhaps the better part of a ton of hard-shelled flesh.

"Mercy me!" Allan exclaimed softly, and lowered himself to the ground. "Off you go. It looks like I've got a fight on my hands."

"What is that thing?" Rex asked softly, as if he knew already that he would not like the answer.

"That is what your people used to call a demon," the dragon explained as Jenny climbed off his back, then straightened. "It is a creature of magic, brought into this world—at least mostly into this world—from a level of existence very different from what you know."

"Your level of existence is rather different from what we know," Rex pointed out.

"What should we do?" Kerie asked. "Can we go around it?"

"It would follow us, I am sure. And I do not want that thing at my back." Allan considered the problem briefly. "I will fight it, but not with sword. Swords, I fear, would be useless against that thing. I must fight it as a dragon."

Leaving the others to guard Jenny, he stepped forward until he stood a few feet short of the base of the bridge. The demon watched him closely but with no outward sign of emotion or even aware-ness, almost as if it were as mindless as a machine. Allan took a deep breath and released a dense tongue of flame, striking it squarely in its armored chest. The demon only stood its ground, seemingly unconcerned about the fires that surrounded it.

Indeed it was unharmed by his flames. Rex lifted his gun and gave the thing a couple of blasts, but to no better effect. Allan lifted his head to stare at the creature, realizing that he had some-thing of a fight on his hands. But not in the big, loose boots he had appropriated. He slipped off one boot and hurled it with all his strength at the demon's round head. It snatched the boot ca-sually from the air with one pincer and popped the entire thing into its mouth, eating it whole. Allan only stared, bemused.

"Well, do something!" Rex said urgently as he stood at the

dragon's side. "Are you waiting for the other shoe to fall?"

Allan stared at him in disbelief, and they both sat down on the stone floor laughing. "I cannot believe you said that!"

"I do regret it, heart and sole," the surgeon answered.

"Bite your tongue!"

"If you clowns don't mind," Merridyn called impatiently.

"Yes, of course," Allan agreed as he rose, chuckling softly. He stood for a long moment peering intently at the demon, which only stared back in its typical bland manner. Just when he had decided that it was not going to press an attack of its own, it began to take slow, ponderous steps forward, raising its powerful pincers. He turned to the Princess. "You should stand back. Better yet, get Jenny and be ready to run."

"Watch out for yourself," Merridyn entreated him as she slipped back to join the others in the shadows of the tunnel entrance.

"That matter is very much on my mind," Allan remarked nervously as he stepped out onto the bridge to meet the demon.

He stood his ground stoically until the demon stood only six feet away, then spun himself around swiftly. The long, golden whip of his tail caught the monster about its thick ankle and its tip curled around an armored leg. He pulled with all his strength, trying his best to toss the demon over the edge as it fell heavily to the stone bridge. The heavily plated creature was nearly six times his own three hundred pounds, but he succeeded in rolling it over the edge all the same as it fell with a thunderous crash.

But the demon, seeing its own defeat, meant to take him with it if it could. One massive pincer locked onto his right forearm with irresistible force, pulling him with it at the very moment that it tumbled over the edge of the bridge. Allan cried out in pain and fear, but at the same time he fought with his free hand to release the coil of cable at his belt, flip open the prongs of the clip at its end and toss that over the top of the bridge. Then he followed the demon over the edge before the others could run to his aid.

By chance the prongs of the clip caught the edge. The twenty-five feet of steel cable played out until it brought Allan up short at the end of the line, attached where the straps of his harness joined. The demon held on, but the shock of its tremendous weight was terrible. Allan gasped with pain as the long bones in his forearm were crushed in the vise of its grip, the serration along the edges of the pincers biting into his flesh. Panting with pain and shock, he reached around left-handed and drew his sword.

"Dragon!" Merridyn cried, peering down over the edge of the bridge.

Allan needed no warning. He brought the sword around in a glowing arc to sever at the wrist the other immense pincer that would have closed on his long, unprotected neck. The demon did not bleed; it was as dry inside its shell as a tree, its clear blood flowing like thick sap. He struck again but his leverage was poor, so that his blade only slipped off the tough carapace. He struck lower, snapping off the second pincer at the joint. The demon plunged into the fissure, as silent as it had been throughout their contest.

But the pincer still held on, almost as if it possessed a will of its own. Allan spread his wings for balance and raised himself with lift magic back to the top of the bridge. Merridyn and Rex were there immediately, taking hold of the heavy claw and pulling it apart until he was free. Kerie stood ready with a length of bandage from their supplies.

"Hold onto that thing," the Princess instructed as she bent to inspect the serration along the inside edges.

"There was no poison," Allan said impatiently, watching as the claw began to evaporate into the very air. "It does not hurt bad enough. Just wrap me up so that we can get away from here. I will not be much good if we have to fight again. Stand back, now."

"Why?" Merridyn asked.

"Because I anticipate saying a few things that might burn your ears," he stated, and the others stepped back. He muttered the words of command; his forearm glowed with a blue light, and the broken bones straightened and set themselves. His cry of pain became a string of rather potent words, fortunately all in Mindijari. Rex took the bandage from Kerie and carefully wrapped his arm.

Allan turned to Jenny, who stood close watching with wide eyes. "Can you walk well enough to keep up? It is not very far, but this dragon might have enough trouble just getting himself there."

"I can do it!" Jenny declared.

"Good girl! If we hurry, we can be out of here in a few minutes more."

Allan's greatest concern was that the Emperor would send more demons to intercept him, as he must have done when he realized that his mortal servants had failed him. Allan was certain of a few things about the Servants of the Dark that he had only suspected when they had arrived, and he now had a much better idea about what they could and could not do. It gave him hope.

And his hope proved correct. Within five minutes they found themselves once again within the chamber where the airship sat just as they had left it. He had been somewhat concerned about what might have become of the ship during their absence, but it appeared unmolested. All except for the scattered remains of a demon's carapace, which were in the later stages of evaporation even as they arrived.

"Oh, there you are," Dalvenjah said, peering over the rail near the bow of the ship, her head extended to the length of her long neck. "So, you have her. Very good."

"I see that they thought to wreck the ship after all," Allan remarked, watching the last of the demon's remains evaporate. "You seem to have had a better time dealing with yours."

"I am your mate and your instructor in the studies of magic," she replied. "And you are still very new at this. It stands to reason that I know a trick or two that you have not yet learned."

"Not if you were a proper teacher," Allan answered, knowing quite well that he was being teased. "Can we get out of here?"

Princess Merridyn was already lifting Jenny up into Marie's waiting arms on the main deck of the ship, although she paused in climbing the boarding ramp herself to give the injured dragon a boost. Kerie Wold was preparing the airship for flight. Jenny would have liked a closer look at this most unusual ship, but she was already being smothered in Marie's backlog of motherly ministrations. Jenny had already recovered from her two-week abduction by the forces of evil, and absence had apparently not made the heart grown fonder.

"Is he gone?" Allan asked cautiously.

Dalvenjah closed her eyes and nodded. "He is gone. But you know that."

"I was aware when it happened," he agreed. "That—I suppose—was not quite the question I meant to ask."

"I understand." Dalvenjah paused as the airship backed clear of the chamber, steering slightly into the wind to counter drift until her masts and vanes were clear of the tunnel walls. Kerie accelerated the ship quickly to full speed. Dalvenjah frowned. "He did not die directly by my hand . . . at least I contrived to spare myself that. All I can say is that I am glad it is done and over.''

"Dragon! What is the meaning of this?" Marie bellowed, dragging Jenny over to where they stood. "Look at this child's hair. Now you tell me why they dyed her hair blue.''

"It is not dyed," Dalvenjah made the mistake of granting a candid answer. "That is now the true color of her hair.''

Without a word of warning, Marie pulled open Jenny's pants and looked inside. Unfortunately, the proof of that test would still have to wait a year or two for puberty. Dalvenjah sat back on her tail and sighed wearily, knowing that she had a fight on her hands. Marie had never said a word to Dalvenjah about turning her brother into a golden-scaled dragon, but she suspected that she would never hear the end of this business about blue hair.

Dalvenjah made some odd gesture over Jenny's head, and her hair returned to its original color.

"That fixes it?" Marie asked suspiciously.

"For now," Dalvenjah assured her. "It will grow out. Then she will need something like you use to make your hair blond.''

Marie glowered for a long moment, but it had no effect on the dragon. She let go of Jenny's arm. The girl ran over to hang onto the rail, looking at the green and blue canvas of the ship's fins and stabilizers.

"Are you trying to tell me that they've changed her in some way?" Marie asked quietly.

Dalvenjah thought about that, her ears twitching like signal flags. "Can this discussion wait until we get home?"

"Why?"

"Because you are not going to like the answer.''

The airship settled almost gingerly on the ledge outside Dalvenjah's mountain home. It was a small ledge and a rather large airship, with four large vanes ribbed with red and blue canvas. Kerie Wold eased the ship down with an expert hand, and the others began taking in the vanes immediately so that sudden winds would not disturb the vessel. Vajerral, who had not at all liked being left behind, was there immediately. Jenny called out to her in delight and dropped over the rail of the ship even before the ladder could be set out.

Dalvenjah's home was indeed her castle. Marie had never known quite what to make of the faerie dragon's contention that she lived in an abandoned mountain fortress that she had converted for her own use, but it was just that. It was hardly Camelot, but it did make a rather sprawling abode even by draconic standards. There were no towers or battlements, just an almost haphazard group of grey stone structures joined together into a single rambling edifice.

The interior was considerably more comfortable; Dalvenjah had a talent for decorating that was subtly exotic without being imposing. She had adapted the main hall into a type of overgrown den. The cold stone of the walls had been mostly replaced by either paneling or heavy curtains. The back wall had been almost completely replaced by a bank of immense glass windows, leading onto a deep balcony that overhung the cliff itself, looking out across the vastness of the forested valley far below. Marie, at least, was interested to note that dragons had glass for picture windows. She had come expecting medieval squalor, but faerie dragons seemed to enjoy nontechnical prosperity without the benefit of mutual bonds and IRA's. Apparently there was something to be said about old-fashioned hordes.

"This is where you live?" Jenny asked as she stared in fascination. There were no chairs or sofas, just firm cushions of immense size and low tables. Rex and Marie took their seats near the two dragons, while the sorceresses disappeared into the kitchen.

"No, this is the bus station," Dalvenjah said as she eased herself onto one of the cushions. "We are awaiting the next trolley back to your world."

Jenny deflated like a sad balloon. "Ah, do we have to go back so soon? We only just got here."

"That will depend upon many things," the dragon replied guardedly. "What do you remember about the ones who took you away? Did they tell you why they brought you there?"

"No, not really." Jenny frowned, apparently having some trouble remembering the incident. "The big dragon said a lot of things. He said that he was my father, but I never understood what he meant by that . . . and I never believed him. He smiled a lot, but . . . but I always felt like he was going to bite me."

"He was not your father," she told the girl firmly. "And faerie dragons do not bite. Are you afraid that I might bite you?"

Jenny thought about that for a long moment. "I think that you would spank me, if I did something bad."

"Don't you do something bad, and we will not have to test that," Dalvenjah said, trying to hide a smile. "Why don't you and Vajerral help the others to prepare our dinner?"

Marie waited until she had disappeared in the direction of the kitchen, then turned back to the dragon. "What is this business about the big dragon being her father? Does she mean your brother?"

Dalvenjah laid back her ears and sighed sadly. "She means the High Priest Haldephren. The High Priest and the Emperor are mortal, but they have lived for thousands of years by taking the bodies of others. With Karidaejan, it was the first time that either one of them had taken an immortal form, and I have destroyed that one. What Haldephren meant was that he had once taken the form of the one you knew as James Donner, who was Jenny's father. That was his way into your world . . . the first time."

"But James Donner died," Marie protested.

"That was his way back out of both that form and your own world," she explained. "At least that is what he said, to make his own claim upon Jenny. I do not know if it is true."

"But it could be?" Marie asked fearfully.

"Yes, the possibility does exist," Dalvenjah admitted. "It explains the only part of this business that I do not understand, which is how Jenny came to be the subject of a prophecy from a very different world. Unfortunately, I do know that the Prophecy itself is true. I saw it in my gold dreams. Almost every Mindijaran sorcerer shared that same dream on that same night, but I could not come in time to stop them from taking her."

"Just what is this prophecy exactly?" Rex interrupted for the first time. "I know it says something about either their destruction or their return to power."

Dalvenjah nodded. "The blade that cuts both ways. You see, once the High Priest and his Emperor were very powerful indeed, but they fell two thousand years ago and have not returned since. They lack the third, the Consort Darja, who was a warrior sorceress even greater than Haldephren himself. She has never returned to this life as they have, and they cannot bring her back as easily as they keep themselves alive."

"Then Jenny is this Consort?" Marie asked, too surprised to be properly horrified.

"No, I really do not think so," Dalvenjah explained, her ears laid back. "I think that Jenny is simply meant to somehow prepare the way. And that is the matter that can decide this business either way. By what happens to Jenny, or perhaps because of Jenny, then the Emperor and the High Priest will either achieve greater power than they have ever held, or else they will be finally destroyed beyond all hope of recovery. But the exact answer is hidden from us even yet.''

Dalvenjah elected to keep the most important question to herself, that of Karidaejan's mysterious part in this affair.

''Oh, my!'' Marie looked very thoughtful, and very frightened, as she considered all the implications of that. The only possible answer was obvious. She looked up at the dragon. ''You have to protect her.''

Dalvenjah nodded. It was better that Marie had thought of that for herself, rather than having it suggested. ''That is a fact. The best that I can do for her is to bring her here, into my own home, even to the extent of making her immortal and a faerie dragon, as I did Allan. That will not stop the Prophecy, but it will make her best able to defend herself. But I would not ask you to agree to that.''

''Is there any alternative?'' Marie asked, a good indication of just how desperate she was.

''She must learn the dragon magic, by any means. I do not doubt that the faerie centaurs are devoted, but their magic is poor and they could hardly drive off another attempt to take Jenny. The only hope I see is for Jenny to remain here, and her command of dragon magic will change her in time, making her immortal in subtle ways.''

Marie looked very thoughtful for a long moment. ''Then you just might as well make her a dragon. Otherwise she will just be stuck between, a dragon in everything except form.''

Dalvenjah nodded reluctantly. ''That is so, although the choice must be entirely her own. I will protect her the best that I can. But if she is to ever be free of the Prophecy, then the day will eventually come that we will have to fight it and see it through to its end.''

''When will that be?''

''Not until she is quite grown up, I'm sure.''

They were interrupted by the return of the others with their dinner. Marie looked at her own suspiciously. It appeared to be roast beef, large rolls with cheese, and beer. But the cheese was rather sharp, the beer was oddly sweet, and there was no way to know just what manner of beast had been roasted. She elected to keep her mouth shut. With dragons, she thought that she should consider herself lucky that it was cooked. Prime cuts of virgin; which would you like, breast or thigh?

She realized that she must have been under a worse strain than she had thought. That sounded like the sort of nonsense that Rex was prone to say.

She glanced over at the dragon. "Will she ever have a life of her own? I mean, what will she have left when the Prophecy is complete, even if everything goes favorably?"

"Her life, I hope," Dalvenjah admitted frankly.

"But the successful completion of the Prophecy is more important than even Jenny's life?" Marie asked with detached candor.

"I do not think that Jenny will have to die for the favorable completion of the Prophecy," Dalvenjah answered cautiously. "If she must, then nothing I can do will prevent it. Because I will do everything I can."

Jenny sat without touching her plate, aware that she was being discussed and that her very life was at stake. She stared back at them both, very wide-eyed with fright.

Dalvenjah softened her gaze, appearing more warmly reassuring. "What of it? Would you like to be a dragon?"

"That means I would never be able to go home," Jenny said, not making a question of that. She had obviously considered this.

"That is so," Dalvenjah agreed. "You could visit, but you could never stay. But you would live here always."

"I would like to remain what I am for just a while longer, if you think I could," the girl decided surprisingly quickly. "Maybe when I'm grown up, like Allan was when he became a dragon."

"Yes, that can be done," Dalvenjah agreed, although she was mystified about the reason why Jenny would be honestly afraid, even terrified, of that suggestion. She would have expected that Jenny would have begged for the chance to be a dragon.

It was easy enough to let matters stand for now. The Prophecy argued that Jenny would most likely be a dragon before the end.

So it was that Jenny began the serious study of dragon magic, and to be a Veridan Warrior. The first true Veridan had come from the mortal world of Morin, in the ancient days when the first sorcerers of the Light had by bitter necessity been warriors as well, battling the Dark in their long war with the Alasheran Empire. The Mindijaran had never had any need for swords until they began to have increasing contact with human folk, mortal and immortal, fighting with the weapons that nature had granted them as dragons. They had established a small colony of their kind in Morin some six centuries before, eventually adapting the ways of the Veridan for their own use.

And so the years passed swiftly. Jenny was an adept student; far more so than she realized, measuring her progress against the standards of the faerie dragons, creatures of magic. She shared their keen telepathy and their ability to memorize instantly, she mastered their immortal magic with ease, and she could even hold her own with the sword. She enjoyed this way of life, and she never regretted her very limited contact with her own kind. And yet she remained unwilling to become a dragon herself, although she would never explain why.

According to the custom of the Mindijaran, Jenny was to be taken into the forest on the night of her fourteenth birthday, where her inner name would be defined. She was growing quickly now, giving clear hints that she would be a tall, long-limbed woman, possessing a noble beauty if just a little large of nose, and her breasts were enlarging quickly. There was no hiding that fact, for she had spent most of her life among the dragons naked as they were.

That night came late in a spring that was warming quickly to summer, although most mortals would have still thought it chill there in the mountain forests, and the stars were frosty bright. Jenny had flown to the small clearing with the dragons. She did possess the ability to fly, using the same lift magic that made their own flight so swift and effortless, although without wings she lacked much of their speed and precision, and her endurance was very limited. Now, with the formal definition of her inner name, her powers would mature even more swiftly than her lithe body.

All objects, animate and inanimate, have their inner name, and people of all types, mortal and immortal, have an inner name that is far more intimate and individual than the one they are given at birth. The inner name, at least its sound, was only an instinctive prop that sorcerers used to identify and control the magical nature of objects. But an individual's inner name gave a sorcerer control over the person as well, granting the ability to command that person or to change their very essence to some creature very different.

But when the inner name was formally defined, it could at that time be set with defenses which hid it against a sorcerer, forbidding its unwarranted use to the harm of that person. All mortal sorcerers set such defenses about their inner names, for they were the most vulnerable to attack. And all immortal folk, whether they studied the higher magic of sorcerers or not, were given the most intricate defenses as well. Ordinarily no dragon could have given a mortal who had studied the dragon magic her inner name, for the dragon would know only that person's inner name as she would have been were she herself a dragon, and immortal. The inner name that Jenny was to be given this night was a counterfeit, incomplete, and not as secure as her true inner name.

"How long?" Jenny asked. She had been waiting in the clearing with Allan and Dalvenjah, while Vajerral did her best to wait patiently with respectful solemnity for the occasion. The young dragon was beginning to grow quickly now that she had entered her ninth year; already she outweighed Jenny.

"Soon now," Dalvenjah assured her. She was an exceptional telepath, even for a faerie dragon, and she clearly sensed that Jenny was very anxious about something, even upset. She rubbed her soft cheek against the girl's in a dragon's sign of gentle affection. "Dear child, what troubles you?"

Jenny shrugged. "Usually we go to my world for my birthday, and we have a party in the cabin by the lake with my parents and the centaurs."

"We will go tomorrow," Allan promised her, knowing how important to her were her two annual visits home. "For tonight, this is important. This will help protect you from your enemies."

"Yes, I know," Jenny agreed. "The Prophecy."

"Do you know the importance of the Prophecy?" Dalvenjah countered.

"All I know is that I have always sensed how very important it seems to be to everyone," she answered. Her telepathy rivalled that of most of the dragon sorcerers. "I know that it seems to be a matter of life and death."

"Life and death, but perhaps of whole worlds, if you fail," the dragon told her candidly. "You know much already, but now is the time for you to understand the full nature of the Prophecy. Please sit."

Jenny seated herself in the dry leaves beneath the trees and Dalvenjah settled herself on her belly to one side, so that they could more comfortably be on one level.

"A matter of life and death," the sorceress mused. "It began on the night when you were captured, now these five years past. On that night I had a gold dream, for gold enhances the magic of the Mindijaran and I am never without it. For so it is, that at times the dragons may dream the gold dreams and see something of the future. But on that night, every dragon sorcerer who dreamed, throughout any world where they might have been, dreamed the same dream. And on the rare times when that may happen we know it to be a warning, a most important prophecy. Many sorcerers of Morin dreamed the dream as well, for the Prophecy concerns most their world, although it may be of importance to every world where folk of any type dwell.

"Centuries ago, more than three thousand years, many of the mortal folk of Morin turned to the worship of the Dark, and in turn they were granted much knowledge of Dark sorcery until they came in time nearly to equal the evil of the Dark Dragons. No other folk would dare even to enter their world, for fear that the evil of the Alasheran Empire might spread if its wizard-priests gained knowledge of the Ways Between the Worlds. But the Light came to the good people of Morin in their desperation and they were given the knowledge of the Light Magic and the skills of the Veridan Warriors, and in time they defeated the Empire and destroyed the worship of the Dark in their world.

"Or so they hoped. For among their many evils, the Emperor and the High Priest learned a type of counterfeit immortality, transferring their spirits into the bodies of new, younger victims. For so long as a coven of the Dark survived with the knowledge to effect this transfer, they could have survived the fall of the Empire. And we know now that they have, that they live even now and plot the re-establishment of the Alasheran Empire and the worship of the Dark.

"For they too knew of the Prophecy, and they saw a chance to use to their own ends. The High Priest Haldephren had his spirit transferred into the body of Karidaejan, my brother. Then, with the advantages of a faerie dragon's immortal form, he was able to steal you away from your world. But they moved too soon, and they revealed not only themselves, but the fact that they now have knowledge of opening the Ways Between the Worlds. In that way the return of the Alasheran Empire has become a threat not just to Morin, but to all the worlds. If the Empire should regain its full strength and form an alliance with the Dark Dragons, then all folk of the Light may be lost.''

"And I am the key to stopping them?" Jenny asked.

"The Prophecy says that you and another are important to the final defeat of the Empire, for you and she will find the way to destroy the Emperor and the High Priest for all time, and break the power of the Dark," Dalvenjah explained, then paused and sighed with regret. "But you are the primary key. For the second part of the Prophecy holds that you may be turned to the Dark, and in that way effect the final defeat of the Light."

"But I am dragon-trained, and I work dragon magic," Jenny protested. "I thought that the dragons cannot be corrupted to evil."

"That is true, but only in part," she explained. "The faerie dragons, like all immortal folk, will not turn from their true nature of their own accord, and we are creatures of the Light. The dragon magic will protect you. But you are not a dragon, only trained in the dragon magic, and still vulnerable. That can be remedied, if you become a dragon."

Jenny frowned. "Soon, perhaps. But not yet. I want to go home one more time before that happens."

Dalvenjah did not pursue the subject. Jenny was as adamant on that subject as ever, whether or not she really understood why.

"I could never be turned to the Dark," Jenny promised, perhaps mostly to herself, but Dalvenjah knew that the Prophecy would come in time to be balanced upon the blade of a sword, ready to fall either way. The girl looked up. "But one thing I still do not understand. Who is the second?"

"When the time is right, your paths will cross."

Jenny translated that to mean that she had just asked another of those all-important questions which Dalvenjah had no intention of answering. She knew that Dalvenjah knew more on the subject than she was willing to say.

Late in the autumn of her eighteenth year, Jenny was finally allowed to return to her own world to begin her college education. Now that Jenny was finishing her apprenticeship in magic and was quite capable as a Veridan Warrior, Dalvenjah deemed it safe enough for her to return for four years. Jenny knew that this would be her last trip home, at least for more than just a rare visit. She believed that the Prophecy would be upon her before she ever got another chance. Once the Prophecy began to sneak up on her, she knew that she would finally have to face her fears and misgivings and accept Allan's choice, becoming a dragon for her own protection.

The important question in her life right now was the subject of her major in her college studies. She was looking for subjects that would be most useful to a Mindijaran sorceress. Allan was little help; his higher education from his pre-draconic days had been limited to music. Her mother still chose to believe that she would eventually return to her own world and a fairly normal, quiet and secure life as a financial advisor. Rex recognized the realities of the situation; he dropped occasional hints that medicine would serve Jenny well wherever she went.

Jenny was primarily interested in mechanical engineering.

The one thing that facilitated the matter of transferring Jenny's academic credits was the fact that the government had, in a very distant and discrete manner, been involved in Dr. Rex's Centaur School of Magic from the start. The two FBI agents Wallick and Borelli had not mentioned it at the time, but they had known all about the centaur colony. The advantage of government sanction was that the necessary texts had been imported for Jenny's education, and Allan had guided her studies to a high school equivalency.

Although this plan remained a complete secret to the general population, certain elements of the government were quite willing to support the plan to return magic to that world. The entire area about Rex's cabin and the lake was now a sealed wildlife preserve. Faerie centaurs were apparently regarded as wildlife, and their very limited numbers in this world made them an endangered species.

The three dragons brought Jenny back to the cabin by the lake, what Allan was inclined to refer to as the scene of the crime. Jenny had grown into a tall, almost lanky girl, still so thin and long-legged that she looked taller than she was, so that Allan was able to carry her on his back for the longer flight between the worlds.

There was quite a party at the cabin in honor of Jenny's return.

The centaurs and their handful of mortal students were there, as well as the two agents Dave Wallick and Don Borelli. It was considered quite an occasion when the Mindijaran came, especially since the dragons visited only rarely and never stayed long. Their powerful magic was too disruptive to the fragile mortal magic the centaurs were helping their students to discover.

Since they arrived a little early for the party, Rex took the dragons outside for a demonstration of the precision skills of an experienced surgeon. He took with him the most important tools of the trade, his clubs and a couple of balls. The problem was the lack of adequate open space in the forest for driving a decent ball, the best being the partial clearing just uphill from the cabin.

"The first time I was here, you were engaged in a very different manner of recreation," Dalvenjah observed.

"Because we have since discovered the convenience of formal cohabitation, I now have time for a little golf besides," Rex said as he stepped up to bat. "This is known as addressing the ball."

"You expect to send it parcel post?" she asked.

Rex afforded her a brief glance, then hauled back and gave the ball what for. It was a really beautiful drive, except that it sliced rather badly and failed to clear the opening through the trees. By some odd chance, it hit with just enough force to bounce off four trunks until it disappeared into the brush. The dragons had dropped belly to the ground with their hands over their heads.

Dalvenjah lifted her head to look about. "Yes, I do understand. Golf is not unlike billiards."

Rex glared at his club, giving it an admonishing shake, then turned to the dragon. "The idea is to get it between the trees. You want to give it a try?"

"It looks damned awkward," Dalvenjah remarked as she took the club. She had a rather remarkable command of the English language. She looked down at the ball that Rex had set on a tee before her. "Just what is the objective of this game?"

"The one who hits it farthest wins," Allan explained. "You get an extra point for each tree your ball bounces off. Rex is ahead by four points."

Rex turned to stare at him. "You know, ever since you were turned into a dragon, you've been a real smartass."

"I quite disagree," Dalvenjah quipped. "He always was."

Before anyone could speak, Dalvenjah drew back the club and

gave the ball everything she had. It was, as she had said, an extremely awkward stance for a dragon. But faerie dragons were also very agile, and tremendously strong for their size. The ball took off like a shot. In fact, it sounded almost like a shot, since her swing had propelled it just beyond the speed of sound. It might have gone the better part of a mile, except that it hit the same tree after only about ten feet. The ball exploded in a shower of bark and the little rubber worms that were packed inside cheap golf balls. The entire tree shook with the impact, and three squirrels fell chittering with fury from the branches. Dalvenjah was left holding a bent club.

"How many points do I get for each squirrel?" she asked as she gestured a brief spell over the club, which straightened itself.

"The idea is to hit the ball several hundred yards and down a hole," Rex told her as he took the club.

Dalvenjah stared at him. "How big a hole?"

"Just big enough for the ball."

"That does take some skill." She turned to stare across the length of the clearing. "Where is the hole?"

"There is none," Rex explained.

Dalvenjah glared at him. "Then why the hell did you have me hit the damned ball?"

"I wish I knew!"

Rex decided that it was time to cook dinner. Vajerral lit the charcoal grill—for old times' sake—and they were cooking within minutes. It made an interesting contrast to their old days around the cabin. For one thing, it was warm summer rather than the bitter cold of late winter. Vajerral was much larger than she had been during that first visit, now nearly as large as her mother. The most noticeable difference, of course, was that Allan was now a dragon himself, tall, serene and proud, very different from the shy Norwegian-born cellist he had been.

That time by the lake, waiting for Dalvenjah's last battle with the evil steel dragon Vorgulremik, were pleasant, warmly nostalgic days in Jenny's memories, although one could argue that—at eighteen—she was too young to be so sentimental. But the fact was that her life had gotten tremendously complicated, even uncertain, almost immediately afterward. She still enjoyed life and delighted in indulging her insatiable curiosity, but the vague but constant threat of the Prophecy had taught her to fear the future.

Other things had also changed considerably, mostly in the company they were keeping these days. The colony of faerie centaurs had grown to over a dozen, two of them of the young and small variety, looking over three dozen mortal students. There was now a regular little community on the other side of the hill from the cabin, although everything had been designed to appear inconspicuous, scattered like a knot of ordinary vacation cottages.

"Do you really want to return to this world?" Vajerral asked privately as they waited for dinner. A growing dragon had an appetite like a bear; Jenny had often referred to her as the sky shark. "What does this place have to recommend it? The reruns of *Gilligan's Island*?"

"It will be a nice change to be among my own kind for a while," Jenny answered, glancing at the young dragon slyly. "And when I come back in four years, you'll have matured enough that I can stand you."

"So, I see." Vajerral looked surprised. She rose to leave.

"Do you realize that you're speaking English?" Jenny called after her.

The dragon turned her head to glance back, a look that was hysterically shrewd and self-satisfied. "Of course. I am quite mature."

Jenny was careful to hide her amusement. The little dragon was indeed growing up, although she still had a lot to learn. Her amusement faded when she realized that her mother was coming up behind her, deep in conversation with the two older dragons. And that the subject of discussion was herself.

"There are any number of advantages to keeping her in your world," Marie was saying. "Not the least was my own peace of mind in knowing that her virtue is in no danger. She could hardly lose her virginity to a dragon."

Jenny lowered her head to hide a very startled and self-conscious blush, and even Dalvenjah was a little fazed. The dragon knew, although not necessarily by personal experience, that a surprising number of things were very possible. She also knew that Jenny had explored such possibilities with a certain polite young dragon. Mindijaran could give such truly magical kisses that other constraints went out the window, and they could usually lay a pretty smooth line on a girl besides.

Of course, Jenny was always willing to try anything, and she was usually one step ahead of the game. She had seduced the dragon.

"It's time to start letting her learn about such things," Allan interceded innocently. "You don't want her to grow up inhibited."

Marie crossed her arms. "Fat chance! The girl is about as inhibited as a typhoon. That's frankly the least of her problems. I just wondered if she is going to be safe."

"She really should be quite safe," Dalvenjah insisted. "I very much doubt that the Emperor Myrkan will attempt to capture her now. Besides, she is a well-trained Veridan Warrior, and she has passed her apprenticeship in dragon magic. As long as she keeps her sword at her side at all times, she should not have to fear magical assailants."

Allan and Marie both fell silent, turning to look at each other. Allan scratched his head and turned to his mate. "Jenny cannot wear her sword in this world. No one carries swords here."

"Yes, of course." Dalvenjah had to think about that for only an instant. "We will just have to get her a gun. I remember that everyone here carries a gun."

Dalvenjah watched a few too many westerns during her original visit.

Marie and Dalvenjah went into the house to prepare dinner—a matter that neither of them was willing to trust completely to the faerie centaurs—and to continue their negotiations, that being the only word to describe their conversation. Marie would think of reasons to worry, and Dalvenjah would assure her that there was no cause for concern. Of course, Marie had never intended to talk Dalvenjah out of allowing Jenny to return. This was her first chance in ten years to spend any real time with her daughter, and it would most likely be her last. Which of course brought up the question of why she was arguing in the first place.

It was part of her nature.

Allan waited until they were gone, then turned to Jenny. "He has asked me to say farewell to you for him."

"He?" Jenny asked. "He, in big letters? Could you be referring to a certain dragon?"

"So just how many dragons have you made love to?" Allan asked succinctly. "Not enough to know better, it would seem. But it is too late for that, I suppose. You are caught, and there is only one solution. So there is only one real question. Why are you running away?''

"So who says that I'm running away?" Jenny asked evasively, then shrugged. "It was easy for you, because it all happened so quick. Dalvenjah Foxfire was ready to go home, and she asked you to join her. She never gave you a minute to think about it. I've had all this time to think about how absolutely final it is, and all the things I'll regret never having done."

Allan frowned. "Is that a reason or an excuse?"

Jenny looked puzzled. "Isn't that the same difference?"

"Not at all. Reasons are the things we know to be true. Excuses are the things we say to satisfy ourselves and others."

Jenny rolled her eyes. "That frightens me more than anything, the thought of spending the rest of eternity inflecting deep and esoteric utterances upon everyone I meet. And in achingly precise grammar, at that."

"We should go for a walk by the lake, just you and I . . . me," Allan said, smiling, as he waited for her to join him. "Actually, Dalvenjah and I were not so different from yourself. It was love at first sight, in that completely magical way that dragons fall in love. She knew it and I knew it, but I was just too frightened and naive to be consciously aware of that fact. I wanted to go home with her so very, very much, and I never could figure out why. More than anything, I was just so relieved to finally understand why I was so miserable to be with her that I could not wait to go. So, do you really like to be miserable?"

"No, I don't like feeling miserable," Jenny admitted, shuffling along with her hands in her pockets. "I just don't like feeling trapped, either."

Allan stared. "Trapped? Are you pregnant?"

"You know what I mean. Ever since this business began, I've been told that I'll have to become a dragon for my own protection. I don't have any choice, and I'm not asking for much time at all, measured against the life of a dragon. You had all the choice in the world."

Allan shook his head firmly. "I had no more choice than you. Not once the dragon magic binds you to an immortal spirit. Just do not stay away too long. Even a dragon can get impatient with forever, and the bond can break when you are worlds away for very long. Or do you want that bond to break?"

Jenny looked startled, even fearful, but the moment faded

quickly into her old uncertainty. "I don't know what I want. I don't really want for him to go away, but I wish this could have waited until the Prophecy was settled and my life was my own. Perhaps then I could have welcomed it as eagerly as you did. Right now it frightens me, since I don't know what kind of life I'll have under this Prophecy . . . if any at all. I can't afford the distraction. I don't want to be hurt, and I don't want to see him hurt."

"It seems rather too late for that," Allan remarked, struggling with his awkward shape to walk upright on the steep slope. "I can anticipate having a certain dragon hanging on our doorstep for the next four years, pining away for his one true love. There really is nothing more miserable than a pining dragon, I can tell you."

Jenny smiled at the thought of a dragon pining for her, and had to admit that Allan probably was not exaggerating by much. She bent to collect a large flat stone from the outer edge of the beach, then gave it a deft flip into the lake. It disappeared in a single enthusiastic plop. She put her hands in her pockets and sighed. "Nice skinnydipping weather."

Allan shook his head firmly. "Your mother has radar, and she was upset enough even before you had tits. Sometimes I wonder that she never makes an issue of the fact that I wear no clothes."

"I suppose so," Jenny agreed, kicking one large stone into the shallow waves. "I guess that I need to start practicing mortal habits again."

Allan twitched his ears. "That is the key word, is it not? Mortal. Keep always in mind that you have been a part of the dragon magic for so long that you are no longer mortal, nor can you ever be again. Play if you will, but do not fall in love with one of them. They are less your own kind now than that golden-scaled fellow with the wings who does love you."

"I can hardly forget that," she said, kicking idly at the sand. "There's no one in this world for me, not even in play. I love him too much."

Allan was startled, actually surprised to hear her say those words that she had never dared to say before. He was not surprised by the tears in her eyes, or the depth of her emotion. Jenny wore a shell of bright eagerness and girlish charm, and in most ways she really was the person she pretended to be. But she could not hide the truth of her inner self from dragons, who were sensitive to the minds and hearts of others.

"Have you ever missed this world?" Jenny asked after a long moment, still looking out across the lake.

"I have broken all ties with this world. You have not," Allan answered obliquely. Dragons did that almost as a point of polite conversation, even born-again dragons like Allan Breivik. He considered it time to change the subject. "Engineering with a biology minor is an interesting combination, but it will serve you well when you are a full sorceress. Have you thought about what you will do and where you will go when you have finished here?"

Jenny shook her head. "Fulfilling the Prophecy is my business in life and I won't allow myself to think about anything beyond that until it's all done. Until then, I have only two purposes. I prepare myself in any way I can for what is to come, and I enjoy life while I can."

"You are wise," Allan agreed vaguely, although he knew better. He knew that Jenny was coming to fear the Prophecy now that her childhood was well behind her.

"There is just one thing," Jenny said, dropping her voice conspiratorially. She glanced back up the hill toward the cabin, where Dr. Rex prepared burnt offerings beneath a cloud of grey smoke. "I've never asked about the Prophecy, but I would like to know when I might expect it to begin."

"And what makes you think I know?" Allan asked cautiously.

"You maintain a unique monopoly on that source of all arcane and esoteric information," Jenny pointed out. "In other words, you're the only person who goes to bed each night with the mysterious Dalvenjah Foxfire."

"I would have it no other way."

"So?"

"I will not betray Dalvenjah's trust," Allan said with a distinct note of finality. Dragons also had an almost instinctive devotion to perfect honor, like Boy Scouts.

"Oh, be that way!" Jenny declared. She slipped her hands back in her pockets and stood for a moment, kicking at the sand. Allan saw it coming, and prepared himself. The forecast was for more hard admissions. She shrugged. "You know, I never said good-bye. Maybe I knew that I would never have the courage to say some things I should. Will you tell him that I love him very much?"

"He knows that, I am sure. But it still bears repeating."

"Nuts! Let's go for broke, and just scare the piss out of him," Jenny declared. "Tell him that we're mates, no less than you and Dalvenjah. I've got things I have to do first, but if he can wait then I will come back to him. Tell him that when he does see me again, I'll be a dragon."

"That seems a lot to promise, for such a long way off," Allan observed.

Jenny shrugged. "You said it yourself. Did I ever have any choice?"

• Part One •

Higher Learning

WHEN JENNY BARKER arrived in Bennasport, the cool, hilly coastal port where she was to study magic with the sorceress Kasdamir Gerran, she arrived in style. She had arrived in the mortal world of Morin the evening before, spending the night at the Academy of Magic in the capital city of Tashira. The airship that brought her down from the Academy was a freighter of considerable size, twice as long as the largest aircraft of her own world. That fact fascinated her all the more when she considered that it was made of wood. The ship settled gingerly for a landing on the stone-paved airship slips near the warehouses, floating down into a pocket of open space between the dark wooden buildings that was hardly any larger than herself.

Jenny had watched the landing from the rail, then hurried to collect her bags and guitar case. She did not have a cabin; the flight had only lasted eleven hours, leaving from Tashira that very morning at sunrise. Returning to the deck, she waited while the boarding ramps were set into place. She realized that she looked rather out of place in this late-Renaissance world of magic, dressed as she was in jeans and sneakers and a machine-knit sweater, with two pieces of vinyl Samsonite at hand.

Even more out of place was her companion. Vajerral had grown into a very lithe and powerful dragon, and an exceptionally pretty one. She was only slightly larger than her rather petite mother, very slender and long-limbed of build. She had insisted upon accompanying Jenny into this world and remaining in the role of bodyguard—at least as often as she could—and Dalvenjah had been surprisingly agreeable to that idea.

Jenny was not about to complain. It was nice to have a familiar face in a strange world. Even a face like that.

"Our new home," Vajerral said, coming up behind her.

Jenny glanced at her. "This is no place for a dragon."

"I have lived in worse places," Vajerral answered succinctly, meaning to imply certain things about the place Jenny came from. "Besides, I can come and go as I like. You are stuck."

"So, here you are, safe and sound."

She turned to face the captain of the airship, who was also the sorcerer whose magic had provided its lift. He was still young, tall and powerfully built, like the handsome, derring-do captain of a sailing ship from some old movie. He certainly did not look like anyone's idea of a sorcerer, at least not anyone from her world.

"We'll have your crates stored in the customs warehouse, for you to collect later," he told her. "They'll take good care of your things, especially when I mention the name of your new mistress."

"I would appreciate that," Jenny responded, still struggling with the language of this world. Her accent left her even more exotic and out of place.

Carrying her bags gallantly, the captain escorted her down the boarding ramp and even managed to find her a ride. It was a freight wagon instead of a carriage, he explained with regret, although Jenny thought that anything was better than walking. Vajerral, of course, had no bags, only her own small crates of books and other goodies. She was also of the opinion that flying was better than riding perched on the crates in the back of a wagon for the entire city to stare at her, but that was exactly what she got.

Everything had gone well enough so far. Jenny had made connecting flights in three different worlds, and she still had all of her luggage. That was a considerable amount, since she expected to be staying in this world for the next couple of years at least. Morin, or at least the northern country Elura, was a place quaintly medieval in appearance, perhaps middle nineteenth-century in technology, and Scandinavian in landscape. The dress and custom reminded her quite a lot of Norway, but with a large amount of middle-eastern thrown in. Bennasport itself reminded her a great deal of Bergen, or perhaps Seattle of a century before.

Dalvenjah Foxfire had insisted upon this, but Jenny could not for her life imagine why. She had taken her apprentice training from the faerie dragons, and she had enjoyed that. Her last four years had been given to her college education, but then Dalvenjah had insisted that she complete her training in magic with Kasdamir Gerran. Since Jenny was trained in dragon magic, that in itself seemed to make little sense. It was like finishing her pilot training with a truck driver.

Jenny had little idea of where her future might lead her. The position of journeyman sorcerer was in some ways more difficult than that of an apprentice. She was no longer just a student; she was expected to do her share of competent work, and not just read and experiment and learn. But her mistress would declare her a full sorceress only when there was nothing more for her to learn. And Lady Kasdamir, according all that Jenny had heard, had a hell of a lot to teach. Jenny could be a journeyman here for years to come. But what choice did she have?

That ultimately led Jenny back to the real reason for that drastic change in both her training and her life. Dalvenjah always had her own reasons for everything, and Jenny was reminded that she was ultimately getting ready for that main goal in her life, that of facing the Prophecy and defeating the High Priest and the Emperor Myrkan. Since Dalvenjah had arranged this, it must in some way be to Jenny's eventual benefit.

The fact that she was here was, in part, her own fault. Her four years in college were to have been her last mortal fling before accepting the greater protection offered by the form of a faerie dragon. And to fulfill the promises she had made to a certain dragon to whom she was tied by bonds of love and magic. But she had hesitated yet again and Dalvenjah had been surprisingly agreeable to yet another delay, sending the girl into this world for special magical studies with the sorceress Kasdamir Gerran. Perhaps the dragon knew that the next time the question came up, the Prophecy itself would force Jenny to accept.

The wagon stopped before a wide wrought-iron gate set in a high brick wall that was half-hidden beneath draped blankets of ivy. Jenny hurried to collect her bags and guitar from the back of the wagon. She had hardly expected to find herself deposited at the entrance to an estate.

Jenny stepped through the open gate and stopped short to stare. She knew that the sorceress Kasdamir Gerran was among the most successful in the trade; Jenny's own abilities warranted only the very best teacher to complete her training. But she had never expected this. Many sorcerers had to sell love potions and fortunes to pay the rent, but the Lady Kasdamir dwelled in a mansion which must rival those of local master merchants. The residence itself consisted of a bulky central structure of three stories dominated by a massive tower of at least five, with wings that angled forward from either side, two stories high with turrets at each corner, framing the loop of the paved drive. Behind that were the stables and a dark, barnlike bulk that she thought must house an airship. Sturdy oaks, newly clothed in the fresh green of spring, drew a still, secure cloak over the yard.

So great was her surprise that she stepped back to the street quickly to check the address a second time. Not only was the number on the polished bronze plate correct, it bore the name of the proper owner as well. All of her previous reservations about this extended visit to a backward world vanished like smoke. This promised to be far more interesting than she had ever anticipated.

Jenny almost hesitated when she saw that some manner of party must be taking place behind those well-lit windows; several carriages were pulled up to one side, and a handful of coachmen seated about a game of cards looked up at her in a very appraising manner. She all but ran up the few steps and knocked, then brushed the long, dark hair out of her face as she waited, hair a blue so dark that it looked black in the dim light.

"Trick or treat!" Vajerral said over her shoulder.

Jenny waved her aside impatiently. "Go suck your tail."

The door opened after a long moment, the warm, deeply golden light of true oil lamps flooding out into the evening. Jenny's anticipation gave way to curiosity and amazement when she saw that the door was held by a very small and frail-looking old woman dressed in the odd combination of the black jacket and long skirt of an abbess of the Wandserian Nuns and high leather riding boots. Her large, dark eyes were bright and her long, silver hair was braided and bound on the back of her head. The Wandserians were civil if not friendly with the mageborn, whom they professed to be demon-spawned, so one would hardly expect to find an abbess of their order answering the door at a sorceress's party. She stared at the caller rather appraisingly for a very long moment before she seemed to come to some decision on the matter.

"Yes, may I help you?" the tiny abbess asked in a voice that radiated professional briskness, as if she was the proprietress welcoming a paying customer into her shop. She certainly did not seem surprised to see this odd pair at her door.

"We've come to see the Sorceress Kasdamir," Jenny answered, her usual confidence returning quickly to her own voice. "I'm Jenny Barker, her new journeyman, and this is Vajerral Foxfire."

"How do you do," Vajerral added quickly. She saw the wisdom in keeping her own mouth shut.

"Oh, yes! We've been expecting you." The abbess beckoned them in as if welcoming the pair into her own home. "Well, I'm Dame Tugg, and I've been Lady Mira's housekeeper since she came to make her residence here six years ago. You do know that we have five buildings on five acres of land, including an observatory, the largest private library on the west coast and an enclosed shed for a one-hundred-and-ten-foot airship."

"No, I didn't know that," Jenny answered, slipping the pack and guitar off her back as the housekeeper closed the door. She immediately perceived that to have been the wrong answer.

"Well, there's more going on here than there might seem from the street," Dame Tugg declared with slight condescendence for the stupidity of the world at large. "Lady Mira is a research sorceress, as you surely know. Sorcerers and scientists and scholars of every description come from all over the world to consult with her. When she's not traveling herself, of course."

"Lady Mira?" Jenny asked. This last part she had indeed already known.

"As the Sorceress Kasdamir prefers to be called."

"Does she have other students?"

"No, of course not," Dame Tugg said in a sharp manner which made the young sorceress feel rather stupid for not knowing something that should have been common knowledge, although Jenny could not imagine how.

"I'm sorry," she mumbled, daunted by that odd personality despite herself. "Of course, I come from another world."

"Well, you'll learn how things are soon enough," the small abbess said, graciously accepting the apology. "If you will come this way."

She led them into a type of sitting room to one side of the entranceway. In the few scant seconds of silence that followed, they were able to take their first good look about. The place was furnished as richly as the home of some wealthy merchant but in a manner that was more exotic at the same time that it was also more comfortable, with heavy, wooden furniture, rich, dark cloth and leather, and statues and paintings of magical subjects. The whole place was delightfully ostentatious, as if the entire house was designed around a mischievous sense of humor, bordering on gaudy.

"You may leave your things here while I inform Lady Mira and prepare your rooms," Dame Tugg said, although she seemed to be in no hurry to do so. "You know, this house was built by my older brother about twenty years ago, when his shipping fleet was in its heyday. We came from a very old family, among the first settlers here nearly twenty-two hundred years ago. But my brother was in poor health and wanted to retire to the country, and so he sold the place to Lady Mira. Of course, I had already retired here after thirty years as the abbess of the Abbey of Wayngot."

And you refused to budge? Jenny thought to herself. Or did your brother sell you with the place? But, by exercising wizardly patience and firmly biting her tongue, she managed to say nothing.

"Ah, yes! So you must be my young student and her dragon friend."

Jenny turned quickly, and knew this woman as the Sorceress Kasdamir by the invisible cloud of latent magic that encircled her like a long cloak. She was not as old as Jenny would have thought for so accomplished a sorceress, surely not much past forty. And she was an elegant woman, in her own remarkable way. She hardly looked elegant, as richly as she was dressed. She was tall, two inches beyond even Jenny's rangy height, with a face that was the model of mature beauty, laughing eyes and an impish smile, and long, red hair tied up behind her head. She sauntered into the room like a sailor in port. And yet she radiated a regal elegance, obviously without trying or even caring, but an elegance that was open and friendly rather than cold and remote.

"Do see to their rooms, Dame Tugg," she said.

Dame Tugg nodded once and left without a word. Lady Mira watched her until she was gone before turning back to her protégé. "Dame Tugg is a dear, but I would gladly toss her out on her scrawny ass if I didn't have a weakness for old people. Well, I'm pleased that you made it, if a bit the worse for wear. You look done in.''

"Time changes from one world to the next," Jenny explained. If she was tired, it was mostly her own fault. She delighted in airships—just as she delighted in almost everything in life—and had spent most of her journey with her head hanging over the rail like a hound in the back of an old truck.

"Well, that's all safely behind you," Lady Mira declared. "What you look like you could use is a nice, hot bath. . . . No, you really look like you need something to eat more. Why don't you freshen up just a bit before you join us for a little dinner?''

Vajerral, with the iron fortitude of a dragon, declined the offer and was sent on to join the party. Lady Mira led her new student upstairs, and even carried one of the heavy suitcases herself. They could hear Dame Tugg blathering blissfully to herself not far away, but the talkative housekeeper did not—mercifully—put in an appearance at that time. The room that Jenny was shown as her own was a luxury beyond anything she had ever known in her life, including Dalvenjah's subdued opulence. It was a complete apartment, with a bedroom, study, even a separate bath, richly appointed but in a more sedate manner than Mira's typical flair for the exotic.

"You just come downstairs when you're ready," Mira declared as she sailed out the door to rejoin her guests. "We'll be waiting for you.''

Jenny was not at all certain that she wanted to be introduced to her mistress's guests, no doubt the cream of Bennasport's high society, at least not this night. But it seemed that she had no choice if she wished to have any dinner, and she thought that she should hurry. She hesitated to think how Vajerral might be enjoying herself at the party.

She washed the dust off her face and changed quickly into the best clothes she had with her, dark slacks with a loose silvery-white blouse and fashionable boots. She had been warned beforehand to bring only pants; there was a cultural prejudice in the Northlands against skirts and dresses, which were considered to belong to the evil and decadence of the ancient Kingdoms of the Sea and the Alasheran Empire to the south. She glanced at herself briefly in the full-length mirror, her old dislike at seeing her own reflection keeping that inspection brief.

"Well, what do you think?" she asked the black-and-white tomcat that had followed her in and had remained behind to watch her dress. Or perhaps he had simply been overcome by a sudden fit of exhaustion, for he had thrown himself down atop a wooden chest. The cat only looked up at her with an expression of droll exasperation for disturbing his rest, and went promptly back to sleep.

Jenny suddenly felt faint from the trials of her journey and had to sit down quickly on the edge of the bed. She sighed heavily. "Oh, my!"

"Put your head between your legs."

She looked up to see the cat staring at her, and it suddenly occurred to her that this was no common cat but its mistress's familiar, a spirit of magic in animal form. "What did you say?"

"I said, put your head between your legs."

"Oh, very well." She did as she was directed with remarkably little difficulty, being a very strong and agile girl. "Now what?"

"Now lick your asshole."

Jenny sat up quickly. "What!"

"Well, it's what I would do, if I were in your position," the cat remarked drily.

Jenny had never had much contact with familiars. For the moment she was unsure whether or not she was being teased. Leaving the cat to his business, she hurried downstairs. Lady Mira intercepted her at the bottom of the stairs, staring at her appraisingly. Jenny realized that, compared to the heavy materials and baroque enthusiasm of this world, her own attire had a simple and rather futuristic look, as if she had just stepped out of a flying saucer. Her dark blue hair hardly helped matters.

"My, you are a pretty thing. And Beratric Kurgel said that off-worlders are all homely," Mira declared. Then she paused to stare intently. "What's upset you?"

Jenny laughed. "Oh, I'm not upset. Just surprised. Your cat says some very peculiar things."

Mira waved that aside. "He's just a familiar. Pay him no mind."

Jenny frowned as she followed her new mistress, wondering why Mira was speaking to her so gently. Did these clothes make her look delicate, or had Mira only received some wrong information about her new student? After spending so many years with dragons, Jenny was hardly delicate.

Jenny stopped short at the door leading into the spacious dining room. She had never seen such an odd assortment of characters in her life, and considering the company that she had kept most of her life, that was saying quite a lot. Of course, most of the three to four dozen people gathered about the tables in small groups were perfectly ordinary merchants. The rest might have been escapees from some storybook, if not an asylum. But there was a very casual, unprepossessing atmosphere to the gathering. Vajerral was enjoying herself immensely, daintily holding a glass of wine and a sandwich as she appalled a group of ladies with some draconic tale.

"Listen, everyone!" Lady Mira held up both hands as she addressed the gathering in a loud voice, commanding imperfect attention. "I wish to introduce my new journeywoman, Jenny. She's only just arrived."

Jenny thought that her embarrassment could not have been more complete, until the entire group actually set down their cups and plates to applaud her entrance. The curious thing was that the cheers actually seemed to be sincere, if not overwhelming. It seemed that being Lady Kasdamir's own student counted for quite a lot. But Mira gave her no time for honest embarrassment, taking her by the arm to lead her right into the center of the group.

"Here you are, dear child," she said as she pushed a plate into Jenny's hands and began piling things on it from the platters and bowls that filled the table. "You need to eat something right away. I'm sorry that the party tonight was strictly buffet, but you should make out just fine."

"Oh, I'm . . ." Jenny paused and took a step backwards at the sight of the two Trassek mercenaries, dressed in full armor and carrying bared swords, who had quietly appeared behind each of Mira's shoulders. One was very tall and very thin, with dark hair and eyes, while the other was short and blond but just as thin. Both looked like mere boys, eighteen or nineteen at the most, beardless and almost comically stupid of expression.

"Oh, pay them no mind," Lady Mira said after a quick glance over her shoulder at the pair. "These are just my Trassek bodyguards, Dooket and Erkin. They understand that they are to serve you as they serve me . . . hopefully better. Say hello to the nice lady, boys."

"Hello, nice lady," they said as one.

"Ignore them," Mira added as she piled the plate to overflowing. "That should do it for now. Will you have something to drink?"

"Oh, nothing stronger than ale, thanks," Jenny said as she did her best to balance the plate. "I don't drink."

"Ale it is," Mira said as she took the full mug from Dooket's hand and gave it to her. "So, how are things going?"

"No luck yet, Lady Mira," Erkin answered. Dooket was still staring at his empty hand.

"No luck? Oh, you poor boys," She evidently understood what they meant, even if Jenny did not. "Well, just remember that these are very important people. You simply must keep a hold on yourselves, no matter how hard it is."

Dooket looked down at his pants. "I'll keep a hold on it, but how did you know . . . ?"

"Bite your tongue!" Mira declared, although half amused. Jenny finally understood what they were talking about. "Go wander about and keep your ears open. I can't imagine this crowd getting out of hand, but some of these dear old gentlemen are drinking quite a lot."

The two mercenaries bowed their heads over the curved swords they held at shoulder level and moved off into the crowd. By this time Jenny had decided that the two of them were not so stupid as they first appeared; they were just energetic but inexperienced kids who possessed the rather wry sense of humor that was required of those who served Lady Mira. She caught a glimpse of Dame Tugg, also wandering through the crowd under the ruse of serving drinks from the wide tray she carried. She appeared to be descending upon hapless victims and boring them half to death with banalities.

"Well, well. The Sorceress Kasdamir Gerran has finally gotten herself a student." A woman of about the same age as Mira descended upon them from out of the crowd. She was small and dark, and by nature seemed rather fussy and self-centered. "It took you long enough to give in to the Academy's demands."

"It took this long to find a student worthy of what I intend to teach," Mira answered haughtily, although Jenny was beginning to comprehend that this cattiness was only play between two old friends. She turned to her student. "Jenny, this is Addena Sheld, the finest concert singer on the west coast—although I would never have her hear me say that."

"I never did," Addena said. "How are you, dear girl? Mine

is another middle-aged face for you to get used to, since I do an even half of my freeloading here."

"I can afford you both, if that's what you want to know," Mira said, blandly condescending. "What I've never understood is how you could have hung about this place so long without learning any real magic for yourself."

"Have I not?" Addena demanded in hurt tones.

"Oh, that's right! You haven't had to ask me for a contraceptive spell in a couple of years now."

"Hm . . . yes." Addena seemed to be at a loss for words. "Well, why don't I talk to the two of you later?"

"When you can think of a few tart comments of your own?" Mira inquired innocently, but the singer made no response as she disappeared into the crowd. Mira stood for a long moment looking quietly amused. Then she spied someone else she evidently knew well, and descended upon a quiet-looking older man with a long, white beard. "Ah, Dardles! Up to your old tricks?"

"Doing well, Sorceress. Doing well," he answered in a thin, raspy voice.

"So, you're the new journeywoman."

Jenny turned quickly to find a young man standing close—too close behind her. She thought him a young merchant by his dress and manner, or perhaps even the son of a wealthy aristocrat; she was very sure that he was no older than herself. He was handsome enough, but he also radiated a smug conceit that she found repulsive. Her first thought was that she was heading into real trouble. Perhaps she was just skeptical, but she simply could not trust the sincerity of someone who was contemptuous of the one they were also trying to score on.

"I'm Jenny," she offered, momentarily at a loss for what to say.

"I'm Lon," he answered. "You know, that old sorceress isn't the only one with something to teach you around here."

"Well, you certainly have a lot to learn," Jenny said coldly. Her first thought, she realized, was quite correct. Besides, she was telepath enough to know exactly what was on his mind. She took what she hoped was a very subtle step backwards.

Lon followed her, and more than made up for lost ground. "I'm sure that I know some things they don't teach at any school for sorcery. If you would care to come to my classroom, I'll . . ."

"You'll get your hands off me right now," Jenny told him. He had taken tight hold of both of her upper arms, as if he meant to crush her resistance with a casual display of strength.

"Hey, don't give me that, little rabbit." He laughed, arrogantly amused. "You say one thing, but I know what you really want."

Jenny rolled her eyes. "I really can't believe you said that."

End of discussion. Jenny had reached the end of her patience. Lon had just reached the end of the line. Whatever happened next happened too quick for anyone to see, except that Lon was suddenly face down on the floor and Jenny was standing over him with his arm pinned behind his back.

Vajerral's furry face appeared instantly. "Good show! Now you skin him, and we'll have a fine supper."

Jenny said a few choice words—in English, for the sake of privacy. Even Vajerral did not know most of those words.

Dooket and Erkin were there immediately. They scooped up the debris in one simple motion and headed for the door, and Jenny never did see Lon again. The guests stared for a moment longer, then returned casually to their previous conversations.

"Very effective," Mira remarked, appearing suddenly behind her. "But you are going to have to be easier on the guests. That's what I pay those two barbarians good money to do."

Jenny laughed. "You certainly know how to throw a party."

"Not exactly the first impression that I wanted to make," Mira muttered in disgust. "This is actually fairly tame for one of my parties, but it's still probably a bit much after the journey that you've just been through. Why don't you two collect your plates and cups, and we'll just step outside for a little air?"

Mira led them quickly through the maze of the large house and out the framed-glass doors of the dining room into the well-kept yard. Already night had fallen; the sky was dark and full of bright stars. Mira stopped short on the stone steps leading down into the lower yard and the airship shed and sat down, leaning well back against one of the posts that framed the top of the steps. Jenny sat down well to the other side, setting her plate and mug on the top step beside her, while Vajerral lay down on her belly in the cool grass, her long neck lifted like a snake.

"I suspect that this was all rather more than you expected," Mira began. "Why, this place is like a madhouse. An obnoxious cat, bodyguards to protect your guests from each other, that blathering old abbess in riding boots . . . and me."

"No, not you," Jenny was quick to assure her new teacher.

"Do you jest? I know that I take more getting used to than all the rest. But when most people get to know me, they still think that I'm damned eccentric." She shrugged, totally unconcerned with what anyone might think of her. "Still, you might just find, if you ever do get to know me well enough, that I am in fact a very practical person. I do not believe in anchoring myself to burdensome conceits. I'll make no claims to being a moral person, but I am by no means immoral; I am, quite simply, amoral. I help those people I can, I leave those who do not want my help alone, and I enjoy myself. And that, dear child, is the closest you will ever hear me come to trying to justify myself to anyone."

"I can understand that," Jenny conceded. "Listen, I'm neither shy nor delicate. I helped to fight my first steel dragon when I was only nine years old. I was raised for nine years by faerie dragons. I've been trained in the dragon magic, and I'm a very accomplished Veridan Warrior besides. I have a degree in Engineering, and I'm a member of the Star Trek Fan Club. I've seen it all."

Mira nodded soberly. "I suppose you can. Do me one favor. Please just wait until tomorrow before you make up your mind. I've never had a student of my own before, but I will do my best for you. And I'll only teach you magic and other forms of higher education, and never require you to understand or adopt my philosophies of life. Also, you'll find that Dame Tugg has quite enough to keep her busy and out of our affairs. The Trassek twins are really two very good, honest boys who will do anything for you. And even J.T. has his dubious virtues."

"J.T.?"

"The cat," she explained, certain reservations of her own quite evident. "His initials stand for Just Trouble, and for reasons that will become quite obvious to you soon enough. What did he say to you anyway?"

"Ah . . . you don't want to know," Jenny said as she turned with renewed interest to her plate.

"Try me," Mira said as she leaned back against the post to stare up at the stars, smiling with mischievous delight.

Jenny hurried downstairs the next morning, wondering if she had slept late. Hardly knowing what else to do, Jenny presented herself at the kitchen for breakfast. Dame Tugg, with an uncharacteristic economy of words, gave her a tray that included a plate

for herself, a porcelain pot of hot water for tea and two cups, and
instructions for their destination. Lady Mira was in her study,
seated at a small round table in a glass-enclosed alcove to one
side of the large room. An open book lay on the table before her,
but she seemed far more interested in the garden outside, bright
flowers of red and deep blue that almost sparkled in the bright
morning light.

Jenny found that she was apprehensive of this first meeting with
her new mistress this morning as she had been for the very first
time the night before. Lady Mira put aside the book and indicated
for her student to take the only other seat at the table, then poured
tea for them both. She measured honey carefully and stirred both
cups to almost meticulous perfection, then took a cautious taste
of her own and sat back with a loud sigh of contentment. Then
she sat up straight, staring at her young student with a curious
intensity that Jenny found disconcerting.

"So, where should we begin?"

Jenny started nervously. "I can't imagine. Surely Dalvenjah
gave you most of the information on my background and training."

"Only what she found valuable, although I saw enough to
convince me to take you on as my journeywoman," Mira agreed.
"You came recommended very highly by some people whose
judgements I trust a great deal. And please do not sit there and
look so surprised. There are certain people in this and certain other
worlds whose thoughts and judgements I hold in as high a regard
as my own, and a few I consider even better."

"What would you like to know?"

Lady Mira seemed quietly appalled, although her student could
hardly imagine why. "Oh, all right. Since you seem to be in such
a confessional—confessory?—mood, why don't you tell me why
such a nice girl like yourself hangs about with dragons?"

Jenny looked genuinely surprised. "Why shouldn't I? Is there
something wrong with dragons?"

"Dragons are wonderful folk! Faerie dragons are just about the
highest and most noble of all the immortal races." Mira paused,
and leaned forward to regard her shrewdly. "So why, then, does
such a remarkable and august dragon as Dalvenjah Foxfire find
you so interesting?"

"Oh, Dalvenjah Foxfire is my aunt."

Lady Mira nearly fell out of her chair.

"Well, there really is a reasonable explanation," Jenny insisted, realizing that what she had said was not entirely reasonable. "You see, Dalvenjah married my uncle Allan Breivik—my mother's younger brother. Only dragons don't really get married, so I guess they're just shacking up."

"Are you telling me that Dalvenjah Foxfire is married—or perhaps not quite married to a mortal?"

"Oh, he wasn't a dragon at the time."

That had not come out quite right. Mira was leaning forward in her chair, her head braced heavily on one arm with the other on her hip, one brow raised in a skeptical fashion as if she had just been offered the movie rights to *Roget's Thesaurus*.

"You see, my uncle Allan was a cellist."

Mira rolled her eyes. "Oh, that explains it! The lady dragons all just swoon over cellists."

Jenny cast a puzzled glance at the floor, as if wondering if she would find her brain there. "Perhaps I should start at the beginning. You see, Dalvenjah was stuck in my world several years ago while she recovered from a broken wing. She went looking for the best wizard she could find, which was my brother. But there were no wizards in my world at that time, so he was working as a cellist. Then they went off into the woods to live in the cabin that was owned by my father, only he wasn't my father at that time. And I guess they must have fallen in love, since she turned him into a dragon and took him home. Let me show you."

She pulled a large wallet from her pocket, one containing money from three different worlds, and flipped open the small group of photographs. "You see? There are my own parents. And that's Allan and Dalvenjah."

"Yes, I see," Mira remarked absently; she seemed far more interested in the process. "Is this dragon magic?"

"No, Polaroid." The next picture, that of a handsome male dragon, seemed to embarrass her considerably. "That's an old friend of mine."

Mira indicated the next. "Who is that rather pretty woman?"

Jenny stared. "Oh, that's Stella Stevens. And that last one is Allan and Dalvenjah with Vajerral when she was still young."

"Are you sure they didn't have to get married?"

"Oh, no. You see, their daughter Vajerral was already four years old when they first met."

"Well, that's certainly a neat trick!" Mira looked as if she had just been hit in the head. "And you were wondering last night that my house was too strange for you?"

Jenny frowned. "No, you were."

"Oh, yeh." Mira shrugged. "So that's the whole story?"

"No, there is the Prophecy."

"Prophecy!" Mira sat up straight. "That frigging dragon didn't say a damned thing about a prophecy. Beratric Kurgel told me to never get mixed up in prophecies, and for once I quite agree. Just how did you manage to get tied up with a prophecy, and what is it about?"

"Well, it all started just after Dalvenjah and Uncle Allan left, when I was nine years old," Jenny explained thoughtfully. "I was kidnapped by the High Priest Haldephren, who had stolen the body of Dalvenjah's brother. He said that he was my father, and even Dalvenjah isn't sure about that. It seems that, according to prophecy, I'm supposed to either destroy the Emperor and the High Priest forever, or else I'll somehow cause the restoration of the Alasheran Empire."

"Yes, I've heard of the Prophecy of the Faerie Dragons. I didn't know that it referred to you." Mira looked impressed, and perhaps just a little frightened. The Alasheran Empire was a product of her own world, gone for the past two thousand years and yet still a nightmare of history. Worse yet, the Empire of the South had been re-established in the past years, growing and prospering rapidly. There was as yet no direct evidence that this was the same Alashera as before, or that the Emperor or the High Priest had returned.

"I should tell you that I had already spoken with Dalvenjah before I ever agreed to accept you for training," Mira continued, tapping her empty teacup absently. "She talked about you as if you were a dragon, which is perhaps the best she can understand. I do think, now that I know about your involvement in the Prophecy, that Dalvenjah is very concerned about this whole affair. She made no real secret of the fact that she is very worried about you. At the time, I couldn't imagine why."

"Do you believe the Prophecy?" Jenny asked, somewhat anxiously.

The sorceress looked rather thoughtful. "I would prefer not to believe it, maybe because I want to reject any thought of predestination as inexcusable interference in one's personal life. But as a sorceress, I know that you can at times see hints of what is to come. You've been raised all your life to believe that you are the pivotal feature in this all-important prophecy. The question is, do you believe?"

She sat for a moment, stirring absently at her tea, while Mira waited with perfect patience and understanding. At last she sighed heavily. "I know that the Prophecy is true. Right now it has me exactly where I am supposed to be, ready for the beginning of the end. Mostly I want it to be over, so that I can finally have a life of my own. But I know that I'm not ready."

"That's the trick, I guess," Mira remarked thoughtfully. "Obviously the deciding factor is whether or not you turn to the Dark. And that depends upon whether or not you find the purpose you seek in life through the Light, or if you surrender to the temptations of the Dark."

Jenny started at what seemed to her an accusation. "But that's just not possible. The Dark doesn't tempt me at all; I'm sure of that. I've always believed that if I do betray our side to the Dark, it will never be intentional. I might do the wrong thing by accident, but never deliberately."

"Hm, I see." Mira thought about that for a moment. "It seems to me that the only way to beat this prophecy of yours is to face it head-on, go after it before it comes to find you. That's the way to use a prophecy to your own advantage, you know. First you discover all you can about it, and that tells you how you can make things turn out the way you want."

Jenny frowned. "I'm not so sure. Dalvenjah has always considered the Prophecy to be a very complex and delicate thing."

"It was also Dalvenjah's idea to send you here, to the very home world of the Alasheran Empire, so she obviously means for you to get busy on solving the Prophecy," Mira said, obviously very pleased with herself for the way she had figured things out.

"Is that what you believe?"

"No, that's just a guess," Mira admitted. "But I'm not so sure that you are in no danger of falling to the Dark. The Dark Sorcerers reject love for hate, goodness for evil, and they make sex a thing of violence rather than gentle sharing. You're not a virgin, are you?"

"Well, no." Jenny somehow managed one of the really spectacular blushes of her life. It came easily, since she had the uncomfortable feeling that her mother could hear her. If Marie Barker ever found out certain specifics about Jenny's sex life, someone was going to find that twenty-two was not too old to be spanked. "Actually, I've sort of promised myself to someone already."

Mira nodded. "We would have had to fix that in a hurry, if you had been. You're going into that time of your life when all the mageborn come to the realization that there never will be a special prince who will change everything in your life. When you realize that no one will ever come between you and your magic— that you cannot tolerate the thought of anyone coming between you and your magic—but long before you realize that the conflict comes from your lack of understanding of your own desires."

Mira paused to take another quick taste of her tea, and frowned. "What it all comes down to is this. Life in general is rough, our romantic and sexual relationships are even harder to keep in any type of order, and the problems are compounded ten times over for the mageborn. Hopefully that makes at least partial sense to you now. Rest assured that, as with all other of the deeper questions of life, the answer will make itself perfectly clear to you at its proper time. And then you will see that the answers to those big questions are actually very simple, since you really knew them all along."

"But that's just the problem," Jenny insisted. "I can't really have a life of my own for as long as I have this prophecy hanging over my head. I don't know when it's going to come, next week or twenty years from now. But when it does come, everything in my life will change. I don't even know if I'll survive. Under the circumstances, I don't dare devote myself to anything, career or personal. I don't want to see things that I've worked for disappear. I don't want to hurt myself or anyone else if things should change, and I don't want to distract myself with the burden of excessive devotions or regret interfering with what I must do."

Mira looked surprised, almost stunned. "Well, there is that. But how can you possibly turn your back on life? Don't you realize that you could be creating just as many weaknesses in your defenses by denying the things that everyone needs from life?"

"I'll try to keep it in mind. I never thought that there was anything lacking in my life. I've always enjoyed myself immensely," Jenny said. That was largely the truth; she had learned long ago to simply concentrate on the simple, short-term pleasures. She did recognize something about her mistress's character. Mira was such a devoted hedonist that the thought of denying herself anything was horrifying to her.

She glanced up at the sorceress. "Ah, do you mean to send me away?"

Mira stared at her. "Why would I want to do that?"

She shrugged uncertainly. "I realize that you never counted on this business with the Prophecy. It's rather a lot to take on."

"Oh, piffle!" Mira declared impatiently. "If I don't take care of you, who will? Besides, let's stop scaring ourselves by looking so far ahead. All I wanted from you this morning, after all, was only a demonstration of your magic."

"Oh . . . Well, what?" Jenny was momentarily at a loss.

"Something that can show me your mastery of focused concentration," Mira said. "That, I suspect, is where you still have room for considerable improvement, as good as you no doubt already are."

"Yes, I suppose," the young sorceress answered, brushing distractedly at her hair. "I still say that I'm very pleased with my life as it is."

"We shall see," Lady Mira remarked as she poured herself another cup of tea, casting a small spell to heat the tepid water. "You're going to find that the more you learn, the more your magic matures, and the more enjoyment you find in life, the more you are going to want. It's an insidious addiction, but a virtuous one."

• Part Two •

High Places

THE FINE LINES took shape on the intricately carved pewter dragon, every one of its scales executed in meticulous detail. Only two hours before it had begun as a round lump of raw metal on Jenny's worktable, until she had employed magic and raw concentration to bend and shape the metal cold. It had flowed in only minutes into the general shape of her subject, a flying dragon, wings spread, as he braced himself atop a jagged pinnacle of rock, the whole thing over two feet high. The slow, difficult portion of her work had been in the finished detail, from the fine lines of each scale to the angry glint of real jade in each eye. Finally she had hardened the pewter with an infusion of other alloys and plated it with gold, all the time working the metals at room temperature.

Jenny was no more reconciled with the subject of the Prophecy than ever, and Mira's opinions actually did not help. In Mira's eyes, everything was so simple. She believed the meaning of the Prophecy to be obvious. Jenny would eventually decide to fight either for the good guys or the bad guys, and that side would win. The answer, therefore, was for Jenny to take an aggressive stance with the Prophecy, go on the attack against her enemies before she had a chance to be tempted to evil. Jenny's dragon training argued that nothing could be that simple. She felt certain that she could never be tempted to evil, and she was afraid that the real danger she would eventually have to face would be less obvious.

But for the moment, Jenny was having the time of her life. The faerie dragons were wonderful people, but they were as a rule reserved and cerebral, quiet and noble. In a word, boring. And she had really had quite enough of her own world. There was real adventure here. Forests that stretched across whole continents, and ancient castles, airships and sailing ships. Lady Mira seemed to know half of the Northlands, and she had her nose quite literally in everything that was happening.

"Well, what do you think?" she asked absently.

Vajerral blinked and began unlimbering herself. She had been serving as the model, and with a exercise of dragonly patience she had somehow avoided any movement for the past two hours. It was so contrary to her nature that Jenny had worried about her mental health. She stretched her arms and legs and long neck, and yawned hugely. Then she turned to look at the sculpture, and stared.

"That is not me," she complained, and blinked. "That's . . ."

"That's none of your business," Jenny said sharply.

Vajerral yawned again, sitting back on her tail. "Just what is the purpose of all this procrastination? Why do you not just go home? Then you could be with him."

"We agreed a long time ago that we would never discuss this," Jenny said sternly as she began putting away her tools. "Besides, I think I know now why Dalvenjah sent me here. A mortal world, with an eccentric sorceress and her demented retinue, and one adolescent dragon for company. This must be her idea of hell. She must be trying to make me grateful to go home and become a dragon."

"Dragons do not believe in hell," Vajerral remarked. "Just recycling. Besides, I am enjoying myself immensely."

"She sent you because you like everything, and to be rid of you." She paused, entertaining a look of profound consternation. "That's right. If I died, would I keep coming back as a faerie dragon like the rest of you?"

"Yes, but Dalvenjah would consider that method of making a dragon of you only as a final resort."

"Mage Jenny?" Erkin called at the same moment he knocked loudly on the outer door of her apartment. "Lady Mira sent me to tell you that Addena Sheld has returned."

"On my way."

Jenny hurried to change. Addena Sheld was, after all, Lady Mira's best friend, and the singer had been away in the southeast giving recitals almost since the young sorceress's arrival months earlier, combining her own business with some judicious spying that Mira had wanted done.

Her mistress had taken her into town only days earlier, insisting that she acquire at least a few new clothes against the coming of colder weather. She quickly slipped into pants, full-sleeved shirt and vest, all in shades of coordinating blue that complemented her hair. She hurried downstairs to Mira's study, finding the concert singer already discussing her exploits.

"Well, I'd never seen anything like it! The Kingdoms of the Sea may have been wealthy two thousand years ago, but they've fallen upon the worst poverty since," Addena Sheld exclaimed as she judiciously added brandy to the cup of tea that Lady Mira had just handed her. She looked up suddenly as Jenny and Vajerral entered. "Ah, so there you are, my dears. I am so glad to see that you're still about the place. Your presence adds a note of normalcy to this lunatic asylum of a house. Although Mira never did help you do something about that hair, it seems."

"It's part of her magic, Addena," Mira reminded her.

Addena glanced at her suspiciously. "Just like you think that you have to . . ."

"We don't have to talk about that!"

Jenny took a seat at the table in the alcove of Mira's study. The day had grown darker than ever, and a cold rain gently chattered against the panes where they sat in the glass-enclosed alcove of the study. Vajerral was sitting back on her tail, staring out the window as if dreaming of bright, clear skies.

"You were telling me about your experiences in the South?" Mira prompted.

"Oh, yes." Addena took a cautious taste of her tea, made a vile face and added more brandy. "I just could not believe the changes in the last eight years, that being the last time I had toured in the South. I'd been there only once before, you know, and I had sworn that I'd never go back. It really just didn't pay, you know. I wouldn't have gone now, except that you had asked me to look about. But this time . . . ! My word, it's like they're in some big hurry to catch up with the North, and then some. They certainly made no secret about their wealth, although they are entirely too ostentatious. You know how new wealth tends to be on the gaudy side.''

"Yes, you have pointed that out to me often enough," Mira remarked succinctly. "I've often wondered how you know."

Addena chose to ignore her. "It's like the ancient times have returned to the Southlands. There were scores of merchant ships and wargalleys in every harbor, but no airships. All the old palaces and forums have been restored and new ones are being built. And the old temples. Now that's the dark side to all of this, and I wouldn't go back to the South for anything. They've rebuilt the old temples, and there are priests and priestesses in black everywhere. Every one of their bright, clean cities has the spookiest feel of anything I've ever known."

"You think that they're worshipping the Dark again?" Mira asked coldly. Jenny was so surprised that she pulled up a chair and sat down to listen. Twenty-five years earlier, the Alasheran Empire had still been in ruins and the Emperor had been in exile in another world.

"Mira, you know that I don't pretend to have a hair of talent, but I know for a fact that something bad is going on there," Addena said in the most serious voice that the younger sorceress had ever heard her use. "It's just this feeling in the air, like something cold and predatory is watching you all the time. All the Northlanders who have been going into the South in recent years say that they're calling demons again, and getting results. But all the Southerners, they just look at you in that cold, superior manner, like they're going to get what they want out of you and then rip you apart with their own hands. Murderous, they all are. For all their faddish interest in the refined arts, killing is what seems to interest them most. They've reopened the old games."

"Great stars! With people?"

"No, not yet. Just with animals now. But they made me go to their games all the time I was there, and I can't recall a game where at least a few people didn't get killed. Accidentally, of course. But the games are vicious enough that they've made that unavoidable."

Mira nodded sadly. "That's very much what they say the worship of the Dark does to a person. Beratric Kurgel has suspected that for the last four years, as far as that goes. It seems to me that the time has come for someone to go down there and have a good look about, before it's too late."

"Too late for what?" Jenny asked, politely ignoring the auspicious name of Beratric Kurgel.

"Too late to do anything to stop it," she explained. "Elura has had the wealth and the benefit of strong magic since the fall of the Kingdoms of the Sea, and in the last three centuries we've enjoyed technological advances that should allow us to stay ahead of the South for some time to come. But we've known that they were going to attempt to re-establish the Empire for the last quarter of a century, and we've done nothing I know of to stop them. Tell me, has the Emperor or the High Priest returned?"

Addena blinked. "I don't know if the Emperor has returned or not, but they talk about him all the time. If he's not there yet, then he is at least running things from wherever he is, and he will be coming soon. But I heard very little about the High Priest. He has a secretary or minister who is doing his work for him—his secular activities, you might say—but it seems that he is not going to show himself directly for some time yet to come."

"I wonder if Dalvenjah scared him so badly that he's afraid she might come after him again if he shows himself," Mira mused. Then she looked up at Addena. "Tell me everything that happened during your tour in the South. I want to know every smallest clue you have to tell me."

Addena feigned extreme reluctance, all the time making it very clear that she would like nothing better than to be the center of attention for the next few hours and relate in detail her successes in the South. Mira made it very clear, however, that this matter was entirely too important, and the singer relented in tolerably good grace. All the same, she did impart her experiences in great detail, concentrating not necessarily on what made a good story but what she thought the sorceress wanted to hear.

Jenny paid strict attention as well, although she hardly knew what to make of it. The worship of the Dark had continued to exist, even in the Northlands, and they were eternally about their work preparing for the "return." But times had changed. Life was far less harsh than it had been in ancient times. The old conflicts, the bands of barbarians in the North and the pirate nations of the Far South, were now at peace. Sorcerers now devoted as much of their learning to engineering and the sciences as to magic, thereby increasing the effectiveness of their talents many times over, and this entire world had prospered accordingly. There simply was no longer any need for the worship of the Dark and its promise of quick rewards through the domination of others.

Except, of course, in the Kingdoms of the Sea. Jenny could see that for herself easily enough, now that she considered it. The North prospered, but the Northlands were rich with resources. The Southlands were rocky, barren islands and coastal stretches bordering rugged mountains. They had very little land suitable for agriculture. There was no timber, no coal and very few metals of any type except for copper. The ancient kingdoms had prospered on copper, but the age of copper was past, diminished by the strength and versatility of Northland steel.

No, the Kingdoms of the Sea had prospered for only one reason. In their time they had overcome their own deficiencies at the expense of others. They had been nations of overlords, conquering and controlling other lands which did possess the necessary resources, until they had come at last to rule the known world as the Empire of Alashera.

The emergence of new sorcerers, those who were slaves to no forces but willing supporters of the Light, had broken the control of the Dark Priesthood, which had grown too bloated and secure in its self-belief. Then the Empire itself had collapsed in a matter of a few short years. With its armies devoid of the support of Dark Magic, they had been broken or driven out of the conquered nations with relative ease.

Addena spoke voluntarily for the better part of three hours, and then Mira questioned her for another hour more. Night had come by that time, and with it a rather violent storm. Jenny could sense the restless forces that gathered in the world that night, as if the very discussion of the Dark had summoned its presence, and she was sure that her mistress knew what was happening as well. It seemed that Addena Sheld sensed something as well; she adamantly refused Mira's offer of a carriage home and retired—or retreated—to the upstairs room that was normally reserved as her own.

"Well, Lady?" Jenny prompted as she took the empty seat at the table. Her mistress was so distracted that she had not even bidden her friend good-night.

"Well, she hardly told us anything that we did not already know," Mira said. "Child, they've all known that it would come to this since they rescued you from the Emperor thirteen years ago. But what have they done about it since then?"

"The faerie dragons have been preparing for war ever since,"

Vajerral offered. "I would have thought that the Combined Academy should have acted as the nucleus of our profession."

"Yes, so one would assume," Mira declared in a voice that spoke worlds of censure. "The Academy is a bastion of learning, and as such it fulfills its function extremely well. As a body of responsible leaders in our hallowed profession, it sucks rotten lizard eggs. Those of us who do form an informal body of responsible leaders have been meaning for some time to make a detailed study of the possibilities. As one of the key members of that body, I fear that I must appoint myself that task. It certainly seems that no one else cares to undertake that mission."

"What task?" Jenny asked.

"Why, finding out if the Emperor or the High Priest has indeed returned to our world, and just how strong a presence the Dark really is."

Vajerral turned to stare, her eyes wide and her ears standing straight up.

"But why you?" Jenny asked.

"Because I am perhaps the only sorceress of the Light who can get away with it," Mira responded, although she did not look at all certain. "I do have one advantage over my fellows. I'm enough of a hedonist to confuse the Dark Priests long enough to discover what I want and slip away with my life. I hope."

Jenny frowned, and glanced up at Mira. "What do you think? Did Addena discover what you sent her to find?"

"I didn't give Addena a clue of what to look for," Mira said. "I wanted her to tell me what she saw, not what she may have thought I wanted her to find. Things have changed a lot in the last few years. We know now that both the High Priest and the Emperor were still alive, that they could open the Ways Between the Worlds and that they had some control over the demons they used to summon by battalions. It's time that we stick our noses back into their affairs, discover if either the Emperor or the High Priest is back in Alashera, and if they have made an alliance with the Dark dragons. Dalvenjah was rather worried about that."

"Then when do we go?"

"As soon as possible, with winter coming on," she replied. "But first, I do want to know all I can about the forces of the Dark. And the living expert on that subject, at least among those of our profession, is my own Master, the Sorcerer Bresdenant."

Jenny searched her own memory. "I don't remember him."

Lady Mira laughed aloud. "Him? He resides at Coot Hall, the retirement home at the Sanctuary of Leyweld. He should know more than anyone about what we should look for. I also hope that he can give us a few hints about how to protect ourselves from the Dark, if we do happen upon something ugly. I just don't like this business about the calling of the Spirits of the Dark."

Vajerral had been all but speechless with surprise, and for the last few moments her ears had been twitching as if they were trying to jump right off the top of her head. "What are you saying? You cannot risk Jenny and her part in the Prophecy for petty spying."

"But this is all a part of the Prophecy," Mira explained earnestly. "It's started now, and the only way Jenny can defeat it is to go out there and fight it."

Jenny did not know what to think. Logically she knew that Mira was right about taking the offensive with the Prophecy, although she was less certain that this was the way. And she was frightened. She had lived in terror of the Prophecy for half her life, but it had always been easy for her to ignore her fear. Now that particular approach to personal stress management was quickly becoming impossible. Her instinct had always been to indulge her fear, to distance herself from the realities of the Prophecy and delay this confrontation until she felt more certain.

She liked to tell herself that she would know when the time had come, that she would feel bold and determined and ready to fight. But she knew that the fear and uncertainty would always remain, and that the day would come when she would have to fight the Prophecy despite herself. She knew that she would only grow more afraid with time, not less. For that reason alone, perhaps this was the time to begin.

Lady Mira knew that the weather would be clearing by dawn, and she had Dame Tugg and the Trassek twins preparing for their journey that very night. She always made a point of keeping *Wind Dragon*, her airship, serviced and provisioned for immediate travel, so that it was a simple matter to load a few perishable items and their personal effects. Addena Sheld agreed to accompany them as far as Leyweld, with the understanding that they would return her to Bennasport before they began their journey into the Southlands. She declared that she had no intention of ever returning to the Kingdoms of the Sea. Dame Tugg and J.T. were remaining to watch over the house.

Since this first trip was over friendly lands, Vajerral seized this chance to run a quick errand of her own. She wanted to have more help at hand before they left for the South, and she had departed for a quick visit to her own world that very morning. She expected to return in a few days in the company of an experienced fighting dragon.

Wind Dragon was rolled out of her shed at dawn, and the Trassek twins immediately set about preparing her for flight. *Wind Dragon* was a tiny ship compared to the round-bellied freighters of over six hundred feet, but the young sorceress doubted that she had ever seen a ship that looked more sleek and swift. Sitting on her skids in the open yard, her vanes not yet deployed, she looked like some oceangoing racing schooner with a flat-bottomed hull, almost as if it had been cut off just below the waterline.

Jenny had flown on these ships often enough in the past, and so she was able to help ready *Wind Dragon* for flight. Her four lift vanes, with their spar-ribbed canvas stabilizing sails, were unfurled and locked into place, and the thrust vanes, the largest that Jenny had ever seen on a ship this size, were mounted in the stern. The smaller stabilizer vanes, of the same bright bands of red and blue canvas as the massive main vanes, were unfurled in the long bowsprit, the short securing masts were stepped in the center of the ship between the vanes and the rigging was pulled tight. The ropes and canvas were dampened by the heavy morning dew, but the ship was prepared for flight in little more than a quarter of an hour of brisk work.

Erkin and Dooket approached this journey with the same enthusiasm of a couple of boys asked to go on a picnic. Jenny was given to wonder if they even knew the meaning of danger, and just what they would do if matters did get rather serious. Either they were too brave to care, too stupid to care, or else they were simply a pair of complete innocents when it came to the realities of their profession. Addena Sheld boarded the little ship as though she was already having second or third thoughts on the subject. Dame Tugg made no secret of what she thought on the subject; she stood below the bow of the ship to evoke the blessing of St. Gurn of the Cows. That only mystified the others, since St. Gurn was commonly the protector of whores; Addena took it to be a personal insult. Only Lady Mira seemed unconcerned. She was

standing on the helm deck pretending to be a pirate setting sail
for the Jade Islands.

"You just watch out," J.T. told his mistress quite seriously.
"There are storms yet in those mountains you mean to cross."

"I know that," Mira assured him. "*Wind Dragon* is as fast as
they come. She can keep us ahead of almost anything."

"She's not that fast," the cat corrected her.

"If any storm does catch us, we can pull in the vanes and ride
it out."

"Just be careful," J.T. repeated himself. "Well, every minute
of clear weather you have counts, so you had better be about your
rat-killing."

Mira joined the travelers who had already boarded the airship
and the Trassek twins pulled in the boarding ladder. From that
time on the sorceress was in complete control of the ship. There
were two large wheels at the pilot's station near the stern, one
controlling the vanes that lifted the ship's nose and the other
controlling the rudder. But magic alone activated and regulated
the lift and thrust vanes that actually got the airship off the ground
and moving. She applied lift until she felt *Wind Dragon* begin to
stir restlessly, then moved the ship forward until the bow vanes
caught the air and raised her nose gently.

"What do you think?" Mira asked her student as the airship
slowly gained speed and altitude, her skids barely clearing the
trees that bordered the estate. She was already spinning the rudder
wheel to bring *Wind Dragon* around to the south, looking for the
first pass through the coastal mountains behind Bennasport.

Jenny only nodded. *Wind Dragon* achieved her cruising speed
of forty knots in less than a minute and continued to climb steadily
toward the pass. The others, she noticed, were completely unconcerned. Erkin and Dooket were still cranking in the retractable
wheels, and even Addena was leaning over the rail near the bow.

Two hours of travel brought them through the coastal mountains
and over relatively open land, although they could already see the
greater range of the Northland mountains farther ahead. The sky
remained clear and deep blue except for a few thick, white clouds
about the peaks, and the air at their altitude was just a bit chill.
But already the two sorceresses could sense the storms that would
soon be building in those distant mountains, wet, heavy storms
full of winds and snow.

"It'll be a race," Mira said, speaking a little loudly to be heard over the wind. "We'll be heading back into the mountains tonight, about the same time this weather will begin to get thick. We won't be able to make half this speed, and we may not be able to stay in the air all that long either."

"We have to land at night anyway," Jenny pointed out. "You're our only pilot."

"A situation that I mean to correct right now," her mistress said. "Only someone trained in sorcery can fly an airship, but then what are you? Feeding the induction vanes is no great trick, and a couple of hours behind the wheels should give you a good feel for steering."

Mira had the airship grounded five minutes later, and Jenny found herself at the helm. She would have liked to have protested, but she found that she had no good excuse for not learning to fly this ship. The force-induction vanes operated by channeling the natural forces in the world, providing thrust either to lift the ship or to move it forward, and it was a simple matter for a sorceress of her caliber to work the simple spells that activated the vanes. Steering the ship with the stabilizers was hardly any more difficult, although she would have to be careful to keep the ship in trim, balanced on its lift vanes.

Since the wheels were still retracted, leaving *Wind Dragon* sitting on her four broad skids, Jenny had to lift the ship straight up, not applying forward thrust until she was well off the ground. And there in the valley, that meant that they first had to get above the trees that bordered the glade where Mira had set them down.

"Just ease her up," Mira urged her. "Just tickle the lift vanes until we clear the ground."

The magic itself was no problem for Jenny. She thought of raising the ship with her own lift magic, the way she would if she was flying with the dragons. She was wrong on at least two points, the most important being that dragon magic was entirely too rich a fuel for these arcane engines. *Wind Dragon* went up like a rocket.

"Ease up on her, child," Mira urged her a little more firmly.

"I wish to hell I could!" Jenny declared rather desperately. "I don't know if I could ease off any more without letting her drop."

"I most devoutly wish that you can learn quickly," Mira remarked, peering over the side. "I know that the air thins with altitude, but I don't recall that anyone has ever investigated just how far the process continues."

Unfortunately, Jenny knew the answer to that. If the problem was in giving too much power to the lift vanes, then perhaps she could divert some of it to forward thrust. *Wind Dragon* jumped in a new direction. As it happened, the elevator wheel was spun almost completely around; the airship curved gracefully up and just kept going. It was most likely the first time that an airship had ever executed a complete loop.

By the time the ship righted itself, Jenny had learned through simple terror how to keep her magic under control. At least only she and Mira had been on deck at that time, and centrifugal force did a lot to keep them there. Mira had been holding on to the rail, while Jenny had entwined her arms and legs in the spokes of the rudder wheel and was still clinging there, upside down. Mira brushed herself off and walked over to spin the wheel, returning her young apprentice to a reasonable attitude.

"That was definitely not the idea," she commented.

Jenny disengaged herself from the wheel and returned *Wind Dragon* to her proper speed and course. Once she began to get the feel of the ship, she actually began to enjoy herself. Airships were never fast compared to the aircraft of her own world, but they had a lot of character.

"Ah, perfect," Mira remarked, peering over the rail at a couple of shepherds staring up from far below. "Bring the bow up just a little more and she'll climb more smoothly. The idea is to search upward until you find a wind traveling in essentially your same direction and allow that to push you along. Ground winds are often unpredictable."

"What about this?" Jenny asked as she felt a cold wind at her back.

"Ah, close enough," the sorceress declared, and ran forward a few steps. "Erkin! Dooket! Hoist the running sails. Let's make all the speed we can, while we can. Helm, full forward thrust!"

"Is this a good idea?" Jenny asked.

Mira shrugged. "I don't know. I've never tried running *Wind Dragon* all out like this before. Beratric Kurgel has always said that an air schooner like *Wind Dragon* was made for running, like a fine race horse."

That caused Jenny a certain amount of consternation. Mira evoked the name of Beratric Kurgel regularly, and claimed to consult with that wise and worldly character all the time. But Jenny had never actually seen any such person, nor could J.T. or the twins testify to his existence, although Mira would claim to have spoken with him over tea only days before. However, Jenny had noticed that any plan that Mira was unsure about had been inspired by Beratric Kurgel, and he was responsible for any idea that went wrong.

Some children had make-believe playmates. Kasdamir Gerran had an imaginary scapegoat.

The two rather versatile mercenaries had both of *Wind Dragon*'s broad, red-and-blue-striped sails unfurled within a couple of minutes. Jenny had her doubts about how much the sails really helped, since the stiff high-level wind was hardly moving any faster than the ship itself. But they were soon hurtling along at fifty knots ∩r more, slightly faster than the airship could have moved without that aid. She did find, to her momentary dismay, that *Wind Dragon* did have a very different feel to her steering when the wind was blowing over the stabilizers from behind.

"Well, you seem to be doing just fine," Mira remarked as she turned and headed toward her cabin. "I'll see you people later."

She was gone before Jenny could say a word, with no explanation of how long she intended to be away or what to do in the event of trouble. Knowing that her mistress had been up most of the night preparing for this journey, Jenny suspected that she meant to stay in her bunk a good, long while. As for the latter consideration, there was not much that could be done when an airship got into real trouble. The idea was to avoid it.

"Pull in the sails!" Jenny shouted her order, wondering only briefly if she had that authority as a student pilot.

Whether she did or not, the Trassek twins certainly saw the wisdom in that action and set about the task as quickly as they were able in this gale. The winds were too unpredictable to be running with the sails unfurled, which interfered considerably with the steering at the best of times. Jenny needed to be able to ride these fierce winds, not fight them, before they damaged the lift vanes and canvas stabilizers. She was trying to control the ship through a combination of manipulating the lift and forward thrust at the same time she was spinning the rudder wheel before her and the smaller elevator wheel at her side.

"What can I do?" Addena asked, shouting over the wind. "Should I go get Lady Mira?"

"She surely knows by now that we need her at the helm," Jenny answered with unconscious authority. "Check on her, all the same. Then take a good look below to make certain that everything is secure.''

''Anything else?''

''Bring my jacket,'' she added. The sky was still mostly clear, even though the sun would be setting within minutes. But the cold was increasing much faster than the coming of night could allow, and there was the feel of fine crystals of ice in the air.

The boys had the sails in a couple of minutes later, loosely tied to their booms to be taken down as time allowed. Now that *Wind Dragon* was no longer fighting the drag of her own sails, her handling improved tremendously and the situation went from critical to merely cautious very quickly. Jenny felt that she had the ship well under control by the time Lady Mira strolled out onto the helm deck, completely unconcerned.

''Ah, you do seem to be doing well enough,'' she remarked. ''I'll go attend to the running lights and stand bow watch. Perhaps we can keep in the air for a few hours yet.''

''Don't you want to take the helm?'' Jenny asked rather desperately. She obviously felt that she could now afford to be frightened, when only a moment earlier she had not had any choice.

''We cannot transfer control of the induction vanes in flight,'' Mira told her. ''At least not under the present circumstances. And you don't seem to be having any trouble just now.''

The matter appeared to be settled. Lady Mira retired to the bow of the airship and spelled the crystal globes hung to either side of the bowsprit. She aimed their beams into the growing darkness ahead and to either side of the ship and occasionally called back instructions and descriptions of the landscape to the unwilling pilot. Night descended within half an hour and Jenny was flying blind, riding the winds as best she could and steering the ship according to what her mistress told her.

Three hours into the night, Mira decided that they had both had enough and directed Jenny into a deep cut in the mountainside, a flat-bottomed ravine so narrow that the ship might not have fit into it sideways, and barely fit as it was. Jenny was alarmed when she saw the walls of the canyon appear out of the misty darkness to either side and heard the occasional thump of treetops against the lower hull.

Mira soon found a clearing just large enough to hold the airship—allowing for the crushing of a few saplings—and Jenny brought *Wind Dragon* down. Settling straight in was no easy task, but the trees prevented a gradual descent. The ravine sheltered the airship from the worst of the wind, but there was still a strong headwind descending through the cut. She had to hold the ship directly over her goal with just enough thrust to counter the effects of the wind and drop slowly to a landing in the darkness below. Erkin and Dooket hurried to fold away the vanes and stabilizers so that sudden gales would be less likely to upset the ship. *Wind Dragon* rocked slightly on the tightly strung springs in her struts until they were finished.

By that time, Jenny was completely exhausted. She had been at the helm for twelve hours, the last three of that fighting the mountain winds, entirely too long for her first time. She was inclined to be rather annoyed at her mistress for leaving her there for so long, but she knew now that Mira had completely exhausted herself in some important magic the night before. Indeed, there was still some question about which of them would be in the best condition to resume the flight the next morning. Jenny thought that she could do it, as long as she got something to eat and a warm bed in very short order.

"We'll share rounds tomorrow," Lady Mira assured her, stepping up behind her out of the darkness to help her down from the helm deck to the cabins below.

She had her student in the galley, stripped of her cold, damp clothes and wrapped in a warm blanket, with a cup of hot tea, a mug of ale and warm bread, cheese and venison at hand while the others were still outside tending the ship. Even Addena, who could be a fussy, self-important performer at any other time, was a willing and silent crewmember on this flight.

"You did very, very well," Mira told her. "I'm sorry that I couldn't help you more today."

"I know why," Jenny said, unconcerned.

"I made a potentially disastrous presumption based upon my belief that you are an extremely capable person," the sorceress continued. "I should not have done that, whether you came through as well as you did or not. It really would have been best to have waited a day."

"It's done, and I've become an experienced pilot in a hurry," Jenny said. "How much longer?"

"Two more days, if the weather turns out as I expect. Starting tomorrow it might take the two of us to fly this ship, one just to sit on the bow and try to navigate the fog and snow in any way that sorcery will allow.''

"That probably places me back at the helm again," Jenny offered, knowing that her teacher was not about to say that her own talents were best for the task of discovering a way through this mess.

The next morning brought not just winds and cold but winter storms. Icy fogs and gale-blown snow hid miles of the highlands, and restless winds shook and tugged at the struggling airship. Lady Mira was often reduced to finding their path as best she could in complete blindness, trusting her talent to show her shadowy images of the hidden peaks and cliffs. The running lights would sometimes pierce the storm at the final moment, illuminating a tree or rocky face just in time for Jenny to evade certain impact. The mercenaries probed below the hull with long poles, feeling for the unseen ground or treetops. Addena, her uncharacteristic silence now entering its second day, alternated between watching from the bow with Mira and assisting Jenny in any way she could.

The storm only worsened as the morning wore on, although it never quite reached the point that either of the sorceresses suggested that they would have to put to ground and ride this out. Probing the mountains at a speed of ten to twenty knots was better than sitting still. But they both agreed that, if either of them felt that they were not doing their best, then they would set down for a rest. They meant to stop for an hour or so at noon under any circumstances.

"Half speed, Jenny!" Mira called from the bow. "The storm is letting up, and we seem to be in fairly open air just now. Some fairly large valley."

"Right, but keep your watch all the same," Jenny answered. Increased speed meant that any impact would result in greater damage, and one wrecked vane was enough to send the airship tumbling from the sky.

"Tea, Addena!" Mira added.

Addena looked up from her work; she was currently sweeping accumulated snow from the decks. "Tea? How can you think of tea at a time like this?"

"This is the first moment I've had all morning to think about tea, and I need it." Mira paused, and turned abruptly back to stare out over the bow. "Stand to! Something is coming toward us through the storm. Some two things, I should say, and making good time. Boys, I want you to string your longbows and get ready for a fight."

Jenny sensed it too, and she strained her talent for a better understanding to the point that *Wind Dragon* began to slow from lack of attention. She knew that something was out there, something of far greater evil than anything that she had sensed in a long time. Something out of the Dark itself. She also did not doubt that they were about to come under attack. The others only looked confused, but the mercenaries hurried below to collect their weapons. Addena accompanied them to find a sword and bow of her own.

The things were upon them before the warriors returned, two black shapes that passed to either side of the ship at the very edge of the storm, vast forms on broad wings just behind a veil of mist and snow. They circled for another pass just as the Trassek mercenaries arrived on deck. They stopped short and stared in awe and fear. Addena came up behind them, only to cower back from the sight of the strange beings.

"I've felt that before, in the South," she said aloud, perhaps for Mira to hear. "They're of the Dark!"

"I know that," the sorceress said impatiently. "But that still doesn't explain what they are."

"They look like dragons," Jenny called from the helm deck. Standing almost in the very stern of the ship, she had been closer than any of them when the two creatures had circled around for their second pass. She had been too preoccupied to feel the intense fright that still had Addena shaking, but she was aware that the hair on the back of her neck was standing on end.

"What?" Mira asked incredulously. "But there are so few evil dragons left in the Northlands. Besides, those . . . those things had a stink of raw, violent evil about them worse than anything I've ever seen in even the worst of the Dark Dragons."

"I know that, but I also know what they looked like," Jenny insisted. Her mistress seemed to be speaking from experience in her observation about Dark Dragons, but she did not consider this the time or place to ask about that.

"We'd better be ready for a fight, whatever they are," Mira declared. "Boys, the two of you had better ready the catapults. Jenny, we need room to run. Head northeast and ascend an additional five hundred feet. Addena, you can forget about that tea for the moment.''

The catapults were in fact crossbows of such immense size that even Dooket had some trouble carrying his. The bows themselves were large steel bars like carriage springs, six feet across and so tight that a large, long-handled mechanism had to be used to draw the braided-wire bowstring back for loading. The bolts looked more like spears, five feet long with iron heads that weighed four pounds. There was three mounts built into the rail on each side of the ship, although the mercenaries fitted their weapons into the mounts to either side of the bow where they could more easily follow Mira's directions. Addena had collected a longbow and shield and hurried to the bow to offer their helm some protection. Jenny wondered how much use a concert singer would be in battle, but this was better than nothing. She certainly could not release control of the ship to defend herself.

The Trassek twins loaded their weapons and stood ready, but the two dark shapes did not return. Lady Mira stood at the bow and probed the storm as best she could, but for the moment all she could detect was a shadow of their presence some distance to the southeast. The snowfall, which had never yet been truly heavy, began to pick up somewhat, driven by a harsh wind. Fortunately the snow was dry and hard, and constant eddies in the wind were continually sweeping it through openings in the rail.

"Stand ready!" Mira called a couple of minutes later. "There's a ship coming toward us through the storm. Jenny, stand by to turn toward them as they approach."

Jenny could sense the ship as well; force-induction vanes had a very distinctive sound or feel, depending upon how one chose to describe it, to those who were sensitive to the flow of magic. The curious and alarming thing was that both of the evil creatures appeared to be pacing the ship, or perhaps even leading it. There was a sorcerer on board that ship as well, not a very strong one. But the feel of the magic about him, driving his ship, was dark and violent. Mira's words seemed to imply a suspicion that they were about to come under attack from this combined force, and Jenny had to agree.

That raised some rather difficult questions of its own, such as what a Dark Sorcerer was doing this far north, where had he acquired an airship, and why did he seem intent upon attacking

Wind Dragon? Jenny immediately had to wonder if this attack was directed at her.

She hoped to be able to find a few of those answers, assuming that they won this battle. If it remained a contest of magic, then she and Mira were more than a match for this rather mediocre sorcerer. But there was also the problem of those evil dragons; *Wind Dragon*'s canvas stabilizers had to be protected from their flames. And she was certain that the other ship would have a company of its own archers. As far as she knew, there had never been a battle between airships before. These ships needed a sorcerer at their helm, and two sorcerers trained in the service of the Light would never fight each other. That meant that there were no proven strategies they could rely upon; they were very much on their own.

A tense minute passed as the enemy ship drew steadily nearer, striving to cut them off. Both of the sorceresses chose to meet the threat rather than run, aware that the two dragons could easily keep them occupied until their ship arrived. The two Dark creatures shot past, silent and evil but seemingly uninterested in engaging in battle themselves. Jenny brought *Wind Dragon* around sharply, and a few moments later the other ship emerged out of the blowing snow.

The enemy ship was larger than *Wind Dragon* by perhaps thirty feet. Her vanes and stabilizers appeared to be no larger, but the ship itself was much wider and deeper in construction, most likely a small freighter rather than a schooner like their own. If it came to a running battle, *Wind Dragon* did have the advantage of speed and maneuverability. But the other ship also had a couple of dozen archers clearly visible on her deck.

"What ship?" Mira called.

"*Blood Hawk*, out of Alashera," the sorcerer at her helm shouted back. "What ship?"

"*Wind Dragon*, out of Bennasport."

"Stand to and prepared to be boarded, woman!"

Lady Mira looked rather indignant. "Stand to and prepare to get your ass whipped, bastard!"

If the Dark Sorcerer had any reply to that, it was lost in the wind as the two ships shot past. Jenny could see the two mercenaries standing by at the catapults and she whipped *Wind Dragon* around as quickly as she could at the same time she increased speed to full, hoping to catch the heavier ship from the side as it

labored through its own turn. Addena, well aware of how she
would serve best in the battle, moved forward to protect them
both with the large shield she carried. At least the Trassek twins
were in a combination of plate and mail armor, hopefully enough
to guard against the missiles from ordinary longbows. Mira stood
at the bow unconcerned; she could guard herself with a warding
spell.

Jenny's judgement was perfect; the enemy ship appeared out
of the white curtain broadside to them and nearly on a level. She
brought *Wind Dragon*'s nose up sharply and climbed at full lift
and thrust, showing the enemy archers the airship's hardwood
hull. The Trasseks waited until they could shoot down from above.
They aimed at the helm station but both of their bolts swerved in
flight, missing both the Dark Sorcerer and the vulnerable controls
to crash through the planks of the deck. Mira loosed a shot from
her own longbow, and the spelled arrow did not swerve to avoid
the warding spells but struck the sorcerer in the chest. He staggered
back and the wheels spun, but he quickly returned to his post.
The spelled arrow had been frustrated by very ordinary armor.

Addena rushed to protect Jenny from behind with her shield as
a small cloud of arrows followed their own ship. *Blood Hawk*
disappeared again into the storm, but Jenny could sense it turning
away to circle around and she quickly leveled out and turned *Wind
Dragon* in the opposite direction, hoping to catch the other ship
broadside yet again. In the bow, Lady Mira considered only a
moment before she turned to the two bodyguards.

"Use the exploding bolts, boys," she told them.

"Lady?" Erkin asked uncertainly.

"Do it, and hurry," she insisted. "We have no hope otherwise.
We can't hide from their arrows forever, and those dragons might
attack at any moment."

The Trasseks were still nervous about this. The exploding bolts
were Mira's secret weapon, something of her own design, and not
yet tested. But they had to do something. The enemy archers were
using fire arrows, although their first volley had been frustrated
by spelled hardwood and the storm, and the canvas stabilizers had
somehow been missed altogether. Addena was still trying to get
a flaming arrow off her shield without burning herself.

The mercenaries hurried to a weapon locker to collect the special
bolts, which they loaded quickly into their catapults. The explosive
bolts had a small metal canister behind their longer but compar-

atively lighter barbs. Then *Wind Dragon* was upon her enemy, the larger ship still struggling through her turn. Jenny brought them around to catch *Blood Hawk* broadside yet again, while Mira laid aside her bow to concentrate on protecting her own ship, warding away the cloud of fire arrows that rose to meet them.

"Try for the base of the forward vane!" she ordered.

Dooket and Erkin shot at almost the same instant, and their aim was flawless. *Blood Hawk* was shaken by two powerful explosions and the forward vane was ripped away, disappearing inside a ball of flames. Lady Mira's knowledge of chemistry and her skill at engineering nearly equalled her command of magic. Unsupported on that quarter, *Blood Hawk* began to dip slowly in that direction, rolling like a sinking ship. Then her critical balance reached a point of no return and she fell, tumbling in flames and smoke from the snow-filled sky.

"Fire and flatulatants!" Mira declared. "I told Beratric Kurgel that it would work!"

The stricken airship crashed unseen on the snow-covered slope. and, from the sound, continued to roll some distance down the mountainside. Apparently she did not shatter on impact, even though she must have dropped six hundred feet; airships were built strong and reinforced with magic. Jenny was already bringing *Wind Dragon* around for a very hasty landing, knowing that the two dragons would probably be upon them at any moment.

She found an open, level space mostly by chance. *Wind Dragon* slid across the snow for a short distance until she pulled to a shuddering halt, and her skids sank down at least a foot. Their advantage now lay on the ground, where her own attention and magic would not be involved entirely with keeping the ship in the air. She might not be a match for Lady Mira, but she was still a formidable fighter and two sorceresses were always better than one.

The dragons attacked moments later, diving toward the ship from opposite directions. Dooket and Erkin were ready, having reloaded their catapults with more of the exploding bolts, apparently assured to their complete satisfaction that the weapons did indeed work. They shot almost as one, again with the same deadly accuracy, but this time to no effect. The bolts passed unhindered through the bodies of the dragons, arcing over to explode somewhere in the storm-shrouded land.

"Those aren't dragons! Those are winged demons!" Jenny declared. "I've seen demons before."

She hurried to join her mistress, using her sword to fend away the cutting whip of a tail, which rang with a sound like very solid steel. They were the ugliest, most alien things that she had ever seen, not at all like the fierce majesty of true dragons. And they seemed to use fear as a weapon, causing the hand that moved sword or shield in defense to hesitate.

"Jade eyes!" Mira exclaimed.

"Where are we going?" Jenny asked as she helped to open the rail and lower the boarding ladder, confused. Faerie dragons had jade eyes, but these demons had eyes like burning rubies.

"To the wrecked airship," the sorceress replied. "Our only hope of stopping these demons lies somewhere in that wreckage, if we can find it."

Jenny had no idea what her mistress had in mind, but she did trust that the older sorceress did have some idea of what to do. The problem with fighting demons was that they were creatures of another existence and not entirely real in this one; they were vulnerable to few forms of attack, either mundane or magical, although they could do very real damage. Being demons rather than dragons, they at least lacked fire. Her own education was rather lacking on the subject, which was not surprising, since sorcerers had not had to fight demons on anything like a regular basis in hundreds if not thousands of years. Even Mira professed to have no effective way of dealing with demons and other forces of the Dark, that being the whole point of the first part of their journey. But she did seem to have some way out of their present mess.

Jenny had at least some idea of where *Blood Hawk* lay wrecked in relation to where she had landed *Wind Dragon*. They could both sense the continued presence of Dark Magic, far weaker than it had been, as if the evil sorcerer still clung tenuously to life somewhere in this storm. At the same time it became obvious that they themselves, and not their airship, were the object of this attack. The demons followed them relentlessly, diving down to lash at their backs and heads with their long, lashing tails. Dooket and Erkin, protected by their armor, turned the attacks time again with sword and shield. The slopes were treacherously steep and hidden beneath drifts often several feet deep, so that they had to force their way forward as best they could.

Half a mile back along *Wind Dragon*'s path they came upon an especially steep section of the mountainside, and Jenny was sure that this was where *Blood Hawk* had fallen. A moment later they caught a bitter trace of smoke on the icy wind, and there was no longer any question. This slope was so steep that it had, in effect, merely deflected the airship's fall, preventing its complete destruction as it rolled into the valley below. They could not yet see the ship itself, for the lower portions of the slope disappeared into the dimness and blowing snow, but bits of shattered wood and shredded canvas littered the mountainside.

Erkin, growing tired with the running battle, suddenly lost his footing and sat down heavily on his shield. He immediately slid off down the snow-covered hillside at an alarming pace, stopping with a loud crash somewhere far below. The others waited in silence for several long seconds, wondering if he had survived.

"I've found the wreck!" he called back at last.

"Well, I'll be screwed," Mira muttered in mild amazement. Then she threw herself down on her rump and slid off down the slope as well, although at a more sane pace since she was able to use her legs to slow herself. Dooket and Jenny looked at each other, then shrugged and followed in the same manner. The younger sorceress could have flown, but she had no wish to meet the demons in their own element.

Blood Hawk lay on her side near the bottom of the slope. She had come up hard against a large outcrop of exposed stone, which had almost broken her into two even pieces. She had lost her vanes, masts and bowsprit, and her deck cabins in the course of her fall. Boxes and bales had been lost from her broken hull and lay scattered with several bodies across the slope. Only one form in heavy black clothes lay struggling feebly to one side, and the two demons had come to ground to protect it fiercely.

"Now what?" Erkin asked, brushing packed snow and pine needles out of his armor.

"We've got to kill that sorcerer," Mira declared. "But how? None of us thought to bring our bows."

"Permit me," Dooket said gallantly.

While the others watched silently, he searched about in the snow until he found a large stone. He tested its weight carefully and then heaved it with both hands toward the dying sorcerer. Jenny doubted that she could have hurled that stone more than a few feet, certainly not the sixty feet to its intended target. It sailed right over the Southerner's head and landed with a heavy thump in the snow at least five feet away.

Muttering obscenities, Jenny stepped forward and stood with her legs braced and both arms held straight out before her. A glow of brilliant blue light surrounded her clenched fists, and a bright beam shot out to strike the nearest of the demons. It was blasted backwards off its claws with a harsh cry of distress, the first sound that either of the creatures had made. Singed and smoking, it leaped into the air, and Jenny repeated the process with the other. Then she seemed to collapse, or at least she had to sit down in a hurry. Erkin prevented her from tumbling over backwards into the snow.

Lady Mira rushed forward without hesitation. She paused long enough beside the sorcerer to snatch something from about his neck, then calmly employed her sword to separate him from his head. The demons screamed again, but for the moment they either would not or could not attack. She hurried over to the rock that Dooket had thrown and placed the object on top, revealing it to be a large piece of jade, pulsing with a sickly green light, which had hung about the sorcerer's neck by its golden chain. She fetched a second stone out of the snow and used that to crush the evil talisman. The two demons vanished screaming in flame.

"You destroyed them?" Dooket asked.

Mira shook her head, panting heavily. "I just sent them back where they came from. The spells that released them into our world were worked into the stone, which the sorcerer used to control them. That much I have heard about the summoning and control of demons . . . tricky business! Jenny, are you quite all right?"

"Oh, fine," she said, brushing her long hair from her face; she still seemed rather disconcerted. She tried to rise and failed, and so she reluctantly allowed Erkin to assist her.

"Well, we've had quite a day!" Lady Mira declared briskly. "But we also need to be on our way, or the storms are going to pin us here for some time. I believe that I'm capable of flying *Wind Dragon* for the rest of the day."

"Oh, I'll be able to fly the ship," Jenny assured her. "I just need to rest a few minutes."

Mira started to protest, but had to consider that. "Actually, it will take the two of us to navigate these mountains, so you might as well take the part you feel most comfortable with, steering or scouting. I'd keep us grounded for the rest of the day if I could. Boys, find us a way out of here.''

"Going up is going to be harder than coming down," Dooket remarked, looking up at the towering slope at their backs.

"If we can't go up, then we might go around. You two see if you can find an easier way back. I want to have a closer look at this ship."

While Jenny sat and rested, sheltered from the icy wind by the airship's broken hull, her mistress took a look inside. Mira would occasionally return to the break to toss something out, but she seemed far more interested in gathering evidence than salvage. Her search was hampered by the fact that she was having to walk on the walls of the ship, which made getting through the hatchways nearly impossible. She returned at last, and sat down beside her student with a heavy sigh.

"It's just as I suspected," she said. "This ship was built in Elura, at Tashira for that matter, and went into freighter service fifteen years ago as the *Sea Wind*. The Southlanders must have stolen it quite recently and renamed it *Blood Hawk*. That indicates to me that they don't yet know how to build their own airships."

"Why did they attack us?" Jenny asked.

Mira shrugged. "For the practice, most likely. If they had taken us, we would have been just a small ship lost in a snowstorm. We were lucky, we took no harm, and we know a few things that we didn't know before. We know that the Southerners are getting aggressive, that they will steal our airships and attack others, and that they are summoning demons to serve them."

"I can't say that I'm pleased to know that," Jenny remarked dejectedly.

"Perhaps, but it's better than not knowing that they are doing it."

• Part Three •

Ale and Old Wizards

THE SANCTUARY OF Sorcery at Leyweld was an unimposing quadrangle of buildings in the hills overlooking that modest town. It was hardly the equal of the Academy at Tashira, being barely a quarter of the size of that great center of research and teaching, lacking most obviously the training grounds for young students as well as the construction sheds for airships. And yet, except for that significant difference in size, the two might have almost been patterned after much the same model.

The Sanctuary filled a few special functions that the Academy could not, as its name suggested. To a small degree, it was a place where sorcerers who had no wish to teach could come to perform special research, although its facilities were limited in that respect compared to the Academy. It was also a place were sorcerers could come for a few weeks to several months of peace and rest, and where those who had fallen victim to ailments of the mind, an occupational hazard, would be cared for in comfort until they were cured, recovered, or died. And it also possessed an entire wing which housed wizards retired after a lifetime of hard work. Sorcerers paid high dues to their guild, but it provided a great deal in return.

"It's good that we were able to arrive so early," Mira declared as the ship descended toward the large building atop the low hill in a clearing of the forest. A small village lay below, about a quarter of a mile away.

"Why is that?" Jenny asked.

Mira laughed. "You have to catch Bresdenant during that brief period of the day between the time when he gets up and before he's had enough to drink to get thoroughly stewed."

Lady Mira brought *Wind Dragon* down in the yard to one side of the quadrangle, since that seemed a most convenient place to land, without a thought for gaining permission. Her philosophy on that subject had always been that it is easier to get people to go along with something after it was already done. They were still folding away the vanes when someone of authority did come to investigate. He may have even come to protest, although Mira never gave him a chance.

"Come with me," she told Jenny softly as they hurried to the boarding ladder. "Ah, Bardas, my old friend! We meet again in bad times indeed, but perhaps it is not yet too late."

"Eh?" The tall, white-haired man paused at the base of the ladder to look up at her questioningly. "Too late for what?"

"Just look at this!" Mira declared. She had not waited for his reply, but had descended the ladder as nimbly as an acrobat. She directed him beneath the ship, while Jenny hurried to follow. "We were attacked, Bardas! Attacked, and in these very mountains. If not for the skill of my two bodyguards and the quick and capable wits of my journeywoman Jenny, my *Wind Dragon* would be lying wrecked on a snowy mountainside rather than their ship."

"Yes, someone sent you a few good fire arrows," Bardas remarked, then turned to look at her in open amazement. "You mean to say that you were attacked by another airship? Do you know who?"

"They hailed themselves as *Blood Hawk*, out of Alashera. And they had two winged demons coursing for them."

"The Dark, then." The old man actually seemed satisfied with that answer, either because it laid that question to rest or because it precluded the disagreeable possibility that one of their own sorcerers had piloted an airship against his own kind.

"But come," Mira said suddenly, turning him back toward the building. "I came all this way to discover what I can about demons and Dark Magic, and it seems that I got a good example on the way. Is Bresdenant well?"

"I suppose, but we had better hurry," Bardas remarked drily. Apparently Mira had not exaggerated about the old wizard's drinking habits.

Coot Hall, Sanctuary's self-contained retirement home, was the portion of the quadrangle that faced south and slightly east to catch as much as possible of the sun in morning and winter. They hurried up the steps leading directly into the middle of that building, and found themselves immediately inside a well-appointed lobby or sitting room of some size. Jenny was momentarily surprised. She had been expecting older sorcerers and sorceresses of high standing, men and women of quiet dignity and great wisdom. What she found was the strangest, most decrepit-looking assembly of backwoods wizards and witches.

"Don't let Bresdenant bother you," Mira warned her student softly. "He really is harmless. Even cute, in a crude way."

"What?" Jenny asked, alarmed.

"You'll see."

Indeed she did. Bresdenant was among the youngest of those gathered in this room, although he still looked to be in his late sixties. He was neither short nor tall but rather thin, his clothing undeniably rich but questionably tasteful and terribly loose and wrinkled. His unruly hair was limp and white as snow, as was his short beard, and there was a slightly wild and very impish look to his dark eyes. He had a noticeable shake, especially to his hands, which Jenny would have thought the effects of a stroke or some other ailment if she had not been warned about his drinking. For the moment he was involved in a very animated conversation with one of the hall's serving girls, who was rather impressed with his charms even if she did not seem to have the slightest idea of what he was lecturing her about.

He paused in mid-sentence and turned to look up at Mira, who was smiling down at him with her own impish smile. He stared at her intently, sitting on the edge of his chair. "Do I know you?"

"Of course you do, you old goat," she told him patiently. "I'm the Sorceress Mira. You set your evil hooks in me a little over twenty years ago."

"Oh, yes! Kasdamir!" he exclaimed in recognition. "You sure were good in bed!"

"You never found out," she told him evenly.

"Oh, yes! No wonder I didn't remember you. Hee, hee!" His voice was not particularly deep, but it had a gravelly edge to it that made it captivating. And his curious laugh held an infectious charm. He reminded Jenny of her Norwegian Uncle Brent, who delighted in annoying his neighbors by pretending that he was going to sexually molest their cats.

Bardas had quietly indicated for the serving girl to be about her work, and now he pulled up chairs for the two guests. "This is business, Brez. These two sorceresses have come a long way to speak with you. I have to be about my morning duties, so if you'll excuse me."

"Oh? What would I know that anyone would want to hear?"

"You used to know more about the Dark than any sorcerer in the North," Mira said as she took her seat directly across from him. "There were so many things that you never would teach me, but now I have to know."

"Why? Do you plan to go against the Dark?" he demanded.

"You know that the Dark has returned," she told him. "You knew that it was out there years ago, growing, but no one wanted to hear that. Well, it's coming to us, now. We fought Servants of the Dark on our way here, and I had to dispatch two winged demons the only way I could."

"Of course they're here," Bresdenant declared. "You didn't have to come all this way to tell me that. I felt them five days ago. They were way up in the air, and they were hunting. You fought them?"

She nodded. "They had a stolen airship. Jenny was flying my own *Wind Dragon* when they attacked us in a storm. Jenny outflew them brilliantly, and my two guards were able to bring their ship down by ripping away one of her vanes. But we still had two winged demons to deal with, and the only thing I knew was to find the body of the wizard who controlled them and destroy the jewel that was spelled with the magic that kept them in our world."

"That's doing it the hard way," Bresdenant said, sitting back in his chair. "Still, if you were caught unprepared, it was the best you could do."

"What could we have done, if we had been ready?" Mira asked.

The old wizard frowned. "You were trained a Veridan Warrior, were you not?"

"Of course!" Mira declared with a note of pride.

"Then you know how to fight demons. Or at least you know how to begin. In the old days all warriors were given weapons spelled with special magic, so that the touch of their blades could reach right into their own level of existence and hurt demons. Sorcerers also knew how to make their own magic to fight the Dark.''

''Jenny shot beams of blue light at the demons that scorched them good.''

''Did you?'' Bresdenant radiated approval. ''But do you know what it was you did?''

''No, not really,'' Jenny answered self-consciously, brushing her long, blue hair away from her face.

''No, of course not. You acted entirely out of instinct. You've seen the Dark, haven't you? You've never looked close enough to learn any of its secrets, but you know how its magic feels and you know how to make your own magic respond accordingly.''

''Yes, I guess so,'' she agreed with great reluctance.

''You mean that's the answer?'' Mira asked incredulously. ''That's how to fight the Dark directly?''

''Of course.'' Bresdenant leaned back in his chair with that sense of triumphant satisfaction of a teacher whose student had just made an important discovery. ''To know how to fight the Dark, you have to look deep enough into its ways for your own magic to get some instinctive feel for it. From that time on, your magic is not only able to recognize an enemy, but it knows what to do about it.''

''But magic isn't a matter of instinct,'' she protested.

''It is when you pit Light Magic against the Dark,'' he told her impatiently. ''You also forget all that I ever tried to pound into that thick head of yours. Wizards and witches differ from sorcerers and sorceresses like us in that they do operate far more by instinct than education. Of course, that is also the reason why their magic is so limited. They don't really have the slightest idea of what they're doing. You get better results by guiding your magic.

''But in fighting Dark Magic, you really can't know what you're doing. If you understood Dark Magic that well, you would belong to the Dark. You let your magic do the fighting for you. Apparently this student of yours has a very good instinct for how to go about that.''

Mira seemed to be somewhat uncomfortable with that idea. As a research sorceress, she had always believed in and supported the theory that all mages benefited from careful training, and that magic worked best when merged with all appropriate sciences. She did not care to have to consider that she possessed any professional prejudices against untrained wizards and instinctive magic, but that appeared to be exactly the case. She had to remind herself to be open-minded on the subject, but this unexpected turn of events had a very bitter taste.

"Ah, crap!" Bresdenant declared, noticing her reaction of distaste. "You know, that's exactly what's wrong with magic these days. All you women took over, and you want everything to run nice and predictable. You've even got the men these days thinking the same way, but I still remember that magic has to come first from the instinct. And that's why you sorceresses don't stand a chance of fighting the Dark."

"We've done well enough so far," she reminded him.

"You were lucky. You were trained all wrong to be able to control the magic you need every time you need it."

"But you trained me."

"Oh." He recovered quickly. "That's quite beside the point. You sorceresses have taken Light Magic from a weapon against evil and made it a slave of your precious sciences."

"Is that so?" Mira asked coldly.

"That's right," Bresdenant declared. "You can't name me one important sorceress working today who couldn't benefit from what I'm telling you right now."

"Not Melithen Reld, or Kerie Wold?" Mira demanded. "Or what about Deiven or Harlayn? Or even Lady Tenika?"

"No, not a one."

"But you trained each and every one of those people," she pointed out.

Bresdenant considered that for a moment, and shrugged. "So? Anyone can make mistakes."

Mira was prepared to launch a major attack when she reconsidered and closed her mouth. She reminded herself that this was not the man that she had known twenty years ago, when she had been a shy, self-effacing journeywoman. Bresdenant had always been a self-important, lecherous ass. Now he was only a lonely, half-senile old drunk who would gladly keep her here arguing all day just for the attention and company. It might be doing him some good, but she had all the forces of the Dark and the Kingdoms of the Sea to worry about.

"That is quite beside the point," she told him slowly and sternly. "The issue will become irrelevant if the Empire is re-established and the Dark Priesthood drives us back into the arctic wastes. I must be on my way into the South as soon as possible, and I must know anything you can possibly tell me that will be useful to that mission.''

"Well, let me think about that." Bresdenant rubbed his beard thoughtfully, and reached for a mug of fruit juice on the table beside his chair. But Mira leaped up and took the cup from his hand.

"What is this?" she demanded, sniffing at it suspiciously.

"Just cherry juice," he insisted, looking rather hurt.

"Cherry juice, my ass!" Mira declared. "This is ale. You're still up to your old tricks, it seems, conjuring alcohol out of the sugar in fruit juice. Why do you think you have to drink so much?"

"Why, to forget."

"What?"

He considered that, and shrugged. "I forgot."

"I'm glad that things are working out for you," Jenny remarked drily.

"Ah, about the Dark . . ." Mira gently tried to get the conversation back on the subject. She had the suspicion that Bresdenant was trying to avoid the matter. She wondered why he had suddenly gotten so perverse.

"Oh, you don't want to go into the south," he told her suddenly. "That's a terrible place for a sorceress, if they're worshipping the Dark again. Do you know what they'll do to you, if they catch you?"

"I'm not going to let them catch me," she informed him. "I've already got a plan that should keep us out of trouble long enough to discover what we want and get back out again. But I need to know anything you can tell me. What about those spells you mentioned to make weapons that we can use against demons?"

"Now did I say that?"

"You most certainly did."

"Well, it's been a long time, and you must understand that I never actually tried any of this stuff firsthand. I'll have to look . . . well, hello there!"

"Oh, you're cute!" Addena Sheld said, tickled with delight, as she stepped up from behind the two sorceresses and sat down on the arm of the old wizard's chair. "You didn't tell me whether or not you needed me to tell this distinguished older gentleman what I saw."

"Ah . . . Addena did some judicious sightseeing in the South for me when she was there on tour this summer,'' Lady Mira explained, looking at her friend questioningly. ''Addena Sheld is a very famous concert singer, you know.''

''Oh, you don't say!'' Bresdenant radiated excited delight like a rat in a cheese pantry. ''So, are you going to sing for me?''

''Right now I need for you to sing for me,'' Mira said impatiently, wondering what in the world had possessed Addena to make such an unexpected appearance.

''Listen, if I tell you all of this, the two of you are going to go running off into the South and get yourself into trouble,'' he told her firmly. ''If what you say is going on down there, then it's no place for a woman.''

''I've been there,'' Addena declared reproachfully, in a way that encouraged him not to disagree with her. She knew an old fart when she saw one; she had been forced to deal with enough of his kind in the past. ''As Mira told you, I've already gone south as her spy.''

Mira noticed that Jenny had the same wicked look in her eyes as she had when she had scorched those two demons.

''Do you really think these two could cavort with the Dark Priesthood and get away with their skins?'' Bresdenant asked her very seriously.

''You don't know these two as well as I do,'' Addena answered. ''They could probably get away with pretending to be Dark Priestesses.''

''Now that's exactly the point.'' He turned to look at the two sorceresses. ''You seem to think that your relative familiarity with the Dark will help you to understand your enemies, hide you from them and perhaps even fight them if you must. But, you see, that's the old trap. To fight the Dark, you must look into the shadows. But once you do, you're easy bait for its true servants. If they get their hands on you, they're going to try to force you over to the Dark. And then you'll find it only too easy to fall, because you have seen the Dark. That's what they used to do with our sorcerers. The very thing that's your advantage is also your disadvantage.''

''I understand that,'' Lady Mira agreed, although the idea clearly bothered her. And it bothered her more for Jenny's sake. ''But we still have to go.''

''Why?''

''Because if we don't, then they're going to come into our lands after us in their own good time. They've already started . . . or do you need to see the arrow damage on the bottom of my airship to believe that? We've got to go now, to see what's going on and what those people plan to do, before it's too late for any of us to stop it.''

Bresdenant looked up at Addena, still seated on the arm of his chair. ''Are you going?''

She took a deep breath and sighed. ''I've already been, remember? And I will go back, if it will do any good.''

The old wizard sat for a long moment, as if trying to reconcile himself to some idea that disagreed with every principle he held true. He sighed heavily. ''Ah, women. They aren't half trained the way they should be, they wouldn't have the slightest idea of what to do in a fight, and they probably don't even know what to look for. But you mean to go, I can see that. And I sure as hell don't see anyone offering to go in your place. I'd go myself, if I . . . Hell, I'm just an old man. I might as well sit around here all day and learn to do something harmless, like basketmaking or weaving.''

''You were weaving when I first knew you twenty years ago,'' Mira remarked with just a hint of mischief.

''Yes, that's a fact!'' He was as quick as anyone to laugh at his drinking habits. He almost seemed to consider drunkenness the major accomplishment of his life. He paused again, and frowned. ''I've got a book where I've collected all the spells and lore I've run across over the years on how to fight the Dark. A lot of that stuff has come down second- and third-hand from hundreds or even thousands of years ago. And I've never been able to test the accuracy of any of it, you must understand.''

''I understand,'' Mira agreed. ''Still, it is better than nothing. What can it tell me?''

''Oh, any number of things you might find useful. I can recall offhand that it does have spells for forcing skulking demons to reveal themselves, and tests to see if someone belongs to the Dark. It has spells to let you shield yourself from the attacks of demons. It has spells that can be woven into the metal of swords and arrows to allow them to bite into demon flesh. Oh, it has quite a lot of useful little tidbits.''

''I need it. But what about magic . . . ?''

''Damn it, I've already explained that to you,'' he said impatiently. ''You develop your instincts until your magic knows how to take care of you. Don't you worry about that, though. There

are a few hints in the book itself that might make that easier. I
don't know. I've never tested it myself. And you really won't
know how well you're learning until your magic has to prove itself
in battle."

"Why don't we go get that book?" Addena suggested, then
gave Mira a beseeching look that suggested that she did not care
to be alone with this old wizard in his room. "You need to start
on it as soon as possible."

"Yes, I certainly do," Lady Mira agreed as she rose to follow
them. Bresdenant, who alone remained seated, looked about in a
bewildered manner, suddenly realizing that he was going to have
all three females alone in his room and wondering what he was
going to do about it. But at that moment the two young mercenaries
made their appearance, moving in to stand protectively behind
both of the sorceresses. Their attempts at looking grim and hard
were laughable, but Bresdenant was in no position to argue. Looking like he had just tasted something terrible, he rose to lead the
way.

"If I had known that we were going to have a damned party,
I would have called for more fruit juice," he muttered miserably.

Lady Mira indicated for the bodyguards to follow behind Addena and the wizard, since she was the one who was placing her
head in the lion's mouth for the sake of their mission. Jenny fell
in close beside her mistress. "Just what is going on here?"

"I wish I knew," Mira answered, seemingly inclined to laugh.
"That old goat was beginning to get obstinate, almost as if he
had decided that he wanted us to fail. Then Addena arrived and
was perfectly willing to play him for the fool he is, and I have to
let her. Letting her keep him too confused and distracted to turn
devious is the only way I know to be able to trust what he tells
us, and I still don't trust him completely. Having that book will
be a big help, and Addena is the only one who has a chance of
getting it away from him."

"He doesn't much like me," Jenny said, confused. She had
always been such an eager, delightful personality that she had
never had to deal with that problem.

"He likes women who are stupid and impressionable, and you
are neither one of those. He especially dislikes women who are
more intelligent than he is. He doesn't much care for my company
right now either, so don't let it worry you."

Bresdenant had one of the larger apartments in Coot Hall—

Jenny was beginning to appreciate that name—consisting of a bedroom, a small kitchen and a front study. Bookshelves lined every wall of that front room and they were packed full, if in a haphazard manner, but half again that many books overflowed the shelves to end up as orphans on the floor, the extra chairs, the vast desk and even the kitchen table. But the books had to battle for any available space with empty mugs, bits of magical paraphernalia, dirty plates, empty bottles and ordinary trash. The visitors picked their way carefully through this maze, although the mercenaries remained on guard to either side of the door. Mira kicked a wad of paper, which deflected off the wall, and the side of the desk and into the large trash basket. That last item appeared to be the cleanest fixture in the room.

"You were a slob when I first met you, and you're still a slob," Mira remarked under her breath.

Jenny looked even less happy. The floor had an odd tendency to crunch as they walked.

"Oh, do you think you can ever find it?" Addena asked with innocent consternation. Mira cleared her throat in a rather obvious effort to keep from laughing.

"Oh, I know it's in here someplace," Bresdenant assured her jovially as he forced his way through the undergrowth to the desk. He happened to glance up at the two guards. "Where did you get those two boys, anyway?"

"Oh, they're just my guards," Mira answered with her own brand of innocence. "The Trassek twins, Dooket and Erkin."

"Twins?" the old wizard asked suspiciously. Dooket was very tall and dark, while Erkin was short and blond. But he decided to avoid arguing the point, fearful of what he might be given as logic for this situation. He began to dig through the upper layers of the desk, then paused to stare at Mira. "I remember you now! You used to be shorter."

Jenny and Addena stared at her in surprise, but Mira did her best to pretend that he had not said that. "What do you mean, you only now recognize me? I was your student for six years."

"Yes, but you were barely four and a half feet tall back then," he insisted. "I remember now. They found you doing cheap tricks and performing as a midget clown in a traveling circus, but you had such talent that they convinced you to go to the Academy. My, but you've grown!"

"I was just late to get my full growth," Mira declared indignantly. Addena had collapsed in helpless laughter atop a pile of books behind the desk; Erkin was biting his tongue, while Dooket stood with his face in the corner behind the door. Only Jenny did not appear amused, although she could not have been more surprised. Mira looked at her, and shrugged. "I got tired of being so short."

"Oh, I can understand that," Jenny agreed. "Magic does sometimes have its benefits."

"Now, if we could take a look at that book . . ."

"Ah, do you think that you can do something about my nose?" Jenny interrupted her gently.

"Your nose is just fine, child," Mira assured her, and turned to glare at the wizard. "If you don't mind."

"Yes, yes. Here it is." He extracted a large but rather thin book from beneath a stack of papers. Mira made her way to his side as he laid the book out on the table, quickly checking its table of contents. It had the appearance of having been machine-printed, except that the style was very ornate; Bresdenant had, at one time, been very meticulous with his magic.

"This looks rather impressive," she admitted.

"The work of a lifetime," Bresdenant declared proudly. "No part of this book is pure conjecture except for those parts clearly labeled so. I still have the source material, although a lot of it has to be spelled to translate the original text . . . and if you can find it."

"Will you let me read through this text?" Mira asked guardedly.

"They really do need to have that book, considering how important it is for them to know how to fight the Dark," Addena added in a rather seductively beseeching tone, moving up close beside the old wizard and holding tightly to his arm. Bresdenant sighed deeply, knowing that he was going to allow himself to be had.

"Now, I'm not about to take the only copy of this text into the South with me, where it might be lost," Mira was quick to point out, although she was surprised to see that Bresdenant probably would have let them have the book. "I can get paper from *Wind Dragon* and spell myself a complete copy in a matter of minutes."

"Oh, well, you can surely do that," Bresdenant agreed pleasantly enough, relieved that he was not going to lose his own copy after all. "How soon do you want to get started?"

"I might as well send Addena after paper right away and get

on with it," she decided. She did not say that she actually meant to make several complete copies, so that at least one could be sent to the Academy. "We really do need to be on our way in the morning, but I would like a chance to read through this material first."

"Would you like to go with me to get that paper?" Addena said, taking the hint to get Bresdenant out of his room. "I'm sure that you would like to see *Wind Dragon*. She really is the most beautiful airship ever."

"I don't much care for flying," Bresdenant said uncertainly as he followed her toward the door.

"Oh, I didn't mean that we should try to get it up."

"Hee, hee! That's what you think!"

"Oh, piffle!" Mira declared impatiently. "You always did have a thing for sex."

"Oh, sure. I just never get to use it." Bresdenant was so pleased with himself that he tripped in the debris, but Dooket caught him before he hit the ground and returned him to an upright position. He stared up at the giant mercenary thoughtfully, rubbing his beard, then hurried out the door after Addena. Erkin closed it behind him.

"My word, I . . ." Mira was caught off guard by a loud burst of giggling from the hall, followed by Bresdenant's rather bacchanal laughter. She glanced up at the door. "And to think, all we have to worry about are demons and the Dark Priesthood."

"Will he . . . ?" Jenny asked nervously.

"Oh, great stars, no!" the sorceress declared. "As far as I've ever been able to tell, he's still a virgin who talks a lot. Why don't the two of you go after them and get that paper? Addena, I trust, knows to keep him away long enough for us to make several copies of this."

"Why do we always got to run your errands?" Dooket demanded indignantly, and Erkin nodded. "We're mercenaries."

"You are two postpubescent clowns whom I pay better than you deserve to do whatever I tell you," she explained patiently. "Begone."

"Did you hear that, brother?" Dooket demanded as they turned to leave. "She called us clowns."

"She ought to know."

"What's a postpubescent, anyway?"

"It means you have a beard, brother." Erkin paused in the doorway to explain.

"Oh." Dooket made an exaggerated grimace, as if he was forcing a reluctant brain into motion. "But I've got no beard."

"Not on your chin, you dolt," Erkin said impatiently. The closing of the door spared the two sorceresses any further nonsense.

"My word, has the whole world gone mad today?" Mira demanded as she sat down in the chair, which made a very unusual squeak of protest. She jumped up, brushed something off onto the floor, and sat down again. She checked the contents of the book quickly and turned to the indicated page. "Yes, here we go. He does have quite a large section on the origins and nature of the Dark and the calling forth of Dark Forces. Although he does indicate that he does not consider the source material to have been absolutely reliable."

"What do you hope to find?" Jenny asked.

"At this point, anything would be useful. Specifically, I want to know how to recognize agents of the Dark from a safe distance, ways to take some measure of the Dark Forces that are gathered in a specific place, and the ways that the Dark Sorcerers work their magic. And, not incidental to all of that, how to get away with our hides. Why don't you prepare a place where we can assemble five copies of this?"

That request fell into the category of things easier said than done, and after some difficulty Jenny had a small table clear enough to lay out the five manuscripts. Dooket and Erkin had returned with all the paper they could find by that time, then retreated to guard the door from the outside so that the two sorceresses could work undisturbed. Mira counted out five sheets and laid them stacked atop the first printed page of the text, then muttered a couple of words with the appropriate gestures. When she picked up the stack of paper, she had five perfect copies of that page.

Jenny watched the process with considerable interest. Mira seemed to have a spell for everything, including cabalistic copying and magical fax.

"Ah, nice," she remarked as she handed the pages to her student, who quickly separated them face down into five separate piles. She was already counting out paper for the next page. "But we do need to hurry. I can imagine what poor Addena is having to put up with, trying to keep one step ahead of that old fart. I had to put up with it for six years, remember?''

"He never caught you?'' Jenny asked as she reached over to receive the second page.

"Brez is a bother, not a danger,'' she explained. "He was younger then, but so was I. And a much smaller target than I am now.''

By that evening, Mira had determined that the old wizard had either never really understood all that much about the material that he had so carefully collected, or else he had since forgotten the better part of it. She saw now that his earlier avoidance of her questions was due largely to the fact that he simply did not know the answers. That also meant that she and Jenny were very much on their own in the matter of finding the answers they needed in that book. And she hoped that the answers they needed were in that book, since they would have to learn its secrets on their way south.

Lady Mira may have hoped for better, but she had honestly expected no more than that. She now had five copies of that very important book neatly bound, one each for herself and her young student, one to remain safely at home, and the last two to be sent on to the Academy. That way all that information would be safe from even the worst of catastrophes, either their failure to return from their mission in the South or the loss of Bresdenant's library to spontaneous combustion.

She considered the first part of this mission to have been very successful; the rest could only go half as well, and they might just come out of this alive and enlightened. Her first inclination was to get *Wind Dragon* back in the sky, return Addena to Bennasport, stock the airship for an extended journey and collect J.T., and be on their way to the southern sea. Addena was quick to agree with that idea; she had reached the limit of both her strength and her patience in dealing with Bresdenant.

The next time she came, Mira meant to bring Dame Tugg with her. Those two strong and extremely peculiar personalities would either murder each other, or marry. And the both of them deserved either fate.

Bresdenant surprised them early that evening by paying a visit to *Wind Dragon*. Addena heard him coming, singing coarsely and telling himself snips of rank jokes, and locked herself in her cabin.

"Well, I don't suppose that I'll ever see you people again," Bresdenant remarked. "I'll regret that. You're not much, but you're all I've got."

Mira's brows did calisthenics. "Really."

"All the same, I will wish you luck in your mission. That book is the best that I can do for you."

"And we appreciate that," Mira assured him.

"Well, I might as well call it a night. It's a night." He turned to leave, but paused to look back. "If you do make it to Alashera, by the way, you might have a look around for the Heart of Flame."

"The Heart of Flame was destroyed thousands of years ago," Mira said, as if daring him to deny that.

"So they say," Bresdenant answered as he leaned over the rail. "The Servants of the Dark were supposed to have destroyed it themselves during the fall of Alashera. But, as you read through that book, you'll see that I've cited three references to the Prophecy of Haldephren, the High Priest of Alashera. He claimed to his followers, before they scattered and left him to his death, that his intention was to seal the Heart of Flame within the chambers of Mount Drashand. There it was to lie hidden until some later day, when the Forces of the Dark would again grow in strength and open the chamber for the new priesthood. It just occurred to me to wonder if they've found the damned thing, or if they've even bothered to look."

"I'll make a special point of that," Mira promised him. "Do you think that the Heart of Flame still exists?"

Bresdenant only shrugged. "I've always thought it possible that the thing still exists, since there was no direct proof of its destruction. I really just don't know. I've never been in the South to have a look for myself, although I always meant to go."

"Will you go with us now?" Mira asked.

Bresdenant thought about it for a long moment, but shook his head. "I'm getting too old for this type of thing, and flying makes me dizzy."

It's because you're a drunk, Mira thought. But she kept that to herself. Matters were getting more and more complicated at every turn, so that their journey into the South was becoming a larger and more complex task every step along the way. But, since that was the way such matters usually turned out, she was not completely surprised.

"Is there anything else I should know?" she asked.

"Well, ever heard of the Prophecy of Maerildyn?" Bresdenant offered.

Mira was astounded. "I've heard of Maerildyn, of course, but nothing about her having a prophecy. Just what does the prophecy purport?"

"Hell, I don't know!" Bresdenant declared. "I don't much think that anyone in the North knows. It dealt with the return of the Empire, and no one seemed to want to think about that. Only traces survive."

"Any hints?"

"Just two," the wizard said, obviously beginning to enjoy himself, as any true sorcerer would during a scholarly discourse. "The prophecy is said to deal with the return of the Forces of the Dark, the re-establishment of the Dark Priesthood, and the second rise of the Alasheran Empire. That seems a fairly safe assumption, under the circumstances during which the prophecy was delivered. Of the second part, all we have is a bare fragment of what is supposed to be the original prophecy."

He rolled his eyes upward as he searched through the cluttered library of his memory.

> "Dragons gold and dragons black
> Seek to gain what each may lack.
> White and black, red and blue,
> Fortune hangs between the two."

"White and black is obvious enough," Mira mused. "But red and blue? Do you have any idea?"

Bresdenant shrugged helplessly. "I have no idea."

"The Empire was coming down on their heads and everyone was busy making prophecies. I guess that they had already called the odds." Mira propped her elbows on the table, rested her chin on her hands and rolled her eyes. "Very well. One more small task in our busy vacation itinerary. Wish you to impart any more gems of information, oh sotted sage?"

Bresdenant spared one of his impish grins. "Have you ever seen a demon?"

"A winged demon?" she offered, as if asking him not to tell her that things got worse than that.

He waved that away impatiently. "The robins of spring, compared to the big beggars I've read about. I'm only glad that I've never seen one, at least not when I was sober.''

"That leaves precious little time for sane enlightenment," Mira reflected to herself, muttering under her breath. She looked over at him. "Can we fight them?"

"As far as I can tell, yes," he agreed, nodding thoughtfully. "People used to do it quite regularly. With the right weapons and a little experience, it seems that you can meet them on fairly equal terms. Listen, why don't just the three of you stop by my apartment later on for a little party? I can teach you a thing or two about having a good time."

By mutual consent between the two sorceresses and the singer, they declined a generous offer of rooms in Coot Hall for the night. They spent the night in *Wind Dragon*, and drew in the boarding ramp behind them.

"More prophecies," Jenny muttered to herself. "I seem to be drawing the damned things like flies. As if the one wasn't really enough."

"Oh, cheer up," Mira told her. "I'm not so sure that we do have more than just the one prophecy. They all seem to be different perspectives of the same thing."

"That's easy for you to say," Jenny complained. "For you, it's just any other professional puzzle. I'm the one who has to put up with blue hair and dire fate."

"You do?" Mira stared at her intently. "I'd never noticed."

Late during the night, a dark figure slipped from one shadow to another as it made its stealthful way across the yard outside the Sanctuary toward the parked airship. It made a sudden dart across the open, disappearing within the dark recess beneath *Wind Dragon*'s hull. Lady Mira had been obliged to crank down the wheels and move the ship to a more suitable location. Now the furtive figure cut the brake cables to each wheel, then pulled out the blocks under the wheels themselves.

The little airship began to move slowly, almost lazily, her long, slender bowsprit swinging around as she followed the gentle slope. Because she rolled on inflated rubber tires with shock-absorbing struts, *Wind Dragon* hardly even shuddered as she stepped gently down off the curb onto the large, flat paving stones of the road leading down toward the village. Fortunately the curb itself was high enough to guide the wheels of the airship. That late at night, no one but an occasional cat observed as the ship lumbered through the very middle of the village.

The really interesting part came on the far side of the village. The paving stones and the guiding curb suddenly disappeared, and *Wind Dragon* seemed destined to crash into a stand of trees past a sudden curve in the road. That might have been better, since the ship was moving at hardly more than an indifferent walk and would not have damaged herself to any great extent. As it happened, she chose that particular moment to wander off the road and her right forward wheel truck ran down a wooden road sign. That had the unexpected effect of turning the forward wheels to the right, and the airship just barely managed to negotiate the turn.

Now she began to gain speed slowly and she descended the gentle slope of the portage road that ran alongside the barge tracks, allowing passage for the teams of horses that hauled the empty ore barges back up to the mines from their long journey down to the coast. Slowly she moved off to the left toward the barge tracks. First the left wheels stepped down into the deep stone-lined trough, and then the right ones followed. It was quite a step down, although the ship was still moving along at no more than an uninspired run and her passengers were used to sleeping in a moving airship.

Wind Dragon was so small and narrow that her wheels fit almost exactly within the confines of the barge tracks. Now that the way was straight and open, the airship began to gather speed steadily.

Jenny awoke early the next morning and stepped out on the central deck for a breath of air. The morning wind seemed oddly brisk, but the air was cool and damp. She took a deep, full breath and released it slowly, and stood at the left rail watching the dark wall of pines whizzing past only a few yards away. Jenny just stood there at the rail watching the forest, which was deep and shadowy with a type of storybook charm, as if the eternal twilight beneath those tall pines hid the little cottages of reticent dwarves and the woodland hunts and banquets of elves. She knew such things from firsthand experience. She took another deep breath and paused.

Now, what is wrong with this picture?

"Mira!" she shouted with the impressive clarity and volume of a trained voice as she hurried to the wheel. "Kasdamir Gerran, you overgrown midget! Get your ass on deck this moment!"

Mira was a good long time in making her appearance on deck, and even then she was wearing nothing except an oversized flannel shirt and carrying a cup of tea in one hand. She yawned hugely. "What is it, child?"

"We're moving!"

"Ah, yes. Drifting gently along on a sea of dreams, the soft breeze that fills our sail bearing us pleasantly away from that fair land of Morpheus." She paused, and stared over the rail. "Holy shit!"

"May I take that to mean that you haven't the slightest idea how we happened into this remarkable situation?" Jenny asked.

"I hope to kiss a pig." Mira hurried to the helm deck, and stopped short. "The brakes are on."

"We have no brakes," Jenny informed her.

Mira looked over Jenny's shoulder to check the airspeed indicator. The dial listed up to a hundred knots, to allow for the measurement of headwinds. A very large percentage of the total lay on the wrong side of the pointer. She frowned. "I wonder how long we've been at it."

"I wonder who put us here," Jenny countered. "I know better than to think that *Wind Dragon* broke all her cables and jumped her blocks."

"And I know better than to think that *Wind Dragon* just happened to wander all the way from the Sanctuary, through the middle of a fairly large village and somehow managed to find herself in the barge tracks," Mira added, and she was never to know just how wrong she was. "I can imagine setting us free to wreck, but I just can't figure out why they did this. I wonder what day this is?"

Jenny stared at her. "What does that matter?"

Mira shrugged. "Probably nothing, since we're in trouble either way. I was just thinking that the ore barges are rolled down to the port in a single group for two days, unloaded for two days and hauled by teams of horses back up for a journey of five days for reloading. The schedule is designed to insure that all the traffic on the line is always moving in the same direction."

"Land ho!" Dooket shouted from the bow. "No, strike that. Water ho!"

The two sorceresses peered ahead. They were just coming over the top of a low rise that began a final long, steep run down to the distant coast. The forest ran unbroken right up to the edge of the sea, which was contained in a narrow bay between two long arms of land to either side. There was a town of considerable size at the end of the line, with sailing ships at rest in the harbor. The end of the line was the part that most occupied their attention, since it was no more than five miles ahead and looked to be at least a mile below. The ship's altimeter, operating by air pressure, insisted that they would indeed descend two thousand feet in a very short time. Jenny thought that, by the time they reached the end of this grade, she was going to find out what it was like to drag race a tea clipper.

"And airships don't have reverse thrust," Jenny said to herself. She turned to her mistress. "Lady Mira, do you know anything about this port? What happens when we come to the end?"

"One of two things," Mira mused. "We'll go right through the warehouses, unless the barges stop us first. That depends upon what day it is. Anticipating your next question, there will be no more than a mile of open ground in which we can swing out the vanes and take to the air. On this slope, even our brakes would never stop us now."

"You'll need to take the wheel," Jenny told her.

"I'll be quick," Mira promised as she headed toward her cabin. She waved to the two mercenaries on her way. "Have everything rigged so that we can swing out the vanes and lock them in place as quickly as possible."

Jenny tried her best to hold the ship to the center of the track, fearful of losing a wheel or even a strut from rubbing against the curb as their speed rose steadily. She wondered about their chances of surviving this while she watched the twins as they prepared the rigging, working to have the vanes as ready as possible to swing out as soon as they reached a space open enough. The increasing wind of their passage was making their work more and more difficult as *Wind Dragon* began to scream down that final slope.

Mira and Addena both appeared soon enough, suitably attired. Addena hurried to help the boys with the rigging, while the sorceress returned to the helm deck to take the wheel. She expected that Jenny would have gone forward to help with the rigging, but that was as ready as it could be. Instead she returned moments later with two ropes, one coiled over her shoulder while she trailed the other across the deck, and a large grappling hook. She quickly tied one end of the coiled rope to the hook and the other looped around both of the stern bracing bits used to tie up the ship.

"You'll only wreck us good if you try to stop us at this speed," Mira observed, although she made that something of a question.

She was perfectly aware that the girl knew that quite well.

"I'm not trying to stop us," Jenny said as she continued her work. "I'm going to try to snag something that will slow us down, maybe buy us more time to get those vanes out."

Mira said nothing more, and Jenny continued her work. They came at last to the bottom of the slope and leveled out at a speed that they guessed to be on the better side of a hundred knots. Jenny stood, bracing herself against the wind by holding to the rail, the grappling hook in one hand, as she looked forward along the left side of the ship for a likely target. *Wind Dragon* emerged suddenly from the depths of the forest into a small belt of farmland behind the town, and she had to take the first target she could find.

Unfortunately, it happened to be a small wagon loaded with round bales of straw that had been left right beside the barge track. There was an explosion of yellow straw, and the little wagon leaped right off its axles to follow the airship. It bounced and skipped at the end of the stout rope, smoking thickly almost at once because of friction from the stones before it suddenly burst into a bloom of flames. *Wind Dragon* began to slow noticeably, although she would still ram herself rather violently into the warehouses only a few hundred yards ahead if she could not get herself off the ground.

Jenny had tied the second rope to the first where it trailed out through an opening in the siderail. Now she cut the end of the first rope, and the weight of the wagon pulled the second rope tight. As it did, it gave a very firm tug on several other ropes and all four of *Wind Dragon*'s vanes snapped out straight and firm. The Trassek twins hurried to secure the locking pins at the joints of the vanes and tighten up the remaining lines. Jenny could not release the burning wagon until they did.

"We've got an open path right through the middle of town," Mira reported, both delighted and horrified by what she could see coming. "There are wide, open avenues to either side of the track. That should give us an extra two hundred yards of running room."

"We're going to need it," Jenny shouted back. "Unless you want to fling this burning wagon right into the middle of the warehouses."

"Damn, this whole town could go," Mira muttered.

"Flight ready!" Dooket shouted from the central deck.

Mira began to apply lift from the levitation vanes, and *Wind*

Dragon began to rise steadily from the narrow canyon of two-
and three-story buildings lining either side of the track. Jenny
leaned over the back rail, watching anxiously until the rope was
reaching almost straight down and the burning wagon slowly left
the ground. It gave the edge of the roof of the first warehouse a
glancing blow, but it did little damage and set no fire.

The only trouble was that Mira had no control over the ship,
since the steering vanes were still retracted. Addena and the Trassek twins hurried to the bowsprit to rig those vanes as Mira took
Wind Dragon out over the bay, allowing the ship to lose momen-
tum. Jenny was about to cut the rope when the burning wagon
collapsed, scattering flaming debris across the water.

Mira's intention was to bring the ship down in the water long
enough for the steering vanes to be rigged. *Wind Dragon* was still
moving along at a fair pace about twenty feet above the waves
when the grappling hook, still trailing underwater at the end of
its tether, suddenly snagged something that was even more reluctant to move than the airship. That brought the line up short,
sending Addena and the two young barbarians over the rail and
into the water.

Finding her ship standing nearly on end, Mira had to apply full
forward thrust as well as levitation to keep *Wind Dragon* from
crashing stern-first into the waves. She was hanging from the
forward wheel, staring over her shoulder at the waves below.
Then, inexplicably, *Wind Dragon* gradually began to make head-
way, rising slowly bow-first into the sky. There was a curious
stirring in the dark waters of the bay as some odd, shadowy form
began to move toward the surface. The waves parted, and a sunken
schooner nearly as large as *Wind Dragon* herself rose above the
vanes. But it would go no farther, since the airship could hardly
lift it into the sky.

"That's one hell of a rope," Jenny observed as she cut the
knot.

That was probably not the smartest move, but they really had
no choice in the matter. *Wind Dragon* shot forward as if she had
been launched from some immense catapult. A long moment
passed before Mira recovered from her surprise enough to reduce
thrust and acceleration. The airship arched over in a neat trajectory
before crashing back into the water with a rather awesome splash.
It was a splash to end all splashes.

Mira picked herself up from the deck, dusted herself off, and stood for a long moment waiting to see if her little airship was going to sink. The vanes and rigging were all still intact, and it seemed that the hull had survived the impact through no fault of its own. She walked over to join Jenny at the aft rail, watching their lost members swimming toward them from over a quarter of a mile away.

"What a distressingly stupid thing to have happen before breakfast," Mira remarked to Jenny, who was still speechless. "What do you say we have some tea before we get back to work?"

• Part Four •

Wind Dragon

ONLY LADY MIRA could pack an airship for an important and dangerous journey and host a party all at the same time. Or so it seemed to Jenny, who had to make frequent trips through the middle of that very party from Mira's study and storerooms to *Wind Dragon*'s shed behind the house. She normally delighted in Mira's parties, and this evening she certainly would rather have been standing around enjoying wine and cheese rather than fetching baskets of supplies out to the airship.

Even Mira found it a bit hard to keep both ends going at once. Ordinarily she could not resist a party, but she had been absolutely entranced with fascination for Bresdenant's book on the Dark. Jenny had to admit that it was all very interesting, but it also made her slightly uneasy. She was even more disconcerted to find that the material all seemed very self-evident to her, while her mistress would have to read the same passage many times and consult other references in her own books before a sudden, startling comprehension would take her by surprise. Jenny's own attempts to explain her own understanding to the older sorceress most often met with failure, since she found it hard to find the right words.

"Jenny, child, I think I have it at last!" Mira declared as her student entered her study, returning from yet another trip out to the airship. "I think I have that spell of release mastered, the one that sends demons back to wherever they came from. I think I'm ready to try it again."

"What, now?" Jenny asked apprehensively, pausing at Mira's side to glance down at the book. Her last attempt at working the spell of release on a "target," small pieces of crystal that had been attuned to simulate the otherworld emanations of demons, had caused a yard-square section of the carpet to unravel itself. Fortunately Mira's magic had been able to put the threads back in place again.

"Yes, now," Mira declared impatiently.

"The practice room?" Jenny suggested. "It has a brick floor and only a few furnishings along the walls."

"Oh, very well," the sorceress agreed, and with no real reluctance. She had no desire to see what other variations of that spell might do to her study.

Jenny noticed that their retreat to the practice room somehow managed to acquire a following. The Trassek twins fell in immediately behind the sorceresses, but that was their duty. Addena noticed that something was up and followed as well, and somehow the entire gathering decided to fall in behind her. Curiosity, according to Mira, was a major cause of accidents, resulted in the wasting of a considerable amount of time, and was the driving force behind most love affairs.

The practice room was simply a large, empty chamber in the back of the house where members of the household could work to develop or maintain their martial skills . . . or even a trim waistline. It was mostly open space, with mats and equipment for exercises and room for fencing and broadsword fighting. The observers remained just inside the door, while the sorceresses advanced to the center of the room. Lady Mira bent to place a small, clear crystal on the floor, then stepped back four paces.

"It's really a matter of translation," she explained quietly to her student. "My last mistake was making 'release' come out more as 'untie' or 'unravel,' since I was wanting to release the spells that bind the demons to this existence. This might work better."

Jenny only nodded.

"Forces of the Dark do shrink, turn out and slip away.
Strip thee of thy protection, withdraw to that cold place

Whence first it did come.
Naked to this world, ye cannot abide!''

"Oh, no!" Jenny half-shouted her warning, but it was too late. The crystal did not disappear, nor did the sense of otherworldliness that surrounded it. But the magic was not without results. The two sorceresses, caught in the backwash of that spell, felt an icy breeze at their backs. And it was all the more icy to the feel, since they were now both completely naked. Even the pins which had held Mira's long, red hair piled atop her head were gone, so that her hair tumbled over her shoulders. Mira turned to her student with a look that dared her to say a word.

"A slight miscalculation," she declared as she turned and headed toward the door, where two score and more of guests stared in calm, quiet amazement. Since they seemed for the moment too startled to withdraw discreetly, the two sorceresses marched through the small crowd in the most casual manner they could contrive. Mira was blushing slightly, although it was not due to her state of undress.

"Where did our clothes go?" Jenny asked softly as they marched through the dining room and headed toward the stairs. Dame Tugg, who was collecting empty glasses, was her usual unruffled self. She appeared to notice nothing. This was actually not a remarkable state of attire for some of Mira's more adventurous parties.

"I don't know for certain, but I have my suspicions," Mira answered. "I just hope those foul demons enjoy my favorite lounging robe."

Jenny ran up the stairs and dressed as quickly as she could, intending to hurry back to Mira's study before her mistress might decide to attempt the spell again. She turned to close the door as she left her room, then turned to see the lithe, graceful form of a faerie dragon standing in the dark hall a few yards away. The dragon stood with his ears alert, staring at her in a rather disconcerting fashion, a fascinated yet troubled look, as if something about herself represented a problem to him.

Then Jenny stopped short. It was Kelvandor.

In all the really weird things that she had done in her life, her curious relationship with Kelvandor had been the worst . . . and in its way the most wonderful. It was also five years past, a time in her life that she now considered to belong to her childhood. She had been interested in her first sexual experience. At that time there had been only the dragons, and she had believed that Mindijaran thought of their affairs only as play, a society without marriage. And Kelvandor had been mature, adventurous and exciting.

But there were a few things that she had never considered. One was the telepathic coupling of a perfect match, that love-at-first-sight manner in which Mindijaran most often began their amorous affairs. What she had never understood was why a dragon would find her sexually fascinating, or why she had felt a compulsion to respond. She had not suspected at the time that love was a part of their odd relationship. Nor had she realized until later that Kelvandor had not thought of her as human, but as a fellow creature of magic who was soon to become a dragon like himself. But Jenny had avoided taking draconic form, delaying that act she both feared and desired. Kelvandor had loved her and she had loved him, and she had studiously ducked the question completely.

It was a classic misunderstanding.

For the moment, at least, they were both too surprised by the whole affair to do anything. Except to be polite.

"It is good to see you again, Jenny," the dragon said politely, his voice a deep, warm tenor, full of honest concern.

"Yeah, you too," she answered uncertainly, scurrying to collect her scattered thoughts. Then she saw another dragon come up behind him in the dim light. "Vajerral! I ought to skin you."

Vajerral looked profoundly surprised. "Me? I've been good."

Jenny regarded her skeptically. "I am glad to have you back, all the same. Let's go see the Lady."

Jenny led the way down the stairs to Mira's study, where she paused to knock on the half-open door. Knowing her mistress's habits, she had to wonder if Mira would have taken the time to dress before returning to her study of the book and its elusive incantations. Mira was already dressed for travel and seated at her desk, reading Bresdenant's book with a pot of tea at hand. She looked up at the dragons indifferently.

"Ah, it's about time that the two of you put in an appearance," she said, then peered at the larger dragon closely. "I say, who's your handsome friend? Your boyfriend?"

"No, Jenny's," Vajerral answered innocently.

Either Mira failed to notice, considered it a joke, or else she had simply reached the point where nothing surprised her. Jenny, however, nearly melted into the floor.

"This is Kelvandor," Vajerral explained. "He is a very experienced fighting dragon, and very close to my mother. He knows as much of what is going on as anyone."

"Wonder of wonders, that Dalvenjah Foxfire should tell anyone what's going on with this mess!" Mira declared, waving her hands. "Not that I question your choice of companions, but just what is the esteemed Dalvenjah Foxfire doing these days? Anything?"

Vajerral employed one of her ridiculously stupid looks; she had long since discovered stupidity as a device for tactical evasion. "When I left, she was trying to talk to a dead dragon."

Mira tried on a stupid look of her own.

"Well, it's her half-brother Karidaejan," Vajerral volunteered when she realized that she would get off scot-free on that one. "He did something during a visit to Jenny's world years ago, but no one has ever been able to figure out what. Mother thought it could be very important to know."

"I dare say," Mira agreed. "I thought that faerie folk were always reborn soon after they die, and Karidaejan's been gone for years."

"The trick is finding out who he is now," the young dragon explained.

Mira looked surprised. "Is he likely to remember?"

"Normally, no. But this was very important, and there are magical means to protect important memories. Sort of like leaving a note to yourself in your next life."

It seemed like a good time to drop the subject.

"Vajerral has explained your plan." Kelvandor managed to get in his first words. "Is this still what you intend?"

"Yes, more than ever," Mira insisted. "The Empire has already begun to move. We were attacked by a captured airship during our last journey, piloted by a Dark Sorcerer with two demons along just for fun."

"Demons." Kelvandor frowned, with a brief glance at Jenny. "That does make things rather more difficult. Vajerral and I can hold our own against demons, and Jenny as well because of her command of dragon magic. But we must now be prepared for anything. What of the rest of you? Did your journey to visit your former master work out for you?"

"We did learn a trick or two. We now have spelled swords, spears and arrows in such a way that they should be damaging to demons," Mira answered, and turned to her protégé. "What did we do with those weapons, anyway?"

"You had Dooket and Erkin load those weapons on board *Wind Dragon* over an hour ago," Jenny replied.

"Indeed? Then let us repair forthwith," Mira said as she rose.

Jenny was interested to note that the appearance of dragons at one of Lady Mira's parties did not seem at all unusual to the guests. That led her to wonder yet again about some of the parties that must have occurred here just prior to her arrival. The sorceress stopped short halfway down the steps to stare intently at some point in that loose gathering of guests.

"Well, I'll be," she muttered in a dire voice. "Addena took up with that professional athlete after all, and I warned her that he's a hopeless bore. Well, it serves her right."

Mira marched right through the middle of the party to where Addena stood in conversation with the biggest, most musclebound man that Jenny had ever seen. He was handsome, but Jenny had to agree with her mistress's assertion that he was an accomplished lover—of himself. Addena was at her fawning best, this time with apparent sincerity.

"Oh, I wouldn't miss the games for anything," Addena was saying, not yet aware of their approach. "You know, I've always excelled at sports, myself."

"Oh, I'll say!" Mira interjected casually. "You should have seen the sport she was with last night."

"Well . . . yes . . . ." Addena sputtered, turning to afford the sorceress an icy stare, and her eye teeth seemed to grow a fraction of an inch. "Maybe you'll feel better about it when the cramps subside."

"Tacky, Addena," Mira remarked as she hurried on her way, well pleased with herself. No one was her equal when it came to puns, barbs and catty remarks, certainly not Addena.

Wind Dragon was secure inside her shed behind the house, with every lamp in the place spelled to full brightness to bathe the ship in soft light. The airship had somehow managed to avoid any serious damage during their previous journey. The fact that the brake cables had all been cut and the blocks removed demonstrated that they had enemies who would do anything to stop them. As a result, Mira had ordered Dooket and Erkin to stay with the ship every night.

The normal store of supplies for an extended journey had already been secured within her holds; the members of the expedition needed only to bring their personal baggage in the morning. Certain things that Jenny had been unsure about, the spelled weapons as well as the special items they might need for fighting demons or Servants of the Dark, still lay on the center deck.

"Oh, I meant for most of this to go into the special holds," Mira said, indicating various boxes and bales.

"What special holds?" Vajerral asked innocently.

"I had some secret compartments built into the interior deck," Mira explained as she began directing the dragons up the boarding ladder. It was tricky going; Vajerral managed to get her leg caught between the slats and fell on her back.

That was enough for Jenny. She turned to walk slowly along the length of the airship. She was annoyed with Vajerral for bringing Kelvandor into this, and with Kelvandor for being his same disarming, ingratiating, delightful self. And mostly with herself, for being so hopelessly foolish.

A large part of her difficulties, she thought, was that she was forever trapped between. Like her uncle Allan, her magic was such that she had never been strictly mortal. Her magical training had only complicated the matter, turning her into a creature of magic, a faerie dragon on the inside but still essentially mortal on the outside. Unable to ever go back, but afraid to go forward.

So there she was. Training to be a sorceress and in love with a dragon, and unable to do anything about any of it for as long as she had the Prophecy hanging over her head. She paused to check the tread on the tires of *Wind Dragon*'s port forward strut. These people were doing their best, but it was stretching the limits of their technology to turn out even a simple rubber tire. Spending half of a long night running down the length of the barge track, rubbing against the stone curbs, had done them no favors. Mira would have liked to replace the front tires before they left, but there were simply none to be had.

Just what was the problem? Was it that she really did not want to be a dragon? She did not think so. She had known most of her life that she would eventually have to become a dragon for her own protection, and that had never bothered her. She was looking forward to it. It would be nice never having to be the outsider, the odd piece, with Vajerral and her other dragon friends, and to finally enjoy her natural intimacy with Kelvandor. Was she just afraid to make that final decision? Although she disliked having to admit it, that did seem to be the explanation. It meant deciding that she was ready to make the decisions that would shape the rest of her existence, not just in this life but in all her lives to come. And it meant deciding that she was ready to face the Prophecy on her terms.

Perhaps that was the key. Jenny's personal philosophy was to be aware of all the options available to her and to use her options wisely. In a matter as important as the Prophecy, she guarded her options like a miser. Actually becoming a dragon required that she had to surrender one of her most important options.

Jenny paused in her absentminded inspection of the forward struts, aware that she was no longer entirely alone. There was a vague magical disturbance in the air behind her that expanded rapidly as a presence began to form behind her. Her first thought was that her enemies had sent a demon after her. She retreated beneath *Wind Dragon*'s bow, ready either to run like hell or call for the dragons to help her, whichever might seem to be the most effective for achieving the desired end of saving her ass.

"Do not fear."

Jenny hesitated at the tone of that distant voice. The misty form that was shaping itself in the air before her was not the dark, massive figure of a demon, but slender and golden. The long, graceful limbs and folded wings of a Mindijarah formed from out of the golden haze. It was a male, of the same size and general appearance as Kelvandor but slightly less powerful of build in the chest and shoulders. He stood regarding her intently, his long neck thrust forward, one hand raised in a reassuring gesture.

"Do not fear," he repeated. "The time has come when you must soon face all the things you fear most, and you must not be afraid."

"What do you mean?" Jenny asked, seeing that the misty figure was beginning to fade. "Who are you?"

"Karidaejan . . ." the mysterious dragon said, and he was gone.

"Karidaejan!" Jenny exclaimed softly to herself, so surprised that she nearly had to sit down.

Well, speak of the devil and he shall appear. Vajerral had said that her mother had been trying to find Karidaejan, to see if he had forced himself to retain any important memories of his visit to Jenny's own world. It was no wonder Dalvenjah had never been able to find him. He had not returned to life in the way of all faerie folk, his magical spirit reborn in a new form. His part in the Prophecy was so important that he had remained between lives until it was done.

But just what was his part? Jenny knew that he had better things to do than bounce around mouthing vague and esoteric warnings. And yet she had to doubt that there were any great secrets to be had. For all Jenny knew, the High Priest Haldephren had come into her own world, quite probably taking the form of James Donner and fathering her in the process. If she had to guess, Karidaejan had discovered the scheme and had followed into her world to stop it. No one but Karidaejan knew what had happened then, but James Donner had died in an accident.

Nor had Karidaejan ever returned, and there had been no hint of his fate until Haldephren had turned up wearing his form. Some things just had a way of adding up. It seemed simple enough, and yet Dalvenjah believed that there was something more. And it seemed that Karidaejan himself had something more to say on the subject. Jenny reminded herself that Karidaejan was Dalvenjah's half-brother. She had never known him herself, but the two of them were probably a pair. Both of them were probably full of their private schemes that they had no intention of sharing until their own good time. She just wished that the two of them would get together and compare notes.

Jenny decided to keep the matter of her unexpected meeting with the spirit of Karidaejan entirely to herself. Out of respect for the departed dragon, she was not going to have Mira perform obscure experiments upon his ethereal essence. And she certainly did not want for Vajerral to go running home for Dalvenjah. If Karidaejan had something to say, he was going to tell it to Jenny only in his own good time.

As it was, the two dragons left immediately on an errand of their own, including the delivery of copies of Bresdenant's book to the dragons at the Academy at Tashira, to rejoin *Wind Dragon* in flight in a couple of days. Jenny was just as glad to see them go. For one thing, it would give her a chance to get used to the idea of having Kelvandor around before it became permanent. Nor was it too soon to begin thinking about what would come after. She did not need to go all the way to Alashera to know that the

Prophecy was already in motion. She had her own personal ghost to tell her that.

"So, what do you think?" she asked Vajerral as they stood on *Wind Dragon*'s deck, waiting for Kelvandor. "Am I finally going to have to give in?"

"Soon," the dragon answered vaguely. She must have learned that from her mother, whose personal philosophies included never giving anyone a straight answer.

"Soon?" Jenny stared at her.

"Not until after this journey, of course."

"Brilliant deduction," Jenny grumbled. "Do you think that Dalvenjah will be coming to join us?"

"She is busy now," Vajerral answered vaguely, quite obviously trying to say less than she knew or suspected. "By the time we return, I think."

Jenny saw her opening and would have pressed the attack, but they were interrupted at that moment as Kelvandor came on deck from below. She had been thinking about matters a lot since the previous night, and she had realized that Kelvandor's presence was more likely Dalvenjah's bright idea than any thought of Vajerral's. That led her to wonder if Dalvenjah had sent him to her to provide incentive, distraction, or because the sorceress knew that he had his own part to play in the Prophecy.

Vajerral took three discreet steps back . . . and promptly tumbled backwards down the open boarding ramp with a startled cry. Fortunately she rolled down the length of the cargo ramp, rather than hitting the usual boarding ladder that would have ordinarily been in place. Kelvandor stared in quiet fascination, and shrugged.

"Well, that was subtle," he commented.

"The very soul of discretion," Jenny agreed.

"Vajerral and I will be leaving now," Kelvandor said rather lamely.

Jenny shrugged rather indifferently. "I will miss you, I suppose. The magical matchmaker will see to that."

"I am sorry," he began hesitantly.

Jenny shrugged. "So, did I ask you to be sorry for anything? Or are you sorry for yourself?"

Kelvandor smiled. "Never for a moment."

He was doing his best. And yet he looked so miserable and eager, like some immense puppy trying desperately to escape trouble, that Jenny had to smile. She thought that if she had to love against her will, she could not have chosen better. She remembered Dalvenjah and Allan and what the love for a dragon had done for him, how much strength he had gained in the company of that golden lady he held so quietly and incredibly dear.

A girl could do worse. Maybe.

"You had best be on your way," she told him. "Just hurry back."

Kelvandor seemed to be beyond words. He stared at her a moment longer as if she represented a puzzle that he did not completely comprehend. Then he turned, leaped atop the siderail and thrust himself into flight. Jenny stood and watched as Vajerral rose into the sky to fall in by his side, and together they wheeled away toward the northeast. She stood and wished that it could have been herself at his side, riding golden wings.

"Why are you weeping?" J.T. asked in complete mystification, walking up to stare at her.

Jenny shrugged. "I suppose that I love him."

The cat was clearly stunned. "Is that any reason to weep?"

She smiled wryly. "It is, when you can see the future."

"I've got it, dear child!" Mira declared as she exploded up the steps from the middle deck. Then, to Jenny's profound consternation, she set a spelled crystal on the deck. "Watch this!"

Jenny did not watch the crystal. Instead she held out her hand as if feeling for rain, scanned the clear and sunny sky for clouds, and tested the wind. J.T., who had been reposed atop the rail, leaped down and streaked away toward other portions of the ship. Mira stopped short to watch this activity, and frowned.

"Oh, piffle!" the sorceress stated. "I've got the damned spell worked out. You're not going to lose your clothes."

"We'll see." Jenny remained skeptical.

Lady Mira did not recite the spell aloud this time, but leaned over the crystal to mutter just a few key words together with several appropriate gestures. Nothing obvious happened to the crystal, but the faint, disquieting sense of magic which surrounded it abruptly vanished. She straightened, quickly felt of her clothes to insure that they were in place, and turned to her student. Jenny was gone. Only her clothes remained in a neat pile on the deck.

"Mira?" Jenny's distant shout came from beneath the airship. "Kasdamir Gerran, I'll get you for this!"

* * *

"How does it look?" Mira called from the helm deck, where she stood at the wheels. A rather threatening bank of clouds was slowly moving in from due north, just off *Wind Dragon*'s port stern. She could see it bearing down upon them menacingly every time she glanced over her shoulder.

Erkin climbed down from the rigging of the forward mast. Needless to say, the airship was not running under sail in this erratic wind. He turned toward the rear of the ship. "All clear ahead for the next two miles or so, but after that the land climbs sharply. It looks very rugged, with quite a bit of mist and cloud down to ground level."

"Oh, well, it's still not as bad as we had it last time," Mira said to herself, although she was not entirely pleased by that report. She turned to her student. "Not to worry, though. If it gets too bad, then I could always put you at the wheels."

"Me?" Jenny was rather alarmed. "Why would you do that?"

"That way, if we do get in a fix and lose the ship, I can always blame you!" the sorceress declared, as if pleased with what seemed to her a perfectly reasonable plan. "I was only teasing you, of course. I'm a good pilot, but you seem to have a tremendous natural feel for this ship."

"I should have stayed at home," J.T. complained as he sat peering through an opening in the rail at the mountains passing far below.

Lady Mira glanced at him impatiently. "What's your problem? Do you need your hairball remedy? You know that every ship needs a cat."

He looked over his shoulder at her. "There are no rats on airships, and there never have been. They know better. By the way, those dragon friends of yours are coming."

"Oh? How soon?"

"Any moment." J.T. rose and stretched. "I think that I'll go below, if it's all the same to you."

A sudden, fierce crosswind shook the ship violently and began to force *Wind Dragon*'s nose slowly around toward the south, where rocky slopes rose in threat several miles ahead. Mira spun the rudder wheel, bringing the ship back around. Fighting this stout wind made the ship difficult to handle but, since it was also a following wind, it had the effect of picking up their speed slightly even if they had no running sails out to catch it.

"Here they come," Jenny warned.

Kelvandor and Vajerral were angling across the wind to intercept them, their broad wings beating in powerful strokes to thrust themselves forward at a hard pace. Mira glanced up at the dragons only briefly, and a new idea occurred to her.

"How are they going to land?" she asked her young student.

"I guess that they could come down here behind the helm, if you swing *Wind Dragon* around into the wind," Jenny suggested.

"Is that how you would do it, if you were a dragon?" She was beginning to recognize just how much she could rely upon her young student's quick mind and tremendous attention to detail.

"I don't really know," Jenny answered. "I can fly very well, but without the benefit of wings—which is not true flight. I just know that it's easier to land *Wind Dragon* facing into a wind."

"Here we go, then!" Lady Mira declared as she spun the rudder wheel, bringing the airship around hard to starboard until they were facing hard into the wind.

Wind Dragon shuttered as she fought the wind. Her ground speed, judging by her shadow on the rocky slopes below, had slowed to a crawl, although her indicated air speed jumped as Mira pushed the ship full speed against the brisk wind. Jenny called for the two mercenaries to assist her, then ran to the very stern of the ship and waved to the dragons as they circled close for a good look at the ship. They appeared to understand what she wanted of them, for they nodded their heads on long, powerful necks in an exaggerated gesture.

"Stand ready to help pull them on board, but stay clear of their wings," she told the mercenaries as they hurried to assist. "Let them go if they start to fall, since they can save themselves."

Turning into the wind seemed to have been the answer, allowing Kelvandor to match speed with *Wind Dragon* slowly as he came up behind the ship. He reached out to grab the rail and used that to pull himself on board agilely, needing no assistance from the others. He moved quickly out of the way, and Vajerral followed him on board a moment later.

"We were followed!" she warned. "Winged demons began to follow us about half an hour ago. And there are airships just ahead. Since they were obviously moving to intercept you, we did not worry about leading the demons to you. It seems better that we make our defense together."

Jenny rolled her eyes. "Oh, great! What is it with this airline? They should have three monitors in the terminals. Arrivals, departures and odds. This is worse than the *Hindenberg*."

Mira turned to the dragon. "What the hell is she babbling about?"

Vajerral only shrugged.

Lady Mira considered the matter a moment. "I don't suppose that we have any choice. Boys, go get the catapults ready, and load them up with explosive bolts. Dragons, you two get your tails overboard and do what you can. Remember that their stabilizers are canvas and will burn. Jenny, I need for you to take control of this ship, and let me help the boys with their defenses."

Jenny stepped forward, obviously reluctant, and took both of the wheels from her mistress. Changing pilots in flight was a very drastic act indeed. Mira released her own control over the induction vanes, and the ship hesitated and began to settle, losing both speed and altitude quickly. Jenny established her own control only an instant later, and *Wind Dragon* responded immediately. She brought the nose of the ship back up, angling over the rough terrain that rose only a mile or so before them. At that moment another blast of icy wind shook the airship.

"Is it coincidence that we always seem to run across these people in the middle of a snowstorm?" Jenny asked.

"J.T.!" Mira bellowed, and the cat stuck his head above the top of the steps leading up from the main deck a couple of seconds later. "What of it, old catgut? Is the Dark behind this storm?"

"They guide the storm towards us, but they did not make it," J.T. said. "That is why their control is not as obvious."

"Can we control it ourselves?"

J.T. shifted his ears around, as if listening intently to a very distant voice. "Perhaps, but that would be difficult."

"Do we even want to?" Jenny asked. "They will be using the storm to cover their attack, and they rely upon their winged demons to guide them. But we can dispose of the demons, then use the storm as our own cover. *Wind Dragon* is most likely a smaller, quicker ship than anything they have."

"A good point," Mira agreed. "Very well. Jenny, you have the helm, and I will organize the counterattack. Lizards, we need for you to get yourselves overboard and lead those demons close enough that we can spell them back to where they came from. Can you hold your own with those monsters?"

"We are faster, and we have our flames," Kelvandor answered with quiet dignity. "This should be simple."

"Oh, certainly," Mira muttered as she turned to leave. J.T. took one quick look around, determined that he probably would not be needed, and decided that he belonged below.

It suddenly occurred to Jenny that they might just be in serious trouble. Three airships, with Dark Priests, archers and attendant demons all in unknown quantities, was hardly a casual matter. If they had come up against such a force a week earlier, they probably would not have survived. Would the formidable combination of Mira's weapons and Bresdenant's spells and counterspells make the critical difference?

It all depended upon how quickly they could dispatch the demons, leaving them free to concentrate their attack on the three airships. She was certain that they could handle either the demons or the airships as separate groups, but both together might be too much for their own rather meager forces. That depended upon whether two faerie dragons could make up for a very big difference in the odds.

A minute passed, and then two, and the leading edge of the storm was upon them. At least there was not much snow with this storm, but an icy mist closed about them with a swiftness that was alarming. Lady Mira, standing in the bow, issued a spell that cleared a pocket of air for several hundred feet around them, so that their enemies could not approach completely unseen. J.T., seized by a sudden fit of responsibility, returned to the helm deck to assist Jenny in locating their enemies in the frosty mist.

"Here they come!" Kelvandor called as he suddenly hurtled out of the white haze, circling the ship quickly. "Demons first, but the airships are right behind them."

"Let's concentrate on getting rid of the demons first," Lady Mira ordered. "Boys, you two go after them with longbows and spelled arrows. I'll do what I can with counterspells. Jenny, do your best to stay clear of their ships, and keep in mind their fire arrows. Dragon, lead those demons in!"

Kelvandor turned and shot away, disappearing abruptly into the curtain of mist. Jenny could now sense the approach of the three airships and angled *Wind Dragon* up to pass slightly above them, remembering their earlier success in using the hull of their own ship like a vast shield. After a moment they heard the challenging roars of the Mindijaran roll dimly through the fog, followed by the harsh, nerve-grating screams of the demons in answer. By the sound, they were already heading back, and quickly. The three archers readied their bows.

The dragons shot out of the mist moments later, a cloud of at least a score of winged demons almost on their tails. The archers began shooting immediately and their aim was predictably deadly, but the spelled arrows, while clearly painful to the demons, did not seem especially damaging. Only one demon fell from the sky, pierced by three shafts including one that transfixed its long, plated neck just below its ridged skull. Its black form burst into flames just before it disappeared into the clouds, leaving a thick, oily trail of smoke.

But the demons were guided by greater intelligence than Jenny would have given them credit for possessing. While the main flock followed the dragons around the stern of the airship and back into the mist, two circled around to attack her. All she could do to defend herself was to wave her sword over her head to fend them away, for she was too involved with keeping *Wind Dragon* in the sky to work her own counterspells. But they abandoned their assault quickly when long shafts began cutting deep into their armored bodies.

Mira rushed up to her side, bearing her own longbow and a large pack of spelled arrows. "Sorry about that. Our mistake was in failing to recall that we need an archer on the helm deck to protect our pilot."

"How did they know?" Jenny asked. "Are they intelligent enough to know that I was vulnerable, or do they recognize me?"

"I just don't know." Mira glanced quickly to port. "Here they come again."

Jenny waited until the very last moment, then angled *Wind Dragon* up sharply, showing the enemy ships her protective hull just as they emerged from the fog beneath her. The Southern archers held off for the most part, although a few fire arrows streaked upward at the smaller ship. Fighting a stiff, cold wind and dragging their burden of burning rags, all of the arrows arched over too soon and passed well beneath *Wind Dragon*'s hull. The sorceress had a quick look at the enemy ships. Two were middle-sized, heavy freighters not unlike the one they had fought and defeated days earlier.

The third was a cargo ship of vast size, perhaps five hundred and fifty feet from bowsprit to stern, converted into a flying fortress by the addition of metal plating on her hull and broad shields raised above the two hundred archers who lined the rails of her deck. She also carried several small catapults, although of the type that launched heavy lead balls rather than the more accurate bolts such as *Wind Dragon* bore. She would be a tough nut to crack for little *Wind Dragon* and her crew of six—not including the cat. But for the moment the fortress held back from the fight, staying well to one side of the other two ships.

"Yarg, what a beast!" Lady Mira declared when she saw that ship, although she did not pause in loading her longbow. Kelvandor and Vajerral returned at that moment, leading the demons on a wild chase between the hulls of the ships.

"Fight, or run?" Jenny asked her mistress even before the enemy ships shot past.

"What do you think?" Mira asked in return.

"Fight," she decided, already spinning the wheel to bring *Wind Dragon* back around. "At least for the moment. The confusion seems to be in our favor, and we need to stay in this open space."

Mira understood what she meant. She was herself too busy to guide the ship through the clouds as she had on their previous journey, and they knew that rough land was climbing very quickly just ahead of them. The demons were easier to pick off as they dodged around the hulls of the ships; an important point, since several telling shots were required to destroy the tough little monsters. The danger, of course, was from fire arrows. Jenny knew that she would have to keep just enough distance to make the task of the enemy archers difficult.

Unfortunately, her own planning worked against her. What had been a very successful strategy against one ship no longer worked against three. The enemy vessels did not return in a group but scattered to move in on *Wind Dragon* from three different directions and at different heights. She saw no hope but to run straight through the middle of it before the enemy ships could converge for a concentrated attack.

At that moment it became obvious that the demons were definitely under some form of direct control. They suddenly broke off their chase after the dragons and descended upon the airship in a furious assault, ignoring the stinging arrows as they concentrated their attack on the helm. Jenny had to duck down behind what cover the two wheels offered, waving her sword over her head. Three of them concentrated on plucking her out of hiding, but Mira came to her defense. She worked the counterspell as

quickly as she could, and the demons scattered screaming. But
they had not been driven back into their own level of existence,
as the spell should have done. She stared at them in mystification
as the three demons retreated, still screaming in fury.

"Lady!" Jenny said urgently.

"What . . ." Mira turned to her young student, standing just
behind her, and stopped short. "Oh, my word, I've done it again!"

Jenny was clinging to the rudder wheel, as naked as a belly
dancer in a Jade Sea pub. Mira paused a moment to reassure
herself that she still had her own clothes.

"Oh, I can't take you anywhere!" she exclaimed. "I'll take
the helm so that you can dress yourself."

"No, there's no time," Jenny insisted, recovering quickly. She
looked up at one of the smaller enemy ships, which was dropping
back alongside *Wind Dragon* just above and about two hundred
feet to the right, half hidden in the clouds. "I'm a winter nudist
from way back. You have to defend the ship."

Mira did not have time to answer. At that moment Kelvandor
looped around *Wind Dragon*'s stern on a swift attack run on the
enemy ship. He saw Jenny standing naked at the helm and did a
startled double take. When he glanced around again he saw that
he was on a collision course with the other ship and snapped his
wings in powerful backstrokes, but too late. He struck the lower
hull headfirst . . . and clung there. Instead of knocking himself
senseless to tumble to his death on the slopes below, he had driven
his eighteen-inch horns half their length into the hardwood of the
lower hull and was stuck.

Jenny immediately cut speed slightly to pace that ship. "We
have to protect him. Once the demons see that he's helpless, they
are going to come after him."

"Right," Mira agreed as she ran toward the front of the ship.
"We need a diversion."

Suddenly another ship emerged out of the clouds, the second
smaller vessel, closing in quickly from the left. *Wind Dragon* was
caught between these two adversaries, and Jenny could see that
they meant to catch their prey between them, perhaps pulling
alongside close enough to board. Rather than force her own ship
on ahead of the two, she held back, waiting for the other to pull
even.

"Hold your arrows!" she called to her crewmembers in the

bow. "Let them come even. I have a plan. Stand by the port catapult."

Mira apparently trusted that she did have a plan, for she indicated for the Trasseks to hide themselves behind the protection of the siderails. The approaching ship came even with *Wind Dragon* and matched speed, above and barely a hundred feet out. Her archers, forty at least lining the siderails on the near side of the ship, held their arrows. Jenny locked the wheels in place and ran to the front of the helm deck, leaping up on the rail where she could steady herself with the rigging for the vane immediately below. She wrapped herself in the strongest spell of raw sexuality she could manage as she showed herself to the archers and crew of the enemy ship, her legs spread wide as she stood atop the rail.

"Hello!" she called alluringly, at the same time with the very uncomfortable feeling that her mother could somehow see this. "Hello, boys!"

The archers gaped, and one leaped so far out over the rail that he tumbled overboard. But so deep were the others in the thrall of the spell that they did not even notice. Jenny was a young and beautiful woman, her brown body lean and fairly well muscled. But beyond even that, she was one mean sorceress who knew how to turn a spell. The icy wind streaked like cat's claws over her bare skin, whipping her long, dark hair.

"Now!" she barely heard Mira order from the bow. "Don't stare, shoot!"

Jenny was concentrating so hard on her spell of sexuality at the same time she worked to keep *Wind Dragon* in the air that she did not dare turn to look. Apparently she had done her work too well; Dooket and Erkin, who had never before afforded her a lecherous glance, were caught in the spell as well. She heard Mira swear softly but furiously. A moment later the braided wire of the immense crossbow sung like a guitar string, and the forward vane of the enemy ship exploded into flames.

But it did not collapse. Jenny remained atop the rail, arching her back to thrust out her breasts as she poured all the magic she could spare into keeping the crew of the enemy ship locked in a fiery enchantment as their vessel began to burn around them. She could hear Mira struggling with the cocking device to load the catapult for another shot. She could see the Dark Sorcerer at the rail, struggling to throw off the effects of her spell, perhaps even preparing a counterattack. Then the damaged vane folded at last, and the burning ship was plunged to sudden death on the rocky slopes hidden far below.

Jenny leaped down from the rail just in time to avoid the raking claws of a demon, already exchanging the sexuality spell for the one that had protected her from the biting cold as she hurried back to the wheels. Mira ran the full length of the ship as quickly as she could, sword and shield held aloft to protect her student from a renewed attack by the remaining demons.

"Sorry to take so long, but I simply could not get that catapult cocked to shoot again," Mira said as she ripped the wing of one bold demon with her spelled sword. She smiled grimly. "Considering the show you were putting on, I'm surprised that it didn't cock itself."

"I hate it," Jenny said with disgust as she angled *Wind Dragon* away from the other ship, swearing in both Norwegian and the language of the Mindijaran.

"You did what you had to do, and you did it well," Mira told her.

"Lady Mira, the stabilizers are on fire!" Dooket called from the bow.

"Oh, damn!" Mira exclaimed and was off again, already working the spell to still the flames that ate ravenously at the canvas stabilizers. But it was already too late. Jenny felt the wheels go dead in her hands as the control surfaces were destroyed, and then the ropes themselves burned through and snapped. *Wind Dragon* was not completely helpless. Jenny could still control their altitude with the lift vanes alone, but she could not steer. Their only hope of avoiding a collision would be to fly above any obstacles.

"Mira, help me set the trim sail!" she shouted. "We don't have time to set new stabilizers, not while demons are harassing us, and we certainly cannot land."

The trim sail was a small triangular sail that was sometimes mounted to the back of the rear mast, corresponding to a spanker sail on an oceangoing ship, stretched between a horizontal spar below and an angled spar above. Under certain conditions it was used to augment the regular rudder, but in this case Jenny hoped to make it take the place of the missing rudder. She doubted that the control it gave would be as precise, but anything was better than what she had. As it was, they could not avoid the enemy ship that was slowly advancing from their right except to outrun it, which she was trying to do. *Wind Dragon* had a tendency to rock and bob at high speeds without her stabilizers.

She glanced over at the other ship in time to see Kelvandor finally manage to brace all four legs against the lower hull of the ship and pull his horns free with a powerful heave. She turned back to her own crew.

"Hold on tight!" she yelled, and gave them to the count of five to brace themselves.

She abruptly cut speed, allowing the enemy ship to streak past, then poured every scrap of thrust she could find into *Wind Dragon*'s lift vanes. The smaller ship seemed to climb straight up like a rocket; Jenny knew that *Wind Dragon* had oversized vanes for her size, and she was not weighed down with crew and cargo. They could not lose the Southland ships with this tactic, but they could buy themselves a couple of minutes to rig the trim sail, and perhaps do something about the dozen or so remaining demons as well. Jenny took the ship up to two thousand feet and leveled off, resuming full forward speed.

"Forget the stabilizers for now!" she called to Mira. "Have them get their bows after those demons."

Mira did not even relay the order, only indicated for the Trassek twins to comply with a brief nod. She joined Mira on the helm deck and, working together, they had the trim sail raised and rigged in little more than a minute. By that time J.T. was laboring backwards up the steps from the main deck, dragging something dark and heavy behind him.

"Bless you, cat!" Jenny exclaimed as she hurried to collect the jacket that he had pulled all the way from her cabin. He could only nod, panting heavily, and hurried off again . . . presumably after trousers.

"Mira, you must take control of *Wind Dragon* for a minute," Jenny said. "I'm going to do something about those demons once and for all."

They exchanged control of the ship as they had before, *Wind Dragon* dropping a few feet before Mira had the vanes in operation. Jenny had pulled on the jacket and hurried to fasten its buttons. Shoes and pants would have to wait, even as cold as it was. Compared to complete nudity in this wind, this was a minor discomfort. She hurried to the very back of the helm deck just as Kelvandor sailed past.

"Send them in my direction," she called to the dragon. He

nodded, too far past to shout back his answer, then turned sharply after a small knot of demons not far away.

Demons might possess some native intelligence, Jenny thought. But they had no patience and they did not learn from the mistakes of their fellows. Kelvandor was able to get them to chase him, singularly or in small groups, time after time. And Jenny would dispatch them with ease, using that same counterspell which gave Mira—and indirectly her young student—so much trouble. It seemed that Vajerral also knew the counterspell, dispatching her own share of demons on the wing. Working together, they sent all fifteen of the remaining demons back into their own level of existence in only three minutes of concentrated effort.

"All done?" Mira asked. "Can you take control of *Wind Dragon* again? J.T. says that those enemy ships are coming up on us in a hurry."

"Let me have it," Jenny agreed, and *Wind Dragon* bounced as they traded control. "Can we take them? You know that I'm not going to be able to steer this ship anything like I can with a real rudder."

"No, you should be lucky just to hold a straight course." Mira considered that for a moment. "Can we outrun them?"

"I doubt it." Jenny brought the ship up to full speed, and it immediately began to buck and shake in protest. She allowed their speed to drop back down slightly. "I'm sorry, Lady. *Wind Dragon* simply is not that stable without those forward control surfaces."

"There's no hope for it, then," Mira said, and walked to the forward portion of the helm deck. "Dooket! Erkin! Come back here and set up two more catapults on the stern. Those enemy ships will be coming at us from behind."

The airship had been more or less riding the wind for the few minutes before they had been able to raise the trim sail, although Mira had been able to hold them on a steady course north by northeast since then. Then Jenny had an idea. After all, what else was the good of being a sorceress with a degree in engineering? She carefully brought *Wind Dragon* through the tricky and rather dangerous maneuver of reversing course until the ship was pointed directly into the wind. Now the combination of the wind of the airship's passage together with the fitful blasts of the storm itself caused the trim sail to act almost exactly like the rudder of a ship, if less precisely. In that time the two mercenaries had mounted catapults into frames built into the stern siderail, and were already loading the weapons.

"You're dented!" Jenny exclaimed, suddenly seeing the deep crease in the plate armor on Dooket's back. "A demon's tail."

He nodded. "The mail inside turned the blow. I would say that my attire has fared better in this battle than your own."

Jenny glanced down, blushing. Then she looked up in alarm, aware that she had been inattentive. "Ship dead ahead! Ready the catapults!"

But it was too late for that. The rear catapults could not be brought about to bear on the enemy ship. Jenny bent every scrap of talent she could spare on the forward catapults, which swung around in their mountings in response to her distant touch. At that same instant the white curtain of the clouds parted and a vast, dark shape emerged out of the swirling mist as the large airship bore down upon its tiny prey, approaching level with *Wind Dragon* and turning slightly to pass to starboard. Jenny released the bolts as soon as she felt she had a good shot at the forward vane of the ship that was on her right, but she shot too soon and the bolts swerved away from their target. Too late she realized that there was more than one Dark Sorcerer aboard that ship.

The immense form of the battleship passed just over *Wind Dragon* like a dark, threatening cloud. As her vast vanes overlapped over their own, lightly armored soldiers leaped down from that structure into the supporting net of the stabilizer's broad arc. They immediately swarmed up the canvas-covered spars and over the siderail, while the Trasseks rushed forward to repel this invasion. Mira stood at Jenny's side, ready to defend *Wind Dragon*'s vulnerable helm.

Then, as the larger ship passed, three heavy grapples crashed to the helm deck just behind the two sorceresses and were pulled back along the deck to catch against the siderail. Jenny cut forward thrust before *Wind Dragon*'s stern was ripped away as the lines went taut. Lady Mira leaped forward to sever the ropes, only to find that they were sheathed in braided wire and spelled to invulnerability. The enemy ship turned tightly as she passed, and *Wind Dragon* was whipped around at the end of her tether. Three of the enemy soldiers were thrown to their deaths by that violent jerk, but a dozen more scrambled over her sides.

"Not on my ship, you don't!" Mira declared, and rushed to

defend the nearest of the short flight of steps leading up from the main deck.

Jenny turned away from the battle, waving to Kelvandor as he circled up from below and pointing to the three cables that tied *Wind Dragon* to her adversary. He nodded and rose above the two ships, then dived to the attack, playing his fiercest flames across each of those cables in turn. Nothing, whether wrapped in steel or spell, could stand for long against dragon flame. When the first cable snapped, Jenny brought one of the two catapults around and released its massive bolt. She had never used a cross-bow of any type in her life, but at fifty feet her aim was good enough. The port stern vane folded upward almost as the bolt exploded in flames against the hull, and the immense ship slowly rolled to that side and began to fall. *Wind Dragon* was pulled after her for an instant, before the smoking cables parted.

With one problem solved, Jenny turned back to the trim sail with the intention of getting under way before the remaining enemy ship arrived, only to find that she faced five soldiers who had cut around Mira's fierce defense to come up the other stairs. She was no slouch with a sword, having been trained as a Veridan Warrior by the faerie dragons. But at the moment she was distracted by the need to keep *Wind Dragon* in the air.

Jenny augmented her natural speed and strength with all the magic she could spare, pressing the attack. She thrust and ducked with lightning speed, mindful of what would happen to her light sword if she accidentally connected with the powerful swing of a heavy broadsword. She could get past their guard easily enough, but their heavy mail frustrated her time and again. Kelvandor had just landed in the stern and charged into battle, wielding his own sword as only a dragon could, while Dooket and Erkin were swordsmen almost without peer and Mira was raw fury with a blade.

Lady Mira dispatched her remaining adversary and turned without a moment's pause to rush to the helm deck, where she joined Kelvandor and her student in sending the Southland soldiers over the rail with little bother. Then she stood, panting as she leaned on her sword, watching as the Trasseks and the dragon made a swift end to what remained of the fight.

"Yarg, what I wouldn't give for a cup of tea!" she declared.

"I'm cold," Jenny muttered, in what seemed to her mistress to be a grand understatement.

"One more?" Mira asked wearily.

"A little one. We can't outrun her, not considering the shape *Wind Dragon* is in. But we can stay ahead for a couple of minutes yet."

"Right. I'll get the rest of your clothes." Mira turned to leave the helm deck, pausing at the steps. "Dooket! Erkin! Get all the catapults ready for battle, and hurry."

Mira rushed to Jenny's cabin and pulled open both of the drawers under her bunk. A rather startled black-and-white cat lifted his head out of one of the drawers and blinked.

"What are you doing in there? Hiding?" she asked suspiciously.

"Of course not!" He sniffed haughtily. "I had climbed inside to get a pair of pants. Then the floor dropped about ten feet and the drawer slammed shut and locked."

"Well, you're missing all the fun," Mira told him as she jerked the pants out from under him, sending the cat tumbling.

She turned to return to the deck and heard the sound of one distant explosion and then another, and assumed that the battle must already be over. She found that she was wrong.

She could make out the dim form of the enemy ship, slightly larger than her own, at the very edge of the fog. There it hung, apparently content to maintain that distance for the time. Occasional arrows arched through the sky between the two ships and Jenny was having a hard time spelling them away, between keeping *Wind Dragon* in the air, watching the trim sail and keeping herself from freezing. Multiple spells were difficult to maintain, and she was reaching her limit of endurance.

"I don't have to ask if both of the boys missed their target," Mira said as she stepped out onto the helm deck.

"They have a second sorcerer on board, and he is deflecting our bolts," Jenny said, turning back to her mistress. "They must have learned . . ."

She suddenly staggered and nearly fell forward, catching herself by the useless elevator wheel. *Wind Dragon* shuddered in response and began to drop, throwing the others off balance as well, but lift returned and she held steady. Mira picked herself up and rushed to the aid of her student. She took hold of the girl's jacket and spelled it off, so that it instantly came away in her hands. A long arrow transfixed Jenny's left side, the point emerging barely an inch above the upper edge of her pelvic blade.

"You make too good a target," Mira told her as she cast the

spell that would deaden the pain. "If you can keep this ship flying for a minute longer, I'll get that thing out of you and repair the damage."

Jenny only nodded as she stood holding the wheel, her legs firmly braced. Dooket and Erkin moved in close, protecting the two sorceresses with their shields and their own armored selves. Mira tried to maintain casual indifference, but inside she was scared half to death. She marvelled at her student's strength and endurance, for this was damage that, if left untreated, would almost certainly be fatal in a matter of minutes. Strong men had not survived such wounds even this long. But Jenny kept to her task, and *Wind Dragon* never faltered.

Mira laid her hand gently on the feathered shaft that emerged from one side of Jenny's back, and the arrow vanished as she conjured it away. That was one problem solved, but only a small problem compared to what followed. With the arrow removed, she began to bleed heavily . . . internally as well as externally, Mira was sure. She worked the complex regenerative spells step by careful step, reassured that this at least was magic she did very well. The bleeding stopped, and the wound began to close. She quickly cleaned away the blood with wet rags that J.T. had brought and helped Jenny to dress, then straightened her back and looked behind at the airship that still followed at the edge of their limited visibility.

"Why did they not take advantage of our vulnerability these last couple of minutes?" Mira asked herself. "Assuming they knew, of course."

"You could have left that thing in me for a few minutes," Jenny said tightly.

"You would not have survived that long," the sorceress told her frankly. "How do you feel? Up to finishing this fight?"

"I have no choice, do I?" Jenny asked. She looked very worn and pale, and she was still holding on to the elevator wheel to steady herself. Still, Mira thought that she might last out this fight on sheer determination, something this young lady had in far greater abundance than she herself knew. Then she would likely pass out in her bunk for the next two days.

"Boys, I can shield us now," Mira declared. "Did you reload all the catapults? Then go find the replacement spars and canvas for the stabilizers and get to work on that."

The mercenaries hurried on their way, obviously uncertain about climbing out on the bowsprit in armor. J.T. recognized where his own greatest potential lay in this battle and went to assist them. Lady Mira stood for a long moment staring back at the pursuing airship, ignoring the infrequent arrows that now swerved wide to avoid *Wind Dragon*. At last she weaved a complex spell, then collected her abandoned longbow and released an arrow at the enemy ship. It sped on its way, straight and true, and one of the dim figures standing in her bow disappeared behind the siderail without a sound.

"Ah, that did it! We can hit them, but they cannot hit us." She turned toward *Wind Dragon*'s bow. "Come on back, boys! We can finish them off quickly now."

But the enemy captain was no fool. He knew exactly what this turn of events meant as well, and he had no intention of tarrying long enough for his former prey to employ their catapults. The other ship suddenly turned away and disappeared into the clouds, and it continued to flee at full speed.

"We can't let them get away," Mira said. "They'll return home before we get there and tell their superiors."

"They don't know that we are heading there ourselves," Jenny pointed out.

"True, but a tale of the destruction of three of their no doubt limited number of airships by new weapons and magic will create quite a stir," Mira said. "Especially when they say that they were defeated by two women and two boys in a rather small ship."

"Help me put this ship about, then. But we must have those stabilizers replaced or we never will catch that ship. We can't run at full speed until we do, let alone fight."

"Right," Mira agreed, and turned to the mercenaries. "Go back and get those stabilizers replaced, and hurry. Where did those dragons disappear to, anyway?"

That was a good question. Kelvandor must have gone overboard immediately after the last fight, and he was nowhere to be seen now. And Vajerral had been gone even longer. But Jenny felt certain that they must have been attending to something important, or they would not have been gone for so long. Working together, the two sorceresses managed to get *Wind Dragon* turned back around and in pursuit of the enemy airship, but the Southlanders had a small advantage in time and distance that they could not yet begin to close. Jenny did not dare force the ship so much that it began to shake and rock, not with two mercenaries and one cat hanging from the bowsprit.

"The storm is breaking!" Jenny observed several minutes later.

"The clouds are thinning," Mira said. "The wind is going to be with us for a while yet."

"The elevator is working!" Dooket yelled from the bow. He was often elected spokesman by virtue of having the biggest mouth. "Give it a try!"

"Are you sure?" Mira called back.

"Well, we think so."

"Very reassuring," Jenny muttered as she released the lock on the elevator wheel and gave it an experimental spin. The nose of the ship lifted accordingly, and she immediately leveled back out. "Well done, but we need the rudder as well."

"Coming up!"

"It's times like this that I long for the quiet life," Jenny said to herself, then turned to her mistress. "Lady, can I ask you a question?"

"What is it, child?"

"Have you always had this capacity for getting yourself into trouble, or is this a recent development?"

Mira laughed. "I've always had a capacity for generating personal disasters that involved only a very few people. These days I seem to be getting more ambitious."

"Your personal disasters must not have been that bad," Jenny observed.

"And why do you say that?"

"Because you never seem bitter about it."

"Ask me about that again sometime when we have a couple of days," Mira said, and she was quite serious. "But the point is, I don't dwell on it . . . and that, by the way, is something I learned the hard way, for the sake of my sanity. . . . "

"Land ho!" Dooket called from the bow.

Mira looked up, startled and mystified. "He must be joking."

Unfortunately, he was not. The clouds were beginning to thin and break, so that they could clearly see, not two thousand feet ahead, the broken line of a rather steep and rocky ridge. They were perhaps a hundred feet to one side of what appeared to be an inviting pass through an otherwise imposing string of steep, barren peaks. But, with *Wind Dragon* handling so sluggishly with only the trim sail and elevator, that was a hundred feet too far, and even then the pass was two or three hundred feet above their present altitude.

"There they go!" Mira exclaimed, indicating the ship that was slipping through the pass. "Hard over, Jenny!"

"What?" the younger sorceress demanded increduously.

"We can make it. I'll pull trim sail, while you bring the nose up to get us through that pass. This is what I get for not sitting in the bow and witching out our way."

Jenny shrugged and did as she was told, reminding herself that Lady Mira was in command of this ship, owned it, and was entitled to wreck it. Mira brought the sail over and did manage to get the ship turned into the pass, although she had to spell a few blasts of well-aimed wind into the trim sail in order to accomplish this. Jenny was not quite so lucky in getting the ship to climb suffi- ciently, however. As they entered the pass, she could see that it continued to ascend for several hundred feet even yet. She thought that they should slide into the snow-covered slope about halfway up.

"I know where we are!" Dooket declared. He was still hanging by the rigging of the bowsprit as he and Erkin worked on the rudder. "This is Murker Pass through the Aydun Peaks."

"And there is a road somewhere under that snow!" Mira agreed excitedly, and turned to her protégé. "If you have to touch down, try to find that road."

Jenny released the lock on the hub of the rudder wheel, engaging the steering for the forward struts. At the same time Mira hurried to the bow to guide their approach as best she could, and to order the twins and J.T. back on board. The ground was coming up beneath them quickly now and they appeared to be well centered over the road, which was barely visible as an even ribbon of depression across the blanket of snow. Which was just as well, since Jenny could no long work the trim sail by herself. She would have no steering control until they were actually on the ground, and she was doing her best to avoid that.

She nearly made it. *Wind Dragon* was almost through the pass when Lady Mira warned of impact, and the front skids bit deep into the snow. The ship shuddered and the nose lifted a little more. Then the back skids settled down as well as the ship slid relatively smoothly across the deep snow, and Jenny found that she could now steer the ship. The only problem was that she could not see ahead. But Mira could and she did her best to guide them on through the pass, ordering full speed when Jenny would have stopped.

"Rocks ahead!" she warned. "Up, up! Take us up five feet."

"Oh, fart!" Jenny declared as she took *Wind Dragon* back into the air just briefly, then settled back into the snow. They were safer trying to negotiate this pass on the ground, where she could at least steer.

Wind Dragon cleared the pass, which was choked with just enough clouds to make things very tense as they ran blind for a few seconds, then emerged out the other side of the ridge. Jenny marvelled that they were still alive and moving, before she saw that several gentle switchback twists lay in the road ahead. Then she discovered something even more alarming as the ship continued to accelerate very quickly even though she eased off their forward thrust, then cut it completely. *Wind Dragon* seemed destined to repeat past mistakes.

Jenny began to engage the lift vanes, then stopped short when she saw the dark form of the enemy ship dropping down almost on *Wind Dragon*'s stern. They had somehow overrun the other ship in the clouds, perhaps when her commander had cut speed to feel his way blindly through the pass. Now he found himself almost directly over his prey, where he could attack while his own ship was safely above the reach of *Wind Dragon*'s catapults.

Lady Mira was just about to order the mercenaries to remove a catapult from its mounting and hold it by hand, but there was no need. The missing members of their party suddenly returned. Dodging arrows, the dragons dived at the enemy ship time and again, playing their deadly flames across her rigging and stabilizers. The enemy vessel was afire in a matter of seconds and it now began to descend slowly until it settled with a heavy crash onto its skids. But her springs somehow survived the impact, and the larger airship now began to close on *Wind Dragon*, pulled by the weight of her greater size and heavier cargo.

"Cliff ahead!" Kelvandor warned as he landed heavily on the back of the helm deck. "You'll never make the turn. Get back into the air."

"I'm . . . trying," Jenny panted, but she was in pain and clearly at the end of her strength.

She spun the elevator wheel, and *Wind Dragon*'s nose began to lift as her front skids left the ground. Then she left the road and shot out into open air as the ground fell away beneath her.

She dipped slightly, then began to climb as the lift vanes took effect. The enemy ship followed a moment later only to nose slowly over, arching a hundred feet out and over six hundred down to crash bow-first into a tumble of massive boulders. It exploded into flaming debris with the force of impact.

A moment later Jenny went limp and fell backwards into Kelvandor's waiting hands. He lifted her gently as Mira hastened to take control of the weaving airship.

"Courage, cunning and plain dumb luck prevail again," she remarked, then glanced over her shoulder. "How is Jenny?"

"The little sorceress seems to have passed out," Kelvandor answered. Jenny made a very limp burden in his arms. He stepped back as Vajerral landed on the back of the helm deck, peering at her friend with concern.

"What has happened?" she asked, plucking at the torn, bloody jacket.

"She took an arrow, but I got it out and did what I could to repair the damage. Take her below and place her in her bunk," Mira directed. "We're going to land in a couple of minutes and spend the rest of the day doing something about the worst of our damage."

"This ship will have to be repaired completely before you can take her into the Kingdoms of the Sea," Vajerral remarked, looking about at the damage. "The bowsprit is charred, the siderail over the stern was chewed to pieces by those grapples, and there are arrows stuck in the hull and deck from one end of this ship to the other."

"Yes, I know," Mira agreed reluctantly. "I suppose that we can lay over a few days at Woody Bog. And Jenny needs the rest even more than this ship needs repairs."

· Part Five ·

In Country Mirth

WHEN JENNY AWOKE some time later, it was to discover that she was in considerable discomfort. Her head was pounding so intensely that she could actually hear the throbbing. There was a fierce, stabbing pain in her lower back that hurt even more. And her bladder was absolutely about to burst, a pint-sized container forced to hold at least five gallons. Well, she could do something about that, since the ship's head—a silly name if ever she had heard one—was adjacent to her own cabin. Assuming that she was in her own cabin . . . she opened one eye and looked around, and saw that she was.

Only an emergency like this could have gotten her out of her bunk, the way she felt. She sat up in bed, wondering whether *Wind Dragon* was still in the air or if it was her own impaired sense of balance that made the bunk sway. She slipped off the side of the bed, steadying herself by holding tightly to the wall, and looked down to find that she was standing in four inches of water.

"Oh, I had a boo-boo," she said to herself, then stared at the door with a look of almost painful concentration. "But if I did this, then why do I still need to? Or again?"

She shrugged, opened the door, and paid her visit to the privy.

By the time she finished, her head had cleared enough for her to know that she could not have made this mess. For one thing, it was obviously fresh water, and she was certain that she had a stronger constitution than that. She was also just a little suspicious of the volume. She returned to her cabin, pulled on pants and jacket, and staggered up the stairs to the main deck. She saw Mira standing at the wheels on the helm deck.

"Lady Mira, we seem to be sinking," she announced.

"Sinking?" Mira looked over the siderail. "Dear child, we happen to be a thousand feet above dry land, in a clear sky. What do you mean, sinking?"

"There's a hand of water standing on the floor downstairs."

"Below," Mira corrected her absently. "Erkin, take the wheels and keep us on course. I'll keep the vanes spelled."

"Right, Lady!" Erkin bounced over to stand by the wheels, looking like a dog that had been invited for a walk.

Mira followed her student back to the stairs, and together they descended to the lower deck. Jenny stepped off into the icy water with complete indifference, but her mistress remained on the step just above its level. The pool shifted back and forth in sudden waves as *Wind Dragon* responded to the changing winds, pouring in and out of cabin doors.

"I didn't do it," Jenny stated flatly.

"Of course you didn't," Mira assured her, wondering what she meant. "The water tank must have broken open. Are you feeling well, child?"

"I hurt like hell," she answered. "And I feel very sleepy and dizzy."

"Oh, you're still half under that sleeping spell I put on you," Mira said, and quickly reversed it. "Better?"

"Yes, much. But that seemed to make it hurt more."

"I'll see about that in a minute. If you don't mind that water—and you obviously don't—then could you go to my cabin in the very stern of the ship, find the drain plug in the deck by the back wall of the room and pull it? Do you feel up to that?"

"Oh, right away," Jenny agreed, sounding very much her usual self. She attended to the task, moving slowly from the stiffness and pain and for once being careful to avoid splashing herself more than necessary. She disappeared into the rear cabin, and a few seconds later a loud gurgling, slurping sound could be heard

But the water level was in no apparent hurry to go down; the drain was rather small.

"That's done," Jenny said as she returned.

"Sinking, indeed!" Mira laughed. "Get yourself out of that water, child. Come up on the deck in the sun, or what's left of it. You've been sick, remember."

"I've been skewered, remember," Jenny said, and looked about as they came out on deck. The sun would soon be setting behind them, and the mountains she expected were nowhere to be seen. They were over rolling hills covered by a heavy forest. "What's left of the sun? Have I slept away the entire afternoon?"

"All afternoon and most of the next day, in fact. Sit down." Mira indicated the steps, casting one slightly apprehensive glance toward the helm and their temporary pilot. "It will take a while for the lower deck to drain, and then the boys will have to mop it out. But you're going back to bed at the first opportunity."

"Oh, I won't argue with that," Jenny insisted. She seated herself on the steps, while Mira leaned back against the siderail. *Wind Dragon* was a mess, even though the loose debris had been cleared away. "What do we do now, Lady? Our first stop was supposed to be Woody Bog."

"And we should be able to get repairs there," Mira said. "Lord Araedyr of Kaendon does owe me a favor or two . . . although he might not remember it quite that way."

"Where are the dragons?"

Mira laughed. "They are both out patrolling or something. Vajerral seems rather nervous and restless. She either thinks or worries a lot. She worried about you a lot, and Kelly was beside himself—although he tries not to show it. Also, I think that flying, under someone else's power, makes him nervous. He turns up when we land for the night. Now, may I ask you a question?"

"Oh, certainly," Jenny agreed, slightly mystified.

"You arrived at my house half a year ago with a rather large guitar in a very stout case. I noticed that you brought it with you on this journey. And yet I've never heard you play it."

"That's three statements, not a question," Jenny pointed out.

"Will you play it?" Mira asked evenly, without a hint that she thought that this was anything but a very serious matter.

Jenny looked down at her hands, wondering if she still could.

"Do you think I should?" she asked without looking up.

"You are a person of many rare talents, of which music is only one," Mira told her. "I would not have you turn your back on any talent you possess. You obviously used to play quite a lot, or you wouldn't still be carrying the damned thing around with you."

"I used to," Jenny said. "I never wanted to be a musician the way my uncle Allan used to be, before he took up being a dragon instead, but I always enjoyed it. I guess that I could try."

"Why don't you?" Mira turned to the bow, where Dooket was standing watch. "Here, you great, skinny lout. Run below and fetch Jenny's guitar for her. We might have a little music."

Dooket splashed about in the remaining inch of water for a few moments, then returned to the deck bearing the heavy guitar case. Jenny took it from him reluctantly and laid it carefully on the deck, then opened the lid. The guitar was large, long but slightly narrow of body and long of neck. It had the look of a well-used but well-tended tool of a professional musician.

Jenny lifted the guitar gently and held it against her as if to play, then gasped as that motion caused a sharp bite of pain from her wound. She adjusted her hold cautiously. She plucked the key string and adjusted it to pitch, then tuned the others to key. Satisfied, she began to run through a variety of chords, hesitantly at first but with increasing speed and certainty.

"I seem to remember how this thing works," she said.

"Lady?" Dooket appeared again, this time handing a smaller guitar case to Mira. Jenny had not known that her mistress played, or that she even had an instrument of her own. When Mira took it from the case, Jenny saw that it was of course one of the small guitars of this world, almost like a lute.

"I'm supposed to be able to do anything, remember," Mira told her, mildly amused. She plucked each of the strings in turn and found that they were still in tune; she had obviously played recently. "Name it."

"What do you know?" Jenny asked. She had heard much of the music of this world, although she had never played it.

"Hm . . . how about this one?" Mira found her key with some experimentation and began to snatch out the main line of a song.

Jenny recognized it almost immediately and began to weave her own themes around it. Then, as they returned again to the main theme, she began to sing. Her deep, warm voice was not as clear as it had once been, but it was still strong. Mira added her own, slightly higher voice to the song as well. It was a song of gentle passion and quiet longing, a song that told no real story but spoke of many things.

"Why did you ever stop?" Mira asked softly.

Jenny shrugged. "I guess I just no longer had the time. It seemed to interfere with my other studies. There's always so much that I want to do."

"Watching you in battle, I've come to realize just how clever and inventive you are," Mira told her. "You think all the time, and nothing seems to escape your notice. Vajerral tells me that you're an accomplished artist and musician, and that you've mastered sciences that make us look like barbarians. You are a person of many talents, but you are a sorceress first of all. You can be anything else you wish, but you cannot force that to take the place of your primary obligation to yourself. Once you are sure of your priorities, perhaps you can begin to enjoy music again."

"Perhaps you are right," Jenny agreed, although she knew that she would not. The guitar had been a private interest during her college years. Soon she would be a dragon, and dragons could not easily play instruments shaped for human use.

Mira set her guitar aside. "Be true to yourself. You just have the same problem that all talented, ambitious people have. We want to be everything and do everything all at once, but you can't. Just know the one thing you really are in heart and spirit, and let everything else be your diversions."

"Never any time to talk," Vajerral said as she joined Jenny on the forward deck, speaking English for the sake of privacy. "You are feeling well? Stuck like as pig?"

Jenny laughed softly. "You never could speak English worth a damn."

"Phooey!" the dragon declared in a remarkable Russian accent. "Phooey on mortal languages."

Jenny shook her head helplessly. "Have you been through the Twilight Zone lately? How are things on Mother Earth?"

"I spoke with your mother on the phone two weeks ago. She says that she loves you."

"I know that, although only the experience of long familiarity allows me to recognize that."

Vajerral just stared at her. "Too many long words. Wallick has gone away. They sent him to a new place in Mexico."

It took Jenny a moment to realize that she probably meant Albuquerque.

They spoke together for some time, remembering years past and all the things that they had done together. They had grown up together almost as sisters ever since that first day, thirteen years past, when Jenny had chased Vajerral around the chair in Allan's house. They had seen a lot since then, faerie centaurs and unicorns, wyverns, dwarves and elves, and dragons of every sort. Vajerral's presence had kept Jenny from ever feeling lonely in a world of dragons. They were both in a form of exile from Jenny's world, since the dragon magic they both commanded was so damaging to the fragile natural magic that was being nurtured there.

Jenny wondered what had happened to her life, when most of the people she loved were dragons.

That brought Jenny's thoughts unavoidably back to the subject of the one dragon she was learning to love best. Her heart told her that there was no question. Her mind provided any number of excuses to avoid any commitments, this one especially. And that, she thought, was her whole problem. She was no longer a person, she was a debating team.

"What is Kelvandor doing here?" she asked, determined to get at least one straight answer out of a dragon. "Was this all your own bright little idea, or did Dalvenjah put you up to this?"

"Oh, my," Vajerral muttered, looking away and laying back her ears.

"Answer me," Jenny said sternly. "We would not want to talk to Dalvenjah about that cute dragon who came to study with your mother and had to go home in a hurry."

Vajerral's ears stood straight up. "That was not as bad as the way you and Kelvandor used to carry on."

"I wasn't eleven at the time," Jenny reminded her. "Besides, Dalvenjah already knows about that. I can't be blackmailed. I have no shame."

Vajerral had no shame, except where Dalvenjah was concerned. She had to think about that for a long moment. "Dalvenjah and Allan were supposed to come themselves this time, but they are tied up with a problem of their own. Dalvenjah seemed to think that the Emperor has a new stronghold somewhere. Kelvandor really is the best choice to come in their place. Of course, I am sure that Mother was aware of certain . . . consequences."

"I'll have something to say to Dalvenjah when I do see her,"

Jenny said to herself. It was, of course, an idle threat. No one took Dalvenjah to task. The Devil himself said "Yes, Ma'am" to Dalvenjah Foxfire. She frowned. "At least Kelvandor is keeping a respectful distance, but he's so eager and endearing, and so damned innocent."

"Innocent!" Vajerral nearly choked to keep from laughing. "Kelvandor is a scrupulously honest and devoted lover, even for a dragon, and he has always been something of a loner. But he has been around. In fact, he is much older than Mother."

"He is?" Jenny still had a hard time with dragons and their long lives.

"He is two hundred and sixty years, at least."

Jenny frowned. Dragons rounded off their age to the previous decade, at least after their first hundred years. Her first serious relationship, and it did have to be with an older dragon. "Then I suppose that he's taken a mate before?"

"Nothing serious that I ever heard."

"What about yourself?" Jenny asked.

Her ears standing up straight, Vajerral glanced in either direction before she dipped her head and spoke softly. "I've been screwing around."

"Oh, ho! Vajerral has a boyfriend," Jenny exclaimed. Vajerral was now seventeen, a time of life when a young dragon's thoughts turned to her severe hormonal imbalance. Heaven help Vajerral if she had inherited either her mother's romantic obsessions or her horniness. "Please tell me it's another dragon."

"Of course."

"Good. There's quite enough debauchery in the family."

Vajerral spent a long moment looking over the rail at the forest far below, her ears laid back. "What will you do?"

Jenny shrugged. "I don't know. I can't say no, and I don't feel free to say yes. I don't have the right to ask him to wait, because I don't know how long it will be. And he expects . . . he deserves an answer soon. What am I going to tell him?"

Vajerral made a helpless gesture. "What are you going to tell your mother?"

Lady Mira demonstrated that she did indeed have a fine sense of the dramatic as she brought *Wind Dragon* in for a landing at Woody Bog. She had brought the airship in low over the nearby village of Welliden, nearly tangling with the mast of a river schooner tied up at the dock and almost causing a riot of startled townsfolk and delighted children. She then swooped in low and fast over the fields, disrupting the autumn harvest. All that time, Vajerral raced and sported about the airship's vanes, chasing horses, stealing apples out of the orchard and otherwise showing off. Kelvandor sat quietly on the back of the helm deck and behaved himself.

Woody Bog was the manor house of Lord Araedyr of Kaendon. This land had once been a small kingdom on the shores of a narrow, northwestern branch of the inland sea and was now a district of the constitutional monarchy that had united the Northlands in the single nation of Elura over a hundred years before. Lords and ladies were now legally the equals of all other folk. Many, like Lord Araedyr, were still major landholders and owners of large, prosperous estates, employing large numbers of the local people their ancestors had once ruled and still looked to as leaders of the local community, if their abilities and behavior warranted such respect. One of the advantages of democracy was that gentlemen of title and estate were much easier to ignore.

Jenny held mixed feelings about the old nobility. On the one hand she found it terribly quaint and romantic, but she was also the child of a society that held very little tolerance for divine right. In her own opinion, Mira, an untitled, illegitimate former circus midget who happened to do magic very well, deserved to be called Lady far more than most who claimed that name. But Mira obviously thought highly of Lord Araedyr.

Woody Bog deserved at least half its name, since the manor house lay just inside the edge of the dense forest that stretched away north and west toward the distant hills. But the bog was now mostly rich pasture land, with only a remnant of the original swamp along the shores of the river four miles away. The name itself was a thousand-year-old carryover. With the old forest closing in closely about the house, there was not much in the way of open ground to land an airship. But Mira was able to drop *Wind Dragon* straight down into the pocket of yard behind the house with room to spare.

The first thing Jenny noticed upon landing was that it was still late summer or early autumn here, pleasantly warm and breezy but not hot. That was especially important to her now, since cold, wet weather bothered her injury, even though nearly all trace of the wound was now gone. The worst damage, of course, had been deep within.

"Let's go ahead and do a complete disassembly of the rigging," Mira directed as they set about closing up the vanes. "We will be down for a few days, and we need everything out of the way for repairs."

"Permission to come aboard, Captain?" someone with a smooth, pleasant voice called from beneath the hull.

"Permission granted!" Mira called back, and looked around for the Trassek twins. Dooket was already unlatching the boarding ladder in order to drop it down, saving her the need to give that order.

Lord Araedyr climbed the ladder as soon as it was down; Jenny had no doubt about who this must be from first sight. He was a most impressive man, in both appearance and manner, which matched the vague thoughts of admiration, warmth and raw lust Jenny sensed from her mistress's thoughts and memories. Araedyr was an older man, at least from the stilted view of the young, with a rough, deeply lined but dashingly handsome face and a full, thick mane of cottony white hair. He was also tall, trim and strikingly broad-shouldered, his body belonging to someone half his sixty or so years. Mira hurried to his side and he took her offered hand with gentle gallantry.

"They sent word that you were coming," he began. His gravelly voice was almost a rich purr, carrying a rather charming trace of the Southlands accent. He stopped before the sorceress and smiled warmly. "It is good to see you again. You look well."

"The only condition I tolerate," Mira answered, as she pulled him forward to make introductions. "You surely remember my boys. This is my new student, Jenny Barker, her cousin Vajerral Foxfire, and Kelvandor."

"Charmed," Vajerral said graciously, bowing fluidly with one hand on her breast. Jenny was suffering through an uncharacteristic fit of shyness.

"You are all most welcome," he assured them grandly. Then he stopped short, having spied *Wind Dragon*'s chewed rear deck and siderail. "Now that looks like battle damage."

"We had something of an altercation with three Imperial airships on our way through the mountains," Mira answered casually.

"You are right to say Imperial," Lord Araedyr remarked, noticing the charred bowsprit. "There is a newly declared Emperor in Alashera, although not all the Kingdoms of the Sea have formally recognized the full authority of either the Emperor or the Senate. I can only assume that you came out the winner of your 'altercation,' since you are here."

"We possessed certain advantages," she explained vaguely. "The trouble is that we need to have this damage repaired before we continue on. If the Southlanders see an airship that was obviously damaged in a fight . . ."

"I'll have carpenters get on this as soon as I can get them here," he assured her. "But I suspect that you will need a completely new bowsprit, and we have no one experienced in ship-work."

"No problem. We'll just pull the old one out and have them make an exact copy. The vanes are the main concern on an airship, and those sustained no damage."

"As you say," he agreed. Then he stopped before Jenny and bowed gravely, one hand on his chest. "I am very pleased to make your acquaintance, young sorceress."

She only looked profoundly embarrassed and muttered something inaudible.

Jenny stayed behind to assist in securing the ship for an extended stay, deciding that they might just as well remove the forward stabilizers at that time and save that delay when the carpenters arrived. They stripped the rigging completely off the bowsprit and began the process of unstepping the long boom, so that it could be pulled out as soon as a frame and pulley could be raised to lift it out. She stayed to work on the ship alone some time after that, sending the two mercenaries away to discover whatever mischief they could find.

She liked Woody Bog. There was a peaceful, even happy feel to the place, and such things were very noticeable to telepaths. The climate agreed with her, and she did need the rest. All the same, she was uneasy, very eager for them to be on their way. As much as she hated to admit it, she had no desire to meet any more new people at this time.

Jenny climbed down from the ship and stopped short when she saw Kelvandor standing under the stern of the airship, talking quietly with Vajerral as they surveyed the damage. For some reason, she was reminded strongly of the time that they had shared, now five years past. There had been a closeness between them unlike anything two mortals could ever know, and she found that she was tempted to share that seductive spell once again.

Kelvandor had been watching her with that same intensity, and now he turned to walk over to join her. "I have not spoken to you. I hardly know what to say."

Jenny shook her head. "You do not have to say anything. I just do not know how to answer."

"Is the answer so difficult?" he asked, the faintest trace of impatience, even desperation in his voice. "You must soon become a dragon; Dalvenjah has said that. Then there will be no barrier between us."

"It goes beyond that," Jenny insisted, frightened seemingly beyond reason. "I must stay free of demands and commitments, or I'll face the Prophecy tied to blinding emotions."

"I have not spoken of demands or commitments," Kelvandor insisted. "I know only the pleasure we have shared in each other."

"I know," Jenny said, turning away.

Kelvandor caught her arm before she could flee. "I would not be the cause of your distress. I will go away, if you want."

"No, don't ever leave me," Jenny insisted, before she realized the desperation in her own voice. "Just give me a little more time to think."

And Kelvandor only stood there, looking up at her apprehensively. But he never spoke a word, chasing betraying thoughts from his mind, meaning for her to make her own decision. She turned and rushed back up the ladder onto the ship, the only piece of home she had in this strange and suddenly frightening place.

Jenny lost herself in her work, thinking furiously as she stripped down *Wind Dragon*'s standing rigging. What was it in Kelvandor that caused her such fear? There was no reason for it. And yet she found herself locked in a limbo between pleasure in his company and terror of the thought of sharing something deeper, of exploring that magical link between them. This was nothing new and unexpected. This link had tied their lives together for five years. They had even been lovers, as awkward as that had been.

She had thought at the time that it had only been play, and now she knew that it very definitely was not. No, she knew what she feared most. She feared the loss of her ability to say no if she thought she must, knowing that she could never send him away once they became that close. She feared that magical link between them, knowing that it would never let her go.

* * *

"Lady Mira, what am I going to do?" Jenny pleaded as she followed her mistress into the house. Night was falling and dinner was being served, in that order, and their presence was expected if not actually required.

"Right now, you'll follow me into the dining room, trying your best to avoid looking like a disaster has just befallen you, and at least make a pretense of eating," Mira answered her impatiently. "Then maybe you can tell me what your problem is, and we'll do something about solving it."

"It's Kelvandor," Jenny blurted out.

Mira stopped short and turned to stare at her. "What about him?"

"I . . . I . . ."

"Oh my stars, you don't say!" Mira looked very perplexed, and just a bit pleased. "I felt that something was going to happen, but I never foresaw this. I really should invest in a crystal ball. Does he . . . ?"

"Well, yes. I'm sure of that."

"And do you . . . ?"

"No . . . well, yes." Jenny closed her eyes and sobbed aloud. "I don't know!"

"Piffle, it's not the end of the world," Mira declared as she turned and led the way. But she had only gone a few steps when she spied a certain black-and-white cat asleep in a chair in the hall. "J.T., what are you doing?"

By a supreme effort, he managed to lift his head slightly and open one eye enough to glare. "I'm minding my own business. How about you?"

"Pray don't trouble yourself," she told him, and started off again. "What can I tell you? If this is something you do want, then it would do you good."

"Are you sure?" Jenny asked suspiciously.

"No, I'm not!" Mira declared. She was surprised to see Jenny carrying on in this manner, when the girl had always seemed so certain of everything in her life. It did not surprise her to see that, when Jenny did let go, she did it with all the proper theatrics.

Further discussion was delayed as they entered the dining room. Lady Mira had been required to go in search of her student at the last moment, and so they were both late; the entire table watched them expectantly as they took their seats. As custom dictated, the host sat at the head of the table with his honored guests at his right hand; Mira, by necessity, took the first seat and Jenny the second. Kelvandor sat on his tail beside Jenny, with Vajerral across from him at Mira's side. Mira tried to break the strained silence by immediately reaching for a tray of hot bread, not waiting for Lord Araedyr to pass the first plate.

"Eat something," she hissed in warning to her student as she passed the tray.

"I'm not hungry," Jenny answered petulantly.

"You'll eat your dinner and you'll like it, or I'll practice that spell that always makes your clothes disappear."

She frowned. "I'll eat it, but I won't like it."

"Well, did you have a pleasant journey?" Araedyr asked in a desperate effort to avert social disaster. Mira afforded him a stare that spoke volumes of censure. "Oh, yes. We have been through that, haven't we?"

"Honestly, I don't care to hear that they've begun the process of trying to re-establish the Empire," Mira said, leaping like a panther into the conversation on another subject to distract attention from present matters. "That, and the fact that they have attacked Eluran airships with their own captured ships, indicates to me that they've reached such a level of confidence in their own abilities that they think that there is nothing we can do to stop them. Kaendon used to be a province of the old Empire. Have they put you under any pressure to join their new Empire?"

"They have inquired politely, if their insufferable haughtiness can be considered polite," Araedyr answered, obviously somewhat angered by the memory of the officious manner of the representatives who had visited him. "Their representative promised vague rewards if Kaendon were to be an early supporter of the Empire. What it comes down to is this. Only the primary city-states have representatives in the Imperial Senate. After that are provincial city-states, which have a voice only in the Imperial Forum, and the Territories, the conquered lands. In the past, Kaendon was only a provincial member of the Empire. If we return now, we can be a primary member and I would have a respected place in the Senate."

"Meaning that they need any support they can get right now," Mira assumed. "Later, when they don't need you as badly, they're not going to give you any more power in their Senate than they can help."

Araedyr nodded. "And if we support Elura, then we are to be

treated as conquered territory along with the rest of their enemies
. . . if and when their enemies are defeated. I signified that I intended to remain neutral for the time, with the indication that I
wanted some real proof from these upstarts that they really could
defy the North and establish their new Empire. My hope was that,
to them, this would look like normal caution on my part before
casting my lot. My real interest was to put some pressure on them
to tip their hand too soon, encouraging them to show their true
intentions prematurely. Then, perhaps, the North would have
something to work on."

"Ah, a wise course," Mira agreed. "You could have done no
better."

"And from what I've been able to discover, the Kingdoms of
the Sea agree on only certain points," Araedyr added. "They all
seem to have turned to the worship of the Dark, and they are all
keeping their borders as tightly closed to rumor as they can. Which
is no small trick, at the same time their trade is beginning to
flourish. But their structure of power and political alliance is new
and incomplete, still very shaky. They do have the unity of all
their people, from the merchant princes in their great palaces to
the beggars in the streets. My casual spies have been unable to
get anything out of them beyond what you already know. You
will be hard pressed to discover anything more."

"But what of the Emperor or the High Priest? Have either of
them put in an appearance?" Mira asked.

"Everything is in the Emperor's name, and his word is heard,"
Araedyr answered. "But he remains absent, and some minister
seems to attend to the High Priest's duties."

"But if they are confiscating airships for their own use, then
are they going to let you take *Wind Dragon* back out again?"
Vajerral asked.

"That really does not worry me," she explained, demonstrating
her own lack of concern. "I have a three-part plan for getting in,
discovering what I want, and getting back out again, all the time
keeping their suspicions diverted just enough to delay them from
taking any countermeasures until it is too late. All it involves is
the proper combination of audacity, cunning and heaping mounds
of bullshit, served up in the proper combination as the moment
requires."

"Meaning that you intend to play it by ear," Araedyr con-
cluded. "Well, if anyone can pull that off, you can."

"I'll take that to be a vote of confidence," Mira said with a shrug, and turned her attention to her plate.

Dinner was over soon enough, and most of the formal guests retired to the main hall to join members of the household staff and others who lived and worked on the estate as they convened for music, conversation and a variety of entertainments. Mira arrived there in Lord Araedyr's company well ahead of Jenny and the dragons. She found that the Trassek twins had already arrived and were deeply involved in the hunt, stalking a pair of local girls who seemed nice enough and were easily impressed if just a bit simple . . . which helped to explain why they were so easily impressed. She disliked interrupting them, although she was not about to let them know that.

"You two run out to the ship and bring back both Jenny's guitar and my own," she ordered.

"Ah, Lady, do we have to?" Erkin whined and wheedled.

"Yes, go earn your pay."

"Can our friends go with us?"

"You can show them the ship afterward," she told them. "If the four of you go now, I can't imagine when or if we'll ever see those guitars. This way, you'll get them here in a hurry."

"She's got us figured out," Dooket told his "little brother," and they hurried off to complete their errand.

"I think we've spoiled her terribly," Erkin countered.

Mira continued on across the room, having a discreet but very good look about. Kaendon possessed many democratic traditions which had been hundreds of years ahead of their time, such as this hall which was open to everyone regardless of wealth or standing. The Lords of Kaendon had always been a rather informal lot, little impressed with rank—even their own. There was a bright blaze built up in the fireplace at one end, although the nights this far south were only beginning to turn chill. Not more than a score of people had arrived yet, but the evening was still young and the keg of ale had not yet been tapped.

Mira leaned herself against a post in a doorway to one side of the fire, surreptitiously watching the evening crowd slowly accumulate. The girls that Dooket and Erkin had cornered were still waiting. She found that to be a mild surprise but a considerable relief, since she preferred not to interfere in their hunting. The boys had been with her just over two years now, and she wondered how much longer they would be around. They were competent warriors and far more mature—at least professionally—than one would suspect from their manner. But there was a big difference between watching over the guests at her parties and the type of work she had for them now.

"It's nice to see that some things never change," Araedyr said as he suddenly appeared behind her, rubbing her shoulders affectionately.

"I was just contemplating that very subject," Mira answered. "Woody Bog has always amazed me, how a place so big and so full of people can also be so homey. It seems to me that all the rest of the world is changing in a hurry these days."

"Troubled times," Araedyr agreed. "Troubled times. But is this old world changing into something new, or just taking a big step backwards into the dark past? All the same, I was speaking of you. Still the same old Mira. Still with your nose in all the world's business, worrying and worrying."

"When nature gave me this nose, I assumed it to be a sign."

"So what are you brooding about tonight, love?" he asked. "Those children of yours?"

"Hardly children," Mira said. "Jenny is twenty-two, and Kelvandor is pushing hard against two hundred and seventy. I just want for them to have something good this once."

"As I said, some things never change," Araedyr said, amused. "Do you ever think of yourself?"

"All the time, I assure you."

She paused, seeing that Jenny and Kelvandor had entered from the door on the far side of the room, so involved in their own conversation and each other that they failed to notice her. They retreated to one side of the fireplace, at the edge of the small crowd gathering there. Mira wondered what they were discussing, and even more what they might be thinking. She wished, and not for the first time, that she possessed her student's rather awesome telepathic abilities.

"Do you still believe that those two need any help?" Araedyr asked. "They seem to me to be doing well enough on their own."

The Trassek twins entered through that same door a moment later, and Mira hurried to intercept them. She took the larger of the two guitars out of Dooket's hands and presented it to Jenny. "This seems like a very good night for a little music. Guitar duets, if you please."

"Will you play with me?" Jenny asked, seeing that Erkin was standing ready with her own guitar.

"I was contemplating a substitution, if he is willing," she said as she handed her guitar to Kelvandor. "And none of your lame excuses, dragon. I've been told by Vajerral that you play quite well."

"I might just consider it, if Jenny will condescend to take pity with rank amateurs," he answered as he took the instrument, holding it to his chest with some difficulty. He plucked the strings experimentally. "And I do mean rank. What should we play?"

"A love song, but something light and hopeful," Mira insisted before her student had a chance to reply. "This is a night for happy songs."

Jenny was looking up at her suspiciously. "What have you got on your mind?"

"As if you didn't know!" Mira answered with a shrug and turned to walk away. A judicious retreat seemed to be in order.

"As it happens, I usually do."

Mira hurried back to rejoin Araedyr in the shadows along the far wall. The two musicians were plucking at the strings of their instruments with slow, careful determination, as if they were having some trouble coming to an agreement. Already the small crowd was beginning to take some notice, and the evening mood in the hall lightened with new interest and excitement. Dragons were rare enough as visitors, and even more so as musicians. Jenny was at last able to make her point clear to her eager but uncertain partner and their fumbling chords modulated into the opening measures of a song. Then Jenny began to sing, the depth and quality of her voice surprising and impressing Kelvandor to such an extent that he almost allowed his part to falter.

"Your new student plays like an honest professional," Araedyr observed after he had listened attentively through half the song. "She's descended of the old aristocracy of the Middle Kingdoms, is she not?"

She glanced at him questioningly. Jenny's dark blue hair had already been spelled to black, in the event that there were Imperial spies about. "What makes you suspect that?"

"I am only guessing, actually," he said. "But only one group of people I have seen have noses quite like that."

Mira looked startled and, a moment later, faintly amused, but she made no comment. She just hoped that Jenny never heard, or otherwise perceived, what Lord Araedyr had to say about her nose.

The two musicians had drawn quite a crowd by the time the first song ended. Jenny was clearly a professional; Mira, who had already played with her, was all the more impressed. So were the locals, to judge by their response. Kelvandor was certainly good enough to get away with playing second guitar with her, and he had not yet had the opportunity to demonstrate his fine tenor.

"They do perform well together," Araedyr remarked, and turned to Mira before she could make some off-color comment that was forestalled between her brain and her tongue. "We are usually responsible for entertaining ourselves during our nightly sessions, such as we are able. This is indeed a rare treat."

The crowd had been debating some point since the end of that first song, and they were now pulling back the benches to make room. Mira paused a moment to watch. "What is this? Are we going to have dancing?"

"That seems likely," Araedyr agreed, then paused a moment. "Ah, yes! They are bringing out the drums."

Mira knew from her past visits that the drums were used for the powerful, relentless beat that thundered the time to many of the exuberant local folk dances, some of which were as old as the days of the Alasheran Empire. She had always enjoyed drum dances in the past, although the combination of noise, excitement and the strong southern wine tended to bring on a swift headache. Lord Araedyr might have read her mind, for he suddenly darted away to fetch a bottle and two glasses. They took their seats on a bench in a private corner of the hall where they could watch the dancing from a safe distance.

Four drummers were stationed at the corners of the dance floor and the captain of the manor guard stepped to the center to mark the opening time, each downward stroke of his sword an echoing beat. Two young dancers, both members of the guard, quickly took their places behind him. Arms folded behind their backs, they began the vigorous and complex steps of the dance. Concentration was intense, not just on the part of the participants but also the audience. Mira had always been uncertain whether these energetic dances were entertainment, an art form or an acrobatic performance. Drum dances had long been a favorite of soldiers, especially the elite household guards, providing good training in strength, endurance and dexterity while giving more experienced dancers a chance to show off their hard-earned skills.

The first pair of dancers surrendered the floor at last and, after a quick but spirited debate between herself and several of the others, Jenny pulled off her shoes and stepped out to the center. Mira's interest and amusement turned to sudden apprehension when she saw four members of the household guard join her, moving with formal, military precision to form a square about the solitary dancer, their long, narrow-bladed swords upraised. As one they knelt and laid their swords on the floor, razor-sharp blades facing up with points touching to form a cross beneath the young sorceress's long legs.

"Yarg, surely she doesn't mean to do the sword dance!" Mira protested, and turned to her companion. "Ary, she can't do this."

"She means to try," Araedyr said. "Surely she has done it before."

"I can't imagine." Privately, Mira was surprised that her protégé knew any of the drum dances. Jenny must have learned some interesting tricks during her years among the dragons. Actually, she had practiced wild acrobatic dances with the best: Jane Fonda.

Jenny indicated for the drummers to increase their beat. The watchers muttered with growing excitement and leaned forward tense with anticipation, the concentration becoming almost tangible like a throbbing counterpoint to the drumbeat. Jenny began the dance, arms folded behind her back, dancing between the blades with lightning-quick steps. It was no variant of the sword dance of this world, but it worked.

"Put a stop to this, before she hurts herself."

"There is no stopping it now," Araedyr said sharply, indicating for her to remain silent. "Nothing must break her concentration until she decides that the dance is done."

Mira had to admit the logic in that, as little as she liked it. Jenny was doing very well indeed, her every move quick, precise and strongly graceful. Mira's apprehension faded—somewhat— as she watched in complete fascination, as captivated as everyone else in the room. Then a look of momentary surprise that crossed her face evolved into her usual mischievous grin.

"Ah, of course!" she said to herself. "Bless her, the dear girl is actually showing off for her dragon."

And when she took a closer look at Kelvandor, she saw that he ploy was working very well at that. He was as captivated by the dance as anyone else in the room, but he also looked very pleased and just a little proud. Mira was just a little pleased and proud herself, enough that she was almost willing to forgive her student for pulling such a dangerous stunt as attempting the sword dance without practicing first. And it was such a daring and impulsive stunt for Jenny, normally so cool and reserved, that her forgiveness was almost complete.

Almost, but not quite. Mira did approve of unorthodoxies and believed that impulsive behavior was a virtue to be rewarded. She would have to consider the matter as she calmed her nerves over a cup of tea.

The night was cool and clear, the air fresh and bearing a shadow of the snap of an autumn evening, an indication that summer was passing quickly even this far south. Mira, standing on the wooden deck of a porch behind the house, drank her tea slowly as she reflected that it was indecent for any land to be blessed with perfect weather. Which was not exactly the case; Kaendon did have rare snowfalls about every other winter, and she had not forgotten the hurricanes that threatened the coastal lands far more regularly. Yes, it was important to keep all things in perspective. That made living in cold, wet Bennasport more bearable.

Mira paused and set her cup on the wooden rail where she stood, glancing surreptitiously over her shoulder. Jenny had just appeared on the brick-paved lower porch and was quietly making her way up the steps of the deck. Mira wondered why the girl thought she needed to be so stealthful, and if she believed that she really was getting away with anything.

"You dance superbly, dear child," Mira said without turning. "I might add that you're about as subtle as a tipsy dragon."

"I'm as quiet as J.T.," her student protested.

"That's not saying much. And I was referring to your behavior earlier, not in your manner in stomping up those steps."

"What about my behavior?" Jenny demanded, feigning surprise and slight indignation.

"You were most definitely showing off for a certain dragon," Mira told her bluntly.

"Who says that I was showing off?" Jenny insisted.

"I say that you were showing off!" the sorceress declared, refusing to be intimidated. "Listen to me, young lady. If you've come here to ask my advice, then you are going to have to admit to a few obvious truths."

"Who says that I've come to ask your advice?"

"Yarg!" Mira pantomimed pulling her hair in frustration, and knocked her teacup off the rail in the process. She peered over the rail after it. "Now see what you've made me do. And I have the suspicion that I'm going to need all the tea I can get tonight. Now, why don't we just get this over with? There are better things we could both be doing tonight."

"You were waiting for me." Jenny conjured the teacup back onto the ledge, only without its tea.

"Of course. Now, I'll start off with providing the answer to a question you might not think to ask. If you didn't love him, then there would be nothing for you to decide. The next question is, how much do you love him?"

Jenny frowned. "I don't know. I've been looking for those answers all night, and I just cannot find them. It's so hard to decide."

"Is there anything to decide?" Mira asked. "Kelvandor is a dragon. How could you possibly make love to him?"

"I've . . . made love to him before," Jenny explained softly.

"Oh." Mira had to hastily reconsider her arguments—at the same time that she was overwhelmed with fascinated curiosity. She would have given five gold crowns to have seen that. "But I still don't understand. There is a difference between amorous and romantic, at least in my book, and I must be too much of the former and not enough of the latter. Kelvandor is a faerie dragon and you are . . ."

Well, that was an interesting question. Jenny had certainly started life human and quite mortal, but Dalvenjah had warned Mira, long before the girl had ever come into this world, what long familiarity with dragon magic had done to her. She had hardly forgotten that Jenny had taken an arrow in the gut with less harm than most mortals would have had from a slight wound to the arm or leg.

Jenny frowned. "I know that I must become a dragon to play my part in the Prophecy. And that, I suspect, will not be long in coming. My uncle Allan became a dragon for Dalvenjah's sake, and they share a deep, quiet love that I can only describe as magical. I can see a distant glimpse of that when I'm with Kelvandor. But I'm not yet ready to commit myself that fully to him. I need more time."

Mira nodded in understanding. "I know that many dragons spend most of their endless lives devoted to a fair number of loves, turning to one or the other as they feel or need. And some mortal folk like myself, who have learned the hard way to be properly circumspect, balance such relationships in our own way. Then, when the day comes that you feel ready to make a permanent commitment, so be it.''

Jenny nodded in mute agreement, but she still did not look completely convinced. She stood for a long moment, leaning on the rail and staring into the dark forest only a short distance beyond. "Love can be so complex and difficult to understand. What do you think? What is your position with men?"

"Usually on the bottom," Mira remarked evenly, but with her sly little grin.

Jenny rolled her eyes. "I should have seen that one coming. I should have learned, after half a year, to beware of how I phrase things with you."

"I can't make your decision for you," Mira told her sternly.

"I'm not asking you to," her student answered. "Talk to me, Mira. Give me the benefit of your vast experience, and we'll see if any of it takes root. I trust you more than I trust anyone in this world."

"Oh, very well." Mira sighed heavily, unaware that the slender wooden rail creaked in warning. "All right, then. This is the first truth I learned, a long time ago, and it has helped preserve both my perspective and my sanity every time I find myself in 'your situation.' There is no such thing as love. It's an illusion. You can't put it in a bottle or the bank, and it sure as hell don't make the flowers grow. You can do without it. You can get through life just fine, and possibly better, all by yourself. You don't really need anyone, not friends or lovers. Just clients."

Jenny looked so scandalized that Mira smiled. "Of course, there is one important thing you do have to keep in mind about love."

"And what is that?" Jenny asked breathlessly.

"It feels good." Mira shrugged helplessly, and shook her head. "And so, keeping firmly in mind that love is something you can do just as well if not better without, it allows you to keep your perspective and watch out for yourself when you do find yourself involved in affairs of the heart . . . or the crotch. Keeping your perspective and watching out for your own interests—and your partner's—is the best insurance against something going badly wrong. It helps you get more out of love, and it tells you when the time has come to get out of a bad situation, with a minimum of friction.''

"That makes sense,'' Jenny agreed. It all sounded very much like her mistress's curious but effective philosophies.

"Which brings us to rule number two,'' Mira announced. "I never allow myself to proceed into a situation where I lose more than my half of the control. I refuse to stay in a bad situation. But I certainly never allow a promising opportunity to slip by. Practical hedonism is the only way to get the most from life.''

Jenny laughed softly. "And I thought that Addena Sheld was a hopeless flirt.''

"She learned from the expert,'' Mira said, pointing to herself. She turned to lean on the rail, and the two of them peered into the night for several long moments.

"It's easier to be a dragon,'' Jenny continued after a brief moment. "Male or female, a dragon is a dragon and they are never at odds. But men and women often seem almost like different creatures, and I don't understand men. It just seems that men only care about what they want, like pleasing them is our only interest and purpose.''

"It seems that way, I do admit,'' Mira agreed. "Men are not by nature self-centered assholes, but an inordinate number turn out that way because they have never had to learn better. They don't know that they're missing the best part of love just to satisfy their lust. And there are certainly enough games that women play, so I guess it comes out fairly even in the end. But there is no reason to ever give in to that. You either get what you're entitled to out of a relationship, or you get out.''

"You make love sound so transitory,'' Jenny observed.

"Do I?'' The sorceress looked startled. "I certainly never meant to imply that. If you ever are lucky enough to find your perfect match, then don't you ever let him get away. It's just been my part to have acquired an impressive string of near misses.''

She paused a moment to lift her cup, then looked within it and realized that the rest of her tea had gone over the rail. She sighed heavily. "Hang me for a nosey old bitch, but I just have to ask. How do you make love to a dragon in the first place?''

"Oh, that's not hard,'' Jenny insisted, rather innocently. "The trick is getting the dragon on his back.''

"Well, yes.'' For once in her life, Mira did not want an answer to her question. "So, what do you think?''

"It won't be long until I'll have to become a dragon for my protection," Jenny mused, almost to herself. "It's not as if I'm becoming a dragon to be with him, as my uncle Allan did for Dalvenjah. But I'm afraid to get involved until I'm done with the Prophecy and have a life of my own. Once I become a dragon myself, this whole situation with Kelvandor will become a lot harder to ignore."

"So who says you should ignore it?" Mira asked. When Jenny turned to stare, she shrugged broadly. "I mean, what is really going to be different? You're going to have that dragon hanging about as it is. If you just go ahead and get it over, that's one less thing you'll have to worry about."

Jenny had to think about that for a moment. Mira did make one good point. If the idea was to avoid distraction, Kelvandor already had her distracted enough. If love itself was the distraction, then she was already in love. She was reminded yet again of Allan and Dalvenjah, and how they both seemed to be stronger and more secure for having each other. Of course, theirs was hardly the deep, magical relationship that Dalvenjah and Allan shared. It came down to a question of the better of two evils, having Kelvandor . . . or not having him. And as Mira said, he was going to be around anyway.

"I'm going to find another cup of tea before I fade away into the night like a shadow," Mira said as she turned back to the door. "Just be certain that you're not making it more of a problem than it really is."

Jenny leaned on the rail, looking out into the night at the dark shape of *Wind Dragon* sitting in the yard beyond. The airship was in a state of partial disassembly, lacking her bowsprit and rigging, as well as the burnt and damaged sections of her deck, rail and hull. The old girl had really taken her lumps in the past couple of weeks. It frightened Jenny just to think about it.

"She is right."

Jenny turned sharply at the sound of that deep, soft voice to see the misty form of a golden dragon standing behind her. She relaxed. "I was wondering when you would turn up again. You are going to have to be a little less mysterious, you know. You could just say what you mean."

Keridaejan looked honestly surprised. "I did not want to frighten you."

"Drifting in and out muttering cryptic messages is your idea of being discreet?"

"Well, pardon me for dying," the dragon said, turning his head away. "I was trying to do you a favor. But never mind that. After all I've done for you and this Prophecy, I should want to proceed as I see best."

"Well, I'm sorry," Jenny conceded grudgingly, turning back to lean on the rail. "It just seems like know-it-all dragons have been running my life according to their own secret plans for most of my life."

"Yes, I can imagine that you would find it frustrating." Karidaejan was reluctantly mollified. He made vague motions of stroking his scales, a nervous gesture that was defeated by the fact that his physical appearance was an illusion. He sighed heartily. "You have been patient, even devoted. You deserve to know the truth, and I know things that even Dalvenjah does not dare to suspect. And you deserve to know everything."

Jenny nodded. "I've always thought that I could do better for knowing what was going on."

"That just goes to show how much you know."

Jenny turned to stare. "You have no intention of telling me a damned thing, do you?"

"The time has not yet come," he explained. "You have an important and dangerous task before you. Once that is done, then I will come to you again and explain everything. But at that time you must become a dragon, for your own protection, before it is too late. Your enemies plan to trap you, and you will be betrayed by one you will not expect."

"And you have no intention of telling me who that is?" Jenny asked as the dragon's misty form began to fade.

"Not on your life."

With that he was gone. A moment later the door opened and Mira stepped out onto the deck, holding a cup of tea. She blinked in confusion. "Who are you talking to?"

· Part Six ·

Jewel of the Southern Seas

FIVE DAYS OF conscientious labor had *Wind Dragon* restored to
perfect condition. The damage to her woodwork from fire arrows,
grapples and the lashing tails of winged demons was repaired to
invisibility. The new bowsprit was set into place, the stabilizers
were rigged and a new set of replacement stabilizers were made
and stored in the hold. The water tank was also repaired, along
with a careful drying out of the contents of the airship's lower
deck. And Jenny was given a new set of clothes to replace what
she had lost to rather unusual circumstances.

Mira was up before dawn, packing for her move back into her
cabin aboard *Wing Dragon* so that they could be away shortly,
but she was interrupted barely halfway through. She was just a
little annoyed to discover Erkin knocking on her door, mostly
because he was knocking so loudly. She opened it impatiently.

"Lady Mira, there's a big, ugly ghost poking around the ship,"
Erkin explained before she had a chance to lecture him.

"What?" Mira demanded. "Oh, piffle! There's no such thing
as ghosts."

"Whatever it is, something is out there," Erkin insisted, un-
convinced. He was, after all, a barbarian. Or what passed for
barbarian in this modern age. "Dooket is keeping an eye on it."

"Oh, let's go have a look," she acquiesced. Ghost or not, she was willing to concede that her two mercenaries were level-headed enough to know that they had seen something unusual, even if they had no idea what it was.

The door across the hall opened and Jenny peered out inquisitively. "What is it?"

"We have a ghost in the ship," Erkin told her, perfectly serious. Mira sighed deeply and rolled her eyes, disputing that.

"Oh." Jenny seemed to get the message. "Mind if I come along?"

"The more, the merrier!" Mira exclaimed. "Lead on."

Now there was one serious misconception being perpetrated, at least on Jenny's part. She knew of only one ghost, and she could not imagine why Karidaejan would be poking about. Any other ghost, perhaps. But not some secretive Mindijarah. She had not heard Erkin's description of the ghost as big and ugly, although she did think that he would know a faerie dragon when he saw one. Even one who had been dead as long as Karidaejan.

They hurried through the dark, silent manor house and stepped out onto the back porch. The sky was only just beginning to lighten in advance of the rising sun. The grass of the lawn was dark beneath a blanket of dew, and the morning air was cool, heavy and wet. *Wind Dragon*'s vast, dark shape loomed only a short distance away. A dog was barking somewhere, but without any particular urgency or alarm, and everything seemed silent and calm. But in contrast to that sleepy, peaceful scene, there was a vague troubling to the native magic of the world. Mira shuttered despite herself, as if in revulsion from some foul touch.

"Over there, Lady Mira." Jenny indicated to their right.

At that moment Dooket stepped out of the open door of a storeroom in the corner of the house, near *Wind Dragon*'s stern, and gestured impatiently for them to come. They hurried to join him, and Mira was surprised to note that he actually looked just a little frightened. Since none of their hair-raising adventures of the past two and a half years had ever come close to achieving that effect, she was surprised and mystified.

"It's in here," he whispered hoarsely. "It glows quite a bit, so you can't miss it."

"Of, piffle!" Mira declared yet again and she conjured a soft blue ball of light above her head and entered the storeroom boldly. "There's no such thing as ghosts. Honestly, boys, you surprise me, trying to tell me such an absurd tale. I'll have you know that I'm a trained and competent sorceress, an expert in matters of magic, and I have no patience for superstitious nonsense.''

Jenny kept her mouth firmly closed on the subject.

She stopped short when something vast and threatening stepped out from behind a stack of crates to block her way. It was well over seven feet tall, so enormous that it barely fit under the ceiling, and it did indeed glow faintly with its own pale, sickly light. In form it seemed like some impossible mixture of man and crab. Its massive body was encased in hard, armored shell, although it walked upright on two short, plated legs and its long, spine-edged arms ended in immense pincers. Its small head seemed to emerge directly from its hunched back, hinged so that it could look to either side only slightly. Two points of white flames marked its small eyes, burning balefully from deep within the shadow of its armored brow. Mira turned to the Trasseks with an impatient gesture.

"What did I tell you, boys? That's not a ghost. That's a demon," she declared, then turned abruptly back to the malevolent monster. "Yarg!"

The demon drew back a massive pincer and took a swipe at them that would have scattered the entire group across the room, except that they had already scattered. Dooket and Erkin stood ready to charge in with their swords, but Mira gestured them away sharply. She did not know if the weapons they carried were those which had been spelled for fighting demons. Then she began working the spell that should have sent the demon back to its own existence.

"Don't you dare!" Jenny declared, one hand held protectively over her breasts. Mira turned to stare at her in astonishment and mystification.

Ignoring her mistress, Jenny stepped forward to face the demon, coldly determined, even as it prepared to attack. She gestured toward the monster, one arm aimed level at its plated chest, and a soft blue glow surrounded her closed fist. The demon lunged ponderously forward straight toward her, but a shaft of blue mist shot out from her fist to impact against its thick shell, blasting it backwards against the wall behind with force enough to crack the brick and shake the very foundations of the manor. It stirred weakly and began to rise, but Jenny caught it with a second blast that exploded the monster, casting plated segments across the floor.

A moment later those segments began to dissolve into thick, creeping mist.

"I do need the practice." Mira pretended to sound aggrieved.

"Well, do it when I'm not about," Jenny answered, rubbing her closed fist. "My word, that tingles. So, what do we do now? Was that thing looking for us, or was it only in the neighborhood?"

"That's a very good question, but I really do not know the answer," the sorceress said. "I don't like the thought that they might be sending demons out to spy upon and intimidate their enemies and possible allies. I like even less the thought that they know who we are and had these things out looking for us. For the sake of our good host and his people, we should get *Wind Dragon* into the air as soon as possible. Let's get to work, boys."

"Right, Lady Mira," Dooket and Erkin agreed eagerly, as if nothing had ever happened, and hurried out of the storeroom to attend to the task.

An hour of hard work found *Wing Dragon* once again in the sky, and in somewhat less than an hour more the airship passed from the woody coast of Kaendon out over the rolling, white-headed waves of the sea. There was a brisk inshore wind that the ship was forced to climb above to maintain her speed, but the sky was mostly clear and the sun bright and warm. With luck, they would not be caught over water by an autumn storm. Mira kept very much in mind that this was the season for hurricanes, and that an airship was just as vulnerable to such violent weather as any other ship at sea.

But for now, matters aboard *Wind Dragon* were quiet enough. Kelvandor was overboard stretching his wings. Jenny stood at the ship's wheels, so lost in her own thoughts that she looked up only every two minutes or so to check the compass for drift. Lady Mira sat on the deck a short distance away, poring over her books with a single-minded interest.

Mira looked up at last, peering at her young student intently. "What great matters are you pondering over there? You're thinking so hard that I can't concentrate on my reading."

"Oh, just thinking," Jenny replied with shy evasion, pushing a ribbon of her long, spelled-black hair away from her face. Mira recognized that nervous gesture and thought she knew what it meant.

"Oh, ho!" she declared. "So, how are things going between yourself and the dragon?"

"Oh, just fine."

"Just fine? Your enthusiasm overwhelms me."

Jenny smiled. "I'm not thinking about Kelvandor. I've got something else on my mind."

"Oh? So what am I, a mind reader?" Mira inquired.

"I hate it when people say that to me," Jenny muttered with a frown, and sighed deeply. "Frankly, I'm worried about that demon the boys found. If it was looking for us, then we're flying into a trap."

"Yes, I've thought about that too," Mira said, solemnly academic but not particularly concerned. "I really don't see how they could be looking for us, specifically. They might have sent their demon to spy upon or terrorize Lord Araedyr, since he is holding out on their offer to join the Empire. But, more likely than not, they are just spying out the countryside for airships they can steal for their own use."

"Oh, of course!" Jenny agreed. "They have to be coming up with airships somewhere, and airship trade into that region has always been sparse. What did Araedyr have to say?"

"What you no doubt suspect," Mira replied. "A certain number of airships have disappeared on routine flights here in the South. The ships are posted missing, and in two cases war galleys have claimed to have found wreckage. Then, a few weeks later, the same ships are seen flying again under new names as a part of the Imperial sky navy."

"Could they possibly be boarding and commandeering ships in flight?" Jenny asked dubiously. "They've attacked us in flight twice, but they seemed far more intent upon destruction than boarding."

"I wouldn't want to try it," Mira said. "I suppose that it is possible to board and capture an airship in flight, as difficult and dangerous as that might be. That sounds like one of Beratric Kurgel's stupid ideas, and how did they capture the first? It seems far easier to capture the airship while it's still on the ground, say the night before, very quietly and secretly. Then they would have had their own crew take the ship out of port and fly it home rather than on to its next destination."

Jenny glanced over her shoulder to see that Kelvandor was laboring to come up behind the ship. She cut speed somewhat and moved as much as she could out of the way while still keeping hold of both wheels, and Mira discreetly withdrew to the starboard steps down to the middle deck. J.T., coming up the other steps at that moment, took one look and turned tail.

"Coming through!" Kelvandor bellowed as he took hold of the rail and thrust himself forward onto the deck, only to trip and crack his chin sharply. He rose and shook his head vigorously. "Hm. That was an improvement."

Mira glanced up from her book, affording him one of her droll expressions. "Sometimes he's so stupid, he even frightens himself. Where have you been, Lizard?"

"Having a look about," the dragon answered, rubbing his chin. "But this little ship is making such speed, I cannot range very far for fear of losing you."

Lady Mira, still seated on the steps, was staring thoughtfully at the dragon. She shook her head slowly. "You know, we can't just fly into port with a pair of faerie dragons on board."

Kelvandor stared at her. "I never thought that we would. Vajerral and I will go overboard as we near the island, to do a little furtive investigating of our own, and generally just hang around in the event you need us for daring rescues. The rest of you can stick your head in the noose, and be safer without us."

"I don't like the way you phrased that, but I believe that would be best," Mira agreed. "But for pity's sake, don't get yourselves caught or do a damned thing that could cast any suspicion on us. I dare say that we'll be in quite enough danger as it is."

"Right . . . Mom," Kelvandor agreed. He was in a playful mood.

Mira rolled her eyes but refrained from answering him. She looked at Jenny, who was quietly attending the helm. "You've remained completely silent on the subject."

"I just wish I knew what you had in mind, once we arrive," her student said frankly.

Lady Mira sighed deeply. "So do I."

Wind Dragon had stopped for the night on the sands of a small island, and Jenny had gone with Kelvandor and Vajerral up the beach a short distance to do the laundry in a broad stream that emerged from the forest. They were bringing in the laundry that they earlier had hung to dry on a line stretched between two trees. Five days in Kaendon and they had not thought to have their laundry sent out. It was interesting that the dragons agreed to the task of washing clothes, since they were adamant about wearing only what they grew for themselves.

Jenny had found a small mirror in one of the pockets of Mira's jacket, and she seemed to have had a morbid fascination with it ever since. Now Jenny had always had something of a compulsive dislike, even fear, of mirrors. She had an intense aversion to seeing her own image, even in those times when she had spelled or dyed her hair black as a matter of necessity, such as the four years she had been in college, and she could not guess why. Now she seemed almost addicted to staring at her own image, as if to make up for those long years of avoidance.

Vajerral paused in folding towels to stare over her shoulder, wondering if Jenny was using the mirror for some magical spell. "What do you see?"

Jenny frowned. "You know, I've had this face for nearly twenty-four years now, and I have never appreciated it. I have just never thought about it. Is it a pretty face? An intelligent face? A kind face?"

"All of those things at once, I am sure," Kelvandor was quick to promise her. When love speaks, beauty is in the eye of the beholder. Even if the beholder is a dragon, and knows not whereof he speaks. "A pretty face, above all else. Very beautiful."

She turned to him. "Are you sure?"

"Oh, yes," he said, then laid back his ears uncertainly. "At least for a human."

"Oh, thanks!"

Vajerral placed a sock on the end of her snout and tossed her head to cause it to swing back and forth. "Look! An oliphant!"

"Oh, enough!" Jenny snatched away the sock and used it to snap the young dragon in the rump.

"What is an oliphant?" Kelvandor asked. He was entertaining the rather outrageous vision of a dragon with a long, obscenely limp nose.

Jenny glanced into the mirror yet again. "I was just thinking that soon I will have to become a dragon. There is nothing wrong with being a dragon, I must admit. But I have become rather used to what I am, and I think that I am going to miss it . . . no matter how much I might enjoy being a dragon."

"Allan always did regret that he never could play his cello," Vajerral agreed thoughtfully. Then she saw that Kelvandor was glaring at her, and she remembered which side of the argument she was supposed to take. "Of course, he does make a very good dragon."

Jenny was staring at the pair of them, thoughtfully. "I am beginning to think that you two were exactly the wrong people to talk to about this."

"Look at that!" Vajerral exclaimed. Trotting on all fours, she hurried across the beach to intercept a curious crawling shell like a horseshoe crab that was being tumbled ashore by the surf.

"Did you know Keridaejan?" Jenny asked. She had been thinking about his warning that she would be betrayed by someone she would never suspect. She wondered if he foresaw that as a part of the Prophecy, or if being a ghost gave him a special advantage in being able to sneak about and discover things.

"Karidaejan was my father," Kelvandor answered simply.

Jenny stared. "I beg your pardon?"

"Long story," he explained. "All old family history. You see, the Prophecy as you know it actually began before Dalvenjah's own birth less than fifty years ago. She was an orphan of circumstance, surrendered by her mother to apprenticeship at a very early age, unaware of the identity of her own father until she was nearly your age. She's a fighter, a survivor, even by the standards of our own kind."

"I know that," Jenny agreed. "And I know that she lost her first mate."

"It was more than that," Kelvandor continued. "You see, my father was her older half-brother, and also her first true mate. They knew each other only a very short time and yet they loved each other dearly, both as brother and sister and as lovers. And do not stare; that is the way of dragons. But they were also so very much alike that they were not completely comfortable with prolonged company. Then Derjadhan came and stole Dalvenjah's heart. The High Priest was able to get at Keridaejan, and Dalvenjah was forced to slay his body by her own hand. She saw her first two loves die within months of each other, but then she also found Allan. That was why Allan was so good for her; it took her three tries to get it right."

"Then you are a consulting sorcerer, like Dalvenjah?" Jenny asked, thinking that he wanted to change the subject.

"In most ways, but not quite," Kelvandor explained, considering his words carefully. "It is, I suppose, a matter of reputation.

Dalvenjah is known for solving mysteries, for finding things or figuring out how things happen. I am a troubleshooter, a solver of obvious problems. I do such things as slay evil creatures, negotiate for enemies or perform quests. I also do a good deal of consulting work in matters of landscape engineering, dams and bridges and the like.''

Jenny bent down to pick up a large spiral shell and hold it to her ear. Kelvandor stared at her intently. "Why are you sticking a shell in your ear?"

"You dragons know nothing about the sea," she declared, laughing. "If you hold one of the larger coiled shells to your ear, you can hear the sea."

"I can do that without the shell," Kelvandor muttered as he stepped over to the edge of the surf to collect an especially large shell, and held it to his ear. A large hermit crab reached out with one pincer to grab his ear.

Jenny laughed as she gently removed the crab, but Kelvandor only glared. "You never told me that things live inside."

"Begone, foul creatures of Darkness!" a strong male voice declared from just behind them. "Unhand that lady!"

They all turned sharply, and Jenny saw one of the more amazing sights of a long and eventful career. There, on the very edge of the forest behind them, stood an actual knight in shining armor. His visor was down and Jenny could see nothing of his features, but he was tall and his voice, a little deep for Errol Flynn, was still well cast for the part. He stood with drawn sword, ready to descend in righteous combat with the two dragons.

"I say, get your hands off!"

Startled, Jenny drew back the hand she had on Kelvandor's shoulder; otherwise neither of the two dragons was touching her. Vajerral was standing over a large crab some distance away, her head down and her back beginning to arch. She had inherited her mother's fighting instinct.

Jenny was beginning to recover her own composure. "What do you mean by this? What manner of fool are you, if you don't know that faerie dragons are of the Light?"

"One thing I've learned, little lady, is that things are not always what they seem." He advanced on Kelvandor, who had to take several steps backwards to avoid getting nasty. "Shall it be you first, or do we save the best for last?"

Jenny drew the long-bladed sword from Kelvandor's harness

and intercepted him. "You leave that poor dragon alone! He's my boyfriend."

"Honestly, Miss, I'm just trying to defend your virtue," the knight said reasonably, then stopped short. They could almost see the whites of his eyes in the shadow of his visor. "Your boyfriend? Oh, my! I might already be too late to salvage your virtue."

Kelvandor glared. "You're starting to get on my nerves."

The knight brought up his sword, and Jenny countered the attack by lifting her own blade. That left the poor fellow at something of a loss. Fighting a dragon to rescue a damsel was one thing, but this damsel was fighting him for possession of the dragon. If anyone should happen by, they might get the idea that he was trying to rescue a dragon from a damsel and that simply would not do at all.

Kelvandor decided to put a quick end to the entire question, whipping his tail around to trip the distracted knight. There was one thing that he knew about knights in heavy armor. They went over like a log, and they tended to stay down for the count. Kelvandor relieved him of his weapons, then stood with one hind paw in the middle of the knight's armored chest.

"Are you prepared to be reasonable?" Kelvandor asked.

"I suppose that we might talk about it," the knight agreed.

Kelvandor stepped back and lifted him, armor and all, with deceptive ease, and the knight pulled off his helmet. He was everything that Jenny would have expected of a knight in shining armor: tall, powerfully built and ruggedly handsome. The only thing that she had not expected was that he was old, at least compared to her Prince Charming image. Actually, he was only. in his mid-forties, slightly weatherbeaten but still quite hale and distinguished. Perhaps she had expected that an experienced knight would not have been running around behaving so foolishly, accosting innocent dragons as they folded laundry with their damsels.

"So, you mean to say that these are real faerie dragons, and that you are not in any danger?" he asked, drawing himself up sternly. "Then who, might I ask, are you, what are you doing here and how did you get here?"

"I'm a sorceress from off-world," Jenny explained, mindful of giving her true name to strangers. "My friends and I came here aboard the airship *Wind Dragon*, laid over for the night. My mistress is Lady Mira, a sorceress of some renown. We are on a quest, a spy mission to Alashera."

"Kasdamir Gerran?" the knight asked incredulously. "Well, why didn't you say so? Mira's an old friend of mine."

Jenny sighed. Here we go again.

The knight swept a surprisingly elegant bow, considering the fact that he was wearing a Toyota. "I am Sir Remidan Ardont Resmaer-Traytess, Son of Sir Talebaern, Son of Sir Raemard, Defender of the Crown and Knight Errant of the Loyal Order of Stewards, Bearer of the Golden Horn of Valor. My card."

Jenny glanced at the card. Sure enough, it said all that.

"Just a moment," he turned to the forest immediately behind them. "Yo! Staemar! Show yourself. We're going to see Mira."

A white stallion of rather impressive size, decked out in saddle, neck and face armor, and sheets of chain mail hung about its form like draperies, stepped into the opening. "Mira? That crazy lady?"

"My word, it's Mr. Ed," Jenny muttered to herself. In fact, the voice was curiously the same, only this horse was a tenor. Staemar must have heard her, because he glared at her through the eyeholes in his face armor.

Remidan seemed willing enough to accompany them back to camp, and he was able to see *Wind Dragon*'s masts above the dunes about a quarter of a mile away once he put on a pair of wire-framed glasses. Jenny stared, fascinated to see that suits of armor had pockets. Staemar seemed less willing.

"These dragons won't eat me, will they?" he asked uncertainly.

Kelvandor looked at him in a very appraising manner for a long moment. "No, I don't think so."

Mira and the two barbarians were standing below *Wind Dragon*'s boarding ladder, staring in complete mystification as Jenny and the dragons approached with their unexpected guests. Mira peered very intently at Sir Remidan for a long moment, and then her eyes widened in surprise.

"Remidan?" she asked. "Remidan, it is you. I haven't seen you in years now. Where have you been all that time?"

"Well, I'm afraid to say that Staemar and I have been ship-wrecked on this island for the past two years," Remidan explained. "I've never been sure, but I've always expected that it was the foul sorceress Queramael who caused me to be stranded here. If she thought that she made an end to me that time, then she is in for quite a surprise indeed."

"Sorceress Queramael?" Kelvandor asked.

"A most evil sorceress and self-proclaimed Queen of the

Shadow Islands,'' Sir Remidan explained, wiping his glasses with a lacy hanky. "Also a childhood companion of mine. We share a bitter and deadly rivalry that goes back these twenty years and more, and she will stop at nothing to destroy me.''

"Why is she so peeved with you?'' Jenny asked.

"He got her pregnant," Mira whispered succinctly.

"Oh." Jenny blinked. "I'd be out for his hide myself."

"It was hardly my fault," Remidan explained, his pride ruffled by this distasteful admission. "It happened during our first great contest, a fierce battle of Dark sorcery against my own finely crafted skills and magical armor. She employed a spell of uncontrollable lust against me, and was then caught in the backwash."

"Professional hazards," Jenny remarked.

"That's quite beside the point," Sir Remidan continued briskly. "Your young protégé has told me of your quest. I should be honored to accompany you on your noble mission."

Mira had to think about that for a long moment. Dooket and Erkin were glowering in the background; they obviously did not like the competition. At last she looked at the knight shrewdly. "This is a secret mission, you know. You'll have to leave your armor and that stupid-looking nag behind. We'll collect them on our way back."

"Under the circumstances, I quite forgive your insults," Staemar remarked. "In fact, I won't mind too much if you never come back, as long as I'm spared a trip to that place. I've heard that they're cannibals."

"The Alasherans are much too proud to eat horses," Mira told him. "I just don't know how I could explain having a horse on an airship. You've been here for two years, you say? Why didn't you eat that horse?"

Remidan shrugged. "Never had to."

The travelers found the early afternoon clouds very obliging, even if they did make for rough flying. The broken cover, only just beginning to build into afternoon storms, would allow *Wind Dragon* to arrive unannounced, or at least unseen long enough to land before the local authorities knew what to do about it. Mira firmly believed that it is far easier to get permission to do what you want if you first go ahead and do it, then ask politely. And she did not want to take the chance that they would be refused permission to land. Jenny privately thought that they were less likely to be attacked if they did not pop in upon the Alasherans as a complete surprise, but she kept that opinion to herself.

The clouds also presented them the excellent opportunity to set two of their numbers overboard with little risk of being seen. They were approaching the narrow, mountainous peninsula that separated the vast harbor of the city from the open sea to the northeast. Sir Remidan looked like he was beginning to regret his decision to accompany them. He was by no means afraid of the servants of the Dark, but it was rather beneath his dignity to pretend to be one of Mira's barbarian bodyguards . . . and even more so to have to dress the part. Even worse, he looked suspiciously like a knight of considerable reputation, dignity and rank pretending to be in disguise.

"Deucedly uncomfortable," he remarked to Jenny as they stood together on the helm deck. "Of course, it's hardly as bad as the time I spent six weeks in the port of Edigan, pretending to be a barmaid."

Jenny turned to stare at him. "A barmaid? How did that work out?"

"Quite well, actually," he explained. "I was too big to sit on anyone's lap, too damned ugly to make a proper whore, and I still made a tidy profit off the business in tips."

"Serving drinks?"

"No, I doubled as a bouncer. Of course, if I had been trying to make a living as a proper harlot, I should have starved."

"Well, we're all ready?" Mira asked as she bounced up the steps to join them. Kelvandor followed behind, bearing a small pack. "My good Sir Remidan, do join me over at the rail. I want to show you something."

"What is that?" Remidan asked suspiciously, confused and slightly reluctant. They leaned over the rail near the top of the steps Mira had just ascended. "What would you show me?"

"How to mind your own damned business and give Kelvandor a chance!" she hissed impatiently.

"Oh? . . . Oh!"

Kelvandor looked at the odd pair with some amusement, then turned back to Jenny. "It would be foolish of me to ask you to watch out for yourself. Just promise me that you'll watch out for the rest of this troupe of clowns."

Jenny tried to keep from laughing aloud; he was unaware of the inside joke. "I will do my best. We'll get back out of here just as quick as we can. I won't let Mira loiter.''

Jenny hesitated only a moment, then grabbed him around the neck and gave him the best kiss that he had had—at least from her—in some time. From a dragon's point of view, humans could not kiss worth a damn, but Kelvandor was not about to complain. She leaned close to his ear. ''When we leave here, then I'll have a real surprise for you.''

Kelvandor blinked. ''Sex?''

Mira kept Remidan looking over the rail until Vajerral came up on the helm deck to join them. She was already wearing one of the larger, heavier harnesses that faerie dragons used when transporting packs. Kelvandor began wiggling himself into his own, while Jenny stood ready to help him with the pack.

''We will stay as close as we dare, so that you can contact us when you need us,'' Kelvandor said as Mira and Jenny attached a large pack of supplies to the straps behind the saddle. He glanced at Jenny. ''Are you certain that you have that much power?''

''From that distance, I could talk to almost anyone,'' she assured him.

A moment later the airship slipped into the clouds. Lady Mira looked around, then gave the dragon a firm swat on his rump. ''Get yourselves overboard, and be quick about it. And be careful!''

''Right, Mom!'' Kelvandor agreed with raw mischief as he thrust himself up and over the rail, disappearing almost instantly into the thick, grey fog.

''I am not your mother!'' Mira shouted after him, rushing to the rail. She sighed heavily. ''So I'm a dragon's mother. Wonderful thing, being a mother.''

Vajerral stepped forward quickly, placing a reassuring hand on Jenny's shoulder. The young dragon looked very somber. ''Please be very, very careful. Remember what your life means to the fulfillment of the Prophecy, and what the servants of the Dark would do to you if you were again in their power. And remember also how I would grieve should anything happen to you.''

''I'll remember,'' Jenny insisted. ''Thank you for everything, especially for your understanding and good wishes.''

Vajerral smiled and clasped her hands firmly, then turned and leaped over the rail to disappear quickly into the clouds. Jenny returned to the wheels and quickly checked their course. Lady

Mira had already hurried to the front edge of the helm deck. "Boys!"

"Yes, Lady Mira?" Dooket and Erkin responded instantly, looking up from their work.

"We'll be landing in a matter of minutes," she told them. "Get all the spelled weapons and all the exploding bolts for the catapults into the hidden storage lockers. I've opened them for you."

"Right, Mom!" They agreed eagerly. Mira flinched, and thought that the barbarians listened to more than was good for them.

Wind Dragon dropped down from the dark clouds into the bright afternoon sunlight, bold as brass as she ran at almost full speed, her skids barely skimming the bobbing waves. Round-bellied merchant ships crept in and out of port amid the vast bulks of Imperial wargalleys, their hulls ornately carved and decorated with lavish designs and with two and three full decks of long, slender oars stroking the waves. *Wind Dragon* was a gaudy little thing, with her blue-and-red-striped vanes and stabilizers, although far short of the blatant, even intimidating ostentation of the Imperial vessels. But she was undeniably the center of attention as Jenny, at Mira's direction, took the little ship right through the middle of the harbor, fleetly dodging in and out between the larger oceangoing ships.

Alashera lay cradled in the protective arms of two long folds that reached out from the towering slopes of Mount Drashand, framing either side of the broad harbor. The city itself seemed to be built upon a successive series of irregular shelves, each one reaching back, shorter and shallower, until they filled the long, narrow triangle formed by the branching of the two towering ridges. Fields and pastures crowded tightly where they could in the rugged lower slopes to either side of the city while terraced vineyards clung stubbornly to the more treacherous slopes. The smoking cone of Mount Drashand stood in brooding challenge directly behind the city, her head lifted a mile and more into the clouds and crowned with her own billowing steam. And yet she was only a fraction of the size of the original volcano that had once risen in the dim, unremembered past and then destroyed itself in some incredible violence, leaving only the broken ring of her lower slopes which now enclosed the broad, deep harbor.

The great city itself lay open in the full radiance of the afternoon sun, as if the fitful thunderstorms which chased about the lower slopes deferred grudgingly to some royal person, not daring to darken her skies or hide her overt splendor from the world. Every building seemed a palace of white marble and bright gold, vast and shining and tastefully immaculate. Alashera was a city of immeasurable wealth, and the inhabitants wanted there to be no mistake about either the riches at their command or their willingness to possess the very best.

"Great stars, do they charge admission to this place?" Lady Mira asked breathlessly, awed by garish pretentiousness beyond her fondest dreams. "Our dear Addena's descriptions hardly begin to do it justice . . . as if mere words would ever suffice."

Jenny quietly bit her tongue.

"And to think that all of this is wasted upon such generally rotten people," the sorceress continued, and consulted the rude map of the city that Addena Sheld had somehow procured. "Straight up the middle of town to that shelf where the two branches of the hills join. That's supposed to be the new Imperial palace, and the Temple of the Dark is built into the mountainside below."

Jenny was concerned about being shot at, although Mira was not. As she explained, the Alasherans were unlikely to shoot arrows or catapults of any type over their own city. Not for fear of danger to the populace; followers of the Dark considered life to be the cheapest and most easily replenished of commodities. But they did have a high respect for property, at least their own, or anyone else's which could be made their own. They kept a fastidiously tidy community.

Whether Lady Mira's strategies had any effect or not, they climbed street by street toward the back of the city and reached the Imperial palace unmolested. She was determined that they should proceed straight to the palace and present themselves to the highest possible authority. Working their way through the rat's maze of local bureaucracy would have taken more time than they could spare, with no assurance that they would ever come anywhere near the top. Jenny had to agree; she did not have to like it.

The Imperial palace was a long, rambling structure in white and grey marble that stretched along the shelf formed by a crescent-shaped cup in a rather steep section of the hillside. There was no apparent form or logic to its construction, just an ill-assembled string of halls, chambers and wide-stepped entrances which enclosed various paved courts and meticulously manicured lawns. Mira referred to it as two wings in search of a building, and its aimless wanderings amounted to nothing more. It was all shiny new with scattered portions still under construction, which was the case with much of this bright, clean city. The only point of real interest to be seen from outside was the fact that much of the central portion appeared to be built into the cliff face itself, as if the edifice followed unknown ways underground.

If Mira was tempted to land *Wind Dragon* on the pale grey flagstones of the court below the wide steps of the main entrance, she restrained her impulse and directed Jenny to a rather plain little stretch of pavement to one side. Not too far to one side, of course. The sorceress wanted it plain that she expected to be treated as an honored guest, with all rights and privileges, not as a servant at the back door. She also had the Trassek twins taking in the vanes and stabilizers the moment they were on the ground, making it plain that she had no intention of leaving until she was good and ready.

"Here they come," Mira warned softly. "Leave everything to me."

Jenny refrained from remarking that she had little choice in the matter. A rather small squad of soldiers, not more than an even dozen, were marching in glittering formation toward the little ship. They were immaculate in ornate armor and brightly dyed leathers which seemed more like costumes from the distant past than modern uniforms. The twins spared them one amused glance before returning to their work; honest barbarians were far more efficient in a fight, although barbarians had seldom won wars.

An official of some undeterminable rank, although certainly not military, trotted along behind this tasteful vanguard. He wore a rich, fashionably cut version of what seemed the local costume, as if the loose, flowing togas of ancient Alashera had been shortened into some manner of oversized tunic and coupled with loose-fitting trousers of the same light material and bright colors. And he was very young, no older than Jenny, tall and thin, although he conducted himself in a very deliberate manner calculated to make him seem older, an air of experience and stern authority so forced that it betrayed its own falseness.

The guards arranged themselves in two widely spaced lines to either side of an imaginary aisle leading from *Wind Dragon*'s boarding ladder and the boy official took his place at the far end.

Mira made some expression of minor surprise which Jenny chose not to try to interpret. It seemed that this was an honor guard to extend formal welcome, not a detail to dispatch trespassers. The Empire, it seemed, extended almost disdainful greetings to a pair of wandering sorceresses.

"Lady Mira, of the *Wind Dragon* out of Bennasport. Permission to come aboard is granted." The sorceress introduced herself formally. She was forcing the local authority to make the first move by having its young representative meet her in her own territory, stating his own position before she parted from the relative safety of her ship.

The young emissary seemed to pause only a moment, no obvious thoughts or emotions disturbing the practiced sternness of his features, then started up the ramp in his usual businesslike manner. Mira glanced at her student, with a quick petition to that nameless spirit of good fortune with the quirky sense of humor who watched over her that the girl would be attentive.

He took one step onto the deck and stood his ground, looking down his long nose at Mira as if using that instrument for sighting his target. "Lady Mira, I am Chancellor Ellon Bennisjen, representing the government of the Alasheran Empire. I bid you welcome to our land, although, as you are a foreigner, I must inquire as to your business."

"Scholarly research," Mira answered without a pause. "Surely not a matter to concern the Empire itself."

"It became the business of the Empire when you landed your ship almost on the doorstep of the Imperial palace," Ellon answered smoothly, although Mira had noticed that his diplomatic manners were rough and awkward. "Is the nature of your research mundane or arcane?"

"Purely mundane," she assured him. "I have been researching the theory that major climatic changes have occurred in the course of recorded history. My student and I have been collecting data from old records from a great many sources, and our search has now led us southward."

"Indeed?" the young chancellor remarked thoughtfully; at least he could figure out for himself what old records had to do with climatic changes. "And I take it that your search has led you to the Imperial Archives?"

"It has indeed," Mira agreed eagerly, and began rubbing in the soothing balm of flattery. "I need records not just from the longest possible period of time but from the widest possible sources. My research in the South quite naturally begins here, in this the oldest and grandest of civilizations. The Empire of ancient days was flourishing long before there even was a North, and it controlled the known world for many thousands of years. I also suspect the present Empire has tremendous access to a variety of resources.''

"Quite logical, of course," he agreed sagely, complimenting her in a condescending manner for arriving at what was to him a self-evident conclusion. "You must first, of course, petition your request to the proper authorities. If you will follow me, we'll see to that immediately."

The little procession of decorative warriors packed itself up without a word and reversed course, this time with the two sorceresses and their own small troop of guards following dutifully behind. The procession entered the Imperial palace through one of the nearer doors and made its way through the seemingly endless series of halls and foyers. The palace was in a far less advanced state of construction on the inside, revealing that much of the exterior was only an ornate shell. Even the finished portions near the center had the look of an empty house, with few furnishings and fewer inhabitants. The rhythmic tread of the honor guard echoed loudly through the polished stone corridors. Mira was constantly finding herself unconsciously falling into time with their step, much to her annoyance.

The honor guard went its own way at last, and the visitors found themselves deposited in a large and rather stately lobby with the polite request that they wait just a few minutes. Chancellor Ellon disappeared through the largest and most ornately carved of a handful of dark wooden doors, having announced himself to the young officer in decorative armor who served as some manner of secretary.

"So, what do you think?" Lady Mira asked as she seated herself on a short sofa well away from any of the doors.

"I'm not sure what to think," Jenny answered as she brushed impatiently at the thick layer of grey dust that had accumulated on the bench. Dust from the construction was settling faster than it could be cleaned away. "Chancellor Ellon is not telling us the truth by half. What is a chancellor, anyway?"

"By Imperial usage, he's the private secretary to some official of high rank."

Jenny nodded. "That makes sense. He's not taken us to the 'appropriate authorities,' as he said, but to his own immediate superior."

"I anticipated that already."

"In answer to your second question, Ellon himself does not know what to believe about your story of scholarly research," Jenny continued. "Both he and his master consider it likely that you are here for clandestine reasons of your own. They also believe that you are no match for them, that they will have some sport at your expense and that you will be sent home emptyhanded, frustrated and embarrassed. And don't ask how I knew what your second question would be."

"I already know the answer to that," Mira remarked.

"I know that you know. To answer your third question, they did not know you were coming until we arrived over the harbor. A description of your ship was transferred quickly, and whoever waits on the other side of that door recognized *Wind Dragon* from past experience. A small group of soldiers is already giving *Wind Dragon* a quick inspection, but they don't seem likely to discover anything we have hidden. J.T. is watching them closely."

"Well, so much for questions four and five." Mira frowned. "You seem to be in rare form today. But . . ."

"I don't know for certain, but here he comes," Jenny warned softly as the door opened.

Dasjen Valdercon was perhaps the last person Mira wanted to see walk through that door. But when she looked up, her inner hunch warning her too late who it would be, that was exactly who she saw, as big as life. He was a typical Southerner, tall and lean but far from gaunt, with long black hair streaked with grey, and just as handsome as on that last night they had spent together amid the golden canals of the port of Serras. That was a time that was now eight years past; a hundred years in terms of her own busy life. But she feared him just as much as she had then, ten times as much to see him standing in quiet authority in this place. And his cold, dark eyes still awakened in her that same raw, animal lust.

A great many things could tickle her animal lust.

"Sorceress Kasdamir! So it is you!" he exclaimed with gentle delight as he executed a courtly bow and kissed her hand. He had always called her by her full name; he knew how she hated it. "Sweet lady, it is so good to see you again."

Jenny stared at first one and then the other, then crossed her arms and sat back in her seat with an exasperated sigh.

"Dasjen, I hardly expected to find you here." Mira retreated into flustered confusion to give herself a moment to think—and to do a little digging. "So what are you up to these days? Court magician for the new Emperor?"

Dasjen laughed politely. "Imperial secretary of magical training and research is my full title, which indicates that I am expected to provide an actual service for my keep and not just entertainment."

"That does sound very important," she observed, looking as impressed as she dared. "You must be very close to the Emperor's ear."

"You will find this a very practical Empire," he assured her importantly; he even bragged romantically. "We have the saying here, that the military is the right hand of the Empire, magic and science are the left, and that it walks in the boots of trade. You will find that we conduct all necessary business with efficiency and quiet dispatch; it leaves more time for more important affairs."

Do you have an affair in mind? Mira wanted to ask. But her first question was already answered beyond any doubt; Dasjen Valdercon was the same person she had always known. They were very much alike in curiosity, learning and their command of magic, but in other ways they were opposites. However mercenary she claimed to be, she treated her own magic as a tool to help and serve others; he considered it a key to wealth and power. She did not wonder that he had ended up here, she only wondered why he had to comprise her reception committee. That quirky spirit of fortune might be letting her down.

"My young assistant tells me that you are studying long-term changes in weather patterns," he continued, and chuckled to himself. "Still the same old Kasdamir. I always was amazed at the wide variety of subjects that could captivate your complete attention. Your wish is granted, dear lady. You may have use of the Imperial library. An assistant will be appointed to help you sift through that rather formidable mass of information."

"Thank you. I do appreciate it greatly."

"All the same, there is a small fee," Dasjen warned. "I ask only that you spare an old friend a few stray moments of your free time. If you and your fair companion . . ."

"Addena . . . Addena Kurgel," Jenny answered quickly, having

to dig for a false name in a very awkward moment. Her true name
was from off-world, and it would have betrayed her as quickly as
her blue hair, which Mira had spelled to deep black.

"I have planned a small gathering for this night," Dasjen continued without hesitation. "I would be honored if the two of you
could join me."

"We would be delighted," Mira answered graciously.

"Then I shall send for you at nightfall," He said. "But for
now, I fear that duty presses. My assistant will accompany you
to your ship, and you shall be shown to suites that we reserve for
honored guests."

Mira did not at all like being separated from *Wind Dragon*, but
she had anticipated that. J.T., who remained scrupulously silent
and acted as dumb as he looked, stayed on guard with the ship.
Remidan and the Trassek twins would remain with them, fulfilling
their roles as bodyguards. The Alasherans did not question that,
since personal guards attended all individuals of importance in
this land as a necessary precaution.

Apparently Valdercon had not exaggerated about their being
shown to suites of their own, or at least one suite of such enormous
proportions that there were apartments for each sorceress and even
a spacious chamber for their guards. It was all richly furnished in
light furnishings with flowing, transparent hangings which glided
over stone walls or rippled across wide windows, all in colors of
white or light pastels. Which was to say that it was hardly gaudy
enough to hold Mira's attention for long. But she was momentarily
impressed, at least.

"They reserve this room for uninvited guests?" she asked as
she stood in the center of the room, looking about. She shrugged.
"This must be the off season."

"You knew this Dasjen Valdercon before?" Jenny inquired.

Mira stopped short, looking about suspiciously. "Is it safe to
talk?"

"I sense no one near, and no magical devices in this suite."

"You are handy," Mira remarked, and attended her luggage.
"Yes, I knew him well enough, eight years ago in Serras. I knew
that he was leaning toward the Dark then. We played a game, he
and I, more dangerous perhaps than I was aware at the time. I
know that he plotted my own corruption at the time, but I felt
secure that I was in control . . . at least of myself. But he knew
the lust he stirred within me, and he could have used that as a

weapon to break my defenses. I would not dare to go to bed with him again. Our stay must be as short as possible.''

"Just how high do you suppose he is in the Imperial hierarchy?''

"He actually avoided answering that question, as much as he pretended to brag,'' she observed as she carried her bags into her room, leaving Jenny to follow. She carelessly tossed the bags onto the vast bed. "He is very high in the Dark Priesthood, I am sure of that. What impressions did you get?''

"That the Emperor is still absent, and that he is relaying his master's orders in that absence,'' Jenny answered, crossing her arms. "He is far more dangerous than you realize even yet, Lady Mira. Be very careful of him. He is, at this time, the most evil and dangerous man in this entire world.''

"I don't like the way he looks at you,'' Sir Remidan growled.

Mira turned to stare at him. "Why, Remidan! I didn't know you cared.''

"Well, I have to, don't I?'' he asked. "I've taken oaths to that effect, and all that rot.''

Jenny peered at him surreptitiously, wondering if he was secretly smitten by more than just knightly oaths. There were knights and then there were nights, and this knight might be interested in working nights. Whether he knew it or not. It seemed that life was full of people who had no idea what they were doing.

Mira blinked, then looked at her student thoughtfully. "I forget that you have met the Emperor and the High Priest before. Would you know them, or sense their presence, if they were here?''

"That was long ago and I remember nothing clearly, but I'm sure that I would know them on sight, whatever form they wear now,'' Jenny insisted. "The Emperor may be the same as he was then; I do not know, for he looked very old and corrupt then. The last I saw of the High Priest Haldephren, he was in the body of a faerie dragon. But Dalvenjah insists that she destroyed that body thirteen years ago. He's most likely in human form again this time, but I will know him when I see him.''

Both sorceresses had the same impression the moment they stepped into the room. It was full of young, beautiful people richly dressed in Imperial fashion, the short togas and pants such as the men wore and women in gownlike togas which left at least one breast bare. They moved with calculated grace and elegance, self-superior and languidly calm. And they were deadly evil, each and every one faithful and favored servants of the Dark. They were, by all appearances, the Imperial court. Or perhaps the lackeys of the High Priest, who was very conscious of his attendant admirers while the Emperor himself was cautious and allowed as few as possible in his presence as he could help. But in the absence of their true masters, they were clearly performing for the favor of Dasjen Valdercon.

"They really have put on the dog," Jenny remarked softly.

Mira made a face of disgust. "My stars! I certainly hope not!"

Not all were professional lackeys; out of perhaps three score gathered at the single long table, there were two dozen older men and women who were themselves ministers. But that appeared to be the full tally of the true Imperial government; the Senate was a body of limited power, but it was not currently in session and its members were mostly away at home. The ministers were the hands and voices of the Emperor, who shared his authority grudgingly, and they all seemed to look to Valdercon for leadership. They were all so quiet, clam and circumspect that the young lackeys overshadowed their presence entirely.

Valdercon himself sat at the head of the table; he had met his two visitors at the door and had conducted them to places of honor, Lady Mira at his left hand with Jenny at his right. The younger sorceress was dressed in the local manner in a long, draped gown of light, frosty blue that had been brought to her room. The color was not her best but she looked astonishingly beautiful in it all the same, with her temporarily black hair brushed full and loose. She copied the manner of the young courtiers but on her own terms, calm and graceful but with an inner nobility and purity that made her shine all the brighter among the shadows of these servants of the Dark.

All the same, she had to wonder what her mother would think if she saw her dressed this way. Jenny was doing a lot of things these days that her mother would surely feel better not knowing about.

Mira was surprised and proud of her protégé, although she tried to hide that in their present company. The girl clearly possessed a radiant charm and beauty which she preferred to keep hidden, for she seemed to reflect the immortal side of her nature that she had inherited from her magical training, like some elfin princess. Mira herself made no compromise; she was her usual gaudy self, dressed in some barbarian robe of brightly woven pattern, red silk pants and high-heeled sandals. Unlike her student, she had no intention of baring a breast in deference to local taste. As it was, they made a team who complemented each other well in incongruity.

"You look as radiant as ever," Dasjen told her earnestly. His eye wanted to rove in Jenny's direction, but he kept his attention studiously focused on his former lover. "Almost one would think that the years could not touch you."

"Oh, you are kind," Mira insisted. "Actually, those last few years and I have been at odds for some time now. They say that they're going to come back some day with a few more of their brothers and give it to me good."

Jenny bit her tongue. Dasjen Valdercon appeared to appreciate Mira's humor, but the others—who had been sitting silently with their ears cocked in that direction like a roomful of cats—hardly knew what to make of that. Jenny thought that if they did indulge in humor, it would be something much more biting, perhaps turned against others but never themselves.

"You people are very busy here," Mira continued as she studied her plate, attempting to make some sense of what it was or how it had been cooked. "I don't know when I've seen such industry."

"This is a busy time for us," Valdercon answered. "We try to get most of the construction done when the Senate is not in session. You see gathered at this table almost all that remains of the Imperial government, for now and for some months yet to come."

"I assume that the Emperor himself has already departed to some retreat for the season," Mira observed with casual innocence.

"You assume correctly," Dasjen answered guardedly.

"Such a shame. I had rather hoped to catch just a glimpse of him, but I certainly did not expect it. I'm sure that he has no time to spare for unexpected guests."

"Oh, I am remiss!" Dasjen exclaimed suddenly. "Lady Kaslamir Gerran and Sorceress Addena Kurgel, may I present Korin Sjeldisan, Lord Minister of the Imperial Navy, and Leridae Felde, Lady Manager of the City of Alashera."

The pair of older officials bowed their heads in polite greeting; Mira was beginning to think that these Southerners must age like granite. She thought that Lord Korin, seated to her left, must be well into his sixties, but like Dasjen he remained handsome, lean and strong, a barrel-chested bull of a man. And Lady Leridae, seated to the other side of Jenny, was at least ten years older than herself, but was slim and shapely in a flowing rose gown which discreetly revealed one breast that remained defiantly firm. Magic could cure a great many sins, even gravity. But neither made any attempt to hide the grey advancing in their hair; indeed, it only served to emphasize their remarkable conditions.

"Yours is a most beautiful little ship," Lord Korin remarked graciously.

"Oh, thank you," Mira responded, flattered. She considered asking if the Imperial Navy was contemplating the use of airships but thought better of it. "I did see the most lovely and impressive galleys as we came in over the harbor. It goes without saying that your new ships are larger, faster and more efficient than the wargalleys of ancient days."

"Oh, quite," he answered, obviously careful of the content of his own replies. "Our modern ships can sail in one day what the ancient wargalleys sailed in a week. And most have iron frames and ribs."

"Sorceress Addena, are you of the South?" Lady Leridae inquired, pointedly changing the subject.

"Oh, no. This is my first journey South," Jenny answered a little belatedly, realizing that the woman was speaking to her.

"I've been in the South many times," Mira said quickly, fending off the subject. "I grew up in the circus."

"The circus, did you say?" Korin was astonished and perplexed; he must be of the local nobility. "What ever did you do in the circus?"

"I'm a midget."

"Oh, I see," Korin said thoughtfully; he obviously did not.

At that moment the handful of musicians who had silently filed into the room began to tune. One frail young musician gave his recorder a loud squawk, as if to clear it of cobwebs, not six feet behind Mira's unsuspecting ear.

"Yarg!" She jumped in fright, and her fork and knife were sent sailing before the eyes of the courtiers. Jenny snatched the fork out of the air deftly, but the knife stuck point-first in the table not two inches from Lady Leridae's hand. Mira had already leaped out of her seat and drawn her sword—she alone at the table was armed—and she seemed about to come to blows with the frightened minstrels. One stout fellow seemed prepared to fend her off with the bow of his viola.

"Oh, mercy!" Dasjen muttered in disgust, rolling his eyes and shaking his head slowly. He made an impatient gesture. "You musicians please remove yourselves somewhat and be about your business. Bring more wine."

Looking like a cat with ruffled fur, Mira waited as Lord Korin recovered her upset chair and assisted her in taking her seat. Jenny quietly returned the fork and knife; Leridae, wide-eyed, was still rubbing her hand as if she had indeed taken a wound. Naked, dark-skinned girls hurried to serve wine to the speechless company.

"Sorry about that," Mira said, but she did not appear at all apologetic. "I just cannot abide people sneaking up behind me."

Jenny had long since figured out her mistress's game. These people were the barbarians trying to mimic genteel manners, but for all their wealth and fine trappings, their nature was betrayed by the bare-breasted gowns of the women, the young, naked servants—male and female—and the generally disorganized atmosphere of this entire gathering. In the court of Queen Merridyn, dinner guests would not have been left to seat themselves in a haphazard manner, nor would musicians have filed in late to begin tuning after the guests were seated. But Mira pretended to be the violent, ill-mannered barbarian, allowing them the luxury of feeling superior and putting them off their guard.

Jenny saw her own part to play, as her mistress's shy, simple student. When handing back the knife, she leaned just a little too far across the wide table.

"Thank you, dear child," Mira said tightly, ignoring for the moment the mess Jenny had made. She turned to Dasjen. "I don't want to make a mess of your little supper. It reminds me of the time that we were traveling in the wilds of the arctic wastes. We lost our corkscrew and were forced to live on food and water for several weeks."

Dasjen chuckled softly. "Kasdamir, you always were such a wit. But I do not recall you drinking anything stronger than tea."

"You never caught me, you mean," she answered, then glanced at Jenny and made a half-hearted gesture, as if trying to be discreet. "Clean yourself up, dear child."

"Oh, my!" Jenny permitted herself a healthy blush. In leaning well over her plate, she had acquired a large glob of some thick, yellow sauce directly on her bare nipple. She dipped her napkin in her water glass and, taking firm hold of her breast, proceeded to clean it.

"Well, yes," Dasjen shifted nervously in his chair, trying not to stare. No one else made that effort. "Ah . . . so, what do you think of our city?"

"Has all this work been done in the last few years?" Mira asked in turn.

"Beginning ten years ago, the old town was systematically leveled and rebuilt," Lady Leridae answered with a practiced recitation after a quick glance at Dasjen for permission. This obviously was no secret. "The work continues at a furious pace, but for the last six years all work has left the confines of the original town and spread into the surrounding hills. Trade is flourishing throughout the Kingdoms of the Sea due to the introduction of modern technology, contemporary magical practices and improved agricultural methods. And Alashera is now, as it was in ancient days, the hub of every major trade route. It is only logical that Alashera should become the capital of commerce and government throughout the South."

"I see," Mira said thoughtfully. Will there be a test after dinner? "You are catching up with the North in a hurry."

"We feel that we are on the verge of surpassing the North," Dasjen himself answered, very serious now. "That is no threat or boast, but a logical prediction of what must be. Elura has the benefit of wood and coal, diverse ores and diverse other resources, and the North shall forever remain strong and prosperous because of that. But the North is also cold and mountainous. Trade between cities is restricted to certain months when the passes are navigable by wagon, and agriculture is even more limited. We foresee that the North shall supply resources to the South at a furious rate in the warmer months, to be stockpiled so that industry may remain at full strength year round."

"Yes, there is some logic in that," Mira admitted. "Except for one valid point. The North has been mass-producing airships for some time, freighters to rival an oceangoing vessel for size and speed, but several times as fast. Ships that are capable of delivering their cargo direct, rather than at some waterfront warehouse of a seacoast town. The strength of the South may be in ocean vessels, but the North has the strength of airships."

"Airship transportation will not endure," Korin told her in a condescending manner, smiling at obvious foolishness. "You people have been very lucky so far, but you will soon learn the hard way that airships are unsafe, unreliable and inefficient."

Dinner ended soon after, and the gathering moved outside to a large moonlit terrace for late-night conversation and dancing to the gentle music of the small band of musicians. This was not a good strategic move for Jenny, since that left her at the mercy of the attentions of Dasjen's young assistant Ellon. She countered this threat by staying well out in the open, between the table of refreshments and the small, bubbling fountain in the center of the terrace. She knew that it would hardly be beneficial to their cause it she was to break Ellon's arm, as much as she was tempted. The dress was something of a hazard in itself; Ellon's hand seemed to have a mind of its own. She decided that if he did make a grab at her bust, she was going to bust him.

Mira tried to keep a protective eye on her young student, but she had her hands full with Dasjen—mostly because he often had a handful of her. These people were not discreet.

"It was the fair goddess Fortune herself who bought you to us," Dasjen said as he brought her another drink. That seemed to be his tactic for the night: imbibe and conquer. He was unaware that she could drink a pirate under the table. "That, and overwhelming curiosity."

Mira smiled at him, feigning ignorance. "Actually, it was my pretty little airship."

Dasjen laughed. "Lady Kasdamir Gerran, you are a sorceress of many arts and talents, but subtlety is not one of your stronger points. You surely know your history. The Alasheran Empire of two thousand years ago belonged to the Dark. You, and every sorcerer of the North, wonders if our new Empire belongs to the Dark as well. That, I suspect, is your true business here."

"Yes, that is the big question over cocktails these days," Mira admitted cautiously, and drained her glass.

"Then you will be answered," he told her. There was not, nor had there been, any hint of threat in his voice. Only amusement. "We inherit many of our ways and manners from the ancient days. You may have heard that we have opened the games. That is so, but they are a tame shadow of the barbarity of olden times. Our servants are naked, and even our beautiful ladies of the Imperial court bare their breasts. Your own student does not hesitate to do the same. This is not decadence, only an expression of our deep appreciation of all things that are beautiful in life and nature.

"Our Empire is based upon industry and commerce, not conquest and slavery. Wargalleys fill our port, but they prey only upon the pirates of the petty kingdoms, further opening fair and honest trade and travel. We build our homes like palaces, but because we would leave something of lasting beauty to our descendants for many generations to come. There was much that was good in the ancient Empire, but much that was evil. We eagerly reawaken all that was good, but we shun the evil just as surely as you good people of the North. No, we are not of the Dark. And we welcome this opportunity to prove ourselves."

Mira was impressed; she knew that he was lying a greasy streak, but he did it most eloquently. She bowed her head slightly. "If you would, many minds would be set to ease."

"Beginning with your own," he said, smiling warmly and reassuringly, and he gently took her hand. "You shall stay here as long as you like, and you are free to go wherever you like. We have no secrets, and we will do whatever you request to prove that."

Mira excused herself as soon as she could with the claim for an early bed after a long day. Dasjen clearly wanted to volunteer his own bed to this worthy cause, but Mira made a hasty retreat. She snatched her student from the jaws of licentiousness and they made a hasty retreat to their rooms.

"I noticed that you declined to dance with Ellon," Mira observed.

"My mother always told me never to dance with my tits hanging out," Jenny answered. "I'm sure that she had something else in mind, but it seemed to apply to these circumstances."

"Perhaps this won't take much longer," Mira said. "I think that you should sneak out tonight and find those dragons of yours. I'd like to know what they've turned up. Let's hurry, now. Sir Remidan will be fretting so."

• Part Seven •

Local Intrigues

LATER THAT NIGHT, a short time after Jenny had gone to bed, she quietly rose again and, without summoning a light, slipped out the window. Her room was three levels above the hard stone walkway below, and that had perhaps been meant to discourage guests from departing in this manner. But that was of no consequence to Jenny. When she leaped out the window, she went up.

Fearing guards below, she moved stealthfully along the edge of the roof until she came to a place where a large tree, growing near the side of the building, offered her some concealment in its welcoming shadows. She leaped from the roof and hurtled across a hundred feet of open air, landing softly close to the massive trunk. She looked about for guards, then hurried through the landscaped grounds of the Imperial palace. Her enhanced vision found her path easily through the protective shadows of trees and shrubs, her bare feet making scarcely a sound on grass or smooth stone, and her lanky body was clad in loose, dark pants and shirt to hide her in the night.

When she came to the edge of the grounds, well to the north where the steep, rugged mountainside encroached, she thrust herself into the night sky and over the wall, coming down in the street beyond. She moved as cautiously as she could, keeping to

uninhabited ways as she hurried through the remote edge of the
city. The buildings, mostly two- and three-story shops, were dark
and silent.

As she worked her way through the long, deep shadows that
filled the streets, the thought of Karidaejan's warning was very
much on her mind. She had given it little thought at first. It had
seemed inconceivable that any of her companions would betray
her, and she had not been in the mood to hear any more prophecies
from the mouths of secretive dragons.

But now she was not so sure. Mira seemed quietly fascinated
with this Dasjen Valdercon, and the two of them had apparently
spent some time together not so many years past. But Dasjen had
a secret only Jenny knew, although she had to think that anyone
who knew him as well as Mira claimed to would also have to
suspect it. Jenny was still not prepared to consider the idea that
Mira would deliberately betray them to their enemies. But she
was not so certain about what Mira might inadvertently do in this
distracted state. Mira was many things, but she was not a cautious
person. Karidaejan had not said that the betrayal would be deliberate.

But he had also ·insisted that the betrayer would be the last
person Jenny would suspect. Mira was at the top of the suspicion
list, which made her the first rather than the last person Jenny
suspected. Who, then? Sir Remidan lived for honor and duty, but
Jenny also considered him quite capable of doing something stupid. The twins were unlikely to spontaneously do anything of any
consequence in their entire lives, good or bad. The two dragons
would willingly give their lives to defend Jenny or the Prophecy,
which probably sent them to the top of the list of least likely.

Jenny paused at the approaching sound of heavy boots on the
flat stones that paved the streets, aware that she had been inattentive. She backed into the shadows of a doorway of one shop,
peering out into the light. The yellow glare of an oil lantern
appeared around the next corner, behind it the black silhouettes
of a patrol of three soldiers. With nowhere else to run, Jenny
turned her attention to spelling open the lock of the door, then
slipped inside the shop. She locked the door again for good measure, remembering from an old movie that policemen were supposed to check the locks of the shops on their beat, then crouched
in the shadows until they were past.

Jenny remained in hiding for more than a minute longer, giving the patrol plenty of time to clear the immediate area. She finally returned to the door and was about to leave when she became aware that she was not alone. Something large was moving stealthfully down the narrow stairs in the far back corner of the room, and the presence she felt was definitely magical. Did the Alasherans release their demons into the streets at night to guard against spying sorceresses like herself? There was no time to wonder. Jenny looked around and found that she was in the front room of a bakery, complete with a stair-step of shelves before her stacked with cakes and pies.

Lacking alternatives, she chose the weapons that were at hand and picked up a large pie. She had always wanted to do this, and it seemed likely to provide enough distraction for her to get out of the shop. When a dark form appeared at the bottom of the steps, she hauled back and let fly.

The result was rather unexpected. The pie flew straight and true toward its target, the mushy side first. But about halfway through its trajectory, it was intercepted by a blast of magical flames. Where the flames would have deflected the pie from its dire course was never to be known, since it exploded. Sticky goop flew everywhere; Jenny was fortunate enough to have been hiding behind the shelves.

But there was something familiar about those flames, something that was not at all hard to place for someone who had grown up with dragons. She also knew better than to stand up, for fear that it was trigger-happy Vajerral.

"Yo, dragon!" she called in English, which should also help to establish her credentials. "Vajerral, is that you?"

"Jenny?"

It was indeed Vajerral. Jenny stood up. The young dragon was standing only a short distance away, with clumps of mutilated meringue and an extraordinarily surprised expression on her face.

"Well, fancy bumping into you," Vajerral remarked. "This might just be an exceptionally good time to get the hell out of here."

"I am with you," Jenny agreed, turning to the door.

A shout from the street sort of put an end to that idea. Jenny had no idea just what type of pie that had been, but it had certainly exploded with a great deal of enthusiasm. They were going to be open for business in a hurry.

"I came in through a door in the roof," Vajerral offered. "I think that I would like to leave the way I came.''

Vajerral declined to wait for an answer; she was already on her way up the stairs. In Jenny's experience, the young dragon was hardly ever right about anything and could generally be relied upon to exercise the most extraordinary bad judgment. This case seemed to be the exception. Jenny was only three steps behind.

''What are you doing here, anyway?'' she asked as she followed the dragon up the dark stairs. She could see nothing except a dim grey light far ahead, at least three stories.

''I was looking for you,'' Vajerral answered. ''What are you doing?''

''Looking for you.''

Vajerral stopped short on the stairs and bent her long neck to look back over her shoulder. ''We must stop meeting like this.''

''I ought to slay you!''

The dragon turned and hurried on. ''Watch out on the roof. It is steep, and the tiles are slick.''

Contrary to her own advice, Vajerral slipped out through the small doorway and stepped out onto the roof, and promptly lost it. Her legs flew out from under her in a rather interesting scrabble, and she tumbled the short distance down to the edge of the roof and away into the darkness of the narrow alley. Jenny observed the less than graceful execution of this maneuver, like a plane shot down the catapult of an aircraft carrier before its engines are running, and made a frantic grab at the only part of the dragon that lingered. Meaning, of course, the end of her long, slender tail.

Jenny braced herself, knowing what was to follow, and she was not wrong in her estimation. Vajerral was a small and rather slender dragon, but she was also well muscled from a very active life; she was still a strapping three hundred pounds. Jenny augmented her strength with magic, but it was traction that nearly got her. She slid down the roof and nearly went over the edge herself, saving herself at the last moment by sitting down hard. That left Vajerral swinging like a pendulum, while Jenny wondered how she would ever pick her nose if both of her arms were yanked off, and what would be the use of sleeves?

''Flap those wings, you rock-headed, lead-assed excuse for a dragon!'' she exclaimed.

''You should look at it from my point of view,'' Vajerral complained. She was head down, hanging in the dark by her tail, and she was wearing an expression that she saved for just such occasions.

All the same, it seemed like very sound advice. Vajerral managed to get her arms and legs braced against the wall, a move that nearly brought Jenny off the roof a second time, then lifted herself cautiously with long, powerful sweeps of her wings. She was rising slowly in a hover, a difficult feat for any dragon even with the aid of lift magic, and the results of that were just as disastrous. This time Jenny did come off the roof, a dead weight at the end of the dragon's tail . . . which was an unhandy place to put it. The two of them disappeared into the darkness of the alley.

Moments later, the pair of them shot out of the deeper shadows of the alley and disappeared into the night. Jenny had remembered, almost at the final instant, that she was able to fly using the same lift magic as the dragons possessed.

Keeping to the shadows, they made their way quickly outside the city and across the rugged slopes of the volcanic island to where the dragons had made their secluded camp. Kelvandor emerged from the shallow cave, hardly more than a deep overhang of rock, where they had taken shelter. His ears twitched with concern.

"So, you found her," he said.

"We found each other," Vajerral answered. "She was already on her way to find us."

"So? Why have you come?" Kelvandor asked. "Has there been trouble?"

"Nothing is wrong, really," she was quick to assure them. "Things go well, if hardly as expected. We were received as honored guests and treated like royalty. But the evil of that place . . ."

"Gently," Vajerral encouraged her. "What has happened? And speak the Mindijaran language, which no mortal of the Dark should understand."

"The Emperor and the High Priest are apparently absent, but we were met by this minister, Dasjen Valdercon," she continued in their own language. "He seems to be in charge. He is an old friend and former lover of Mira's. She says that she thought him of the Dark then. Everything went just fine through dinner. Later, Valdercon told us that he is aware that we are spies. He says that the Empire had nothing to hide, and he has challenged us to stay on as long as we want, until it is proven to our satisfaction that they are not of the Dark.''

''But we know they are,'' Vajerral remarked, laying back her ears. ''Do they think that they can pull that off?''

''They seem to think that they can, since so little of the Imperial government is present. Then we will be sent on our way, to spread the misconception that the Empire has no business with the Dark.''

''Then you are safe enough?'' Kelvandor insisted. ''Already you know that the true Emperor and High Priest are not present, do you not?''

''But that is the thing,'' Jenny explained fearfully. She looked up at the dragon anxiously. ''The High Priest Haldephren is here. I remember him from before, and I knew that I would recognize him if ever I saw him, whatever form he wears. There is no question in my mind. Haldephren is masquerading as Dasjen Valdercon, pretending to be his own servant.''

''Does he recognize you as well?'' Vajerral asked sternly. She had no intention of permitting Jenny to return to the palace if it meant that she could be identified and captured by the High Priest.

''I really don't know. His mind is closed to me, but not his strongest emotions. If he has recognized me for who I am, he did not betray himself with delight or pleasure. And yet I could sense his pleasure with the ruse he thinks to perpetrate on Lady Mira. I sense his lust for her as well. And his lust for me is blatant.

''This is the very part that worries me,'' she continued, and frowned. ''I am afraid that Mira may be, shall we say, quite smitten with Dasjen. She has no idea who he really is, but she is definitely captivated by his charm. Mira is, in many ways, a rather unsophisticated person, and she might not see that he knows how best to manipulate her. Frankly, I do not trust her to be logical even if she did know the danger.''

She started to tell them of Karidaejan and his warning, but she thought it best to keep that secret for just a little longer. The two dragons were likely to take the cautious approach and refuse to allow her to return, leaving Mira, Remidan and the boys to save themselves. She felt a moment of guilt, knowing how annoyed she was when the dragons kept their secrets from her. But this was different.

Vajerral turned to Kelvandor. ''The map.''

The male dragon nodded once and came forward to spread a large map atop the slight curve of a low, flat boulder. Vajerral

summoned the merest fragment of light, enough for the keen eyes
of the dragons to see it clearly.

"We have been busy ourselves," Kelvandor said, indicating
the map. "The Empire must have a healthy respect for either
airships or Mindijaran, for there are many things hidden on this
island, not to be seen easily from the air. We have found them
easily enough all the same.

"Look at this. The Empire makes no effort to hide the might
of its traditional navy, and seems inordinately proud of its wargalleys. The things are worthless, easy prey to the dropping of
explosives from high above. But here, a quarter of the way around
the coast, is a great holding of airships of many types, and most
appear to be quite new. We suspect that the Empire is building
its own."

"How are they hidden?" Jenny asked.

"Vineyards," he explained. "There are vast trenches beneath,
and great racks bearing vines that can be pulled away. I do not
know if there is ever a true frost here, but the vines are rather
thin all the same. But we have yet to find what we think to be the
construction yards for airships here on this island."

"They do not seem to be using these ships?" Jenny asked.

"No. All are sleek military ships, and all are kept in waiting,"
Vajerral said. "Remember this place well, and avoid it. Do not
seek their secrets too hard and ignore what you may see, or they
cannot allow you to leave."

"Play stupid?" Mira asked when Jenny conveyed that warning
the next morning. "I don't know if I can play stupid. I am not
naturally equipped. But I agree with the dragons. The plans have
changed. They can do the spying, if we do nothing else but keep
our hosts occupied."

Jenny said nothing. She had discussed the subject with Vajerral
for some time, and they had decided not to warn Mira that Dasjen
Valdercon was in truth the High Priest. They both agreed that
Lady Mira might be a sorceress of many talents, but she was a
poor actress. They also wanted to have her well away before she
learned that she had once been the lover of Haldephren himself.

Jenny had so many secrets going at once, she was beginning
to think that she would make a very good dragon.

"So we just let them give us the grand tour until the dragons
are finished with their spying, then we make a glorious exit ex-

tolling their many virtues," Mira continued, and turned. Jenny was still arranging the elaborate folds of a local gown, one of several more gifts that had arrived with their breakfast. She must have made some impression; four of the five left both breasts bare. Not to disappoint her hosts, she wore the least conspicuous of those four, a rose-colored gown. Mira nodded. "You do look grand. I admire your nerve."

"You would be a real distraction in the blue one," Jenny answered.

Mira chose to ignore that.

"Saint Gurn protect us!" J.T. declared as he leaped up on the bed. Dooket had been sent to the ship early to "check on the cat," and to bear the message that J.T. was wanted. He had eaten at his leisure, given himself a spit bath, and made his way unobtrusively into the palace. Jenny glared at him; Gurn was the patron saint of whores. Then she hurried to complete her makeup; another morning's gift. She had wore none the night before, nor did she require any.

"You behave yourself or I'll have you neutered," Mira told him sternly. "I want you to hang around the palace all day and be a cat. Sir Remidan and the twins will watch the ship today; they can keep themselves busy in our absence."

J.T. cocked his head inquisitively. "What do you mean, be a cat? Do you suggest that I poke my little button nose in all the back rooms and corridors, where you cannot?"

"Precisely," she agreed. "If they are worshipping the Dark, and we know they are, then there will be a temple somewhere."

"Where should I look?"

"In ancient days, the Great Temple of the Dark was inside Mount Drashand itself, and a passage connected it with the Imperial palace. I don't know if the present palace is in the same location, but you can bet that they've reopened the Great Temple. If we cannot find a passage from here, the dragons are going to have to hunt for it down the neck of the volcano itself."

"Got you! Anything else?"

"Do you speak the local language?" J.T. tried to make a face, but cats are impeded by their lack of brows. Mira took that for a no. "Be on your way, then."

J.T. leaped from the bed and ran from the room, his tail in the air. Mira turned away and walked over to the window to wait. She seemed rather pleased with herself; with a slight change of plans, everything seemed to be going exactly the way they wanted. She certainly did not appear apprehensive. She also had no idea that she was playing her games under the very nose of the High Priest Haldephren himself.

"Finished!" Jenny announced a minute later.

Mira turned to view the results thoughtfully. Jenny had some experience with the use of makeup. Her intent now was to demonstrate a vague and slightly novice attempt without agitating her natural effect on the sexual instincts of the local males. Aping the courtesans, she had shadowed her eyes heavily, and her brown nipples were now a bright rose.

"J.T. may have been right," Mira observed thoughtfully. "All the same, I do approve. Can you confuse some of the local boys with teasing hopes while maintaining your distance?"

"I never was a flirt," Jenny admitted self-consciously. "But if need and opportunity present themselves, I will do my best."

"Under the circumstances, you might find more opportunity than you wish," his mistress observed. "Let's not keep them waiting."

The day was bright and clear for early winter, even here in the South. Dasjen Valdercon himself met them at the steps, gallantly indicating the way to a large open-air carriage waiting below. He afforded Jenny only one brief lecherous glance before he turned his attention back to Mira, who was herself dressed rather provocatively—at least by Northland standards—in her own barbaric finery.

"A grand morning to you both, my beautiful ladies," he declared with an elaborate bow. "I had thought that we might begin with a comprehensive tour of our fair city."

It seemed that he meant to conduct this tour himself, without benefit of a retinue of either guards or courtiers. Dasjen led Mira to the carriage but Jenny hesitated on the steps, suddenly aware that Ellon Bennisjen was descending quickly on a course to intercept her and that he was to be her appointed companion. She detested him. Dasjen was dangerous and predatory but he was also charming and witty, but his young assistant was a scavenger, cold and hungry and quite mad. He had not been at dinner the night before, but she now foresaw that she would not be free of him while they remained.

"Here's my pretty lady!" he said as he slipped around her shoulder to stand before her, so close that she had to look up at him. His imitation of his master's charm was half-perfect, lacking only any depth of sincerity. "My Lord Dasjen thought that you might be lonely."

"I had not anticipated a companion," she answered, hiding her revulsion and apprehension in teasing. "But my mistress seems to be engaged herself, and I feared that this might be lonesome duty."

"I know a cure for any loneliness, day or night," Ellon said suggestively.

Jenny had to force herself from backing away, and not only in disgust and fear. Ellon was in a twisted manner the most sexual man she had ever met, for all her conscious disgust of him. But she knew that he would take and never give. She was somehow reminded of creatures which killed their mates; here, for the first time, she saw that in the male of any species.

She knew that Ellon expected her in his bed that night, and then she would belong to the Dark. She was also beginning to think that this whole affair was getting too complicated for words.

For now, at least, there was no immediate problem. They filed into the carriage to sit in the deep, soft seats across from Mira and Dasjen. While Jenny did have to sit beside Ellon for the rest of the day, he did conduct himself very circumspectly while they were with the others. Although Jenny did also have to endure being discreetly molested by him as opportunities presented themselves. By pure will she forced her fear and misery from her mind, knowing that she could not betray herself to Dasjen Valdercon's suspicions.

The carriage proceeded to the docks and a quick lesson on the economic philosophy of the Empire. What Dasjen had to say on the subject was essentially the same thing that they had heard before; the real lesson was to be learned from what they saw.

"I've never seen so many ships," Mira observed. Which was the truth; there were over a hundred merchant ships in port at that time, loading and unloading so quickly that the harbor was choked with their coming and going. "More of the native population must be employed as stevedores than anything else, with rowers close behind."

"Almost all of our menial labor is performed by slaves," Dasjen answered absently, then saw her startled glance and amended himself. "Criminals condemned for serious crimes, some for life, but others only for the term of their punishment."

"You must have. . . ." quite a lot of criminals, Mira began to say. She caught herself. ". . . quite a strong industry to support this trade."

Dasjen nodded once, gravely. "That is so. Alashera is, needless to say, a center of development of modern technology. Raw materials come in for the use of industry, and agricultural products as well as items of low technology come in for use of the population."

Apparently the Empire held a somewhat different idea of high technology than the North. Merchants were always eager to boast of their wares, but most of what was touted for the edification of the two visitors were things they found to be of very common design, although of generally good quality. A very large quantity of ordinary but very well-built and well-designed weapons seemed to be pouring out of the city for all portions of the Empire; nearly every ship, no matter what its cargo, had at least a crate or two of weapons.

Their morning's expedition was interrupted at one point by the ringing of bells throughout the city. The entire population abruptly fell silent and sank to their knees as they stood, heads bowed . . . almost cringing, as if they expected to feel the bite of a whip across their offered backs. Even Ellon copied this gesture, with a very fervent, religiously ecstatic look on his face, his eyes closed. But Dasjen only looked angry and impatient. Jenny caught the distinct impression that he had made arrangements for this not to happen, just as he had arranged that the streets be conspicuously empty of the black-robed priests and priestesses they had seen when flying over the day before. There was no doubt that they were seeing the calling of the devoted to a moment of worship to the Dark, and everyone in sight responded with the same intense, eager reverence.

"Funeral bells." He muttered an explanation, hardly seeming to care if they believed him. "A local merchant ship has been long overdue. The city has awaited news for days, and that news was not good. This is a dangerous season to sail."

The Dark Priesthood might be keeping itself out of sight, but Dasjen could not hide one important item. This beautiful city of his was also replete with temples to the Dark, although none were clearly identified as such and they were all closed and silent. But temples they were, all the same, and there was nothing that Dasjen could do about that. There were no temples of the Light as such,

208 *Thorarinn Gunnarsson*

but citadels of learning, from universities and academies of magic to simple village schools. Knowledge and understanding were the tools of the Light; ignorance and fear were the weapons of the Dark.

Another thing that was obvious enough was the large numbers of soldiers—not constables of law but actual warriors—who endlessly patrolled the streets. Mira thought that there must be an impressive army of infantry, perhaps ten thousand strong, stationed inside the city itself.

The afternoon was spent in a lengthy ride through the hills about the lower slopes of Mount Drashand, above and to either side of the city. That was uneventful enough to be boring, except for the distraction of the beautiful scenery. Jenny was unable to let her guard down for a moment or Ellon would have his hands somewhere they did not belong. But at the same time she did not want to discourage him with a flat refusal; he was more harmless for his quiet, frustrated infatuation. Mira knew quite well by that time what was happening and she found the subtle advances and even more subtle defenses quietly hilarious, and in that way she at least was amused.

They dined that night in Dasjen's villa far above the city. It was a small place and very unassuming, a dark, secluded dwelling hidden back among the trees well off the road, with a vast tract of vineyards to the south. But there were also cooks and servants with dinner waiting, and musicians to play, and a respectable garrison of soldiers who seldom spoke but seemed to be everywhere. Both of the sorceresses feared that they were expected to stay the night; but when Mira casually suggested that it was getting late, the carriage was brought and they were returned briskly to the palace.

Which was just as well for them. J.T. was waiting, and he was not happy. He lay in the middle of Mira's bed, his tail thrashing and snapping, and he gave them a very dirty look. Sir Remidan looked hardly less frustrated as he stood with his arms crossed, looking likely to take matters into his own hands.

"So, here you are at last," he accused. "You leave me here all day long to do your dirty work, and then you have the nerve to stay out half the night while there's work to be done."

"Calm yourself," Mira told him with no concern for his pique. "It's a good two hours short of midnight yet, and you know it."

"That's exactly the point!" J.T. declared, leaping up. "I've found what I think is the entrance of the tunnel leading to the heart of Mount Drashand and the ancient temple.''

"Oh, of course!'' Jenny declared, stopping short and looking so thoughtful that both Mira and the cat turned to stare. "Dasjen and Ellon both were very interested in a quick return to the palace.''

"A midnight sacrifice?'' Mira asked herself. She stood for a moment with her head thrown back, holding the bridge of her generous nose with one hand; a rare gesture of hurried concentration. "But of course. The moon set early tonight; we saw it going down across the harbor on our way back. Dasjen might order the Dark Priesthood to discretion during our visit, but he would not attempt to stop the ordained practices. He wouldn't want to. He is also the highest representative of the Empire in Alashera at the moment, or so we have assumed; he would have to officiate at any important ceremony in the Great Temple of the Dark. Could you not get in there?''

"That's what I need you people for!'' J.T. exclaimed, his back arched. "I don't even know for certain that this is it. There are doors I cannot open, and I waited hours for someone to come through. Then, about an hour ago, it seemed that the entire Imperial government was filing through those doors and not coming back . . . and they all wore black!''

"It must be the temple, then,'' Mira told herself.

"I couldn't get through then . . . got kicked when I tried to run through,'' The cat continued. "Now it's quiet again.''

"I would have gone with him, but I am followed whenever I leave these rooms,'' Remidan added. "If you had not come, I would have done something.''

"I could go,'' Jenny offered softly.

Mira turned to look at her. "Is that safe? Safe for you in particular, if you know what I mean?''

"I do know what you mean, but I am safe,'' her student assured her. "I am not altogether of the Light as you know it, but I reject the Dark even more. Nor do I intend to watch the ceremony, only take enough of a look down that passage to know beyond any doubt where it leads.''

Mira considered that very carefully, and nodded. "I don't like sending you, of all people, on to the Great Temple of the Dark, but I also think that you have the best chance of getting in and out again without being seen. You do have something in mind?''

"I do," Jenny insisted as she shucked her gown in a single swift movement, then hurried over to the dressing table. Sir Remidan, who had been scandalized enough by her attire, now looked about nervously with the beginning of a very boyish blush. The fact was that Jenny had forgotten about him in the excitement of the moment; the faerie centaurs had made an indifferent nudist of her at an early age.

She dipped a cloth in a bowl of water and began washing the makeup from her face and breasts. "I know a trick or two that the dragons taught me. I can't take any weapons with me, but nothing mortal will even be aware of my presence. And the idea is to get away without a clue that I was ever there."

"You know what they will do with you, if they catch you," her mistress reminded her. "What are you going to do?"

"Disappear," Jenny insisted as she finished drying her face on a towel. She turned and grinned, and abruptly vanished as she stood. J.T., who had been seated on the edge of the bed, leaped up and swore briefly and brilliantly; even Mira looked impressed. The girl returned after a moment.

"Yes, I think you can do it," Mira agreed. "Just keep your distance."

A minute later Mira opened the door to allow the two spies into the corridor outside, although any watcher would have thought that she was only putting out the cat. J.T. did his best to imitate the nightly wanderings of a true cat, although not so much that he delayed too long in reaching their goal. Jenny followed him closely and silently, her bare feet treading softly on the smooth stone floor with no betraying rustle of clothes to warn of her presence. She had washed off the makeup with its less than subtle scents, and the perfume that she had used with deliberate profuseness had mostly faded.

They slipped quickly through the still, dark halls to the more central portions of the palace, so far not passing a soul nor even hearing a sound to indicate that the place was even inhabited. For the most part, it was not. The only tight moment came when they found themselves caught on a wide staircase as a troop of guards ascended, making their endless rounds. J.T. slipped deftly through their legs and waited on the steps below, but Jenny did not dare move. The stairs were thickly carpeted and the impressions of her feet were clearly visible in the heavy pile, even if she was not.

She hopped up on the bannister with the intention of sliding to

safety, only to discover something that she had not considered.
Bare bottoms did not slide on varnished rails, at least not without
protest. Her initial launch propelled her only a few short inches,
with the unexpected result of a very loud and incredibly rude noise.
The other result was a friction burn to an exceptionally tender
portion of her anatomy. She let out a startled squeak and jumped
off the rail.

"What was that?" the captain of the guard asked.

"I think I stepped on that cat," one of the soldiers answered.

"So who farted, you or the cat?"

"Jenny?" J.T. called at a whisper when the guards reached the
top of the steps.

"Beside you." Her voice came from just above him. "I hurt
myself."

"Is that all?" the cat asked impatiently. "Should I kiss it and
make it all better?"

Such a question asked in perfect innocence required no answer.

The cat turned and ran down the remaining steps, turning at the
bottom to streak away into the shadows of the back portions of
the palace. Since much of its east side had been built into the face
of the steep mountainside behind, none of the eastern chambers
had windows but were in fact underground, although the palace
did not cut deep into the mountain. J.T. reported that there were
more levels below ground; even the storerooms had simply been
cut deeper into the mountain, where temperatures were low and
constant.

Well behind the stairs, in the back of the palace, they came
upon a short, wide corridor that led quickly to a pair of heavy,
double doors. Jenny paused at the doors; at least J.T. assumed
that she did, since the doors did not open and he heard no sound
of her movements. What he could not see, due to the short stature
of felines, were the wide louvered vents set in the shadows above
the door.

"This leads to the core of the volcano," Jenny observed.

"How do you know that?" J.T. asked.

"There is a wind," she explained. "Hot air rises up the neck
of the volcano, and it draws cool air after it. There is enough air
being drawn through this corridor that it would hold the doors shut
if not for the vents."

"Then we are almost there?"

"Oh, no. We must be at least two miles from the core at this point. We must hurry if we hope to reach the temple by midnight. In fact, I would prefer to be out by midnight, but I have no hope of that.''

One of the two doors swung slowly open of its own accord, or so it seemed. J.T. leaped back, arching his back and hissing, then rushed forward to poke his head through the doorway for a quick look beyond. He slipped through, having seen no one beyond, and Jenny followed, opening the door just enough to squeeze through. The passage beyond was dark, featureless and endless, descending at a noticeable rate, the grey stone tunnel disappearing within a couple of hundred feet into the shadows. The doors closed slowly, silently behind them.

"Now what?" J.T. wanted to know.

"Now we hurry," Jenny insisted, although she remained where she was for the moment. She seemed to be looking around. "As I thought, the wind brings all the dust of the construction through. You can see that many people came through a couple of hours ago, and then just a few more as the dust began to settle again.''

Jenny said no more, and the cat suddenly realized that he had been left behind. He ran to overtake her, only to run nose-first into the back of her leg and bounce back. Shaking his head, he was about to employ a few choice words when he saw what had caught the girl's attention. The tunnel could be seen to end just a hundred feet beyond in a wall of solid stone, without door or passage. As they went on, they saw instead that it turned to the right to open upon a much larger tunnel, this one of vast proportions. It was big enough for two wagons to be drawn abreast; indeed, the smell of horses indicated that it was used for that very purpose. It descended in the opposite direction, rising slightly toward the heart of Mount Drashand but sloping gently toward the harbor, where it gave every indication of leading. And like the smaller tunnel, it was dimly lit by glowstones.

"We don't have time to explore in both directions tonight." Jenny seemed to be arguing with herself. "Cat, you follow it back down. Try to find every major exit along the way. If my guess is right, it will lead you to some hidden port down at the docks, possibly on the sea itself.''

"Yes, I believe so," J.T. agreed. There was a modest breeze moving up the tunnel, a breeze wet and heavy with the chill night air right off the sea, and the smell of the harbor.

"You can surely get yourself out there and come back through the city," she continued. "I'll go on up to the temple, take a quick look around, and come back out here. Watch out for yourself."

"I'm a cat," he reminded her succinctly. "You watch out for yourself. If something were to happen to you, Lady Mira would skin me alive. And then your dragons would skin Lady Mira."

"I'll remember," Jenny promised, her soft voice already receding up the gentle slope of the passage. J.T. shrugged—cats have good shoulders for that, but seldom use them—then turned and hurried on his own way.

The passage up was long and uneventful, for it was now well inside the mountain itself and she expected no chambers or passages to intersect this one until they neared the core. She was tempted to run, except for the betraying slap of her feet against the smooth stone, and so she kept her pace to a brisk walk. She could have flown, but not even the dragons could lift and maintain invisibility as well for long, and remaining unseen was far more important to her now. She reminded herself forcefully that she could afford to take no chances, that her role in the Prophecy vastly overshadowed even her own need to know the current state of the Great Temple of the Dark.

The heart of Mount Drashand lay two miles inward even of the palace; her vague mental map of Alashera had been proven true. Such a walk was of no consequence to her except for the time it took, for she could have easily run that distance without difficulty. The members of the Imperial court had not walked this distance; there had been carriages brought to provide their passage, for the smell of horses was fresh and heavy. That meant as well that there would be horses ahead. The beasts did not need to see her to recognize her presence, for they could hear and smell her.

For herself, Jenny hardly knew what to think. She knew already quite enough of what lay ahead, and she was ambivalent about what else she might learn. She yearned to be free of the Prophecy, to lead a life that was entirely her own for the first time in her own memory. At the same time she dreaded the supreme effort the Prophecy would surely demand of her, the hint of sacrifice she feared. She dreaded the beginning of the end, knowing that she could no longer afford to make a single mistake.

She paused when she saw the tunnel open into some wide chamber just ahead and listened carefully, but all she heard was the sounds of several horses. Expecting keepers watching over the beasts, she proceeded cautiously and quietly, but there was no one about. The chamber was vast, of size and shape like a large warehouse. Several carriages were parked in a row to one side and horses stood alone in their individual wooden stalls built along the south wall, tended and abandoned. Then it occurred to Jenny that the Great Temple was sacred ground indeed where no one but the sorcerers and servants of its very select coven were permitted, at least during important ceremonies.

The horses were nervous, restless. Jenny did not blame them. The sense of weight and time pressed down upon her, as if her anxious spirit struggled to support the great mass of the mountain above her. The darkness closed in upon the chamber tightly, slinking on tiger's paws around the desperate vigilance of outnumbered glowstones. There was something vaguely familiar about this place, a feeling that she had been here before.

And then she knew. The memory returned to her, thirteen years past, a forgotten memory that forced its way back into her consciousness as clearly as if it had only just occurred. It was not a clear memory, telling nothing specific, just the sense of a place like this but many times as strong, dark and dangerous. Dalvenjah and Allen had come for her then, and they had taken her away from that terrible place where life itself seemed to gasp for breath. This was a lesser den of the Dark, but one she hardly dared to face alone.

And it welcomed her. It was not yet consciously aware of her invasion, but it welcomed her all the same, seeking to pull her in, whatever evil will animated this place, turning the heart of the volcano into a thing alive. Or was the force acting upon her will entirely of her own design, that part of her own self that belonged to the Dark and sought its own? She hoped so, for she could easily control the Dark within herself. But she dared not match the strength of her own spirit against the immense, impersonal will of this place.

She made her way cautiously along the wall farthest from the horses, then slipped along the corridor beyond. The presence grew stronger, for she was not only making her way closer to its heart but the closeness of walls and ceiling seemed to funnel that force in upon her like the wind which raced down the length of the passage. Now she began to see the trappings of wealth such as she did not remember from that other place. There was a strip of dense carpet on the smooth stone floor, further muffling her footsteps. Her enhanced sight could make clear the designs and symbols inlaid in gold and silver into the stone itself.

And all of it very, very old, at least the original work, although it all bore evidence of recent and extensive restoration. The gold and silver was new; the etched designs in the walls were not. This, she thought, was in fact that ancient Great Temple of the Dark. History claimed that it had been destroyed, but she saw now that it had merely been abandoned for the last two thousand years. Or perhaps it had never been abandoned at all, only kept from complete decay by impoverished followers until the fortunes of their master improved and they began to prepare for his return.

This was one question for which she hoped to find an answer, although that was hardly vital. Of far more importance, at least to her mind, was the question of whether it was coincidence that the followers of the Dark established their greatest strongholds within these live but tamed volcanos, and if so then why. Did they in some way find access to elemental forces stronger and deeper than the Light knew how to command? She had to see the heart of the temple, the core of the volcano. In spite of her promises to Lady Mira and the cat, she was going on.

The corridor began to branch shortly, once and then again and again, but still the passages turned and wandered like tunnels rather than the straight halls and sharp corners of a true building. Jenny wondered about the purposes of these side corridors and what lay within the closed chambers she could see, their heavy wooden doors locked. Storerooms, or perhaps the cells of resident priests and their novices. Or even a school of Dark Magic, an evil parody of the Academies of the North, but not currently in use from the look of things. Which presented a question in itself; where did the Empire train its Dark sorcerers?

She came deeper into the heart of the Great Temple, and now the passages did more closely resemble a conventional building in form. She also lost the light breeze which had been her guide for so long, now that it had any number of outlets to the core. But her sense of direction did not fail her, for she now had a more certain guide. She could sense the pulsing heart of the Great Temple just ahead, not more than a few hundred feet away. The place had seemed utterly deserted until now, but she was suddenly aware of a regular rhythm that coursed through the air and the stone itself, a regular, frantic pulse. Drums. She knew then that she had come nearly to the core of Mount Drashand, and that its sorcerer priests were even now practicing their midnight ceremonies.

She had no fear of the priests, but the conscious, living presence of the temple itself would find her quickly now that she was deep within its own familiar ground. It was preoccupied with its own affairs, drawing in the rich, evil powers evoked by the priests and radiating them forth again like the vile warmth of some sickly flame. But it would sense her own magic the moment she came within its terrible presence, and her only hope in going on rested in her ability to hide her own powers. She belonged to the Light, but she was also trained in the dragon magic, something alien to its hungry, violent nature.

Jenny allowed her spell of invisibility to slip, drawing in her talents and calming them to complacency, now becoming magically rather than physically unseen. She hurried on, wanting nothing more than her one quick look before she got herself from this place as quickly as she could, trusting now to the shadows of these dimly lit passages to hide her. She felt naked now like she had never felt in her life, in all her draconic upbringing.

The passage ended in a pair of doors, and she carefully pushed through to find herself standing on a wide, narrow balcony which overlooked a second balcony or alcove, a long, deep slot cut into the wall of the volcano's wide core. The core itself lay just beyond, falling away quickly from her limited view except for a dim orange glow from far below and drifting clouds of vapors and hot steam that ascended the shaft. Three long, slender tongues of stone leaped out from equal points along the perimeter of the shaft, one just below her, to meet in the very center of the core.

The tongues of stone supported a thin circular platform that had the look of polished stone. An immense crystal hung suspended above the pit that opened in the center of that platform; three slender posts of stone or dark metal formed the platform to surround the crystal, smaller bits of crystal mounted in the tops of the post that somehow held the larger crystal suspended by some force which interacted between them. The crystal itself was perfect and clear of substance, almost white in its translucence, but in its heart pulsed a light that was blood-red tinged with black. Jenny knew that she looked upon the heart of the temple, a thing that had taken on a life of its own with the centuries of lives and thoughts of the priests who had sacrificed to it.

And on the platform itself, the Dark Priests were assembled.

Jenny looked closer and saw from the figures atop it that the platform was wider than she had thought, at least a hundred feet across. Drummers lined the perimeter of the platform, endlessly beating the great kettle of the drums before them with a relentless precision which was almost mechanical. A single row of black-robed priests formed a second ring just inside the drummers, and before them perhaps two score young, golden bodies leaped and danced naked to the frantic pulse of drums and raw magic.

The limp form of victims were lashed to each of the three inner posts of stone, standing in wide pools of their own blood. Their bellies had been opened wide from crotch to ribcage, their organs already ripped free and cast into the fires below. Jenny thought that she could see fear frozen in their dead eyes; they had not been willing victims. They were all male, young and strong and handsome. Dasjen Valdercon, the High Priest Haldephren, stood beside his victims with a long-bladed knife still in one hand as he watched the dancers with a gloating, sated look, himself naked and bathed in blood.

Looking upon this scene, Jenny understood the secret, innermost nature of the Dark, the secret that the sorcerers of the Light had hidden from the world in horror twenty centuries before. For that great crystal was the Heart of Flame that Bresdenant had warned them of, a great repository of Dark forces. Its servants had worshipped it and nourished it for countless years, as it drank in the violent emotions of their sacrifices, the raw, vicious lust of the orgies that would shortly follow, their very souls, until it assumed a counterfeit life and consciousness of its own. It fed upon them, and they fed it willingly, coven after coven tearing out pieces of their souls to abate its insatiable appetite, until it burned them dry . . . and a new coven would begin again.

And Haldephren took part in that feeding, not feeding the Heart of Flame itself but sharing in its feast. He enhanced his own talents through that psychic cannibalism; he was himself a thing not unlike that massive crystal behind him, lesser in scope but greater in personal awareness, wrapped in a living form. Jenny sensed all this beyond any doubt. She understood him now, and she knew now why she feared him. If he had ever been a living man with a mortal soul, that part of him had been burned away long ago— or perhaps he had left it behind the first time he had taken a new form.

Then she saw Ellon Bennisjen standing near his master, also

naked and holding a knife, his young, lean body sleek with blood.
And she realized this, too, to her horror, numb as she already was
with new terrors: He was no simple chancellor but the favorite of
his master. He was here to learn; for him these ceremonies were
the lessons that would make him like the Emperor and his own
master. Already he was learning to feed as his master Haldephren
fed, but as yet he could only taste the powers that sported like
whirlwinds in this place.

She feared him less than she feared his master, but she hated
him more. She remembered the murderous hunger within him,
the practiced cruelty, and suddenly she could bear this place no
longer. The immortal magic that had become infused with her
very spirit rejected this place, and the relentless drums seemed
likely to burst her head with their thunder. She reeled back, found
the doors by chance in her blind haste and slipped through. Then
she turned and ran as swiftly and silently as she could, turning
her back on the echoing drumbeats, the lust and hunger of death
and violent sex.

Jenny ran, and as she ran she slipped unnoticed from the vile
attention of the Heart of Flame and left its evil behind her. She
felt almost as if she had forgotten herself in the eternity of perhaps
ten seconds when she had looked upon the Dark, so that now she
slowly became aware of her own being and the world around her.
Her first returning awareness was that of her left hand lightly
following the stone wall, guiding her through the deep shadows,
of the beating of her own bare feet on the smooth, cool floor and
the soft, sea-tainted breeze that tickled her skin. At that moment
she could have wept, with either the horror of what she had seen
and felt or else the relief at leaving it behind.

But she was not allowed that luxury, for she was suddenly aware
that she ran from one horror into the embrace of another. She
stopped short, sensing the evil thing just ahead of her and knowing
it from her own distant past, when Allan had fought such a thing
and nearly lost. She wrapped herself in invisibility and shrank
back against the wall just as the massive armored form of the
demon stepped ponderously around the corner just ahead and
paused, filling the generous passage. It was sheathed in its own
pale luminescence, and Jenny feared that it could see her in that
sickly light. Indeed it did seem aware of her presence, or at least
troubled, seeking something it did not yet know but sensed as
alien.

There was no hope to win past the demon. Even had it been of stone, she would had needed to squeeze past its immense form with care. As it was, those powerful pincers could have snapped about her waist and crushed the life out of her in an instant. She retreated, slowly and cautiously, never turning her back on it, and as she receded it became more confused and uncertain, taking a few hesitant steps after her.

Then she found the corridor behind her at last and ran, desperate to cut through the passages ahead of the demon before it could cut her off, even if it was aware of her by now. She hoped not. She could have fought this demon and won; she commanded such magic. Her goal was to escape clear detection altogether, before the demon was certain of her presence, for destroying it would have only told Haldephren beyond any doubt that enemies had penetrated to the heart of the Great Temple itself. And there would be no doubt about what enemies were prowling around these days. The lives of their entire party depended upon her quiet escape.

Jenny circled around, leading the demon, until she returned to the main corridor and knew that it was behind her. She paused a moment, probing the path ahead with keen senses. Then she ran, swiftly and silently and very mindful of the fact that she was not out of danger yet.

By the time she returned to her suite in the palace, all Jenny wanted to do was to jump in bed, pull the covers over her head, and pretend that it had all never happened. Perhaps, somewhere near dawn, she might finally fall asleep, but not if she could not forget that she would have to endure Dasjen Valdercon and Ellon Bennisjen the next morning and pretend that her glimpse of them beside the Heart of Flame had never been. She certainly did not expect to find Lady Mira waiting for her, anxious as a mother on her daughter's first date, demanding a full explanation of every moment that had passed. But that, unfortunately, was exactly what she got.

Jenny despaired of putting any of it into words, and so she did something that she had never before done with a mortal. Locking her mind to Mira's, she relived those terrible minutes inside the Great Temple, and so Mira saw those images directly from her own memory. The faerie dragons did this regularly and thought nothing of it, and hers was dragon magic.

Lady Mira was, needless to say, suitably impressed. In fact,

she looked as shaken and repulsed as her student felt. The only
thing that Jenny amended from that report was that Dasjen was
in fact the High Priest Haldephren. If she had her way, her mistress
would not be made aware of that disturbing fact until they were
on their way home. Mira paid strict attention, making no comment
and asking no question. In the end she had only one thing to say.

"Where did you leave the cat?" she asked simply.

"Oh, hell!" Jenny exclaimed with a very impatient gesture.
"He went the other way when we came to the main passage below
the palace. We thought that he would come out somewhere near
the harbor. He'll be along later."

"I trust so, since he could not have found the type of trouble
you courageously struck your nose into," Mira said as she jumped
up from the edge of Jenny's bed and began to pace. "Well, at
least we know what we came to find, and more than I had hoped
to come away with. Do you think . . . ?"

She paused, seeing that Jenny had fallen back on the bed, sound
asleep. She chuckled softly and gently pulled the girl up until she
was fully on the bed with her head on the pillow, and pulled the
cover up around her neck. Mira finished by casting a simple spell,
making the appropriate gestures over the girl's head.

"Pleasant dreams," Mira said as she turned to leave, then
smiled fondly. "At least I hope you like them. Some of my
favorites."

· Part Eight ·

What More Can Happen?

J.T. RETURNED THE next morning, looking like something the cat had dragged in. He sat at the door and meowed until Dooket let him in, then staggered across the floor mumbling and cursing in a low voice. He went directly to Mira's room, leaped up on her bed and threw himself down with a loud, weary sigh. Then he opened his eyes and looked up at the sorceress.

"I'll have baked fish and a bowl of milk, if you please," he told her.

Mira looked at him quizzically. "You'll have what the servants brought this morning: fried mutton strips, breakfast rolls and fruit wine."

"Atrocious!" The cat declared, making a face. "I'll have a roll and wine."

Mira looked up at Dooket and Erkin, standing in the door. They nodded briefly and left to prepare a plate. She sat down on the bed beside J.T. "Are you well? You look done in."

"Oh, I'm fine," he insisted impatiently. "What about that girl of yours? Did she make it in safe?"

"Here I am," Jenny answered for herself, entering from the other door at that moment, still buttoning her shirt. "I made it in some time ago."

"Real clothes?" Mira inquired, staring at Jenny's usual pants and shirt which replaced the revealing gowns of the last two days. "Poor Ellon is going to be beside himself, not to mention Dasjen's disappointment."

"Too bad," she said caustically. "I've realized that these open-breasted gowns are imitative of their ceremonial orgies. Besides, I've had too much of Dasjen's eyes and Ellon's hands as it is."

"I don't blame you," Mira agreed emphatically, to show that she had never expected that Jenny should have to wear the things. She took the plate that Erkin handed to her and set it before the cat. "Eat. Enjoy. The boys cut the mutton into tiny little bits for you. But speak."

"Not much to say," J.T. reported between a few quick bites. "That tunnel leads straight to an opening at the waterfront where cargo can be unloaded directly during low tide, although the end of the tunnel floods during high tide. I know. I had to wait. There are actually several openings here at the palace itself, including one not far from where the ship is parked that is immense. There is another group of openings about a third of the way down to the harbor, but I could not get through. I came back through the city and found an Academy. I guess that you could call it that. It is a school for Dark Magic."

"That answers my last question," Jenny said. "I knew that there had to be a school somewhere in the city, since they've moved it out of the Great Temple itself. So we also know that the temple is in use, that the Heart of Flame still exists, and that the Emperor is not here."

"Now that is interesting, since the servants reported that the Emperor has arrived and that we are to be taken into his presence later today," Mira mused. "Not the real Emperor, I am sure. You will have to go back into one of those open-faced gowns, but you will have company this time. They brought three for me so that I can 'choose the one I want to wear for the occasion.' I take that to mean that I had damned well better have one on."

"You do get used to it," Jenny assured her.

"Oh, under other circumstances I would probably enjoy it. I plan to take mine home with me for my next dinner party." Mira sat down on the edge of the bed, deep in thought. "I wonder what the others have discovered? A shame that we could not get in touch with them last night."

"Lady Mira, let's get out of here as soon as we can," Jenny

insisted. "We know enough, more than we expected to find. We won't gain anything by staying any longer, not balanced against the danger we are in."

Mira gave her an appraising look, and she was certain that Jenny was completely earnest . . . and on the verge of panic. That impressed her more than anything, for she knew that the girl was calmer and far braver than herself. She nodded. "We will go as soon as gracefully possible. But not today. Now we are stuck with having to go through with our audience with this make-believe Emperor and the welcoming dinner. But I intend to be impressed and cooperative and claim to have seen all I need to see, and with any luck we will be on our way tomorrow."

"No, we really can't get out any sooner," Jenny agreed reluctantly. "But we must be very, very careful. There is tension in the air today, violence and expectation. This entire city is about to explode."

"Now that would be an interesting sight!" Mira remarked, grinning. "And I can't think of anything that would do it more good."

"She is right," J.T. affirmed. He sat back to wash his face, but he was quite serious. "Walk like cats."

"Really, Dasjen," Mira insisted. "It's certainly too much trouble for the Emperor to come all the way here just to see us."

"Unfortunately you are right," Dasjen Valdercon agreed as he courteously assisted her in dismounting from the carriage. "As much as we wish no misunderstanding between ourselves and the North, the Emperor is a busy man. He has come to attend to his own business. When the Senate is not in session, he is the sole government of the Empire and must be present to attend to his many important duties."

They waited as Ellon offered Jenny the same assistance in stepping down from the carriage. Jenny found many such local customs distasteful, but she endured such things as necessary evils. At least they had been encouraged to attend the reception at the docks in Northern dress; Jenny had no intention of baring herself in public yet again and Mira not once. But the formal reception at the palace later that evening was another matter. Jenny was dressed plainly by local standards in her best pants and tunic, her narrow-bladed sword belted at her waist. Mira wore black pants with a tunic that was a glory of glaring colors in abstract designs . . . her usual self.

They walked slowly down the length of the stone pier where the Emperor's ship would tie up, the rough, scarred flagstones now cloaked in carpets of Imperial red. The Emperor's ship had only just arrived in the inner harbor, an immense wargalley with three complete decks of oars and four masts with bright sails, flanked by two ships of identical size and design but less ornate in decoration. Mira frowned and reckoned that the better part of half an hour would pass before the ship was secured at the pier, and heaven only knew how long the Emperor—or his counterfeit—would take in actually departing his ship. That much at least was in their favor. The real Emperor would hurry on no one's account, but this imitation would probably pop out as soon as the plank was thrown down.

As she thought about it, Mira decided that she preferred that the Emperor and his High Priest were absent during her own visit. She doubted very much that she could be calm and polite in the presence of such evil . . . creatures. She could find no words to describe the revulsion she knew that she would feel for those two on sight.

"One moment, please," Dasjen said graciously, and hurried away to confer with the small delegation of dignitaries who waited nearby. Mira recognized all of the ministers, chancellors and local officials they had met so far, but only half of the resident courtiers—those people whose only function seemed to be to attend ceremonies and look pretty, but who were in fact the principal members of the coven of the Great Temple.

Ellon looked at Jenny and started to say something, but bowed his head and hurried after his master. Mira watched him for a moment longer, then stepped closer to her student. "What do you make of all of this?"

"The real Emperor is not on that ship," Jenny reported. "Dasjen is pleased with himself, but Ellon is scared half to death. I suspect that he is planning to do something his master may or may not approve."

A large troop of Imperial warriors, resplendent in snapping new leather and polished armor of bronze and silver, rounded the corner from the street to march with mechanized precision along the length of the pier. The two sorceresses withdrew to the back of the pier to give them room, crowding against the stacked boxes and bales. This whole affair might be a glorious farce, but the farce would be carried through in proper form to the smallest detail. The honor guard split into two long lines, their heavy boots keeping time with their pace like drumbeats, loud enough to drown out casual conversation. They halted in the center of the pier, paused for a long moment, and snapped smartly to their right to be facing the galley when it pulled alongside to dock, all without a single spoken command.

"Yarg, what rude, noisy people!" Mira exclaimed. "I'll bet they chew with their mouths open."

She turned to say something to her young protégé, but Jenny had abruptly disappeared at some point during the confusion.

Mira happened to look back to the small group of the Empire's commanding ministers in time to see the end of some argument between Dasjen Valdercon and his chancellor. Ellon seemed to have won his point; Dasjen gave reluctant consent, then watched with obvious misgivings as Ellon turned and hurried along the pier back to the city. Then Dasjen turned to stride quickly back to where she stood, threading his way through the motionless guards.

"My, you look worried," Mira observed. "Is there any problem?"

"No, I trust not," Dasjen answered. "My chancellor feels that he should return to the palace to insure that the plans for the reception there proceed properly."

"A great deal of fuss, for the off season."

He laughed heartily. "So it might seem, after the informality of the North. But Elura is old and secure. We are new and young, and we need formalities such as this to form our foundations, our own new traditions. The history and traditions we have inherited from the past are not things that we wish to maintain, nor even recall. Besides, this is only a shadow of the reception that our Emperor would receive if the Senate was in session."

Or if it happened to have been the real Emperor. But Mira kept her ungracious thoughts to herself, whether they were true or not, and reminded herself that this was all for her benefit.

"The past is one subject that I wish to discuss with you," she said after a moment. "Assuming that our meeting with the Emperor goes well—and I see no reason why it should not—then I will declare that I have seen enough to set my own mind at ease. The season is getting on and the weather less predictable, both here and in the North. By your leave, I will be on my way home in the morning."

Dasjen was obviously dismayed, but he struggled to cover it.

"So soon, my pet? After all these years, I do admit that I bask in your presence."

"You haven't gotten me to bed yet?" she assumed, teasing at first, then grew serious. It was the best acting she had ever done. "That would not be a good idea, I fear. My home and my duty are in the North, and you belong here. Let's not ask for trouble."

"I know better than to ask a commitment of you," he assured her.

"You need not," Mira told him, turning the blame on herself in gallant self-sacrifice. "I am the victim of temptations which I cannot afford to contemplate. I never expected to see you again. I certainly never expected to find you here. But it is my own heart I break, now as I did seven years ago. The fault was never your own, except in being too perfect."

Mira pulled a silk hanky from the top of her tunic, where it had been stuffed down her bosom, and mopped delicately at her eyes, pleased with herself and blissfully unaware that she was serving up enough ham to feed an army. But Dasjen seemed compelled to buy the whole hog, as long as she continued to stroke his magnificent ego in the process. He gently, graciously took her hand and kissed it lightly.

"Forgive me, my pet," he offered, serious and full of regret. "I fear that I have misjudged your heart from the start."

"You have done nothing that requires forgiveness. I only hope, when my little ship is riding the dawn winds away from your fair island, that I might be able to forgive myself." She paused and turned away with a shuddering sigh. "Leave me, please, for just a minute. I have no wish to meet your Emperor with tears in these foolish eyes."

"Of course, my pet." He gently kissed her hand again before letting it slip from his own, slowly backing away. Then he turned and, with a sigh of vast relief, hurried to rejoin the other ministers at the front of the pier. Mira was a remarkable woman, but he had never contemplated keeping her.

She waited until he was safely gone, then turned to her body-guards. There was not the slightest expression to be seen on the young faces of the two barbarians, in spite of the extraordinary scene they had just witnessed. She made a mental note never to play cards with these two.

Sir Remidan was obviously moved by the performance.

"Jenny is in trouble," she told them. "I know it. Don't ask me how; I just know it. Go find her."

"Yes, Lady," the twins agreed without hesitation, and departed. Remidan looked like he wanted to go running to a bold rescue, but he seemed to have not the slightest idea how.

Mira frowned, suspecting that it was already too late and wishing that this silly charade was over. She could not imagine what danger Jenny could have gotten herself into so quickly, but she suspected that Ellon had something to do with this. He would surely get what he had coming; given half a chance, Jenny was perfectly capable of making short work of him. But Mira wanted to be ready for anything.

Jenny came suddenly and completely awake without ever having been aware that she had slept, and knew instantly that she had been caught unprepared by a spell. Her last awareness had been standing on the pier and suddenly sensing Ellon's presence behind her. Now she lay on a smooth stone floor in some warm, dark place, a place where the air itself seemed to hum with the tension of incredible evil. Ellon stood over her now, one hand extended above her face. He had only just finished the final gesture to remove the spell which had held her unconscious and defenseless.

"Ah, with us again." His voice was a velvet purr, a poor imitation of his master's charm and sophistication. "Very soon, my pet, you will be with us forever."

"I'll fry you to a cinder the moment you touch me," she told him, and that was no idle threat. She knew already that she was held by more than physical restraints. She could not turn her magic outward, but no one could violate a sorceress and survive except a far stronger sorcerer. And Ellon was hardly her superior.

"You will accept me willingly," he told her with smooth satisfaction as he leaned over her to stroke loose hairs away from her face. "You know, I suspect, just who we are. Just now you are held by the coven of the Great Temple of the Dark, and we do recognize our own. Nothing you or your wise mistress can do will ever return you to the Light. But the Dark extends a welcoming hand to orphans like yourself."

"The Dark cannot force me to its will!" Jenny declared, feeling the first tremor of panic. She knew the test he meant to set upon her, and she had no desire to confront it. She distrusted her own resolve.

"The Dark has no need to coerce or beg," he corrected her patiently. "The Dark offers a sorceress like yourself knowledge and power in exchange for your loyalty. It offers pleasure and contentment in exchange for your devotion. And you will accept because the will is within you to accept."

"That remains to be seen."

"And soon it shall be seen." He rose and stepped back, then made a brusque gesture in her direction. "Take her."

Priests in black robes appeared at either side to take her under her arms and lift her effortlessly, her hands still tied securely behind her back in a cruel grip. Priests who were young, handsome of face, large and strong of body. A third caught her bound legs and lifted her up so that they could carry her flat between them as they marched with slow ceremony through the dim passages of brown stone.

Jenny looked about as much as she was able, realizing for the first time that she knew exactly where she was. Ellon had told her that she was within the Great Temple, but only now did those words become clear to her. The evil of this place grew by that recognition, becoming heavy and suffocating like the thick sludge of shadows that flowed through the ancient passages. She knew where they were taking her.

Lady Mira had warned her often enough that she did not want to be taken alive. Vajerral had imparted that same warning, as if she had ever needed it.

She was going to the Heart of Flame. The coven would surround her, making her the object of their ceremony as they attacked her resolve with their relentless temptations, making her desire the destruction and the raw, perverted lust they practiced as an art. And the horrible, alien consciousness of the Heart of Flame itself would recognize her for what she was and strip away her defenses. And then, when she was weakest, Ellon would force his body into her own and show her the delight in the very perverse pleasures that repulsed her now. Then she would belong to them, and they would control the Prophecy of the Faerie Dragons through her.

Jenny knew that she could not hope to resist. Dasjen Valdercon possessed the powers to force access to her inner name, and with that he could command her or reshape her into anything that pleased him. She knew that she could not fight him, the High Priest Haldephren least of all. Every indication was that he was her father, and not even Dalvenjah could ever promise her that he was not.

Jenny could not see much, upside down and surrounded as she was by billowing black robes. But she knew when they carried her out onto the wide, deep shelf recessed into the wall of the core of Mount Drashand. Then Ellon led the way as they carried her up the slender tongue of stone that leaped out from the edge of the shelf to support a third of the broad round platform. There the priests untied her, although they held her arms tightly until they had secured her once again to one of the three inner posts which supported the Heart of Flame, her hands held high and wide above her head by the manacles which had held the sacrificial victims the night before. The crystal itself slept not six feet behind her, dim and dusky except for a faint translucent pulse of ruby light within its core.

Only the cold pillar of stone at her back hid her from its sinister presence, and it was small comfort indeed. She shrank from it with far more fear and loathing than she had ever felt from Ellon Bennisjen or even his master. They might be a threat to her in both body and spirit, but this thing knew only one purpose. It would consume her.

"There you are, my pet, nice and cozy." Ellon continued his pathetic mimicry of his master's geniality. "Not to worry. The coven will convene as soon as possible. The others assemble at this moment. Then we will be done with this whole uncomfortable affair, and have you down from there."

Jenny paid him little mind, too consumed with her own thoughts. There had to be a way out of this. Too much was at stake.

Perhaps it was not over yet. Mira was a Veridan Warrior and the Trassek twins were capable warriors in their own right, but they could not take on the coven of the Great Temple. But add a knight and two Mindijaran and matters would be very different. They were compelled to come for her, valuing her life even above their own. She regretted this turn of events. She should never have come here, exposing herself to even the possibility that allowed this to happen.

Her only consolation was that this was all Mira's big, fat, stinking idea to begin with.

"Ellon!" Dasjen Valdercon said sharply as he marched out onto the platform, a black ceremonial robe over the elegant pants and flowing tunic he had worn at the reception. He was by no means pleased. "What is this foolishness? What have you done?"

"Master, I trust that I have not erred." Ellon was no longer gloating and vain, but humble and circumspect as he bent knee before his master. "She belongs with us; you have said so yourself. I know that we can convert her, and I wish to do this thing myself. I desire her."

"You will have that rare honor, although we will discuss later how you may atone for a greater presumption than you realize even yet," Dasjen remarked, already dismissing his young chancellor from his thoughts as he watched Jenny appraisingly. "A very desirable young lady, yes. She will be turned to the Dark, and you are most worthy of that gentle duty. But after that you will have to be very respectful of her desires."

Jenny edged back as well as the immobile stone behind her would allow, knowing only too well what he meant. But she was loath to see in his thoughts that he had known all along that he had only been playing his own game with her, just as she had pretended not to recognize him.

"Ah, you do know exactly what I mean," he said with satisfaction, standing close and menacing. "We have met before, Jenny Breivik, although you were very young and I wore a very different form. But you recognize me all the same, just as I would know you despite the present color of your hair."

He made an impatient gesture over her head, effortlessly stripping her of the spell that had kept her long hair black. In the dim, ruddy light of the core of Mount Drashand, the difference was hardly noticeable. But a few errant strands of hair caught the honest light that filtered down from above, glowing darkly blue.

"Proof enough, if not for the very feel of your presence," Dasjen said, bitter and impatient with the deception. He turned quickly to Ellon and the rest of the coven, gathered as close as they dared. "Behold, my children! Before you stands Jenny Breivik, the blue-haired child and the important half of the object of the Prophecy of the Faerie Dragons. My daughter!"

"That was ever a lie!" Jenny declared hotly.

"Believe what you want, my child," he told her tolerantly. "Soon enough you will know the truth. The full coven will be gathered any minute now. Then the Heart of Flame will tear away your feeble defenses. You will belong to us, and we will have the other immediately after. You will bring her to us."

"The other?" Jenny asked, heedless of her own fears for the moment. She was beginning to comprehend that matters were far more complex than she had ever anticipated, and that there were portions of the Prophecy that she had never known. She remembered now Dalvenjah telling her of the other, the second one needed to fulfill the Prophecy.

"Yes, have you truly not heard the words of the Prophecy of Maerdilyn?" he asked guardedly, watching her closely. "Dragons gold and dragons black seek to gain what each may lack. White and black, red and blue, fortune hangs between the two."

Jenny could not hide her dismay. She knew now exactly what the Prophecy of Maerdilyn meant, the full meaning of the Prophecy of the Faerie Dragons.

"Ah, you do know!" He savored her discomfort. "You are the blue, and the blue shall be the bait for the red. Only together could you have defeated either myself or the Emperor. But you will belong to the Dark, and Mira will be dead, both before this day is done."

She turned away from him in pain, from his hot, eager breath on her face. Dalvenjah had known all along. That was her reason for sending Jenny into Lady Mira's keeping. Mira was the second half of the Prophecy, her ignorance of that fact being her primary protection over the years. They had been thrust together for this very reason, blue-haired Jenny and red-haired Mira. She could have wept.

She was lost.

At that moment she happened to catch a glimpse of a small black-and-white shape streak across the floor of the ledge to the base of the stone bridge. Mira, Sir Remidan and the Trassek twins followed close behind, swords drawn and ready for battle. Jenny looked but could not see that any of them carried a bow, the one real hope they had of ending her own life and preventing her fall into the Dark. Mira and Remidan had both come intent upon a daring rescue, and the two barbarian bodyguards simply failed to see that the four of them together might not be equal to the task.

Dasjen turned almost casually to regard them with droll amusement. He made an impatient gesture, and six of the priests stripped away their long black robes to reveal strong young men in armor and well armed, sorcerers no doubt trained in their own equivalent of the Veridan. They positioned themselves at the top of the arch of stone, the only way up to the platform. Dasjen stepped to the edge just to one side, serious but unconcerned; as he saw it, the bait was taken and the trap was ready to spring. Ellon held back, sword in hand, still humbled before his master but eager to prove himself.

"Lady Kasdamir, you tried to deceive me," he said in aggrieved tones. "You bring my daughter to me and you make her pretend to be someone else."

"It's a trap!" Jenny warned her mistress, and no one made any move to stop her. "Dasjen Valdercon is really the High Priest Haldephren. He has been here all along."

"No shit!" Mira was plainly surprised by that bit of news.

"You can't fight him!" Jenny added. "Do what you have to do and get away from here."

"Dear child, things are hardly that desperate!" Mira admonished her. "Did it not occur to you that your friends would all come running to your rescue?"

Jenny caught the subtle hint, as subtle as Mira ever got, and understood that the sorceress was stalling for just a little more time. She had anticipated this herself, but she had never guessed that things would be so well organized. Mira glanced up briefly into the neck of the volcano, then lifted her sword and stepped forward for battle. Sir Remidan and the twins moved to join her.

The six guards beside Dasjen drew their own swords and stepped out onto the arch of stone to meet that attack. But Mira's advance was only a ploy, meant to attract the full attention of Dasjen and his followers toward herself and away from the core of Mount Drashand over their own heads. Mira paused a step short of the arch and held her ground, not wishing to fight on the narrow span itself if she could help it. The warriors of the Dark had a similar idea; they advanced quickly to meet her at the base of the bridge.

Kelvandor suddenly descended upon that unsuspecting knot of armored guards like a falcon, hurtling down to scatter them from the span with a well-aimed fireball. He circled around quickly and landed lightly on the platform itself a moment later, drawing his long sword. Vajerral quickly circled around to land beside him, completing their line of defense.

Kelvandor turned to Jenny, and the manacles that held her wrists snapped open in his large, powerful hands as he forced the catches. She stood for a moment, rubbing her abused wrists, then took the long, narrow sword the dragon drew from his harness to offer her.

Dasjen stood for a moment to regard them, examining his own

position and reckoning his chances. He commanded the larger force, but for the moment two Mindijaran stood between his forces and Jenny. He saw no immediate chance of either regaining the girl or preventing her rescue. At that moment he needed to generate a little confusion, delaying for time until his own guards arrived, and he was not opposed to sacrificing the entire coven to achieve his ends.

"Take the rest of our people who are armed and attempt to force those dragons from the platform," Dasjen told his chancellor softly. "I will take these six and rid us of that interfering sorceress."

"I understand," Ellon agreed, plainly frightened. He had no liking for a real fight. "What of the girl?"

"Slay her if you must, but capture her if you can." He cautiously worked his way backwards through the small crowd, then lifted his sword. "Now!"

Many of the priests whipped swords out from beneath their robes and rushed the dragons, while those who were unarmed, mostly the naked dancers, retreated quickly to avoid the battle. Dasjen led his smaller group of warriors down the arch of stone to attack the group at the base. Their initial lunge had scattered the four attackers, forcing them off the bridge, even though they lost two of their own number in the attempt.

One thing became obvious soon enough. The Dark Sorcerers might have been trained similarly to Veridan Warriors but something essential seemed to be lacking. They fought with determination but their magical enhancement barely made them the equals of Dooket and Erkin, two well-trained barbarians. Mira, Jenny and Sir Remidan could make short work of the lot of them, while no mortal could compare to Mindijaran. This battle gave every appearance of being a brief one.

At least until a troop of two score Imperial guards suddenly erupted from the inner passages of the temple to rush the rather precarious position that Mira and the boys were trying to hold.

Vajerral saw no hope for it. She muttered an oath that would have made her mother's ears twitch and leaped from the ledge, gliding down to reinforce their position below. Kelvandor could see that the responsibility for protecting Jenny was now largely his own and assailed the remaining defenders with a vengeance. He did possess two distinct advantages; his enhanced strength was appalling and his thick scales were proof against the sideways blow of any blade, although he was vulnerable against thrusts. Considering the fact that he was wielding a six-foot blade, no one was likely to get that close.

Jenny kept one eye on Vajerral and her mistress, and saw that things were not going so well below despite the dragon's help. Dooket and Erkin were back to back and doing their best just to stay alive, while the Imperial guards were pressing in on Mira relentlessly, heedless of their own losses. Sir Remidan was making a very good showing of himself, despite the lack of the armor that he had been obliged to leave on the island.

"Kelly!" she shouted, and saw the dragon shift his ears in her direction. "I can hold my own now. You have to help the others before Mira or the boys get hurt."

"I cannot leave you," he protested, bending his neck around briefly to afford her a quick glance.

"Save Mira!" Jenny insisted. "She is the other half of the Prophecy, and she is in far more danger than myself."

"What?" He turned to stare at her again.

"Do it!" she shouted. "We can hold on here."

"Nuts!" Kelvandor muttered darkly, and hurled himself toward the side of the platform. A final, powerful sweep of his long tail scattered half of the remaining defenders, sending a couple over the edge.

Jenny rushed to the attack, taking advantage of the momentary confusion. There were not above six trained fighters left in the group, although several of the ineffectual courtesans had taken up the weapons of the fallen to add to the confusion. Unfortunately Ellon remained and he was the greatest threat, for Jenny was certain that he was under orders to either capture her or kill her. He now came to the front of the battle, facing Jenny directly. Seeing that his supporters were disappearing around him, he knew that he had to press his remaining advantage while he still possessed one. No help seemed likely to come up the bridge from below for the present.

"You should have submitted when you had the chance," he hissed at her, and his hatred was sincere, no bluff or ploy to unnerve her. "You have cheated me of my desire, and I mean to make you pay for that. You think that you can defeat me?"

"I'm supposed to be good enough to defeat the Dark itself, remember?"

That was blasphemy, to his ears at least, and it only infuriated him all the more. He stepped up his attack yet again, pushing himself beyond his limits in his blind hate. Jenny fell back before him, slowly but deliberately leading him out from his supporters toward the center of the platform.

Ellon was silent now, his entire existence focused upon the single goal of destroying Jenny. But the young sorceress looked unconcerned; she remained calm and confident, knowing that she would kill him in her own good time. She drew him on, waiting for him to make a fatal mistake, permitting him to think that he was winning.

Then she allowed herself to be tossed back a step after blocking an overhead strike from his heavier blade. Ellon closed eagerly, but he had not reckoned Jenny's cold fury. She ducked under his attack and drove straight into the middle of Ellon Bennisjen and his three remaining supporters, hailing blows and thrusts at Ellon so furiously that the four of them were pushed to the limit fending off her attack. She ignored the guards, striking at Ellon so savagely that she pushed him right through the knot of his defenders.

The three priests tried to come at her now from behind, attacking her undefended back. But Jenny had not been careless in her fury. She ducked under their blows and caught one in the belly, then turned on the other two. They retreated before her wrath, only to find themselves trapped between her and the Mindijaran sorceress. Vajerral had been keeping one eye turned in Jenny's direction, and she had come in a hurry when she observed the girl's attack. Ellon only stood with a sorely diminished band of the naked, helpless courtiers, knowing that he could not face the two of them.

The courtiers scattered, seeing that his presence was no safe place to be at that moment. For Ellon's part, he saw that he would be facing Jenny alone and considered that he still had a chance. He was desperately afraid of death, but his devotion to the Dark remained resolute and he would still give his own life without hesitation just for the chance to take her with him.

Ellon raised his sword defensively, and Jenny dealt him a blow that almost flung him backwards off his feet. She battered his defenses again and again, forcing him back near the edge of the platform. Then, when he lifted his sword yet again, she cut in from below to drive her blade deep into his belly. Even as he died, he tried to strike her one last time. She dodged the feeble blow easily and then forced him back by the blade that transfixed him until he stumbled backwards off the edge of the platform, pulling out her sword as he fell into the fires far below.

In the need of the moment, Jenny did not even pause. She turned to stare at the pitiful group of courtiers, looking frightened and defenseless as they clustered at the top of the arch. Less than a dozen remained; these were the few who had lacked the courage to take weapons and join the attack, and they certainly had no interest in fighting now. She made a threatening gesture in their direction and they fled down the arch past Dasjen, who had been holding the span from both directions. He stepped back, as much as the narrow passage would allow, looking somewhat bewildered at this turn of events.

Perhaps it was finally beginning to occur to him that he was going to lose this battle.

The fight below was winding down as well; Dooket and Erkin were assisting Kelvandor in putting a quick end to the remaining score or so of the Imperial guards. Mira quietly walked over to stand at the base of the bridge, looking up at Dasjen. Jenny took her own position at the top. The High Priest stood in the middle of the span, glancing back and forth at the two sorceresses in an indecisive manner. They were at either end of the bridge and he was trapped between. Very much on his mind was the fact that the two of them together were supposed to be a match for the Emperor—more than a match for himself. He made his choice and turned to face Mira, taking a firm grip on his sword; he considered her the easier of the two to defeat, considering the fact that she was firmly mortal and not dragon-trained.

"Watch him, Lady," Jenny quickly warned her mistress. "He is really the High Priest Haldephren."

"Yes, you told me that," Mira said, not greatly perturbed.

"He cannot afford the risk that you might escape," the girl added. "You are the other half of the Prophecy."

Now Mira did stop short to stare. "What?"

"Remember what Bresdenant said? White and black, red and blue. That is us, our hair. You are red and I am blue. He knows it. He can defeat the Prophecy by killing you."

"Is that so?" Mira frowned, more determined than ever. She afforded the High Priest an icy stare. "You're stuck between a rock and a hard place, you know."

"All the same, you cannot kill me," he reminded her coldly. "I'll take one of you at least with me, and then I'll come back for the other."

Dasjen raised his sword and stepped forward to meet her, at the same time calling upon the Heart of Flame to lend him the magic he needed to be certain of his victory. The massive jewel responded, awakening to a blaze of life, extending without hesitation the power he requested. But it never reached him. Jenny stood between and she had intervened, shielding him from that flux of power. He turned to glare at her, knowing at the same time that his position was far more desperate than he had anticipated.

He turned back to Mira and advanced, with good reason to believe that he could still defeat her on his own. Mira made no move to meet him, but she returned his first strike easily enough and then pressed her advantage. The arch was narrow, steep and treacherous and she was below him, her own swings and thrusts coming up from beneath so that he had to bend or crouch to defend himself against her. He was in no position to strike or thrust at her in return. He retreated before her, hoping to lure her up the arch to the platform where they would be on even ground and he could press his own advantage.

It was a foolish strategy, and he did not realize his mistake until he heard Jenny step up behind him. He turned swiftly to counter her attack, and Mira's blade cut deep into his unprotected back. Immediately she used the steel blade to channel a charge of destructive magic into him, seeking to blast him not only in body but in soul. She knew how to destroy him, not just this once but for all time. In a last desperate attempt to save that one part of himself that was immortal, he flung himself forward off the blade, collapsing heavily on the arch directly at Jenny's feet.

He lay there for a moment, panting in pain and fear, then looked up to see that Jenny was about to strike again and finish what her mistress had begun. Seeking his one chance to escape, he threw his sword at her wildly, forcing her to draw back just long enough for him to thrust himself over the edge of the arch. He fell for several long seconds, and the fires took him into their embrace.

"A pity," Jenny remarked dispassionately. "With only a little more luck, we could have been rid of him forever."

"This was not the time," Vajerral said as she stepped forward to join them. "Dalvenjah accomplished no more in her own time. He escaped into the heart of the volcano even then."

Jenny looked up at her. "Did you know that Mira was a part of the Prophecy?"

The faerie dragon shook her head emphatically. "I did not, although I imagine that Mother did. She was, after all, the one who sent you to Lady Mira. For my own part, I was opposed to that."

Mira afforded her a droll expression, but made no further comment. None was needed.

"I mean no disrespect by that," Vajerral assured her. "I expected no harm to come of it, but I did think at the time that Jenny belonged with us. There were designs that I could not foresee."

"I suggest that we get out of here, while we have the chance," Kelvandor remarked.

"That's a fact," Jenny agreed with a weary sigh, pushing her blue hair out of her eyes. "Why don't the two of you start up the volcano? The rest of us must go back for *Wind Dragon*."

Vajerral cocked her head, her ears alert. "Jenny . . ."

"I'll go with the others," she said firmly. "They came all this way to help me, and chance has been kind to us so far. I owe them any help I have to give in getting back out."

Vajerral considered that only briefly, and nodded. "I know better than to argue with you. We will await you outside."

"No, get yourselves away from here," Mira added suddenly, quite determined. "This might soon be no safe place for quite a few miles around. You can meet us on that uninhabited island where we left Staemar."

The two dragons spread their broad wings and lifted themselves into the air, their forms surrounded in a pale blue glow. They employed their lift magic to the fullest, levitating more than actually flying to ascend the core of Mount Drashand. The warm air rising up the shaft beneath their wings helped all the more.

"Ready?" Mira asked innocently as she turned to descend the arch.

"Do you have something in mind?" Jenny asked suspiciously.

"I think you know."

"Be glad that those dragons don't suspect. But I do agree."

They paused at the base of the arch, finding scraps of cloth from the fallen to clean their swords. They returned to the base of the bridge, standing one to either side with their drawn swords held between them.

"Ready?" Mira asked, and Jenny nodded. "Then strike an arch."

A strand of blue flame, glowing like a sliver of lightning, jumped between their blades. Jenny fed it, making it stronger, and then Mira added what she had to contribute, and they slowly stepped back until the blue arch was as thick as a faerie dragon's arm, buzzing and snapping between the blades. They slowly lowered the swords until the base of the bridge was caught between the two blades, and the arch of magic wrapped itself about the slender tongue of stone and ate away at the structure.

The stone crumbled and split after a long moment, the arch shattering under the weight of the platform it supported. With that one support gone, the platform above bent slowly in their direction until the two remaining legs bent and then fragmented as well. The entire platform broke free and collapsed into the center of the shaft amid the hail of broken stone.

Mira did not even pause to watch an instant beyond that point. She sheathed her sword and turned to run, sending the Trassek twins and J.T. running ahead of her while Jenny followed close behind. They quitted the ledge in a hurry and did not stop running until they had slipped through the maze of dark, close corridors that formed the Great Temple itself to reach the vast chamber that held the stables. Mira paused only a moment to catch her breath.

"Well, that bit of unpleasantness is done," she remarked much the same as if they had just finished cleaning the bathrooms. "We might have a few minutes before the heat shatters the Heart of Flame. J.T., get us out of here and back to the ship. Jenny, follow him closely. Boys, you stay behind me."

"Right, Lady Mira," Dooket agreed eagerly. "We'll bring up your rear."

She turned to afford him her most droll expression. "Do you think that the two of you can lift it?"

"The horses!" Jenny exclaimed suddenly. There were also two score or so horses saddled for riding who stood in a dejected knot in the center of the chamber; they had no liking for the underground passages.

"Oh, there's nothing that we can do for them now, child," Mira told her compassionately.

"They're not even proper horses," Sir Remidan added. "They can't talk."

"No, the horses!" the younger sorceress insisted.

"Oh, piffle!" Mira declared to herself with an impatient gesture, then waved to the cat. "Come back, J.T. We can ride out."

J.T. cared little for the idea, but only a moment later he was seated in a saddle between Jenny's legs. Mira rode ahead, leading the way, while the two barbarians followed close behind. In this way they reached the side passage leading into the palace in only a few short minutes. Which was just as well, for they had just leaped down from their saddles when the first of a series of tremors shook the passage, raising a cloud of grey dust, and the rumble of distant thunder echoed through the stone itself. A moment later the light breeze in that smaller corridor became a sustained rush of wind. The core of Mount Drashand was aflame.

"It must have worked," Mira observed as she paused a moment to look back, as if she could see through miles of rock to the core of the volcano.

"Knowing what that thing was and the power it possessed, I don't doubt it," Jenny told her. "We're in a fair amount of danger."

Mira's only acknowledgement of that was to hurry even faster. They entered the palace through the hidden doors behind the stairs, the two halves now flung half-open by the sweep of wind through the passage. For once the vast structure did not seem so vacant; servants and workmen were in the process of a swift and frantic retreat. They did not likely know of the fall of the High Priest or the destruction of the Heart of Flame, but the entire island knew by now that Mount Drashand was about to erupt violently. That was not a comforting prospect, considering their proximity.

J.T. permitted them only a brief pause to look around before he streaked ahead, leading the way through the chaos of the palace halls. The distant rumblings of the volcano had become a sustained, fitful roar and tremors now shook the island every few seconds. The polished stonework of the palace was cracking and crumbling, so that chips and splinters rained down with every tremor and a cloud of dust filled the passages like thin grey smoke. The entire structure seemed likely to collapse under any additional stress, and the quakes only became steadily worse and more frequent.

So far they had not been challenged; the guards were as desperate to abandon the palace as the rest. J.T. suddenly came to an interception of corridors and came to an abrupt halt, pausing only a moment before choosing the hall to their left. Only a few steps led them to doors which opened upon the paved square where they had parked *Wind Dragon*. He stopped short to look around, ears and tail standing straight up in alarm. The airship was nowhere to be seen.

"Damn them, they took my frigging ship!" Mira exclaimed in dismay. She turned to look at the clouds of thick, dark brown smoke pouring out of the volcano above them. Already a cloud of grey ash was beginning to darken the afternoon air. "So now what? We go down with the volcano?"

"I think I know where it is," J.T. announced as he turned and ran to their left toward a long, high section of well-tended hedge several hundred feet away. Many miles of such tall hedgerows divided the palace grounds, enclosing walkways and quiet gardens.

But when they rounded the hedge at the far end, they found not the garden they might have expected but a broad ramp leading into some subterranean chamber or passage far below. The ramp was ordinarily covered by the long, narrow leaves of a door which fit over the top, the two halves now standing open. The doors were wood reinforced by metal and covered on the top by some material made to look like paving stone, now propped open by the metal arms of some mechanism in the darkness below.

"The doors are open!" J.T. declared, then turned to look up at them. "I found this on my search of the underground passage. There are several very large chambers cut into the rock below, perhaps warehouses. Wagons of supplies were surely brought up this ramp."

"And they rolled *Wind Dragon* down the ramp to hide her below?" Mira asked dubiously. "We are discussing a very big ramp and a small ship, but this is something of a tight fit even with the masts down."

"We can only look," the cat insisted as he trotted down the ramp, his tail standing on end. They had no choice but to follow him.

The ramp was certainly steep; Mira had to wonder that anyone would try to negotiate several tons of airship through this opening while descending such a steep incline. There was indeed a chamber below, the stone overhead thick enough to sustain the unsupported roof. The chamber itself was vast, poorly lighted by glowstones. The main passage leading from the Great Temple down to the harbor bisected the chamber, dark and suspiciously foggy with brown, acid smoke.

Wind Dragon stood in the near half of the chamber, her masts unstepped but otherwise unharmed, although she appeared to have been the center of some activity that had been hastily abandoned with the start of the eruption.

Then, even as they paused at the base of the broad ramp, the mountain was shaken by the most violent tremor yet. They were thrown to the floor by the force of the quake, fearful that the heavy roof of the chamber would come down on them any moment. That held, surprisingly, although the mechanism which raised and lowered the doors on the ramp pulled loose of the wall and fell, pulling one door closed and bringing the other down with it, ripped from its heavy hinges. The tremor lasted for at least half a minute, but Mira leaped up the moment it began to subside.

"That was the eruption of the volcano," she reported absently as she surveyed the damage choking the ramp. "Yarg, we could never clear that in time, not even with our powers of levitation combined."

"Straight down, then," Jenny volunteered. "J.T. reports that the passage is open all the way down to the sea."

"Was open," the older sorceress corrected her. "We can't trust it after that last tremor."

"This chamber held," Jenny countered. "The passage has a much smaller ceiling area unsupported, so it probably came through."

There was no arguing with that; *Wind Dragon* was not going out the way she had come in, and they were going nowhere without *Wind Dragon*. Mira climbed the boarding ramp after only a brief pause to consider their very limited options, heading straight to the helm deck while the others prepared the ship to travel. There was little to be done; they could not raise and rig the masts or extend the vanes inside the passage, and the ship was fortunately already sitting on her wheels, extended slightly below the skids.

Using the smaller thrust vanes, Mira began the slow, careful steps of turning the ship so that her length was aimed down the gentle incline of the main passage, leading toward the sea. Her task was complicated by the fact that she could not steer while the full weight of the ship was resting on the wheels, only when the ship was in motion. Jenny had joined her on the helm deck and stood staring up the darkened passage leading into the core of the mountain, alarmed by a distant grumbling, roaring noise. She suddenly knew what it was she heard.

"Mira, we have to get under way," she said. "The volcano has erupted."

"I was aware of that some time ago," the sorceress answered impatiently.

"Are you aware that lava is rushing down the tube behind us?"

Mira glanced over her shoulder and saw the glowing mass of red and black rushing down the tunnel behind them. She indulged herself with some creative swearing, although she did not pause in her efforts to get the ship turned. Jenny hurried over to assist her in turning the reluctant wheel as the airship began to roll slowly forward yet again. Her long bowsprit missed the corner of the wall by inches as the ship aligned herself with the passage, and Mira began to apply heavy thrust even as she straightened the wheel. There would not have been time for another try; lava was already beginning to fill the chamber behind them.

Jenny watched behind, since her mistress was too preoccupied with keeping *Wind Dragon* to the narrow confines of the passage to look for herself. The lava poured into the chamber even as the ship disappeared out the other side; she could feel it like a dragon's breath following close behind them. It filled the chamber in seconds, the pressure behind the glowing mass enough to shoot it down the tube at a speed that threatened to overtaken them.

"Step on it!" Jenny exclaimed.

Mira stared at the deck. "Step on what?"

"Faster!" she entreated desperately. "It's almost on us."

"Faster?" Mira asked herself. "We're already pushing twenty knots."

She brought their speed up to thirty all the same, and at Jenny's frantic urging she pushed the vanes to their limit to increase their speed to forty-five knots. At that speed she expected one of the frequent tremors to send the ship sliding into the walls any time, and the stone ceiling of the tunnel streaked past less than two feet above their heads. But they had no choice; it was a matter of fly or fry.

"Light ahead!" Dooket called from the bow where he and Erkin were watching. "Half a mile at most, clear passage all the way!"

"J.T.!" Mira bellowed at her loudest. "Is the end of the passage flooded with seawater?"

He streaked to the rear deck, panting. "Not at low tide. I don't know what it would be now."

"The false Emperor's ship came in on the rising tide, but there's no telling how things stand with the island shifting and shaking," Mira mused. "If we hit water, it's going to slow us down."

Fortunately they were gaining on the lava, moving steadily ahead. At that speed they would be coming up on the end of the tunnel in less than a minute. Already they could see the daylight ahead, and the mercenaries in the bow soon reported that they could see waves rolling well up inside the passage itself. They thought that it would be a tight squeeze. Mira was less worried about that than about the prospect of hitting the water at forty-five knots.

When Dooket reported water a hundred feet ahead, she cut all thrust from the vanes and began riding the brakes. *Wind Dragon* slowed quickly, and a moment later the tunnel was filled with a cloud of spray as the wheels entered the water. The sorceress fought the wheel, hoping to steer as best she could as the ship's wheels lost contact with the solid floor, but the ship slowed even more abruptly under the drag of water flooding over the wheels and skids. She applied thrust again, fighting the pull to keep up some speed, and *Wind Dragon* shot out the end of the passage into open air just below the wharf, hurtled off the end of the ledge to settle full into the sea with a tremendous splash.

Mira brought the thrust of the vanes back up to full, putting as much distance as she could between themselves and the tunnel. A moment later the lava hit cold water with an explosive rush of steam which flowed up around them like a wet, heavy fog. But the fiery touch of the lava itself missed the ship, carried even farther away by the boiling waves as lava continued to shoot out the tube behind them.

"We're free!" Jenny reported as they left the tunnel behind.

Mira did not answer at once, pausing for a quick look around. Thick smoke from the volcano was descending upon the entire island along with a rain of hot ash and a hail of burning stones. She could hear the cries from the people trapped in the burning city, see them lining the waterfront. Some had even leaped in after the few remaining ships; most of the vessels were already away, both merchant ships and sleek Imperial galleys pulled far ahead by long, desperate oars. The harbor was choked for miles with the frantic exodus of ships of every size and type. She glanced over her shoulder for another look at the volcano, sensing that their greatest danger lay in that direction.

"She'll blow for sure," she said grimly, and turned back to her scant crew. "All hands crank up the wheels!"

Dooket and Erkin hurried to attend to the front wheels, while

Sir Remidan assisted Jenny with the back wheels.

"Hold on tight!" Mira declared when they had finished. "Once we're under way, start to work on the vanes and stabilizers immediately."

Taking firm hold of the rudder wheel, she coaxed full thrust into the drive vanes. The ship shuddered, gaining speed quickly until she slowly, gracefully rose up clear of the water, actually skiing on the skids of her struts, the troubled waves parting in arcs of spray at the base of each of her four broad, stiffly braced struts. Within moments *Wind Dragon* was leaving even the swiftest of the true ocean ships behind, hurtling along at more than forty knots.

"It worked," Mira said, glancing over the side. "So, Beratric Kurgel was right. For once."

"We've made it," Jenny observed.

Mira glanced at her. "I don't stop worrying about live volcanos until they are a long, long way behind."

For the moment, however, Jenny felt very safe, the safest she had felt in a very long time. All possible dangers lay behind them, not ahead . . . assuming of course that they did not hit something substantial in the water and knock a strut off *Wind Dragon*. The airship's flat-bottomed hull would float; they had already proven that. But the shallow draft, top-heavy vessel was far from seaworthy in rough waves. What was not to say that she did any better planing over the water on her struts, but at this rate she might at least avoid trouble before it overtook her.

Mira deftly steered *Wind Dragon* between two Imperial wargalleys that closed to intercept them, a maneuver that was accidental rather than intentional on their part. She could not imagine that the fleeing Alasherans would pause long enough to trouble an airship that was moving too fast for them in the first place, and the fact that neither arrows nor catapults were loosed in their direction seemed to prove the point. After that they were in open ocean surrounded by the wide ring of islands, the better part of three miles from the harbor. There were many other ships even farther out, but too widely spaced to present any problem.

Mount Drashand continued to rumble like thunder, ejecting masses of thick, brown smoke and burning stones, some as large as houses, to crash in flames upon the slopes. The entire city was engulfed in flaming ruin. For the time Jenny was too busy helping rig the ship for flight to worry much about the two dragons. She only hoped that the eruption of Mount Drashand would not bring them back to investigate.

At that moment Mount Drashand exploded. Jenny happened to be looking in that very direction as it happened. For a moment the volcano shot a tremendous column of smoke and flame straight up, and the slopes of the mountain began to fold inward and roll away in immense landslides, stripping away the cone layer by layer. They had all turned to watch by that time, the ship hurtling over the water untended for the moment as Mira leaned against the wheel. In a final convulsion, Mount Drashand collapsed inward upon itself before it exploded upward and outward in a sustained surge that carried the entire island into the troubled sky.

Mira swore to herself and turned back to the helm; she was pushing the ship to its best speed, and she wished for more. They were ten miles or more from the former harbor, at least fifteen miles from the center of that blast and possibly more. She hoped that would be enough, because at forty knots *Wind Dragon* was only going to gain another mile or two before the fiery, ash-laden shock wave of that explosion overtook them. She waved for the crew to join her on the helm deck.

"Be ready to hold on," she told them quickly. "If I can see the shock wave overtaking us . . ."

That question became academic as a wall of furnace-hot air struck *Wind Dragon* like an invisible fist of fiery, bone-shaking noise, nearly lifting the ship from the water with a blast like the worst thunderstroke they had ever heard. She turned back and saw the wall of grey ash moving out across the harbor like a vast curtain, but she felt certain that they could outrun at least the worst effects of that. She was more concerned with the flaming boulders thrown out by that explosion, already arching down toward them like burning meteors, trailing billowing grey smoke.

"Stand by with buckets of water," she continued with her amended instructions. "If we take a hard strike, be ready to go overboard."

Dooket and Erkin hurried off in search of buckets, but they were interrupted as the first boulder crashed into the sea not half a mile away, so hot that it exploded on contact with a small thunderclap loud enough to be heard over the relentless roar that pursued them. Boulders continued to crash into the sea around them for the next half-minute, most farther away and none so close as to endanger the ship. The hail of smaller stones that Mira had expected, an inescapable hazard, never materialized.

Soon enough it seemed that they were well out of danger. The sky above them was clear, and *Wind Dragon* still promised to outrun the diminishing wall of burning dust that followed. Mira ordered the boys back to the task of preparing the ship for flight.

"You knew that this would happen?" Jenny asked as she paused a moment in her own tasks to join her mistress on the helm deck.

"I had good reason to suspect," Mira told her, looking just a little self-satisfied with her cleverness. "We're even now in the center of a ring of islands that once formed the fringe of a much larger volcano. A volcano that, in the distant past, exploded with many times the force that we've just witnessed. Mount Drashand was the modern offspring of that ancient volcano, but for two thousand years ago and more the servants of the Dark set the Heart of Flame in its core and that has served like a magical cork ever since. That volcano had a couple of thousand years of serious mischief to catch up on, all of it in one immense bang."

"And the city?"

Mira frowned. "I can't say that I have no regrets. Tens of thousands just died from my actions. But they were servants of the Dark, one and all, the evil citizens of the capital of the Dark. They would have carried a thousand times that destruction through the known worlds."

Mira paused, seeing her student stare in disbelief at the destruction behind them. She turned to look, instantly aware of the wall of water that had only just emerged from the grey curtain of roiling ash. It was perhaps five miles behind and closing steadily.

"Yarg!" she exclaimed. "I forgot that the collapse of the island would cause a tidal wave like that. Tsunami, I believe they're called. Boys!"

"Ship ahead!" Erkin called back. "Imperial galley."

"Ignore it!" she shouted impatiently. "Get the vanes out and at least the main rigging in place. We're either airborne in the next minute or else the survivors will be swimming."

They needed no more urging than that. Jenny hurried to assist them, and even J.T. did what he could to pull ropes. They had the vanes folded out within seconds, but enough of the standing rigging had to be in place or they would never bear the weight of the ship. Mira divided her attention between watching their progress and that of the wave that was gaining on them, determined to get them in the air at the last minute no matter what.

She did not like to see Jenny climbing around on the vanes themselves to assist in the rigging, not with the ship so unstable, but the girl was the lightest and quickest for that task. Jenny also figured that, if anyone risked falling overboard, then it should be herself; she could fly. Indeed, she had no intention of going down with the ship, as hard as it would be for her to abandon the others. She tossed the final ropes to Dooket even as *Wind Dragon* shot past the Imperial galley, the larger ship laboring forward under frantic oars, doomed already.

Mira hazarded a glance back. They were coming to the far side of the ring of islands that marked the boundaries of the ancient volcano, and shallow water compared to the vast depths of the core. That slowed the wave somewhat, but it also began to climb as it found the bottom. Already it towered a hundred feet or more above the sea, overtaking the Imperial ship. The fore part of the wave lifted the galley as if it were a toy, and the main body of the wave sucked it in. Its splintered debris would emerge in the troubled sea after the wave was past.

"Ready!" Jenny shouted over the wind as she ran back along the top of the left rear vane, the Trasseks waiting to pull her in.

Mira unlocked the elevator wheel and spun it all the way over, at the same time coaxing thrust into the lift vanes. *Wind Dragon* responded sluggishly, her nose lifting slowly until the entire ship stood poised on her rear skids. The wave rose like a mountain behind her, waiting to swallow her whole. Then the ship was entirely airborne with a final shudder that caught J.T. by surprise as he sat on the rail watching the wall of water; he disappeared overboard with a startled cry, lost in that instant. *Wind Dragon* continued to climb steadily, rising up the height of the wave even as the spray and cold wind of its thunderous passage closed about her.

And with a final surge she climbed above, the crest of the wave passing within three feet of her rear skids. *Wind Dragon* continued to climb into the afternoon sky on broad canvas wings of blue and red, fiery destruction to her back and the golden light of the descending sun to starboard. Dooket and Erkin returned to the task of completing the rigging while Jenny hauled up a trailing rope, bringing on board a very wet and frightened cat clinging fiercely to its frayed end. And all the while Mira stood at the wheels of her proud ship, grinning like a pregnant monkey.

· Part Nine ·

While the Getting's Good

JENNY RETURNED TO the helm deck, carrying J.T. wrapped in a towel. She had gone below to dry the cat as well as she could, and to soothe his shattered nerves with something good to eat. He had looked very wet and ragged after his ordeal, shaking with fright and furious with injured dignity. They paused for a long moment to stare back at the rolling grey cloud which marked the destruction of the capital of the Alasheran Empire. Arcs of lightning rippled through and across the creeping bank of clouds and the sound of distant thunder echoed occasionally, although that thunder more than likely marked continued volcanic activity rather than lightning. The prevailing wind carried the worst of the eruption away to the southeast.

"Not a bad day's work for two itinerant sorceresses," Mira remarked without turning away from the wheels.

Jenny did not answer, but she thought that the destruction of Alashera was something of which she could never be too proud. Not even when she recalled the place of complete and ruthless evil that it had been.

J.T. suddenly shifted impatiently in her arms. "Put me down, please. I want to go fluff my fur in the sun."

She did as he requested, setting him on the deck and watching as he stalked off toward the bow.

Mira glanced over her shoulder at the girl. "Why are you so sad, child? It's not every day that you get to kick the Empire in the knee and get away with it."

"Oh, it has nothing to do with that," Jenny insisted. "It's just that, now that it's all over, I have to go ahead and become a dragon."

"Great stars, whatever for?" Mira exclaimed in obvious horror, as if she could imagine a fate no less dire . . . and had not known this herself for the past half year.

"Any number of reasons, really," Jenny explained. "What it all amounts to is that I must do this for my own protection. I've possessed dragon magic for so long that I'm no longer mortal, but I won't have complete command of my own magic until I do become a dragon. Also, when I do submit to the transformation, my inner name can finally be secured against any attack. No one, not even Emperor Myrkan himself, will be able to command me against my will."

"But you still don't like it," Mira pointed out.

"Not, it's not that at all," Jenny insisted. "There are many advantages to being a dragon. It's my real nature, so I'll actually be a little more at peace with myself. I look forward to it, without regret or reservation."

"Except one."

"Except one," she agreed reluctantly, even sadly. "Why do I feel like I'm losing an old friend?"

Mira scratched her head. "Who?"

"That person I've looked at in the mirror every day for the past twenty-three years," Jenny exclaimed. "Can you imagine the identity crisis involved in turning yourself into something completely different? I mean, it can be upsetting enough just having a facelift."

"I dare say," Mira agreed, nodding slowly. She was trying hard to figure out just what in the hell a facelift could be. "And then again, there is Kelvandor."

Jenny nodded. "Yes, that's upsetting too."

A sharp crosswind stirred her long, dark blue hair. She caught an errant handful and stood for a long moment, fondling it between her fingers while she studied the color in the afternoon sun.

"Kelvandor," she said to herself, and sighed. "It used to be that my way of living with the Prophecy was to never try to look beyond its completion. Now I have that dragon waiting to see what comes after, and I don't know if there will be a future for me. I hate commitments. I have so little control over my own life, it's so hard to know the best thing to do.''

"It always is," Mira told her. "When it comes time to dump the chamberpots of your heart, you just get it over with and spare everyone the stink.''

Jenny looked up at her suspiciously, but the older sorceress only stood at the wheels with her usual look of patient bliss. She shook her head slowly and smiled. "Do you waste time pondering these words of wisdom, or do you just make it up as you go?''

"I make it up as I go, along with the rest of my life," Mira responded without the slightest hesitation. "I ignore the nonessentials, and I refuse to take anything else at all seriously. It saves worry and needless wear on the digestive tract. But I don't know what to tell you, because now I'm sad, too. I suppose this means that you'll be going away.''

"I don't think that you're going to be rid of me quite that easily," Jenny said. "You're a part of the Prophecy yourself, remember. I'm afraid that you are going to be on board for the duration.''

Mira shrugged with almost exaggerated indifference. "Someone has to come along and keep you out of trouble. Those two dragons obviously can't stop you from doing stupid things.''

She had meant that as a joke, but Jenny took it seriously. She stared at the deck, frowning fiercely. "I never should have put myself at risk in the first place. I never should have gone.''

"Ah, but the risk proved worthwhile, and we accomplished far more than we had ever hoped. Consider that practice for greater things yet to come." Mira paused a moment, and glanced back at her shrewdly. "Just how much of all that dribble was true, anyway?''

"All of it, if I understand what you mean," Jenny insisted. "Dasjen Valdercon was the High Priest Haldephren. And he was when you first met him years ago, if he seemed unchanged to you.''

"He was," Mira admitted with considerable regret. "What happened to him? Will he really be back?''

"Soon enough. But I don't have to tell you that. You know more about the ancient wars than I do." Jenny licked dry lips, and sighed with regret for past memories. "I remember him from before, when he wore the Mindijaran form of Keridaejan. He seemed exactly the same person then, for all his vast differences of appearance."

She turned and stared over her shoulder for a long moment, watching the ripple of lightning over the rolling banks of grey clouds. She thought of many things past, and of things yet to be in a very uncertain future. She did not believe Haldephren's claim that he was her father, but she could not entirely ignore it either.

There were many questions in her mind. But she doubted that Vajerral knew those answers, and Dalvenjah would not say. All the same, she very much wanted to see Dalvenjah Foxfire once again.

"It's not over," she said at last. "I have the terrible suspicion that it has only just started. If the Prophecy of the Faerie Dragons holds true, we will have to face Haldephren again, and the Emperor Aressande Myrkan, and destroy them both. And I've never heard the slightest hint of how we are supposed to accomplish that."

"We take it as it comes," Mira answered with her usual lack of concern. "We blundered through this part, and I suspect that we did well enough. Heaven only knows what we can accomplish when we set our minds to it. I do have just one regret, though."

Jenny turned to look at her mistress. "What is that?"

"That I wasn't consulted about this prophecy business first."

"And you think I was?"

Mira glanced over her shoulder. "You grew up knowing the part you have to play, with time to prepare for it."

"Time to get thoroughly sick of the whole affair," Jenny said with considerable disgust. "I only wish that it was done and over, and that I could finally have a life of my own."

"We'll just take it all as it comes," Mira said. "But there is just one thing I would like to know. Do you suppose that we might possibly be spared a little rest before this affair of prophecies starts up again?"

Lady Mira knew that of all life's questions, many answers are self-evident by the nature of the question, some mysteries are not meant to be known, and some can only be proven in time. She suspected that the latter case applied here.

She also knew quite well that fate was an untrustworthy friend at best.

*   *   *

Daylight was fading swiftly as *Wind Dragon* came in low over the waves before settling into the soft sands well up onto the beach. This group of islands, the first that they had passed over since leaving Alashera, showed a fair amount of damage from the waves generated by the destruction of the volcano. Alashera now lay more than a day and a half behind, although the airship had spent the previous night riding out the gentle waves of the open sea. Curiously, the little ship had survived its adventure without sustaining any apparent damage.

Even more surprising, the crew had survived without apparent damage.

The two dragons glided down for a landing on the beach even before the airship had settled onto the sand, and the horse Staemar raced up to join them while they were still securing the vanes. The dragons were glaring—in the way only dragons could glare—and Jenny had no wish to face their wrath. Of course, it would be good practice for facing Dalvenjah's wrath. Mira had no such concerns. The older sorceress was still disgustingly pleased with herself.

"Are you quite finished?" Kelvandor asked when the two sorceresses finally saw fit to quit the ship.

"Yes, I think so," Mira agreed amiably. "There didn't seem to be anything left that we could do."

Jenny just stood behind her, cringing and shifting nervously. She had never destroyed an island before. Mira was so unconcerned about the whole affair, it was easy to assume that she had done this before. Jenny did not consider that entirely outside the realm of possibility. To listen to Dame Tugg talk about it, some of Mira's parties were that raucous.

A fire was lit in the sand and they cooked their dinner outside that night in spite of the fact that *Wind Dragon* had a complete galley and no one except Mira liked sand in their food. The sky darkened to velvety black and the stars came out bright and clear. The evening wind was soft and cool; autumn had come even to the South.

"This reminds me of my father's cabin in the mountains . . . heaven only knows why," Jenny commented after dinner. "Late on cool nights like this we would put marshmallows on sticks and roast them over an open fire."

Sir Remidan stared at her in shock. "Great stars, woman! That sounds horrible!"

He somehow had the idea that marshmallows were a variety of small crab.

Vajerral, who alone knew the true nature of the elusive marshmallow, had a hard time not laughing aloud. Mira looked at each of them in turn, concluding with a rather perplexed expression. "Jenny, why don't you take your dragon for a walk before it gets late?"

It seemed like a good idea to Jenny. Not so much because she wanted to be alone with her dragon, but because she was getting heartily tired of the constant company of Lady Mira, her dippy bodyguards and smart-mouthed cat, and a certain self-important knight. There were rare times, usually no more than once a year, when Jenny did spend a few minutes thinking about her home world. Perhaps their recent adventures reminded her of Krakatoa. Then she would come to her senses.

Jenny pulled off her boots and took Kelvandor for a long walk along the deep sands of the beach. Late though it was in the year, she had grown up in the mountains of the dragons and had a high tolerance of the cold. Kelvandor walked beside her in silence, as he often was when alone in her company. She had to wonder what he thought about this whole affair, whether he was amused or resentful, or just confused by it all. Whether he honestly accepted her as she was or if he was just waiting for her to become a dragon, a form far more accessible and acceptable to him.

As it was, Vajerral elected to follow along behind. Jenny watched the two dragons surreptitiously, reviewing in her mind what she thought about faerie dragons in general, those she knew in particular . . . and what she thought of herself in relation to them. No, there was no question in her mind that this was what she was meant to be. She watched Vajerral sporting at the edge of the surf, the child in her unable to resist the unfamiliar temptations of the sea, and Jenny thought how right and comfortable it would feel to wear that powerful, long-limbed body or dart over the waves on broad wings. Almost she felt that she had ridden golden wings before, in that hazy déjà vu that all dragons had of their previous lives.

That moment of warm belonging faded quickly, replaced by her ever-present doubt. What if that was only a ploy she used to force herself to accept something that quite frankly scared her half to death? She would have to wait and find out what Dalvenjah intended. After all, Dalvenjah had been threatening to turn her into a dragon for nearly fourteen years, but the dragon had always been suspiciously willing to accept any delay. Jenny had to admit that this could just be one more of Dalvenjah's strange, evasive ploys.

"I wonder what happens now," Jenny speculated after some time.

Kelvandor bend his long neck to look at her. "All I know is that we are to meet Dalvenjah now. Whatever she might have in mind, she will not say."

Jenny stopped to stare at him. "Do you think that Dalvenjah knows more about the Prophecy than she is willing to admit?"

Kelvandor seemed amused. "That goes without saying, but she will never share what she knows or suspects. She insists that common knowledge of the Prophecy would defeat it, and I know that she is correct. I do think that the time has come when she will begin to guide you safely through the completion of the Prophecy."

He stopped short, staring into the darkness. "Jenny! Vajerral! Something is coming."

Jenny felt it herself but, unlike the dragons, she recognized that curious magical presence immediately. Indicating for the dragons to remain calm and perfectly quiet, she turned to face the low rise leading inward from the beach. The forest beyond was dark and silent, disappearing into the deep shadows of the night just beyond that first fringe of bushes and low trees.

That familiar golden form took shape quickly, more so than in his previous visits, standing before them only a few paces away. Vajerral held back as if fearful of the unexpected apparition, peering cautiously over the shoulders of her two companions. Kelvandor recognized that strange figure and was plainly startled, taking a small, hesitant step forward.

"Father," he said softly. Jenny glanced at him, moved by the pain and quiet longing in his voice. He had never known what had become of his father.

"It is very good to see you again, my son," Keridaejan responded. "I am pleased to see that the two of you have reached an understanding based in love and companionship. You are good for each other, and Jenny will need you in days to come."

He turned then to the girl. "I would suppose that you know why I have come."

"You said that I would have to become a dragon as soon as

our mission was over," she answered. "You also said that I would be betrayed by the one I suspect least."

"You may well be, yet," he agreed. "Time is very short, so listen well. You know that Haldephren claims to be your father, and that he and I once met in your world. What have you always supposed from that?"

"That he really is my father, and that you followed him to my world to destroy him."

Karidaejan nodded sadly. "Hear now the truth of this matter. It was a necessary part of the Prophecy that a faerie dragon be reborn in mortal form, and left to the fates that have guided this Prophecy, it came to happen. And yet something went wrong, for the chosen one was born a male and so unsuited to the Prophecy. Even so, he was still a dragon in spirit."

"My uncle Allan?" Jenny guessed.

He nodded again. "That is so. I knew him well, in my own time, although he never knew me for myself but for the one I pretended to be. For I dreamed the gold dreams and so was warned of the mistake, and of the part that was my own to play. I went into your world and took mortal form, and in that form I sired the one who would be the true object of the Prophecy, using my magic to guide her coming so that she would be female. I am your father."

It all made perfect sense. Jenny suddenly felt that she very much needed to sit down, but Kelvandor was there immediately, his strong, supporting hands on her shoulders. She glanced at him, aware that she had suddenly gained a brother. It was a good thing for them both that incest was not applicable to dragons.

"So you see that nothing was entirely chance," Karidaejan continued. "Not Dalvenjah's meeting with Allan, nor your own meeting with Kelvandor. But you were wrong in your supposition. It was Haldephren who followed me into your world, where I had remained as your secret guardian. I destroyed him then, for it was his body that was found in the wreckage of the automobile. But he was able to overpower me in my mortal form, and so took my own body."

Jenny frowned. "Mother said that you died an alcoholic."

"Your mother's memories were not entirely accurate. She never suspected my true nature, and it was better that she did not."

"She loved you," Jenny added, then glanced up at him. "Or was that only what she was supposed to remember?"

"Such memories are too precious ever to be tampered with," he told her. "I loved her, in my own way. It was not simply to watch over you that I stayed as long as I did. That was something I never intended."

"And Dalvenjah . . ."

"Dalvenjāh never knew," Karidaejan insisted, his manner suddenly becoming more urgent. "But your time is almost gone. Your enemies are at hand, and you must become a dragon now or you will be betrayed. Come, my child."

He held out his hands to her, ready to begin the transformation. But Jenny hesitated. "Who? Who is the traitor?"

"I cannot answer that," he said, desperate now. "Please, child. Your time is nearly gone. You must begin the transformation now."

Jenny took his word for the truth, as if the memory of these things had always been hidden within her mind and heart. For the first time in her life, she was not afraid of becoming a dragon. She stepped forward to join him, reaching out to take his hands.

Their world suddenly exploded in a flash of blue light. Jenny was hurled several paces by that silent explosion to lie senseless in the damp sand, her motionless form trailing wisps of blue mist that turned to a thick, sickly black before they evaporated into the cool evening air. Kelvandor and Vajerral both lay where they had fallen. Even though the worst of that blast had been aimed at them, they still clung to the very edge of consciousness.

Karidaejan stood where he was, watching them sadly.

"I warned you that you would be betrayed by the one you would suspect the least," he said sadly, and his form began to fade. "I am so sorry that it had to be me."

Vajerral had kept her distance from the spirit of Karidaejan, and she had only been stunned. She lifted her head and shook it uncertainly, then opened her eyes. Before her stood a dark figure hidden within the deep folds of a grey robe, stepping slowly forward with one hand raised to stand before the dragon. That long, withered hand began to move in the slow gestures of a silent spell, but Vajerral was too stricken by the earlier spell to resist. Two bright eyes peered out from the depths of the hood, and Vajerral had a momentary glimpse of a face twisted into horrible lines by evil magic, a face that was now as much canine as that of the man it had once been, a demon in mortal flesh.

Vajerral reeled under the effects of that more subtle spell, fighting to hold to the edges of consciousness, her limbs seemingly held in invisible bonds. The dark figure turned and walked almost casually over to where Jenny lay sprawled on the beach. He stood over her for a long moment, again working his subtle magic, and the girl's form glowed briefly. Then she stirred and turned over on her back, and he held out a hand to assist her.

"Welcome back, my pet," he said, his voice harsh and threatening even though he spoke softly.

"My Lord Emperor," she answered, looking about uncertainly. "It has been a very long time."

"Two thousand years and more," the Emperor agreed. "It could not be helped. But come. Haldephren has made rather a mess of things in his ridiculous efforts to bring you back. I was prepared for that, at least. Then the spirit of that dragon tried to betray me in the end, and it was a narrow thing."

She paused, looking back over her shoulder at the dragon, struggling desperately in the sand. She reached to the side of her belt but, finding no sword, dismissed the matter from her mind. The two dark figures turned to walk calmly down the beach to where an immense black shape was drifting gently down to the sand. It was an airship of vast proportions, five times as long as *Wind Dragon*, its hull dull and dark, with vanes and stabilizers that were as black as night. Running without light or sound, it settled like a black cloud to the beach just long enough for the two passengers to ascend the ramp, then rose to head out over the waves.

Vajerral broke free of the spells which held her then, rising and shaking her head briskly a final time, then hurtled herself into the night sky. She shot out over the sea after the departing airship, already half a mile or more away and gaining both height and speed. A ring of fire began to open just ahead of the dark airship, burning back the night until the passage became a vast oval. Fighting the cold winds that poured through the Way Between the Worlds, the airship disappeared down that long, dark tunnel through the void.

Mira and Sir Remidan arrived only a moment later, making use of Staemar's long legs to get them there in a hurry. Mira leaped off the horse's back and rushed over to assist Kelvandor, who was only then just beginning to recover from the shock.

"Kelly, what is it?" she asked anxiously as she countered the lingering traces of the Dark spell. "Who was that?"

"We were talking with the spirit of Karidaejan," Kelvandor answered, still weak and uncertain. He glanced up, seeing that Vajerral was winging down to land. "Then someone else came. I think it was Emperor Myrkan."

Mira frowned. "Where have they taken Jenny?"

"I've got Jenny," Vajerral insisted as she landed lightly in the sand beside them

Mira stopped short. "I beg your damned pardon?"

"I am not entirely sure, but Jenny apparently had the spirit of another entity within her," she explained. "Emperor Myrkan himself had come. He expelled Jenny's spirit from her body, then brought the dormant spirit of the other forward to take her place."

Then she paused, a distant but vaguely startled look on her face. The others watched her in mystification.

"Of course," she said, almost to herself. "The Consort, the missing part in this puzzle. Dalvenjah wondered if Jenny's part of the Prophecy, at least in that variant in which she serves the Dark, was to somehow prepare the way for the return of the Consort, the sorceress Darja. She was closer to the mark than she thought, it seems. Jenny did more than just prepare the way for Darja's return; she has carried the Consort's dormant spirit for years. They must have placed Darja's spirit within her when they had control of her thirteen years ago."

"That's all very well and quite fascinating, but what about Jenny?" Mira demanded impatiently. "Is she dead?"

"No, not at all," Vajerral assured her. "When the Emperor expelled her, I got her."

"Yes, you did say that," Mira declared. "Where the hell did you put her?"

"Oh, there was only one place I could put her. She is within me."

Mira was so stunned that she sat down in the sand.

"Ah, it's very simple, then," Sir Remidan exclaimed. "All we have to do is find a new body for her."

The two dragons just stared at him. Even Staemar stared at him.

"Just a moment, and I'll see how she is." Vajerral sat back on her tail and assumed a very distant expression. "Jenny? Are you there? You are safe now. Please speak to me."

She entertained a brief, errant thought about area codes, and bit her tongue. After a moment she stirred and bent her neck to look down at herself, running her hands over her scales.

"It worked!" she exclaimed. "I really am a dragon."

The she paused, assuming a more serious expression. "You and I need to have a long talk."

She sat back on her tail, obviously preoccupied. Kelvandor glanced at Mira. The sorceress appeared to be utterly devastated by this unexpected turn of events. And he knew what she was thinking. Mira had been very, very wrong. She had thought that she understood the Prophecy well enough to control it, to shape the future to her desired ends. She had been so busy thinking that she was having her way that she had been neatly and quite simply outmaneuvered.

Sir Remidan was also quite miserable, knowing that he had failed a damsel when she had needed help the most. Kelvandor knew that the shock of his own loss would awaken soon enough. He was a dragon, and as such his initial response was to fly and to fight, to hunt down his enemies and get Jenny back.

"The only thing now is to find Dalvenjah," he said gently. "She will know, if anyone does, what we can do."

"Yes, Dalvenjah," Vajerral agreed, speaking aloud again. "We will take you to Dalvenjah right away. She'll be able to do something to help you, if anyone can."

She paused for a long moment, her head down.

"Yes, but what can she do? It's not as if there are bodies just lying around waiting for people to pop into them, and I would really like to have my own back. Can she make me one out of magic?" The dragon paused again. "It might well be that she can. If not, we will recover your own. Dalvenjah and Allan are the best of all the faerie dragons. They rescued you once before."

"Yes, that's right," Mira agreed eagerly.

"I don't want anyone to risk their lives for my body," Jenny spoke again, looking at her. "Damn! Now I know how Charlie McCarthy felt."

"I do think that we should get back to the ship and get away from here for now," Mira continued, recovering her composure but still rather subdued. "I don't want to be surprised a second time. And just one of you try to walk."

Vajerral rose to follow the others along the beach, seeming to have little trouble walking but still quite distracted, obviously trying to converse with her new other half. Kelvandor walked at her side, the only one of the group with the size or strength to offer her any real support, while Mira walked at her other side.

"How are you making out?" she asked cautiously.

"The body remains my own, and I am in complete control," Vajerral explained. "Only if I withdraw myself can Jenny control any movement herself."

"Is there any real hope of ever getting me back?" the dragon suddenly asked herself aloud, and answered. "We will have to see. Perhaps Dalvenjah can work something out."

Mira turned to the dragon. "I don't wish to seem uncaring, but can't the two of you talk to yourself?"

"That will take a little practice," Vajerral answered. "Yes, a lot."

They returned quickly to the airship, and Mira had Sir Remidan and the Trassek twins set to work on rigging *Wind Dragon* for flight. Vajerral was taken below, to the larger hold that was hastily converted into a cabin for the two dragons. The boys gave her one of the assortment of pies that they had acquired during their stay in Alashera, but Jenny detested berry. Erkin remarked that if they had known that the whole island was going to explode they would have stolen the pies. Vajerral was tired from the ordeal and was ready for bed, but Jenny remarked that she was not sleepy. Vajerral politely pointed out that she was not likely to ever be sleepy. They finally worked out an arrangement in which Vajerral slept with her eyes open so that Jenny could read.

That left only the problem of getting the horse Staemar on board the ship.

Mira had *Wind Dragon* in the sky soon enough. Staemar stood in the exact center of the middle deck, his legs braced wide on the boards and his eyes rolling with fright. Mira was too distracted by her personal guilt and misery to be interested to note that horses had a mortal fear of flying. Kelvandor returned to the helm deck a few minutes later, peering over the back rail. The island was now far behind.

"Have we lost?" Mira asked suddenly. "Was that the meaning of the Prophecy, that Jenny would betray us to the Dark whether she wished it or not?"

Kelvandor shook his head. "No, it is not over yet. They may be stronger for the return of the Consort Darja, but not greatly. They certainly have not defeated us yet. Remember also that we have hurt them considerably in ways we did not expect. And I will tell you that Dalvenjah and Allan are exploring their own lead in finding the secret stronghold of the enemy. After this defeat, we could move against them quickly and crack them like a nut."

"If we're lucky," Mira correct him. "Remember that the Prophecy holds that it's up to Jenny to destroy the Emperor and his pals, and right now she's just a figment of Vajerral's imagination."

He nodded. "We do have to do something about that."

"Now what?" Mira asked. "Can Dalvenjah really get Jenny her body back?"

Kelvandor turned to look at her. "I do think that there is hope. Jenny does have the prior claim to that body."

"Prior claim?" Mira asked incredulously. "What are we going to do, sue them? Besides, if it comes to that, possession is nine-tenths of the law."

Kelvandor smiled. "What I mean is that there is a link between Jenny's spirit and her body that can never be broken. Perhaps Dalvenjah will know how to trace that link to its other end, and use it to force the Consort out of a body that is not her own."

"I've never heard that the true owner has ever been restored to his rightful body once a Dark Sorcerer has stolen it," Mira mused.

"That is because they are careful that the spirit is released to true death, even though the body survives," the dragon explained. "But Jenny is a faerie dragon and always has been, no matter what form she has worn. Also, Myrkan released Jenny's spirit into the night, and Vajerral was there to intercept her spirit and give it sanctuary within herself. Perhaps that has never happened before. How soon can we return to your home if you and I take turns flying this ship without stop?"

"Three days at least," Mira replied thoughtfully. "And then?"

Kelvandor twitched his ears. "First we get ourselves to the world of the faerie dragons as quickly as we can, and then we must ferret out the proper trail in this mess and make an end to this business."

Mira seemed content, but Kelvandor knew that it would not be so simple as that. He now demanded a double accounting. The first was for Jenny, whom he counted as his mate. The second was for his father. They had not only destroyed Karidaejan and stolen his body, they had held his spirit captive, even forced him to betray and trap Jenny. Now Kelvandor had two tasks, to win back both Jenny's body and his father's spirit. The Prophecy of the Faerie Dragons was far from complete; there were still too many pieces on the board to consider the game over. Jenny had been betrayed to the Dark, but she was still alive and on their side. And Mira still had yet to play her own part in the Prophecy.

No, they had not lost yet. But they were a long way from having won, and he feared what else the Prophecy may demand from Jenny before it was done.

CLASSIC SCIENCE FICTION AND FANTASY

___DUNE Frank Herbert 0-441-17266-0/$4.95
The bestselling novel of an awesome world where gods and adventurers clash, mile-long sandworms rule the desert, and the ancient dream of immortality comes true.

___STRANGER IN A STRANGE LAND Robert A. Heinlein 0-441-79034-8/$5.95
From the *New York Times* bestselling author—the science fiction masterpiece of a man from Mars who teaches humankind the art of grokking, watersharing and love.

___THE ONCE AND FUTURE KING T.H. White 0-441-62740-4/$5.95
The world's greatest fantasy classic! A magical epic of King Arthur in Camelot, romance, wizardry and war. By the author of *The Book of Merlyn*.

___THE LEFT HAND OF DARKNESS Ursula K. LeGuin 0-441-47812-3/$4.50
Winner of the Hugo and Nebula awards for best science fiction novel of the year. "SF masterpiece!"—*Newsweek* "A Jewel of a story."—Frank Herbert

___MAN IN A HIGH CASTLE Philip K. Dick 0-441-51809-5/$3.95
"Philip K. Dick's best novel, a masterfully detailed alternate world peopled by superbly realized characters."
—Harry Harrison
